DRUNK ON A BOAT

THE MISADVENTURES OF A DRUNK IN
PARADISE: BOOK 2

ZANE MITCHELL

Drunk on a Boat
The Misadventures of a Drunk in Paradise: Book #2

by
Zane Mitchell

Copyright © 2019 by Zane Mitchell

ISBN: 9781794606111
VS. 3132019.02

To my dad,
The best man that ever walked the Earth.
Thanks for making me the person I am today.
Without you, I'd be nothing.

CONTENTS

SNEAK PEEK - DRUNK DRIVING

1

"Drunk."

Facedown, I felt movement. The earth was shaking.

"Drunk, wake up."

A shrill sound blared in the distance, as if a sonic weapon designed to burst my eardrums and implode my skull had been deployed.

The shaking intensified. I gripped the surface beneath me tightly, afraid I was about to fall off the face of the planet. Panic surged through my body. My limbs were heavy, and my eyelids felt bolted down and unable to budge. A finger jabbed into the fleshy part of my shoulder, the skin-to-skin contact giving me the distinct impression that I wasn't wearing a shirt.

"Drunk!"

Was that a voice I heard?

"Hmm…" I groaned.

"Wake up. Your phone's ringing."

There went that damned sonic blaring again, drilling into my eardrums and making my temples throb. Even when the noise stopped, my ears rang with its distant echo.

I tried to swallow, but my mouth was turned inside out. My tongue was thick and heavy. I gagged a little.

"Should I answer it?" The voice was low, but feminine.

Rolling onto my back, I swiped a puddle of drool from the corner of my mouth. My foot slid sideways until I found a cool spot between the sheets. Spread-eagle, I stretched my arms out over my head. My hand touched a pillow.

I was in a bed.

A very comfortable bed.

But despite the bed's plushy comfort, the claws of death still knifed into my skull.

I pulled the pillow to my side and curled into it.

"Five more minutes," I mumbled around my lead tongue. Even to my own ears, the words were a garbled incoherent mess.

"It's Artie."

I shifted again, trying to find a way to lie that didn't press against my bladder. This time my foot made contact with someone else's bare leg. There was someone in bed with me!

The cogs in my mind suddenly clicked into place, and my eyes popped open.

Bright morning rays of sunshine streamed in from my open window, searing my retinas like death rays of torture. Squinting and throwing a hand up, I turned to look at the face behind the voice.

A woman lay in bed next to me. Young and fresh-faced with big brown eyes and a wild mess of curly brown hair, she had the better part of my bedsheet wrapped around her bare, voluptuous breasts.

I grinned groggily at the familiar face. "Mornin', Mack."

She responded with an easy smile, "Good morning, Drunk." She handed me my phone as it rang again. "Your phone's ringing. It's Artie. Hey, listen, I'm gonna use your shower. Do you mind? I have to get to work before Mari fires my ass for being late again."

I ignored the ringing phone and stared at her through squinty eyes. "Work? What? It's too early for work."

The husky undertones of her laughter softened the shrill sound my phone continued to emit. "It's not too early for work. It's almost eight." She eyed the ringing phone. "Aren't you going to answer that?"

"What? No! Don't go!" I yelled at her as she climbed out of bed, stealing my bedsheet right off of me, leaving me naked and now *fully* awakened. Mack was leaving? How was the night over already? It felt like it had just begun. "Oh, come on! No morning kisses?"

Pressed up against the bathroom's doorjamb, Mack shot me a sexy little pout. "Nope, no morning kisses."

"*Rawck! No morning kisses. No morning kisses. Rawck!*" The screechy echo radiated out from my bedroom window, effectively shooting a piercing dagger through my temples.

I blanched.

Mack giggled. "Sorry, Drunk. We both have to work today. You wanna hang out later, though?"

"Later? Oh, come on, Mack," I begged. I propped myself up on my elbow and patted the empty spot next to me. "You know what they say. There's no time like the present."

Smiling, she tipped her head backwards. The long tendrils of her curls reached down to sweep the curve of her backside. "Yeah, well, my aunt Doris always says better late than never."

I chuckled. "Okay, well, *one*, Aunt Doris is wrong. And *two*, I'm pretty sure the saying is better late than pregnant."

Mack rolled her eyes at me. "Oh my God. You wanna hang out later or not?"

My phone made the familiar shrieking sound again.

Every vein that delivered blood to my brain throbbed in unison.

Fuck! I needed to change that damned ringtone!

My bottom lip plumped out, expressing my disappointment that we weren't going to lie in bed all morning until the throbbing in my head subsided and I was ready to have another go of it. "Of course I wanna hang out later."

"*Hang out later, hang out later. Rawck!*" went the echo.

The sexy sound of Mack's laughter trailed behind her until I heard the bathroom door click closed.

"Ugh," I groaned, grabbing Mack's pillow off the other side of the bed and launching it blindly at my open bedroom window. "Shut up already!"

"*Shut up already. Shut up already. Rawck!*"

My phone trilled once more.

I clamped a hand on either side of my head and squeezed in an attempt to keep my head from rupturing and spewing splushy, vomit-inducing sludge across the room. Surely the resort cleaning staff wouldn't want to come clean up a mess like that.

I closed my eyes and sucked in a deep breath. The morning was not off to a great start. Slowly, I let out the breath, swiped the little green phone symbol, and put the phone to my ear. "Yeah, Artie, what's up?"

Pressing my thumb into my other ear, I almost couldn't hear the echo across the room: "*What's up, what's up, what's up.*"

"Drunk, sorry to wake you so early. I know you probably had a late night, but listen, I need you to come in. We've, uh, got a bit of a situation."

I pulled the thumb out of my ear and ground the pads of my fingers into my eyes. I could hear the sound of the water turning on in the bathroom. "Hey, Artie, I got company this morning. Can't we do this later?"

"Yeah, I'm sorry about that. I wouldn't have called if it wasn't important enough to warrant you coming in."

I had no interest in going into work at this hour. All Little Drunk and I wanted to do was to go join Mack in the shower, knock off a quick one, and then crawl back into bed and ooze into unconsciousness. "Right now?" I pressed.

"*Right now, right now. Rawck!*"

I'd had enough. I bolted up in bed, sending a searing pain through my skull. My eyes met those of a yellow-bellied, blue-bodied, green-headed, zebra-faced parrot. "Shut the hell up!"

"Drunk?" Artie bellowed into the phone.

The parrot bobbed back and forth in the window, doing a little dance on the sill. *"Shut the hell up, shut the hell up. Rawck!"*

"Not you, Artie." I grabbed my own pillow off the bed and flung it at the parrot.

The bird ducked as my pillow sailed over its head and out the window. *"Rawck!"*

"It's this fucking parrot. Ever since you moved me into this cottage, it won't leave me alone."

"Oh. That's Earnestine."

"Earnestine? Fucking thing has a *name*?"

"Yeah. Hey, Drunk, how long before you can get here?"

I scratched my head and looked around. My quilt was twisted into a ball at the foot of the bed. Clothes were strewn all over the room. Empty shot glasses and tequila bottles lined my nightstand, and condom wrappers littered the floor. My head pounded—a memento of the wild night before. But oh, had it been worth it. My first night with Mack was everything I had hoped it would be and more.

It had been epic.

A real killer of a party.

I glanced back at the time. It wasn't even eight yet. I was pretty sure Mack and I had crawled into bed a little after two, but the festivities in my cottage had gone on well into the morning. I was guessing I hadn't gotten to sleep until after four or maybe even five. I wasn't sure. I didn't even remember falling asleep.

"Artie, it's not even eight yet, and I gotta work tonight. Can't whatever it is wait?"

"I'm afraid not. I've got a woman here who's demanding to see you. She's kinda making a scene, Drunk."

I slumped forward in bed and ran a hand through my thick, unruly hair. If I had to guess, it was Alicia. Or maybe it was Gigi; I could see her being a vindictive one. Or maybe Mari had discovered I'd gone through her girls at the same speed I'd binge-watched *Breaking Bad*, and she'd run to Artie to tattle. I let my head fall into my free hand and groaned. They'd all been over eighteen and willing participants. I hadn't had to coerce a single one of them.

Charmed them, yes.

Coerced them, no.

Fuck.

"Hey, listen, Artie, I can explain…"

"No need to explain, Drunk. Just get in here ASAP."

Something in Artie's voice had me curious now. "Come on, man. You're not even gonna gimme a heads-up?"

There was a pause.

I could hear a woman screeching in the background. The voice sounded vaguely familiar, but it was too muffled to hear it well.

The phone crackled and then became suddenly hollow-sounding, as if Artie had wrapped his giant mitts around the receiver. "If I tell you, you're not going to want to come," he whispered breathily into the phone. His raspy voice made him sound like a stalker straight out of a suspense thriller flick.

I sighed. It wasn't like I needed this job anyway. After the $6.9 million windfall I'd received a few weeks prior, I was set for life. The head of security job at the Seacoast Majestic was as laid-back as jobs came, and in all reality, I was mainly doing it for shits and giggles, and so I had a reason to hide out on a tropical island instead of returning to the States and having to come face-to-face with my cheating ex-fiancée again. But if Artie wanted to fire me over sleeping with the help, he sure as hell was welcome to fire me. I'd get over it.

I groaned. "I need a shower."

"Fine. Shower and then come in."

"Have a Dr. Pepper waiting for me, will ya?" I was going to

need some caffeine if I was going to be worth a shit for the day.

"A Dr. Pepper?"

"Yeah, and a candy bar." I *had* saved the man's life, after all. The least he owed me was a damned soda and a candy bar.

"A Dr. Pepper and a candy bar?" repeated Artie like he was writing it down. "What kind of candy bar?"

"I don't care. Nothing with coconut. I fucking hate coconut."

"I fucking hate coconut. I fucking hate coconut. Rawck!"

2

"This better be fucking good, Artie."

After a quick shower, I'd thrown on a pair of tangerine athletic shorts, flip-flops, and an orange-and-yellow tank top that read "Sun's Out Guns Out." Then I'd snuck in through the resort's back entrance to avoid whatever disaster awaited me in the resort lobby, and now I was slouched down on a chair in front of my boss's desk. I was hoping I'd resolve this "issue" quickly, as I had a long day of nothing planned, and I preferred to start it sooner rather than later.

I pulled off my sunglasses and tossed them onto Artie's desk but left on my black fedora. I hadn't taken the time to shave or to put any product in my hair, so not only did I have a full day's growth of dark hair covering my jaw, but I was also sure that the mess hiding beneath my hat would look just as unkempt as I felt.

Artie took one look at the suitcases under my bloodshot eyes and shoved the bottle of Dr. Pepper in my direction. "Well, shit, Drunk. You look like hell."

"You think? The fucking band didn't stop playing until midnight. By the time I signed out the security staff, it was after two."

"You mentioned you had company this morning too?"

I waved a hand in the air dismissively. Now that I was awake, I didn't want to talk about that. I wasn't sure how Artie felt about members of his staff getting busy with one another, and with the way my head was pounding, I was in no mood to deal with getting chewed out.

"Oh, never mind that," I said, swiping my Dr. Pepper off his desk and unscrewing the cap. "Fill me in. What's going on? Who's the chick in the lobby?"

Artie lifted one of his rump-roast-sized shoulders while I guzzled a third of the bottle in one swig. "You're not going to like this."

"No shit? So you're telling me this woman's *not* here to throw a party in my honor? Damn." I shook my head, a small chuckle on my lips. "Listen, Artie. Every single woman I've been with since I've been to the island has been a consenting adult. I guarantee you. I don't understand why this woman feels the need to harass me at wor—"

"It's Pam, Drunk."

The rest of my sentence hung in the air between us, my mouth gaping open. I snapped my mouth shut and tilted my head sideways. Perhaps my alcohol-induced haze had affected my word recognition skills. "I'm sorry. What did you just say?"

"Pam's the woman in the lobby. She's demanding to see you."

"Pam?" The word almost sounded foreign to my ears. It was the last thing on earth I'd expected him to say. I shook my head, stupefied. "As in *my* Pam. Pamela Calcara, the cheating slut I almost married, Pam? The woman that ripped my heart out and fed it to the goddamned wolves, Pam?"

Artie looked unsure. "I mean, she just said Pam. I assumed..." He picked up a folded-up white towel from his desk and wiped big beads of sweat from his lower brow.

Artie Balladares, my boss and the owner of the Seacoast

Majestic Resort on the tiny Caribbean island of Paradise Isle, was a big man. Sumo wrestler big. He was also bald. He covered up his bigness by wearing expensive linen suits, and he covered up his baldness with a big white Panama Jack safari hat with a black band around the crown. Even though he sweated profusely beneath the hat, it was his signature piece, and he never took it off. In fact, I'd only seen him without the hat once, and he'd looked ridiculous, so even though it meant Artie looked like a snowman in heat most of the time, I much preferred him wearing the hat.

"You *assumed* that she was my Pam?"

Artie cleared his throat. "I don't know, Drunk. She's a tiny blonde lady. With big, you know, umm... assets." He cupped his hands out in front of himself.

"And an ass grown men would kill for?" I asked, bobbing my head up and down knowingly. Yes, I could recall those assets well.

Artie's mouth gaped, and he shifted in his chair uncomfortably. "Well, Drunk. I mean, I wasn't exactly looking at her—"

I waved a hand in the air. "It's okay, Artie. Most men never get past her tits. I get it."

He nodded. "So I have to assume it's her."

Fuck.

It was Pam all right. What in the hell was she doing all the way out here? It wasn't like she could be all, *Oh, I was just in the neighborhood and I saw your car so I thought I'd stop in and say hi.* Hell, I was damned near to the equator—not exactly across the street from her hairstylist. In addition to that, I didn't even own a car out here.

I let my head drop in front of me. "Fuck. This is *not* what I need right now, Artie." My head hadn't stopped pounding, and the gurgling in my stomach made me feel both nauseous and like I could destroy the nearest bathroom at any minute.

"You're telling me," sighed Artie. "She's been screaming at

the girls ever since she got here because they wouldn't tell her where you're staying."

I made a mental note to bring the front desk girls an extra box of chocolate.

I rubbed the pads of my fingers against my temples. "She'll go away eventually. She can't stay in the lobby forever."

"She said she's not leaving until you show up."

I threw a hand up in the air. "Fucking call security on her ass, then."

"*You're* security, Drunk."

My head bobbed as I slammed a palm against my knee. "Shit."

"Yeah."

"You can't call the island cops?"

"She's *staying* here, Drunk. She rented a room. She's a guest. I can't have the cops here making an even bigger scene than she is. It'll be all over social media, and that's not the kind of reputation I want for the resort." He sighed and lifted his barely-there brows. "As much as you don't want to, you're just going to have to go talk to her, I'm afraid."

I crossed my arms over my chest and shook my head like a petulant five-year-old. "Hell no. Ain't happening. Uh-uh. You can't make me, Artie."

3

WITH MY ARMS CROSSED OVER MY CHEST, I STOOD IN THE CHILLY epicenter of the navy-and-white nautical-themed resort lobby. By my definition, the lobby was posh. Perhaps some hoity-toity city gal might disagree, but it was enough to impress this Missouri transplant. A wide, curving staircase led to two stories of balconied hotel rooms, which opened to a vaulted ceiling. There were nicely cushioned rattan chairs set atop fancy rugs, and hand-painted vases sat on the tables. Aside from the check-in area and guest suites, the main resort building housed a gift shop, a high-end boutique clothing store, the vacation excursion office, a Japanese restaurant, a gym, a bar, two conference rooms, and of course, the main dining room where the big buffet style dinners were held.

It was check-in time, and new guests were being hauled in from the airport by the dozen, so the space around me buzzed like flies on a cow pie. I felt only slightly self-conscious about my business being put on display, but I wasn't about to take it *somewhere less public*, as Artie had suggested. Nah, that was tempting fate, and I wasn't about to be lured into perpetrating a murder.

My six-foot-four-inch frame stood tall as I stared down at

the petite blonde in front of me. She smelled like coconut oil and mango and wore a pale pink strapless mini romper that stretched tautly across her fake boobs and exposed the underside of her perfectly rounded bottom.

My bloodshot eyes narrowed to pinpricks. "What the hell are you doing here, Pam?"

"Hi, Danny. I came to see you," she said, a cautious smile playing around her mouth.

My head tipped sideways as I pursed my lips. "No. Fucking. Way." I could feel my insides heating up. "Next you're gonna tell me that sharks shit in the ocean."

She ignored my sarcasm. "Be serious, Danny. Isn't there somewhere private we could go to, you know… talk?" She held up her room key. The expensive piece of hardware I'd given her when proposing marriage sparkled on her finger beneath the lobby's chandelier lighting. "I got a room. We could go there. Or if you've got a—"

"I'm not going anywhere with you, Pam."

"But, Danny! We need to talk!" she begged. The soft sweetness of her voice had turned into a whine. "You never answer my calls, you don't respond to my messages. Your folks say you're suddenly moving to the island? What's that about?"

I grimaced. I'd specifically asked my mother to stop talking to my ex. I palmed my forehead. "Stop calling my mother, Pam. That's not normal."

"I didn't call her, Danny. I bumped into her at the supermarket. What am I supposed to do? Just ignore her? Pretend that I wasn't almost her daughter-in-law? I love your mom."

"Yeah, well, she gave birth to me. So I get to keep her in the breakup."

"I'm not trying to steal your mom. I just wanted to be in the loop since you won't call or text me back."

"You don't get to be in the loop anymore. And I don't respond to your calls and texts because I blocked your number."

She grimaced and looked down at her long aqua-colored fingernails. "Yeah, I figured."

Of course Pam had actually managed to get around the block by using other people's phones to call me or by using star sixty-seven to block her number. It had only worked a few times, until I'd finally caught onto her tricks and stopped answering calls from restricted numbers and numbers I didn't recognize.

"You couldn't take the hint that I didn't want to talk to you? Instead you had to fly thousands of miles for me to tell you to your face? Fine. Then I'll tell you." I leaned over to sneer in her face. "I don't want to talk to you, Pam!"

"But, Danny, all I want is a chance to explain what happened."

I wrinkled my nose. "Oh, I know what happened all right. You fucked Steve fucking Shitwell in my bed. My new fucking bed, Pam! On the night before our wedding!"

People were staring at us now. Perhaps it was the profanity. I saw Mariposa, the head of the front office and maid staff, raise one bushy black eyebrow at me disapprovingly.

"Sittell, Danny. His name was Steve Sittell, and I'm sorry! I was having cold feet."

"Then you should've put on a goddamned pair of socks, Pam! What you *shouldn't* have done is screwed around behind my back!"

Pam's face was red as she pouted. "I admit it! All right? I made a mistake! Haven't you ever made a mistake that you regretted?"

Fury that I'd stuffed down for the past month and a half bubbled up from the pit of my stomach. The venom burned as it crawled up my esophagus and spewed out my mouth. "Yes! Pamela! I *have* made a mistake that I regretted! *You're* the mistake! Don't you get it? You are the biggest *fucking* mistake that I've ever made in my entire life. I regret meeting you. I regret wasting a year and a half of my life with you." I grabbed hold of her left hand and shoved the ring I'd given her in her face. "I regret giving you this ring and asking you to marry me. And most of all, I regret that you're standing in front of me right now!" I let her hand go, and her arms dropped to her sides.

Pam's mouth gaped slightly. She looked stunned. Like *I'd* hurt *her*. She had to be fucking kidding me.

We stared at each other while I panted, slightly out of breath from the adrenaline rush and the exertion of yelling at her.

Finally, she took a step backwards. "You regret meeting me?"

I wagged a finger in her face. "Don't."

"Don't what?"

"Don't try and get me to feel sorry for *you*. That's what you do. You play the *victim*. You're not the victim. *I'm* the victim, okay? Got it? *You* made *me* the victim, so you don't get to make that sad face and look all shocked and offended."

"I—" Her mouth snapped shut, like she didn't know what else to say. "Danny, I still love you. I'm sorry that I hurt you. I didn't mean to hurt you."

I swallowed back the rock that was in my throat. "But you did, Pam. And we will *never* get back together. So get it through your thick skull. We're over. So why don't you just pack up your bags and go home."

"But I got a room for the night."

"Just for one night," I repeated. I hardly believed her. There was no way that Pam had flown all the way to Paradise Isle to stay for only one night. Back home, they were still dealing with the last remnants of an April snowstorm. The consistent eighty-two-degree temperature in Paradise was too perfect to leave after only one day. No, I didn't believe that for a second.

She shrugged lightly as her cheeks flushed. "Well, I mean, I'd hoped that we'd…"

My eyes nearly bugged out of my head. "You can't possibly

mean that you thought that..." I drew a line with my finger between the two of us. "That we... that you..."

Her face crumpled into a pout. "I mean... I hoped. There wouldn't have been any sense in getting a hotel room for more than one night if we were going to get back together. Then I could just stay here. With you." She stepped forward then and threw her skinny little arms around my waist. The top of her head went as high as my collarbone. She tucked her chin into the hollow, cavernous region just below my rib cage and stared up at me, her big blue eyes shining angelically. "We can still stay together. No strings attached, Danny. I mean, at the very least, I owe you that."

I swallowed hard. As crazy and outlandish as it sounds, in the year and a half that we were together, Pam and I had never consummated our relationship. When we'd met, I was going through a phase. I'd had the distinct feeling that something was missing in my life. I'd spent my late teens, my twenties, and my early thirties having only shallow physical relationships with women. And after all of my buddies had married off, started families, and focused on their careers, I was still partying hard and bringing home randoms.

But when I'd hit thirty-two, I'd come up with the idea of re-virginizing myself in an attempt at finding *the one*. I'd quit drinking, I'd joined the police academy, and I'd made the decision to save myself for marriage.

And a little over a year into the new and improved me, I'd met Pam.

She'd been a setup. A friend of a friend of my mother's. Crazily enough, we'd been introduced at church, and we'd gone to coffee. Which is partially why it had come as such a shock to find my *good Catholic woman* screwing her ex-boyfriend on my bed, in my apartment, the night before our wedding.

Completely broken, I'd dropped everything and gone on the honeymoon she'd planned for us. Which, in a nutshell, was what had brought me to Paradise Isle and the Seacoast Majestic.

I stared down at her. She was a beautiful woman. There was no denying it. Any red-blooded man on the planet would tell you that. But now, the sight of her repulsed me. And to have her hands wrapped around my waist? It made me even more nauseous than I already was.

She grinned up at me as I contemplated the exact thing I wanted to say to make her leave. It was a sexy little smile. One that had been so damned hard to resist during our courtship. One of her arms unwrapped itself from my back and she slid her hand down, against the front of my athletic shorts. "It'll be my way of apologizing to you, Danny," she whispered seductively.

I quirked a brow and glanced up at the front desk. Despite the steady line of new arrivals, all the uniformed girls kept one eye trained on me. I was sure they all saw Pam's hand now cupping my junk right there in the lobby. One girl in particular didn't seem to appreciate the scene we were making.

Miss Maclynn Rush, aka, Mack.

She shot me the stink eye. Now not only was Pam pissing me off, she was cramping my style.

Furious, I swatted Pam's hand away, then reached down and grabbed her by both arms. I hunched over slightly, so I could look her directly in the eyes. With her nose less than an inch from my nose, I think she expected me to plant a kiss on her. But in a calm, rational, even voice, I said, "Not if you were the last woman on earth, Pam." I let go of her and took a step back.

Her mouth hung open, her eyes pinched together and her brow creased. It was as if she couldn't believe her sexual advance had been thwarted.

"Call the airline, get your ticket changed to tomorrow's nine o'clock flight. First thing in the morning, I'll send the hotel shuttle to your room to drive you to the airport."

With that, I strode away. The adrenaline, mixed with the hangover, mixed with the physical reaction of *hating* Pamela to my core, gave me the sudden, immediate urge to vomit. I headed for the men's room and promptly purged the contents of my stomach.

4

THE LOBBY'S GLASS DOORS SLID OPEN, AND A BLAST OF HUMID island air reached out and embraced me in a warm, much-needed bear hug. I moved my knock-off Ray-Bans from the brim of my fedora to my eyes and stood in the doorway for a split second, drawing in a deep breath and trying to squash down the emotions that had me so on edge.

An airport shuttle full of new guests pulled up beneath the porte cochere. The sight of the guests inside the makeshift shuttle bus made me crack a smile for the first time since laying eyes on Pam. The vehicle was less shuttle bus and more flatbed truck with bench seats welded onto the back and a makeshift aluminum frame holding up a corrugated roof panel to block the sun. I'd been surprised when that had been the ride that picked me up at the airport on my arrival. But after having been on Paradise Isle for several weeks, I now viewed the shuttle as a quaint introduction to a simplistic island, and I realized that I wouldn't have wanted to be greeted any other way.

All around me, palm trees swayed against the tropical breeze, airport shuttles, cabs, and resort cars zipped around the circle driveway, and guests in bathing suits and flip-flops strolled the property. Several of the resort valets nodded and smiled at me as I walked around the shuttle bus.

"Good morning, Mr. Drunk," said a tall gap-toothed man with short dreads and broad shoulders. He wore a concierge's uniform and waved as I passed his assigned outdoor station.

"Hey, Desi. Beautiful day."

"It is always a beautiful day in Paradise, Mr. Drunk," he said in a clipped accent, following up his words with a hearty laugh.

I stopped next to him and pulled a fifty out of my wallet. I slapped it into his hand. "Hey, Des, I need a personal favor."

"Anything for you, Mr. Drunk."

"There's a woman staying here. I'm not sure what her room number is, but I'm sure Mari can hook you up. She needs a ride to the airport first thing in the morning. Can you handle that for me?"

Desi's eyes widened as a slow, knowing smile crept across his face. "Ahh, the woman that was looking for you earlier?"

I sighed. "Yes. Her."

"She said she was your fiancée," he added. "I did not know you were going to be married, Mr. Drunk."

"I'm not going to be married, Desi. We broke up. So, listen, can you please just make sure to get her room number from Mari and then send someone to pick her up in time for the nine a.m. flight, and have them make sure she gets on a plane?"

"Yes, I can do that."

"Ask Mari to leave a message for her so she knows what time the car is coming. Her name is Pam Calcara."

Through his perpetual smile, Desi gave me a stiff little bow. "Yes, Mr. Drunk. No worries. I shall handle it."

I clapped him on the back. Desi was a good man. I knew if I asked him to handle something, he'd make sure it got done. "Thanks, Des. I appreciate it."

"No problem, Mr. Drunk. Enjoy your day."

"You too."

On the other side of the driveway, I noticed Al Becker at the wheel of a sleek black golf cart. Al was a youthful eighty-seven-year-old retired Case IH implement dealer from Nebraska who, along with his wife, Evelyn, had recently moved to Paradise Isle to live full-time. I'd met Al on my first day on the island. Not only had we become friends, but we'd become known as a bit of an odd couple around the resort.

Al was a small man that had gotten smaller over the years and now he barely measured in at five feet tall. Over a white tank top, he wore a blue short-sleeved button-down shirt patterned with pink and green hula girls. His thin bird-like legs poked out of a pair of khaki shorts, his white socks pulled clear up to his knobby knees, and he wore white New Balance sneakers at all times, even on the beach. For the most part, Al was bald, but he kept tufts of white hair behind his ears, just to prove he could still grow hair, I guessed. One might think he sounded ridiculous, but he tended to blend into the rest of the geriatrics that lived full-time at the Caribbean resort.

Looking at him now, hunched over the steering wheel of the oversized six-seater Black Panther golf cart, he looked especially tiny. The golf cart was a recent purchase, and he'd already told me twice that he'd sprung for the six-seater because he was going to have to haul my ass around now that I was officially living on the island too. I knew that in Al speak, that meant that I was now part of the family. I didn't feel too guilty. The guy was loaded and lived full-time on a Caribbean resort—what else did he have to spend his money on?

Approaching the cart, I gave Al a sideways glance. He was quiet, but the sun reflected off his glasses, so I couldn't tell if he was sleeping or deep in thought. Considering that he tended to nod off without much effort on his part, I had to assume that it was the former. I put a hand on the side rail and gave the cart a shake. The jiggling roused him.

He startled but didn't miss a beat. "Finally! What took ya so long?"

I grinned at him. "You were waiting for me?"

"Eh?" He cupped the back of his ear.

"You were waiting for me?" I yelled.

"Course I was. Artie called and said you were havin' a bad day and thought you might wanna talk." He glanced down at his watch. "It's hardly even nine thirty yet. How does a guy have a bad day this early?"

"I'm just one of the lucky ones, I guess."

He thumbed the passenger's seat. "Get in."

Walking around to the other side of the golf cart, I climbed in next to him. "Were you napping?" I said loudly.

"Napping?" he repeated.

I nodded.

He swatted a hand at the air. "Eh, who knows. You know what they say, regular naps prevent old age."

"Yeah, I've never heard that before."

"No, it's true. Especially if you take 'em while you're driving." He chuckled at his own punch line as he put the golf cart in gear.

I fought the urge to smile and instead lifted my brows. "Was that supposed to be a joke?"

He shot me a scowl.

"You know, you Germans really should throw a pie after you tell a joke. That way the rest of us know when to laugh."

"Such a smart-ass," mumbled Al. "You know you really coulda been a comedian."

"You think?"

He nodded his head as his foot fell heavily on the gas, forcing the golf cart to lurch forward. "Yeah, the only thing you're missing is a sense of humor."

I rolled my eyes at him as we breezed down the cobblestone hill. "Why aren't you wearing your hearing aids?"

He glanced over at me. "Eh?"

"Your hearing aids!" I shouted, pointing at my ears.

"Gall-darned batteries died. Evie said she'd run into town later and pick some up for me."

"Tell her to pick up extras. Your age is showing," I shouted. I hated hollering at him. Al was youthful until he took out his hearing aids, at which point he instantaneously became an old man.

"Yeah, yeah," he mumbled, cruising along the cobblestone street that snaked between the main resort building on the right and the three-storied motel buildings on the left. Palm trees provided shade along the beautifully landscaped corridor. Lizards played in the mulch and among the low shrubbery while birds chirped overhead. Desi was correct. Every day was indeed a beautiful day on Paradise Isle. Even days when my ex showed up uninvited.

Our pace picked up towards the bottom of the incline just as we began to see the Pepto-Bismol-pink cottages poking out from around the back side of the resort. Cottages one and two were quiet. When we passed cottage number three, we both gave a wave to Al's wife, who was shaking a rug out the side door of their duplex.

I pointed at the fully restored sky-blue 1978 Toyota Land Cruiser parked in the driveway of cottage number five. "I see Gary got his Land Cruiser fixed."

"Yup," said Al. "Can't even see the bullet holes anymore. It's good as new."

"I bet Gary was happy."

"Happier than a camel on hump day."

Then we passed my old cottage, number eleven. Vic and Shirley Hoffman had come back from their monthlong trip to the States, thereby kicking me out of my old place, which was how I'd recently ended up living in employee housing on the back side of the resort, next door to Artie.

"Shirley say anything about that broken vase?" I asked Al.

Al's puffy eyebrows shot up. "Oooh, that woman was hot. She said it was a gift from her sister."

"Did you tell her it wasn't my fault?"

"I tried. She didn't seem to care much. I'm sure she'll have a word to say to you about it." We both jerked sideways as Al cruised over a speed bump at forty miles an hour. "How do you like your new place?"

I shrugged. "It's bigger. And Artie lets me use his pool, so that's nice. But I miss my beach view, and I've got a parrot problem I need to deal with."

We got to the end of the resort property, and Al cranked the steering wheel and we veered left to make a U-turn at the end of the resort property. He backed up and hit the tire of his new golf cart against the brick edging. "Dammit."

"You're gonna wreck this thing before you can even put insurance on it."

"I already put insurance on it. Dang price of insurance was ridiculous. It's a gall-darned golf cart, not a Lexus. You know I got the extra-long cart for hauling your ass around the resort."

"So I've heard. In other news, did you know that old men tend to repeat themselves?"

"Old men?" He scowled in my direction. "You see any old men around here?"

I pretended to look around. "Nope. I guess not."

He nodded. "Dang skippy."

Headed back in the same direction we'd just come from, I leaned back in my seat and extended my long legs over the front of the dash until they poked out the side of the cart. "We just taking the Panther out for a joy ride, or are we going somewhere in particular?"

Al lifted his newspaper off the seat beside him and reached over and smacked my legs with it. "Whatsamatter with you? Didn't your mother ever teach you any manners? This is a top-of-the-line nine-thousand-dollar high-tech piece of equipment, kid, not some dirty old La-Z-Boy you picked up at a yard sale for a song."

I groaned and scooted upward, planting my flip-flops on the floor. "Whatever you say, Grandpa." I needed a nap. The vomiting had helped ease the symptoms of my hangover, but it hadn't eased the exhaustion that now plagued me. "You didn't answer my question. Where are we going?"

"We're going to the one place that'll make your bad day all better."

"You're taking me to bed?" I gave him a lopsided grin. "I mean, Al, don't get me wrong. I like you and all, but I'm not sure that we're *there* yet."

He backhanded me. "I'm taking you to the swim-up bar, you moron. Now hang on tight. I'm gonna open this thing up."

5

Bouncy Caribbean music poured out of a pair of fifteen-inch JBL speakers down by the pool. The tropical sun shone brightly, reflecting off the serene, glassy blue water and making it sparkle like aquamarine set in a concrete band. Fifty feet ahead sat Angels Bay, an inlet off the Caribbean Sea. After a few weeks of residence on the island, I'd come to learn that the Seacoast Majestic shared its sprawling man-made sandy coastline with two other large resorts in the bay: Crystal Point Resort and Margaritaville. But as the only non-chain resort, we boasted better oceanfront views and a more laid-back, authentic island experience, which I gladly attested to.

As Al and I made our way from the golf cart parking area, I scanned the scene. To my left was the resort's clubhouse, a big white farmhouse style building with a covered wraparound porch. Inside was the fancy dining restaurant called The Beachgoer, Club Seven, where Freddy Garcia held his singles dance classes on Thursday nights, a sports bar, a few party rooms, the men's and women's restrooms, and some public use computers all the way in the back. Only a handful of guests sat on the porch, sipping brightly garnished mimosas and nibbling on fresh fruit and croissants while taking in the breathtaking oceanside view.

A few early-rising guests sat sprinkled around the beach and the pool in lounge chairs, absorbing the morning sunlight. Trinity and Alora, the girls that worked the snack shack over by the hot tubs and miniature golf putting greens, were setting up shop for the day. Seagulls already flocked to their windows, waiting for the fries they'd snatch off plates and the cast-off pieces of food that would be left for them to fight over.

On the far side of the pool, next to the waterfall grotto, was a swim-up bar covered by bright blue umbrellas. The bar had two sides, one that faced the pool for the swimmers and one that faced the ocean, so people coming in off the water or sunbathers could walk up and get a drink without having to track sand into one of the many indoor bars. Al and I took our usual spots on stools in front of the bar.

"Manny, how's it hangin', man?"

The bartender offered me a fist bump across the counter. "It ain't just hangin', it's draggin', Drunk. Same as always." Manny, who hailed from Puerto Rico, was a short, stocky man whose shoulders rode up high, next to his ears. The man, who had a smile for everyone that visited his bar, was chock-full of rhythm. Both he and his customers enjoyed the spontaneous dance moves he broke out from time to time. Next to Al, Manny was my favorite person on the island. Al and I visited him several times a day. Manny turned his attention to Al. "How you doin', Al? You good? You wanna drink?"

Al shook his head, but smiled. "Nah, Manny. It's too early for a drink."

"Oh, come on, it's five o'clock somewhere."

"Yeah, well, it's nine thirty here. Evie would have my hide if I started drinking this early in the day."

I shook my head. "I'm gonna have a talk with Evie. The woman's cutting you off at the knees! How can a man live like that?"

"How 'bout you, Drunk? What's it gonna be today? A Cool and Deadly, a Bay Breeze, a margarita on the rocks?" Manny pulled a tall glass out from under the counter and waited for my order.

"I'm just gonna have to keep it simple and go with a shot of tequila, Manny," I said.

Manny lifted his brows in surprise. "Straight tequila?"

Al pounded his fist on the counter. "Oh, for Pete's sake, Drunk, pull yourself together. You're not drinking tequila shots at nine thirty in the morning. I don't care *how* hungover you happen to be."

I turned to Al and squinted at him. "Remind me. Did it hurt when you gave birth to me? I'm just curious." I held a palm up. "Oh, wait, that's right. It *didn't* hurt because *you're not my mother*."

Manny winced, widening his onyx eyes. "Ay, ay, ay! What's the matter with this guy?" he asked Al, thumbing over his shoulder in my direction.

Al shook his head. "I haven't the foggiest. Artie just told me to pick him up. Said he's having a rough day and could use a friend, but he hasn't said a word about what's going on."

Manny turned and looked at me then. "Oh, does this have something to do with that little mami that was in the lobby with you earlier?"

I tipped my head sideways. "How do you know about that? That was literally like fifteen minutes ago."

"Hey, man, word travels fast around here. You should know that."

"Apparently." I shook my head. "How's that shot coming?"

Manny pulled a shot glass out from under the counter, but Al shoved it away.

"Manny, give the man a mimosa for crying out loud. He doesn't need a shot of tequila this early in the morning."

I stared at Al but didn't say anything. If he wanted me to

start with mimosas, I could start with mimosas. The tequila could come later. What difference did it make to me?

My silence was all the permission Manny needed, and he set about making me my drink.

Al swiveled on his barstool so he could face me. "So, all this…" He drew a little squiggle in the air with his gnarled hand. "This is about a woman?"

I didn't say anything. I really didn't feel like talking about it. In fact, all I wanted to do was to forget about the fact that Pam was even on the island.

"Which woman?" he pressed. "The one that Mariposa just hired? That you were schmoozing last night at the bar?"

I shook my head and let out a deep sigh. "Nah, it wasn't Mack."

"Who, then?"

When I wouldn't say anything, he turned to Manny. "You know who it was, Manny?"

Manny slid my bright orange drink across the bar.

The ocean seemed to sigh, pushing a fine spray of salty ocean water across my back. The lukewarm mist felt good against the heat. I slid a finger down the sides of my glass, drawing a line in the condensation. The cold against my warm fingertips felt good too. I lifted it to my mouth and took a long swallow.

Mmm. Refreshing.

And in that single, solitary moment of bliss, I remembered that I lived in fucking paradise. Nothing else mattered anymore. I let out a long sigh.

"No, I have no idea who it was. All I know is that she grabbed him." Cupping his hand, Manny grinned from ear to ear. "You know. She grabbed his cojones. Right in the middle of the lobby during check-in time." He laughed like it'd been the funniest thing he'd heard all week.

Al's brows hoisted upwards, wrinkling his bald, liver-spotted forehead. "Oh my. I bet that caused quite the stir. No wonder word made it down here already. Now we just need to know who the little dame was." Al looked at me as Manny's head bobbed.

I sighed. They weren't going to let it go until they solved the big mystery. My upper torso crumpled forward onto the bar top. "Ugh, it was Pam, all right?"

"Pam?" said Al, in shock. "You don't mean the woman who stood you up at the altar, do you?"

I sat up sharply. "She didn't leave me at the altar, *Al*!" I barked. But he knew that already. I wondered if it was his eighty-seven-year-old memory that had made him forget, or if he was just fucking with me. If it was a game, I certainly didn't want to play.

Al held his hands up defensively. "Hey, don't get mad at me! *I* wasn't the one who did it."

"I caught her cheating," I muttered, as if that made it much better in anyone's minds. I know it certainly didn't make me feel any better. More than hating the fact that it had happened, I hated talking about it. Being cheated on by someone that you thought you loved hurt. Probably more than I cared to admit. Not only did it burn something deep inside of me, it was embarrassing. *I* had been cheated on. *I* wasn't good enough. The whole thing made me wonder why I'd even wanted to grow up and be in a relationship to begin with. Now that I'd been burned, I truly didn't see the point in monogamy. No. I wasn't ever punching my relationship card again. I was going back to the old Drunk. That guy was more fun anyway.

"And now she's here? On the island?" asked Manny, grinning. "You two gonna get back together?"

I puffed air out my nose. "Oh, hell no! No, I'm putting her on a flight back to the States tomorrow. This island isn't big enough for the both of us." I lifted my fedora and smoothed back my hair. Popping it back onto my head, I drained the rest of my mimosa and slid my glass forward. "Hit me."

Al shook his head sadly. "Boy, she really did a number on ya, huh, kid?"

Before I could respond, a familiar thick Caribbean accent piped up behind me. "Hiya, Drunk."

I swiveled on my barstool to see Trinity, the snack bar girl, standing behind me with a beige bussing tub propped up on her aproned hip. Trinity was a beautiful girl, with big green eyes that sparkled when the sun hit them just right and dark, almost obsidian skin that looked smooth as satin. She and I had a playful relationship. Perhaps she'd flirted with me a bit over the last few weeks, but I'd never made a move on her. She was twenty-two years old but looked like she was barely legal. I think if I'd touched her, I'd have felt like a pedophile, so I'd kind of subconsciously relegated her to kid sister status.

"Morning, Trin," I said with a grin.

Her smile back at me was playful and curious. She turned her green eyes onto Al. "Good mornin', Mr. Becker. How are ya feelin' this lovely mornin'?"

"I'm feeling well, thank you. And yourself?"

"I'm feelin' just fine," she said, the rhythm of her speech hypnotic. She turned to me. "So, whatcha know, Drunk?"

"What do I know?" I quirked a brow. If I had to guess, word about the scene in the lobby earlier had traveled to her ears as well. But I'd play it cool and feel her out. "Not much. You?"

"I heard ya got a woman from the States came to see ya this mornin'."

"Did you?" I shook my head. I wanted to slam my fist into a wall. Now I'd be explaining Pam away to every single woman at the resort.

Fuck.

"I did. Sounds like she was *very* interested in ya."

"It was his fiancée," interjected Manny with a grin.

"Ex," I said pointedly. "Ex-fiancée. She's leaving tomorrow."

Trinity's eyes brightened, as if she'd just been fed an even juicier piece of gossip. I wanted to reach across the bar and slug Manny. "Is she now? Why so soon?"

"Pressing obligations in the States," I lied, nodding my head. I certainly didn't need every woman in the resort knowing I'd been cheated on. That could have a negative effect on some of the girls I'd been messing around with. You know? It might lower my stock. "She couldn't stay. She just flew out here so we could say our goodbyes properly."

"I see." Trinity swept her long black braids over her shoulder. "Well, I hear she's a pretty little thing."

I nodded. That she was. I couldn't deny it. I gave Trinity a tight smile and a little wave. "She sure is. Well, you have a good day, Trin. Lemme know when you got your grills fired up. I'll stop over to the snack bar for one of your amazing grilled chicken wraps."

She nodded at me, a slow smile pouring across her face. "You have a good one too, Drunk." She smiled at Al and Manny. "Gentlemen, I'll talk to ya all later."

She sauntered away. I was thankful to get rid of her. I hated the fact that everyone at the resort was going to have their noses all up in my business now. Was nothing sacred between a man and his slutty ex-fiancée anymore?

"Is that why she came out here?" asked Al. "So you two could say your goodbyes properly?"

"No, she came out here because she wanted me to take her back," I snapped.

"And?"

I looked at Al with my mouth gaping. "You really think I'd take her back?"

Al shrugged. "Some men do."

"Well, I ain't some men!" I bellowed. "*Shit!*"

Al held his hands out flat in front of him. They hovered just above the bar top. "All right. Settle down. No need to get all riled up. I was just asking."

"Yeah, well, I'm a little on edge today, if you hadn't noticed."

"We noticed," Al and Manny said in unison.

Manny slid another mimosa in my direction. "Maybe it's time to break out the tequila after all?" He looked at Al.

Al swatted the air. "He doesn't need tequila. What he needs is to let it go."

I looked at Al incredulously. "Let it go? Let what go?"

"Everything!" said Al, waving his arms up around himself. "Let go of the past. Let go of the anger. Of the hurt. Of the pain. Let Pam go. Just let it all go."

I shook my head as I sipped my mimosa. "I can't do that." How was I supposed to just let that go? I was far too angry.

"Al's right, Drunk. Hate's a double-edged sword, man. You can't cut her without cutting yourself. And the deeper the wound, the bigger the scab." Manny shook his head. "And you don't wanna be some big ole crusty scab, man. That shit's hard and nasty. That ain't you."

"People tip you for that kind of advice, Manny?" I asked, hiding my anger behind a wry smile.

Manny grinned and pointed at the tip jar in the middle of the counter. "Hey, man, tips are always welcome."

I leaned forward onto my elbows. "I'll give you a tip. Leave the psychologizing to the professionals." I swallowed the rest of my mimosa. My stomach growled fiercely, and my head still throbbed. It was a combination of a tension headache, a hangover, and low blood sugar. I turned to Al. "You had breakfast yet?"

"Yeah, I had some oatmeal and toast earlier."

"You up for second breakfast?"

Al chuckled and patted my arm. "I'm eighty-seven years old with nothing to do for the rest of my life. I'm always up for second breakfast, kid."

6

"BUT WHAT'S SHE *DOING* HERE?"

I pulled my shirt off and tossed it onto the pile of dirty clothes on the hardwood floor. I stood in the doorway between my bathroom and bedroom with my arms over my head, leaning against the door frame. My tanned stomach glistened beneath the soft glow of the moonlight streaming in through my window.

"Fuck if I know," I groaned. The conversation was quickly making my buzz disappear.

Maclynn Rush kneeled upwards on my bed. Dripping wet from head to toe, she still wore the white mini sundress she'd worn down at the pool and clubhouse area while I'd worked security. But now, the dress clung to her heavy breasts, emphasizing the fact that she wasn't wearing a bra and that, when wet, a white sundress became sheer. Her usually curly brown halo of hair was also soaked, and water dripped from the tendrils that were just now fighting to resume their curly natural state.

It was late now. Or early, if you thought of it that way. A little after two in the morning. I'd stuck around down at the clubhouse long enough to dismiss Marcus and Charles, my two night shift security guards, and to make sure the club-house and swim-up bar got locked up properly. Mack had waited around for me while I'd shut off lights and checked doors. When I'd met her back at the pool, where she promised she'd be, I'd found her waist-deep in the center of the pool. She'd curled a finger silently at me, beckoning for me to join her.

Whether it was the alcohol I'd imbibed while working, the stress I'd felt from being on the same island with Pam, or sheer horniness, I wasn't sure, but I'd dived in without even bothering to remove my clothes and met Mack in the center of the pool.

Without saying a word, she'd kissed me. The kiss was both sweet and tender, but also seductive and sexy as hell. I'd returned it, and when I'd reached around and grabbed her ass under her sundress, I'd discovered she wasn't wearing any panties.

That was all it took, and before I knew it, I'd christened the Seacoast Majestic's swimming pool for the first time since arriving on the island. If I'd been a smart man, I'd have just left her there. I'd have made my excuses and been on my way back to my room alone. But I wasn't a smart man. I was a greedy one.

I wanted more.

So I'd invited Mack back to my place for an encore, and on the way, that was when the questions had begun.

"So I heard that woman you were hugging in the lobby this morning is your fiancée."

"Ex-fiancée."

"You aren't together anymore?"

"Nope."

"Then why is she here?"

I shrugged. "You'd have to ask her."

"How long is she staying?"

"She's leaving first thing in the morning. Desi's gonna have a car pick her up at eight."

"But she just got here?"

"Yup." I felt like I couldn't breathe.

"Then why's she leaving so soon?"

I crumpled forward. "Why do you need to know all of this, Mack? Doesn't the fact that we just got busy in the pool tell you that Pam and I are over?"

Mack lifted a shoulder before crawling, dripping wet, onto my bed. One of the spaghetti straps of her dress had fallen off her shoulder and cut across her bicep. Her round, hard nipples poked against the sheer fabric. I didn't want to be talking about Pam when I could be tearing that dress off of her.

That was when she'd whined at me. "But what's she *doing* here?"

I threw my arms out on either side of myself. I was tired of talking about Pam, thinking about Pam, and feeling her aura nearby. I needed to bathe myself in another woman to bury everything I felt. "Fuck if I know, Mack. I guess there were some unsaid things."

"And you said them?"

My mouth hung open a little as I searched for the words. Mack didn't need to know all the gory details of our split. She didn't need to know that I hated Pam with every fiber of my body. She didn't need to know that I had had *nothing* to say to Pam and that I'd ordered her to leave the island. So I merely nodded and tried to placate the woman whose body I very badly wanted to ravish.

"I did," I promised. "I said everything. She said everything. We hashed it all out. We're in a good place."

"A good place, as in I should be worried?"

"No! A good place as in the split was amicable. We'll always love each other. You know, shit like that."

"Oh," she said in a muted tone.

The lie I'd told made my mouth taste bad. To tell the

universe a whopper like I would always love Pam was like putting bad juju into the air. I strode over to my nightstand, poured myself a shot of tequila, made the sign of the cross, and threw back the biting liquid.

"What was that about?"

I slammed the shot glass down on the nightstand and crawled onto the bed like a black panther stalking its prey. "I wanted God to forgive me for what I'm about to do to you."

"Oh," she giggled. "Well, in that case, amen."

7

"*RAWCK, NO MORNING KISSES, NO MORNING KISSES, RAWCK!*" THE screechy sound came from my window.

Facedown on my bed, I pried one eye open. An empty pillow lay beside me. *Fuck*. Mack was already gone. I forced my open eye to focus on the glowing red numbers a few feet past her pillow. Eight thirty-seven. Holy shit, that had happened fast. I felt like I'd just closed my eyes a few seconds ago.

"*Rawck!*" Earnestine cried from my windowsill. "*No morning kisses, no morning kisses,*" she chanted. I could hear her little nails clicking on the wood as she danced.

"Shut it!" I grunted.

"*Shut it, shut it, shut it,*" she cracked, changing her chant just to annoy me.

I rolled onto my back and stared up at the ceiling. Where was a fucking BB gun when a guy needed one?

"*Shut it, shut it, shut it.*" Tap-tap-tappity-tap went her feet on the sill.

A tap-dancing fucking parrot. Just fucking fantastic.

I sat up. Slumped over, I stared at the bird. She was a pretty bird. Her head was a bright lime green color, and her zebra face was interesting to look at it. It was like something I'd only seen in a zoo.

"At least you're a pretty bird."

"*Pretty bird, pretty bird,*" she sang.

I rolled my eyes and stood up. My head thumped slightly, but not as bad as it had the morning before. I strode over to my window and shooed Earnestine away, but I left my window open. I appreciated the fresh ocean breeze that flowed through my room. When my window was closed, the nasty scent of sweat mixed with dirty laundry made me feel intoxicatingly claustrophobic.

My phone rang.

I walked across the room and found a note scribbled on Seacoast Majestic stationery lying on top of my dresser. "Drunk, left to go to my place to get ready for work. I'll talk to you later. Mack."

I glanced down at my phone. The number had been blocked. "Restricted," I said with a bit of a chuckle. No doubt it was Pam calling from the airport to tell me she was leaving. I waved at my phone as I dropped it onto the dresser. "Buh-bye, Pammy."

Just the thought of saying goodbye to Pam buoyed me slightly. So much, in fact, that when Earnestine landed in my windowsill again, I didn't even shoo her away.

"*No morning kisses, no morning kisses, rawck!*" she screeched as it rang again.

I laughed at the phone as I pulled a clean shirt and a clean pair of underwear from my dresser. "Sorry, Pammy, nobody's home. Enjoy your ride back to America. Hope your plane doesn't crash."

I strode into my bathroom and started the water. I was suddenly ravenous and couldn't help but hope that Al was ready for another second breakfast.

8

SEATED AT A TABLE ON THE MAIN DINING ROOM'S OUTDOOR balcony with an omelet and plates of French toast, sausage, bacon, toast, fried potatoes, fresh fruit, and rolls covering the table in front of me, I looked like a king about to devour a feast. Behind me, the ocean broke against Paradise Isle's rocky western coastline, firing up white bits of foam and spray into the soft breeze and filling the air with the perpetual, rolling sound of the surf. Birds flew in from the sea and landed on the white-painted iron balcony railing, searching for uncleared tables and remnants of food while the uniformed waitstaff largely ignored their presence.

I rubbed my hands together over the food as if the plates were a fire that warmed my frigid skin. I felt lighter than I'd felt in days and had a sudden insatiable appetite that I couldn't wait to quench.

Al shook his head as he stared at me incredulously. "You seriously gonna put all this away, kid?"

My head tipped sideways as I grinned at him. "Do fucking spiders spin webs and creep me the hell out?"

Al's bushy brows lifted. "You must have a hollow leg or something."

I shoved a piece of sausage in my mouth and quirked a salacious grin. "I got a fairly large middle leg, if that counts." And after the second night in a row that I'd been with Mack, I badly needed to feed the beast.

Al's head jerked back as if he'd just been hit in the head with a Nerf football. "Oh, for Pete's sake, Drunk. I didn't need to hear that," he said through squinty eyes.

I chuckled. "You know what, Al? I think today's going to be a fucking great day."

"Boy, it's like a whole new Drunk." Al leaned in closer to me. "What happened to you?"

"Can't a guy just be happy for once?"

"Well, sure, a guy can be happy. You just usually aren't that guy."

"Thanks a lot, Al."

"I mean, if someone asked me for a word to describe Danny Drunk, it certainly wouldn't be happy."

I chewed on a syrupy bite of French toast. "Yeah? What would it be?"

Al shrugged. "I don't know. Indifferent comes to mind. I can't put my finger on it just yet. I mean, yesterday you walked around all day like someone'd peed in your Cheerios."

"That's because Pam was here," I said. "But you know what, Al? She's long gone by now. Long fucking gone. She's probably sky-high over the Atlantic by now. And I couldn't be happier." I pointed at him with my fork. "Ya like that?"

Al looked at his watch. "It's only a little after nine, Drunk. What time did she leave?"

I shrugged. "Desi was going to make sure she took off early this morning for me." I shook my head while dunking my powdered donut into a puddle of syrup on my French toast plate. "Great guy, that Desi."

"Yeah, Desi's great," said Al. He tapped me on the shoulder. "Speak of the devil." He pointed towards the dining room entrance, where Desi stood conversing with Carla, the restaurant's hostess, stationed on the other side of the all-windowed wall.

"Ah! The man of the hour. I need to talk to him." I stood up and walked to the glass doors separating the dining room from the balcony and waved him over. "Hey! Des! Over here!"

Desi stopped talking with Carla and made a beeline for me and Al. His usual smile was faded, and there was a sharp crease between his dark brows. "Mr. Drunk, I need to speak with you."

"I need to speak with you too, Desi. Do you know if Pam's over the Atlantic yet? What time did her flight leave?" I glanced down at the Smith & Wesson watch on my wrist. It was exactly a quarter after nine.

"That's what I wanted to speak with you about. Her airplane is still on the tarmac. They finished boarding ten minutes ago."

"Oh." I frowned. "Well, what's the holdup? Mechanical problems?"

Desi shook his head. The look on his face said it was more serious than that. "No. I have a friend that works for the airline. I'd asked him to let me know when Ms. Calcara boarded the flight. He just called to tell me that she hasn't arrived yet and they cannot hold the flight for one passenger. They have almost completed their preflight checks, and if she is not there in the next couple of minutes, they will leave without her." He looked at me curiously. "But I have no way of getting a hold of her."

Tension froze my muscles. Pam hadn't left yet? I shook my head and dropped my napkin onto the table. "I don't understand, Desi. You were supposed to get her to the airport on time for her flight."

Desi nodded. "Yes, I asked Akoni to drive her. Yesterday I spoke to my friend at the airport and discovered that she was scheduled for the nine o'clock flight. I asked Mari to let Ms.

Calcara know that they should leave at six o'clock this morning to make it on time."

"Okay?"

"Akoni waited for her, and when she did not arrive, he went to her room. He said that he knocked, but no one came to the door, so he asked one of the maids to check her room to make sure she hadn't overslept. But all of her things were already gone."

"She was already gone?" said Al, who now had a set of fully functioning hearing aids in his ears. "Where'd she go?"

Wide-eyed, I parroted Al. "Yeah, where'd she go?"

Desi shook his head. "Akoni assumed that Ms. Calcara had made other transportation arrangements. But now that we know that she did not make her flight, I do not know where it is that she went."

I frowned. This was seriously not happening. "Fuck," I said, bobbing my head in disgust. I shook my head. "She decided not to fly out. I knew something like this would happen. Dammit, Pam!"

"Are we sure that her new transportation arrangements just didn't break down on the way to the airport?" asked Al.

Desi's hands went up in a perplexed shrug. "Without knowing who she received a ride from, I do not have any idea."

My phone rang. I pulled it out of my pocket and stared down at it. Another restricted call. Now it made sense. Pam had skipped out on her flight and had tried calling me, either to gloat that she wasn't leaving on my schedule or to insist that we meet up before she went back to the States. I gritted my teeth. I didn't want to hear the sound of her voice, much less what she had to say. But I needed to find out where she was so I could send Akoni to pick her up and get her on the next flight out. I'd pay triple the airfare if I had to to get her back to America by lunchtime.

"Where the fuck are you, Pam? You missed your goddamned flight," I hollered into the phone.

"Hello, Daniel," said a deep male voice.

I paused, taken aback. It hadn't even occurred to me that it might not be Pam on the other end. "Who's this?"

"Let's just say it's not Pam," said the man.

My temperature was escalating quickly. Pam was trying to stay on the island, and this guy was gonna play with me? "No fucking shit, Sherlock."

"But I have a feeling you might be looking for her right about now."

I looked at the phone, stunned. Was this a friend of hers? Then it hit me. "Shitwell, is this you?" My pulse was on a high boil now.

"Nope. Not Shitwell either."

"Where's Pam? Is she with you?"

"Now you're asking the right questions."

"Who is it, Drunk?" asked Al.

I waved a dismissive hand at him. "All right, then. If you know where Pam is, then spill. She's late for her flight back to the US."

"Oh, now, Daniel, don't go getting ahead of yourself. First things first."

"First things first? What the hell's that supposed to mean?"

"Well, first we have a little *matter* to discuss before I tell you where Pam is."

I shook my head. "A little matter? What the fuck are you talking about?"

"I'm so glad you asked. Allow me to explain. I recently received word that you've managed to come into possession of quite a large windfall."

"I don't have any idea what you're talking about," I said through a clenched jaw.

"Oh, I think you *do* know what I'm talking about. Thanks to the spike in the price of Bitcoin, I think you made out quite nicely. And despite the recent drop-off, I have reason to believe you cashed out before it dipped too low."

"Yeah? Who told you that?"

"Oh, I think it's kind of common knowledge, don't you? The papers told of your involvement in the cryptocurrency crime ring and the invaluable assistance you provided to the Paradise Isle Royal Police Force."

"So you can read, big fucking deal. You wanna gold star or an extra recess?" I was starting to get an uneasy feeling in the pit of my stomach. The papers knew about my involvement in the scene that had played out at the airport just shy of eight weeks ago, but only a handful of people knew about the money.

"No, as a matter of fact. What I *want* is a piece of the pie."

"Is that right?"

"Yes, actually, now that I think about it. You know what I'd like instead of a *piece* of the pie? I think I'd prefer the *whole* pie."

"I'll give you a pie. Right in the fuckin' face, I'll give you a pie."

"Tsk, tsk, tsk, Daniel. You should be nicer to me than that."

"Yeah? And why's that?"

"Because I have something I know you'll want."

"I doubt it."

"Oh, but I do, Daniel. Because *I* have Pam."

9

Stunned, I gave Al a funny look from across the table. I shifted in my seat. "I'm sorry, what did you just say?"

The gravelly voice purred slightly. "Ohhh, I think you heard me. *I* have Pam."

"With you?" I asked incredulously.

"Yes, with me. Would you like to speak with her?"

Thinking about it, I frowned. Was this seriously happening right now? Was this lunatic implying that he'd *kidnapped* Pam? And then the realization hit me: perhaps *Pam* herself had set this all up. Less than two handfuls of people knew about the money—my parents, Al, Artie, Manny, and a few of Al's geriatric squad members being the entirety of those people. But if Pam had recently spoken to my mother, like she said she had, it was more than likely that *Pam* also knew about the money. Maybe this whole thing was a setup, staged to do two things. One, to get her grubby hands on my money, and two, to somehow win me back.

I swallowed and shook my head. "No. I don't really care to speak to her. Thank you."

"You don't want to speak with her?" The man sounded like I'd caught him off guard.

I shrugged. "I'd prefer not to. If she's there with you, you can fill her in on our conversation, can't you?"

Now the man didn't sound quite so confident. "Oh, well, I suppose—"

I cut him off. "Okay? So what's the plan? You keeping her?"

"Well, that's up to you now, isn't it?" said the voice, trying to resume his previous menacing tone. "If you want her back, it's going to cost you. Seven million dollars, to be exact."

I fought back a chortle. Seven million dollars or Pam? He couldn't be serious. "And what if I don't want her back?"

There was a pause, like the guy on the other end hadn't expected that question. Finally he spoke. "Simple. Then I'll have to get rid of her."

"Get rid of her!" My free hand covered the smile that had begun to creep across my face. I took a long pause, trying to compose myself. Finally, I could hold it in no longer. *"Deal!"* I breathed into the phone. "Thank you, thank you, thank you! Get her cheating ass off the island! I never want to see her face again!"

"Daniel, I don't think you're catching my drift. I didn't mean that I'd give her an all-expenses-paid vacation back to wherever the hell she came from," croaked the voice. "I meant if you don't pay up, I'll be forced to kill her."

I lifted a brow. "Just out of curiosity, is Pam sitting right there next to you?"

"Well, she's in the other room. I can get her if—"

But I didn't let him finish. "Oh, good. Here's the thing. Pam's a little *squeamish* when it comes to blood, you know—or dying," I said with a wrinkled nose. From across the table, Al's watery blue-green eyes stared back at me incredulously. I held a finger up to him to stop him from interrupting. "So you're probably not going to want to let her know what's coming ahead of time."

"Excuse me?"

"I mean, I don't know how you plan to do it. Knife, gun, rat poison, chain saw, shark attack…" I thought about it for a second. "You know, if I were you, I'd probably skip the shark attack thing. She might literally lose her shit if you put her in with some sharks. We watched *Sharknado* once and the woman didn't sleep for a week. I mean, if you're gonna kill her, there's really no sense in giving her nightmares. That's just cruel. You know what I'm saying?"

"Drunk," whispered Al from across the table. "What's going on?"

"Shhh," I mouthed, holding a finger up to my lips. I pointed at the receiver and added, "This guy's got Pam."

"Daniel, I don't think you understand the severity of the situation," said the man on the phone. "I will literally *kill* this woman if you don't bring me my seven million dollars by the end of the day."

That was when I'd had enough. My jaw set. There was no more playing around. "No, buddy. I don't think *you* understand. Pam Calcara is my *ex-fiancée*. They put the *x* in there for a reason. It's to signify how low down the alphabet the woman is in my life. Now if she'd been just my *fiancée*, then she'd be higher on the alphabet. You see? Because *f* comes before *x*. But she isn't. She's my *ex*. She's a low-down, dirty, no-good cheating slut that I made the mistake of giving a five-thou-sand-dollar engagement ring to. That's what she is. So if you want to keep her, by all means. Keep her. I can promise you, she's nothing but a headache. She'll spend your money, make you wait a year to marry her, and then on your wedding night, she'll fuck her ex-boyfriend on your brand-new Sealy Posture-pedic. Okay? It's that simple." I shook my head. "If I were you, I'd send her back to the US, because you know what? She ain't worth the hassle." And on that note, I hung up the phone.

I sucked in a deep breath and noticed both Al and Desi

staring at me. I looked out over the food in front of me and picked up a particularly tempting piece of extra-fatty bacon and bit off half of it. "Mmmm. Anyone else as starving as I am?"

10

ARTIE BALLADARES LEANED ACROSS HIS OVERSIZED DESK ONTO HIS meaty elbows. "You can't be so flip about this, Drunk."

Al's shoulders stooped over as he looked up at me. "Artie's right, Drunk. That's just not right."

I leaned against Artie's file cabinet and shrugged. "First of all, I feel like this is something Pam set up. She's probably not even actually kidnapped. She probably hired someone to make that phone call. She just wants to get her fake nails into my money, and fuck if I'm about to let that happen."

"But, Drunk!" said Al. "You don't know that Pam did this. She could *really* be kidnapped. Whoever has her might actually hurt her. You can't let that happen. You've got to do something!"

I let my head fall back on my shoulders as I groaned. "You guys are being so dramatic! It's not that I'm *letting* anything happen. I mean, you know if this *is* a real kidnapping, and I refuse to pay them, they'll probably just put a bag over her head and drop her off at the airport or something. Why would they want to hurt her if they're getting nothing out of the deal?"

"And if they don't want to let her go?" asked Artie.

I shrugged. "I mean, if they don't let her go, then we'll turn it over to the island cops. They can handle it. I'm not a cop here on this island, you know." I'd learned that lesson the hard way. Paradise Island cops didn't care for Americans, and they *extra* didn't care for American cops, never mind the fact that I wasn't that great of a cop to begin with.

Artie sliced the air definitively with his hand. "Nope. We can't report this, Drunk. Business *still* hasn't gotten back to normal since that whole Jimmie fiasco. Finding a dead body in one of our rooms was definitely bad for the bottom line. If folks hear that there's been a woman abducted from resort property?" He shook his head. "They'd *never* come back."

I looked from one man to the next. "Look, fellas. I don't know what you want me to say. I'm not paying these fuckers seven million dollars for Pam. She ain't worth the price of a stamp, much less seven million fucking dollars. Besides. I didn't even get seven million dollars. I got six point nine million."

Al lifted a brow. "You invested in those accounts I told you to, didn't you?"

I raised a shoulder uneasily. "Yeah, so?"

"Then you should have much more than six point nine million dollars by now. You should have considerably more than seven by now. Those accounts have been doing gang-busters this quarter."

It was true. I'd picked Al's brain for a week straight, trying to figure out where to invest my money. Al was a whiz with the markets, even considering himself a personal friend of Warren Buffet's although he'd never actually met the man. So, thanks to Al, I actually had *more* than they'd asked for. The market was up and so was my nest egg.

"But I spent some of it," I argued weakly.

Al looked at me with narrowed eyes. "Oh yeah? On what?"

I shrugged and tugged on the hem of my tank top. "I bought some new threads." I'd bought an entirely new wardrobe, actually, since I'd tossed all the clothes that Pam had bought with my money for our honeymoon.

"Anything else?"

"And I just ordered a new big-screen for my new bachelor pad. Oh, and I got myself the new PlayStation and a few games." I had to have something to occupy my time when Al was napping and there were no women willing to party with me.

"That's it?"

"Pretty much," I said, bobbing my head. I wasn't much of a big spender. Besides spending money on alcohol and living expenses and occasionally a fancy dinner for a female companion, I'd never really spent much over the course of my lifetime. And here on the island, as part of my compensation package, Artie took care of my rent and put me on the all-inclusive plan when it came to food and drinks. It was quite the setup, and another reason I had yet to bounce back to the States.

I held up a finger. "Oh! I almost forgot. I signed my mom up for a meat of the month club, and I had a new grill shipped to Pops. It's a grill *and* a smoker. He's gonna love it. Of course he won't *tell* me he loves it, but I'll know deep down in his heart he does," I said, nodding. I didn't add that I'd actually had the money for all of that stuff in my savings account *before* the seven-million-dollar payout.

"That stuff couldn't have cost you more than five grand," said Artie, shaking his head. "Look, Drunk, it was found money anyway, I think you need to pay the guy."

I shook my head. I didn't care if it was found money or hard-earned money. That was my nest egg. That money gave me the freedom to take the Seacoast Majestic job or leave it. It gave me the freedom to tell anyone at any time that they could go fuck themselves. It meant I didn't have to go back to Kansas City or anywhere near Pam Calcara. That money was my freedom. "Nah. Not happening, guys. I mean, I'll put in a word with the big guy in the sky. I can't promise it'll be a good word, you know, there's not many nice things I can say about the woman, but I'll ask him to do his best to get her out of her present situation. That's the best I'm gonna be able to do for her."

"Oh, come on, kid. These guys might not be playing around. They could kill her!" said Al, his hands splayed out in front of him.

"We don't even know if they really have her. Maybe she staged all of this. Maybe she *did* find her own transportation. Maybe she caught a cab and stopped off down at the strip to do a little souvenir shopping and, you know, take advantage of the duty-free shops and shit. And then she lost track of time."

"They said they'd put her on the phone, Drunk. They've got her."

"We don't know that," I said. I knew I was grasping at straws, but I didn't know how else to disengage myself from the situation. "I tell ya what. Let me do a little investigating. I'll run down and talk to the maid that Akoni talked to. Maybe she saw Pam leave or something."

Al nodded. "That's a good idea. Find out if any of the maids saw anything. You could check the surveillance tapes too."

I shrugged. Now he was getting carried away. I didn't feel like spending hours holed up in the tiny little shoebox of an office Artie had assigned me and watching grainy black-and-white footage of lizards fucking in the streets and whatnot.

"Yeah, we'll see. Lemme go talk to Mari and find out which one of her girls helped Akoni out. All right?"

"And if she really *was* kidnapped for ransom? What then?" asked Artie.

I swatted the air with my hand. "Let's not go jumping the gun if it ain't loaded, all right, fellas? Lemme do a little snooping around and see what I can't dig up."

11

MARIPOSA MARRERO, THE HEAD OF THE CLEANING AND FRONT office staff, was a forty-two-year-old single mother supporting three children who ranged in age from eight to seventeen. Having been raised in Guanajay, Cuba, in a family of tobacco farmers, she'd eventually immigrated to Paradise Isle to give her children a better life. So she took her position at the resort very seriously.

From the very beginning, Al had advised that being tight with Mari was like having a key to the whole resort, so I'd made it my personal mission to figure out how to get on her good side. But no matter what I did, winning the woman over seemed like an impossible feat. And I'd tried almost everything to charm her. I'd started by picking her up after her shifts in one of the resort golf carts and driving her to her car in the employee parking lot down the hill. Then I'd found out how she liked her coffee, and I'd brought her a cup every morning for two weeks straight. And when I'd discovered our mutual love of chocolate, I'd spent a pretty penny importing an array of fine chocolates that I could share with the woman. But I still hadn't managed to warm her up to me.

"Mari," I said, raising a hand to stop her from boarding the elevator in the lobby. "Hold up."

Mari was a short woman with a large bottom and thick thighs that rubbed together when she walked, leaving a little zipping sound trailing behind her wherever she went. She had dark black hair that was always pulled back into a sharp bun. Her pudgy cheeks dimpled when she smiled. And because she never wore even an ounce of makeup, there was nothing to hide the scowl that she wore when she saw me coming.

In fact, today she sighed when she saw me jogging slowly in her direction. I had a feeling that talk of my indiscretions with her girls had made it to her ears. "What do you want, Drunk? I need to get upstairs."

"What's going on up there?"

"One of the girls said the water isn't working in room two fourteen," she said with a sigh.

"You want me to call Hector and have him come over and fix it?"

"I'll handle it. What do you want?" She looked at me impatiently, her hand on her hip.

"Want?" I swallowed hard. For the life of me, I couldn't understand why it was that I could talk to any beautiful woman without so much as a weak knee, and yet one scowl from Mariposa Marrero made my adrenaline spike and my limbs heavy. "Oh, yeah. Uh, Desi was handling getting a woman off to the airport this morning. He said he was working with you. You know anything about that?" Unable to meet the ferociousness of her glare, I kept my eyes trained on the framed portrait of a salty old sea captain on the wall behind her.

"Yeah, I know something about that," she said, tapping her foot on the ground and crossing her arms over her chest. "What I know is that you shouldn't let your personal business interfere with resort business."

"But she was a guest!" I blurted. "I simply asked Desi to

handle getting a guest from point A to point B. That's what we do around here. We help guests out. And besides, that's Desi's job! He's the concierge. He finds guests rides to the airports and to the shopping centers."

She wagged a finger at me angrily. "I don't consider your sexual conquests to be resort guests."

I swallowed hard. "Mari, I can *honestly* say that I've never slept with that woman."

Mari narrowed her eyes to pinpricks and came at me with a pointed finger. "Oh, please, Drunk. I'm wise to your ways. And don't think I don't know about you using my girls as your own private welcome wagon. You know, I don't hire girls just for your personal pleasure."

"You don't?" I said, finally meeting her eyes with a smile.

She didn't think that was funny. Her black eyes flashed at me as she frowned. "No, as a matter of fact, I don't. How long has the new girl been here, Drunk? A week, week and a half, and you've *already* managed to get her into your bed."

I held up two hands defensively. "Listen, Mari. I don't ask you what you do on your time off. Why is what I do on my free time up for discussion?"

"Because it could be considered sexual harassment in the workplace!"

"*How?* I'm not her boss. I don't have any control over her hiring and firing. Besides, Mack seduced *me*. I didn't even realize that you'd hired a new girl until she introduced herself to me down at the swim-up bar one night."

Mari's cheeks flushed. "You know, just because you have more money than God doesn't mean you don't have to take your job here seriously, Drunk."

My eyes widened as I stared at her. "More money than…"

"You heard me! *Some* of us have to actually work for everything we have. We aren't all best friends with the boss. We have to *work* if we expect to have a job the next day. And we aren't all sitting on a pile of cash to tide us over if we do get fired!"

"Wow," I said with lifted brows. "Tell me how you really feel." Her words actually kind of stung. I'd done nothing but try and get her to like me, and now I was finding out how she really felt about me.

Clearly annoyed with me, she swiped a hand in the air as if to erase the conversation. "Whatever. What do you want?"

"I just wanted to know if you talked to the guest yesterday about her departure time this morning."

Mari put her professional face back on. "Yes, I did. I spoke to Ms. Calcara last night. She had a nine o'clock flight this morning, so Desi asked if we could pick her up at six."

"And what did Pam say? Did she say that was okay?"

Mari nodded. "Yes, she said that was just fine and that she'd be ready."

"And did you tell her where to meet Akoni?"

"Of course. I told her to stop at the concierge's desk at a few minutes to six and her ride would be waiting for her."

I frowned. "And she understood that?"

Mari shrugged. "She seemed to. Why?"

"Desi just informed me that she didn't make her flight. Akoni told him that he went to her room and knocked, but there was no answer. He asked one of your girls to check her room when she didn't answer. She found that Ms. Calcara had already checked out. Do you know which of your girls he would have asked to open her room?"

Mari thought about it for a second. "Gigi Flores is cleaning that area of the motel. I assume she was the one that he saw."

I groaned inwardly. Gigi and I had had a bit of a brief *thing*. Of course, she hadn't appreciated it when I'd simultaneously had a *thing* with Alicia, one of the front desk girls. How was I supposed to know that the two of them were friends and they'd eventually swap sexual escapades?

"Okay, thank you, Mari. I appreciate it."

Wordlessly, she lifted a brow and pressed the button on the elevator. "I'll be keeping an eye on you, Drunk."

I grinned. "Feel free to make it two eyes." I walked away, but as I heard the elevator ding and the doors open, I turned around and pointed at her. "Hey, Mari, I just ordered us some new chocolate from Switzerland. It should be here next week. I'll bring it by when it comes in."

She rolled her eyes as the doors shut.

I'd win that woman over to the dark side yet.

12

I FOUND GIGI FLORES'S CLEANING CART IN FRONT OF A ROOM ON the ground floor of the second motel building. I knew it was her because I could hear her slightly off-pitch singing pouring down the corridor between the hotel buildings and the resort. I approached the motel room with ease, careful not to scare her. The last thing I needed was for Gigi Flores to be even more pissed at me than she already was.

Knocking on the door frame before entering, I called out her name. "Gigi? Hey, Gig," I said, peering into the room. I didn't see her in the bedroom, but then I heard her voice again, coming from the bathroom. I knocked on the bathroom door. "Gig?"

I walked in to find the woman leaning over the tub, head-phones in her ears, singing in Spanish. Her curvy bottom moved in time to the rhythm of the song she sang. I stared down appreciatively at the badonkadonk that had first attracted me to the woman in the first place and bit my knuckle.

Damn.

"Gig," I said.

When she didn't turn around, I gingerly tapped her on the shoulder.

"Ahhhh!" she screamed, jumping to her feet, a spray bottle and a scrubbing pad in her rubber gloved hands.

I flinched, curling up my arms over my head as she aimed the bottle at me. "It's just me!" I screamed.

Her earbuds fell from her ears and dangled around her neck. "Drunk!" she bellowed, her voice echoing off the tile walls. "¡Ay, carajo! You scared the hell out of me!"

"I'm sorry! I knocked! You didn't answer."

"That's because I had headphones on!" she snapped angrily, now holding a hand to her chest. "My heart is racing!"

I wanted to say that I had that effect on women, but I thought better of it and instead decided an apology was my best course of action. "I'm really sorry. I didn't mean to scare you. Want me to go get you some water?"

She scowled at me and strode towards her cart just outside the motel room to put her cleaning solution and scrubber on the cart. "No, I don't want any water. What do you want, Drunk? Are you here to rub it in that you used both Alicia and me for sex and then pounced on the new girl the second she arrived?" She stared at me with her head tipped sideways.

Ouch.

"Oh no. Official security business, actually," I assured her.

She peeled off her yellow gloves and dropped them onto her cart before folding her arms over her chest. She tapped her foot on the floor impatiently.

Taking that to mean that she was listening, I continued. "Akoni mentioned that you had helped him look for a guest this morning because she never showed up for her ride."

"Yeah," said Gigi. She pointed up the corridor. "She'd already checked out. Why?"

Relief that Gigi didn't seem to be aware that the woman in question had been my ex washed over me. That was one less person I had to explain things to. "The woman never showed up for her flight. I'm just checking around to see if I can find out what happened to her."

"I have no idea what happened to her."

"You didn't see her leave her room this morning?"

Gigi shook her head. "Nope. But I did see a guy knock on her door about a quarter to six this morning."

My brows lifted in surprise. "Yeah? Recognize him?"

Gigi frowned and shook her head. "Not at all."

"He wasn't an employee here?"

"Nope. I've never seen him before."

"Well, what did he look like?"

She shrugged. "I don't know, he was skinny. Tall, but not as tall as you. Maybe six foot even. He had a ponytail. Dark hair."

"White guy? Black guy?"

She shook her head. "I'm pretty sure he was white. I didn't get a very good look at his face," she admitted. "I didn't realize anyone was going to ask about him or I would've paid more attention."

"No, no, it's all right, I understand. So, he knocked on the door. Did she answer?"

"Someone did. I saw the door open and then I went about my business, cleaning the room two doors down. I was in there for about five minutes, and when I came out he was gone."

"But you don't know if she left with him?"

"No, I have no idea."

"Do you remember anything else about the guy? Clothing, jewelry, tattoos?"

She thought about it for a moment before nodding. "He did have a cross tattooed on his forearm."

"A cross? What kind of cross? Can you describe it?"

She made a face. "Yeah, it was kind of gross."

"A cross was gross?"

"Yeah, it was about this big." Gigi extended her forearm and kind of sketched out the rough size of it with her other hand, approximately eight inches by three inches. "And the two pieces of the cross were like wooden daggers. The one going up and down looked like it pierced through his skin and had some blood colored in. It was very realistic looking." She made a face as if recalling it disgusted her.

"Ahh. And do you know what he was wearing?"

"Jeans and a t-shirt?" she guessed.

"Shoes?"

She shrugged. "Can't say I even looked at his shoes."

I nodded. "Okay, anything else you remember?"

She shook her head. "Nope. Like I said, I just saw him knock and then I went to finish cleaning the room I was working on." She tipped her head sideways again. "You think something bad happened to this lady?"

"Nah, I don't think so. I'm just trying to find out who gave her a ride."

Gigi nodded. Then she looked at me a little more closely. "So. How are things going with you and the new girl?"

I lifted a shoulder. What in the hell was I supposed to say to that? "Fine, I guess."

She took a half step towards me. The seductive way she'd looked at me right before we'd begun hooking up returned. "Only fine? Maybe you've forgotten that being with me was waaay better than just *fine*."

I smiled at her before shooting her a wink. "Oh, trust me, Gigi. I haven't forgotten."

13

Now, ARMED WITH THE KNOWLEDGE THAT SOME UNKNOWN GUY had actually gone to visit Pam, I was forced to do what I absolutely hadn't wanted to do. I sat in my tiny shoebox of an office, staring at my computer screen. My fingers clumsily clicked buttons on the keyboard, trying to remember how to access the new security system I'd had installed after being appointed to my new position. Technology wasn't exactly my forte. Not that being a police officer back in the States had exactly been in my wheelhouse either, but this was even *less* familiar to me than that was.

There was a knock at the door.

I glanced up to see Al tottering into my office. "Figure anything out yet?" he asked, his voice phlegmier than usual.

"A few things," I sighed.

"Yeah? Like what?"

"Well. For one, I learned that somehow Mari knows about the money."

Al looked stunned. "How in the world does she know about that? That's privileged information!"

"Hell if I know. But she made a comment about me having more money than God. So, someone told her."

Al groaned. "That's not good."

"No, it's not."

"Well, I sure as heck didn't tell her."

I nodded. "I know you didn't, Al."

"And I know my buddies didn't tell her either. I swore them all to secrecy," said Al. "I knew what kind of hassle it would be for you if everyone here knew you had some money. And I didn't want to see that happen to you."

"Yeah, I don't know how she found out. But I also spoke to Gigi Flores. She was the maid Akoni asked to open Pam's room. She told me that she saw a guy knock on Pam's door a little before six this morning." I gestured towards the chair in front of my desk. "Have a seat. I'm gonna go through security footage to see if I can't track down the guy. Maybe that's who Pam left with."

Al put a hand on either side of the chair's armrests and carefully lowered himself down. "Did Gigi recognize him?"

"Nah, she said she'd never seen him before." I leaned my chin on my fist as I debated which security camera had the best angle of Pam's room from the list of options on my screen.

"You know what you're doing there?"

I didn't take my eyes off the screen. "Meh, I'm making it up as I go along. Fake it till you make it and all that, you know?" I clicked the camera, and when the footage showed up on my screen, I moved the position slider slowly backwards to the appropriate time marker, so I could see any motion near Pam's door. As it began to play, a woman exited the room two doors down from Pam's. Her face wasn't visible, but I pointed to the screen. "I'd recognize that ass anywhere." I zoomed into the area. "That's Gigi's cart. Looks like I've got the right camera."

Al stood up and dragged his chair around the perimeter of my desk to sit down next to me. "Which one's Pam's room?"

I pointed at the screen. "Right there. Now we just wait until this guy shows up and see what happens."

"So, what else did the maid have to say?"

"Not much. Just that she saw a guy knock on the door. He's a white guy, about six foot, long black hair in a ponytail, and a big tattoo of a cross on his forearm. He was wearing jeans and a t-shirt."

"That's something."

I nodded. "Yeah, but she didn't see if Pam left with him or anything."

Al pointed at the screen. "Yeah, but we're about to find out. Look."

Sure enough, the exact man that Gigi had described approached Pam's room. I could see Gigi standing in front of the room she'd been cleaning. She watched the man for only a second before carrying on with her business. The angle of the camera obscured the man's face, but I could clearly make out the tattoo in the picture.

"Recognize him?" asked Al.

I shook my head. "Never seen him before in my life."

We watched as the man stopped in front of Pam's door and knocked. Seconds later, Pam appeared in her doorway. There was no volume, so we could only infer what Pam was saying.

"She doesn't seem to recognize him either," said Al.

I swished my lips to the side. Reluctantly, I'd have to agree. She didn't fully open the door and instead kind of poked her head around the corner like one might do when they weren't expecting someone. "Yeah, maybe. If she'd have known him, you'd think she would have just opened the door up wide."

The man took a half a step backwards and pointed up the hill towards the circular driveway in front of the lobby. And then Pam smiled and nodded. She held a finger up to him as if to say "just give me a minute." The man nodded and left her room, heading in the direction he'd just pointed. A minute later, we watched as Pam rolled her suitcase out the door, hoisted the strap of a carry-on bag up on her shoulder and shut the door behind her.

"She's following him," said Al.

My heart lurched slightly. Pam wasn't seriously stupid enough to follow a stranger, was she? "Ugh," I groaned as she moved off my computer screen. I clicked to the next camera and matched up the times to see her heading towards the lobby. Finally, I selected the loading area camera. It was right in front of the lobby and caught all of our guests coming and going, loading into taxicabs and hotel shuttles. I reversed the time slightly so we could see where the long-haired man had gone.

"There!" Al pointed to the top of the screen.

A white car with no markings on it was parked at the top of the circle driveway. Why Desi hadn't asked it to move along, I wasn't sure. It certainly wasn't a hotel car, and it didn't have the markings of a cab. We watched as the long-haired man got into the driver's seat and opened a magazine. He waited patiently until two minutes later, when Pam showed up with her suitcase. The man got out of the car, loaded her suitcase into the trunk, and opened the back door for her, and Pam slid inside.

Less than twenty seconds later, they were gone.

Fuck.

"Who the hell was that guy?" I asked, turning to look at Al.

He lifted his bushy brows but had no response.

I shook my head and lifted my walkie-talkie from my desk, promptly summoning Desi to my office.

14

"I HAVE NO IDEA WHO THAT MAN IS, MR. DRUNK," SAID DESI, wringing his hands in front of his body.

"You allowed him to sit there and wait," I said, pointing at the screen.

"We got a shuttle bus in from the airport. I was helping the passengers unload and pointing them in the right direction. He slipped in while I was distracted."

"How'd he get past the gate security?"

"It is not difficult, I'm afraid. If he told them he was picking up a guest, he only had to know her name and room number."

Still seated in front of my desk, I let my head fall into my open palms. "Ugh, Desi!"

"I am very sorry, Mr. Drunk. We do have people on the island picking up guests from time to time. It is not unusual by any means."

"I can't believe she just rode off with him," I said.

"Perhaps she knew this man," said Desi. "Perhaps it was a friend of Ms. Calcara's."

I shook my head. "Pam wouldn't know anyone on the island. And we watched the man knock on her door. Just by her facial expressions, it was obvious she didn't know him, and she seemed surprised that he was early. It's my guess that he posed as her ride to the airport and she bought it, hook, line, and sinker."

"But who would want to kidnap your fiancée, Mr. Drunk?"

I groaned. "Ex-fiancée, Desi. And I have no idea. That's what I'm trying to figure out." Desi had no idea how much money I was worth. And there was no way I could explain it to him without having my business spread all around the resort. I didn't feel like talking about the situation any more with Desi present. "Desi, do me a favor?"

Desi's head bobbed immediately. I could tell he felt bad, like somehow it had been his fault that Pam had been taken, and he wanted the chance to make it up to me. "Anything, Mr. Drunk. How may I be of service?"

"First of all, once again, keep all of this to yourself," I said, reminding him of my earlier request.

"Yes, of course. I shall not mention this to a living soul."

"And second of all, keep your ear to the ground. If anyone mentions Pam or seeing that car or that guy, I wanna know about it. All right?"

"Yes, yes, of course."

I stood up and patted Desi on the shoulder. I knew it wasn't his fault, but I felt that perhaps I'd given him the impression that I thought it was. "Thanks, Desi. I appreciate it a lot."

"Anytime, Mr. Drunk."

"All right, you're welcome to go."

Desi nodded at me and then at Al and slipped out my office door.

When he was gone, Al inhaled a deep breath and then exhaled it slowly. He scratched the back of his head. "Well, at least we've gotten a look at the man and the car. I'm fairly confident that was a Crown Vic."

"Yeah? Could you tell what year?"

Al shrugged. "It had to be a ninety-eight or newer. Ford

quit making the Crown Vic in twenty eleven if I'm not mistaken."

"So we got a car and we got a guy. That's a start. But Artie doesn't want us to go to the police." I threw my hands up in the air and rocked back on my squeaky office chair. "Then what the hell are we supposed to do? My hands are tied."

"Now, that's not entirely true, Drunk. You could pay that guy the money."

I grimaced. "I'm an American citizen. Americans don't negotiate with terrorists."

"But, Drunk—"

"In case I wasn't clear, Al, that's not happening."

My phone rang once again. One glance at the caller ID told me it was likely the guy who claimed to have Pam. I groaned and slumped back against my seat back. "It's him."

Al's eyes widened. "Well, answer it for heaven's sake!"

"Here, you answer it," I said, shoving the phone in Al's face. I had no interest in speaking to that douchecanoe again.

Al shoved it back. "No way. You answer it."

"Ugh, fine." I pushed the button on my phone and held it up to my ear. "Yeah, whaddaya want?" I growled, reaching down into the lowest register I could find.

"Well, hello again, Daniel."

"Hello, psychopath."

"I thought now that you've had a chance to digest the situation and perhaps come to your senses, I might give you a call to see if you've had a change of heart?"

"A change of heart? Regarding Pam?" I chuckled into the phone. "Why? Has hell frozen over?"

The pause on the other end of the phone gave me the sneaking suspicion that hadn't been the answer the caller had anticipated. Finally, he spoke, his voice a bit froggy now, "Well, then, you leave me no choice, Daniel. I'll have to kill her."

I shrugged. "Hey, man, that's the breaks. I've got a video of the abduction that I'll be turning over to the island police.

We've got both the Crown Vic and the dude with the ponytail and tattoo on camera. It's not gonna be hard to find you. You kill her and you're going to prison for murder. So, that's your call. I mean, I hear some guys enjoy the extracurricular activities that go on behind bars, so you do you, man. But the fact of the matter is you're not getting a buck outta me. So, have a nice life." With that, I hung up the phone and turned to see Al shaking his head.

"What have you done, Drunk? What have you done?"

15

"YOU'RE NO FUN TONIGHT, DRUNK. WHAT GIVES?" WITH MY bedsheet covering her bare skin, the curly-haired brunette propped herself up on one elbow and looked over at me.

I was seated naked on the side of the bed, nursing a fifth of tequila, but I could feel her eyes burning holes into my back. I raked a hand through my hair as my head slumped between my shoulder blades. "Sorry, Mack. It's just been a long couple of days."

I'd invited Mack over for a playdate as a way to push thoughts of Pam's kidnapping and potential murder out of my mind. Unfortunately, it hadn't worked. Because ever since I'd seen the security footage and been forced to believe that Pam truly had been kidnapped, I'd found myself feeling conflicted and unable to get the situation wiped from my brain.

While I *hated* the woman with every fiber of my being, something deep inside of me, whether it was the little Catholic schoolboy who knew right from wrong, or the Boy Scout who'd taken an oath to help people at all times, or the cop who'd promised to serve and protect—whatever it was, something told me I just couldn't let her die. I had to help. But I didn't *want* to help. And I certainly didn't *want* to give up my seven million dollars either. But what was a guy to do? Artie didn't want the authorities alerted. And while I'd been a cop back home, I wasn't a detective. I certainly didn't investigate kidnappings and ransom cases. I was out of my league where this case was concerned.

"Does this have something to do with *her*?" asked Mack, no doubt referring to Pam.

I glanced over my shoulder at her.

She was on her side, my bedsheet pulled across her breasts, held in place by her arm, and her head propped up on her hand. She stared at me curiously.

I sighed. "No, Mack. It really doesn't have anything to do with Pam. Not like that anyway."

"Then... like what?" she asked, her big brown eyes sparkling with curiosity. I actually found her sweet, innocent gaze to be endearing. She seemed genuinely concerned about me. Had I *not* had a chip on my shoulder when it came to women, I might have actually wanted to *date* the woman. Mack was intelligent and witty, and she could carry on a conversation beyond discussing the intricacies of her favorite nail polish or her beauty regimen. She was absolutely stunning, and her assets were out of this world. Plus, she was an island transplant, just like I was, having only recently moved to the island from Bear Creek, Wisconsin after a particularly frigid winter. So we related well to each other.

Plus, Mack lived in a vacation villa only a few klicks away. Her aunt and uncle owned it and had given her permission to use it until she got herself established in her job and found her own place. I liked the fact that she was so close by. It meant it didn't take her long to pay me a visit, and she could leave after a playdate and still be home in under fifteen minutes.

But, all that being said, the truth of the matter was, I *did* have a chip on my shoulder when it came to women and relationships. So all I was in the market for now was meaningless no-strings-attached sexual encounters. And if that made me a bad guy, then paint me red and slap a pointed tail on my ass. I was happy to take the title.

I put the bottle of Patrón on the floor and rubbed my face with the palms of my hands. I really didn't want to talk to her about Pam again. We'd already been through the topic once, and now things were only more confusing. "You just have no idea, Mack. It's a really, really, really long story," I said.

"Well, as luck would have it, *playtime* went quicker than anticipated, so we have a little extra time on our hands."

I glanced back at her over my shoulder to see the sly smile she had on her face. I let out a little sigh. "I said I was sorry."

She laughed and reached out to swat me playfully. "Kidding, Drunk. Geez. Lighten up! I was just trying to make you smile."

"Thanks." I rolled my eyes as I turned away from her. There were few men I knew that enjoyed being teased about their short performance time. Me included. But I'd had a lot on my mind, and I'd found it difficult to put it out of my mind during my performance.

We were both quiet for a while when she rolled onto her back and stared up at the ceiling. "You're still in love with her, aren't you?"

"With Pam?" I bellowed, jumping to my feet to spin around. "Hell no! Not even a little. You've gotta believe me, Mack."

"I don't know, Drunk. She pays one visit to the island and you're acting all shook up."

"It's not that, I promise. Honestly, our relationship didn't end as well as I'd led you to believe earlier," I admitted. I couldn't tell her about the kidnapping, but at the very least I *could* tell her the truth about my relationship with Pam.

"Then why'd you tell me it ended well?"

"Vanity, I guess," I said with a wince. "The truth is she cheated on me."

She was quiet for a couple beats. Finally, she plumped out her bottom lip at me. "Oh, geez. I'm really sorry. That sucks. I've been cheated on before, so I know how it feels."

I shrugged. I didn't want her pity, and I didn't want to commiserate about our similar experiences. I just wanted to clear the air and take back the statement I'd made the day before about knowing that I'd always love Pam. It was as if that statement had brought bad juju upon us. "I found her in my bed with her ex."

"Shit."

"Yeah. So, I have no idea what she thought she was going to accomplish by coming to the island, but it got me a little pissed off, I guess. I'm just trying to forget she was ever here," I said through a clenched jaw. Tension radiated through my shoulders and into my back.

Mack saw it. She patted the edge of the bed. "Sit down."

I didn't feel like sitting. I felt like pacing the room until the answer magically appeared in my brain. But Mack looked so sweet sitting there. I felt bad in that moment, using her as my magic eraser. So I sat down. Immediately, she crawled behind me and began to massage my shoulders.

"Wow. You *are* tense."

Her fingers kneaded expertly into my muscles. I closed my eyes and tipped my head from side to side. "Yeah."

"You really don't love her anymore?"

"It's not that I don't love her anymore. It's more than that. It's that I *loathe* her now. Like truly *loathe*."

"She left the resort this morning, right?"

I let out an uneasy sigh. "Yup. She left all right."

"So, then forget about her, Drunk. She's over. The two of you are done. She's not around anymore. The relationship is history. It's time to move on." I felt her lips on the slope of my neck. Her hands slid down over my shoulders to massage the raised outline of my pecs.

I turned my head slightly to the right, to meet her dark eyes. "Move on?"

She nodded, her face barely an inch away from mine. "Yeah. Move on." Her breathy whisper had barely left her lips before I found them on mine.

16

"*Rawck, no morning kisses, no morning kisses, rawck!*"

My eyes fluttered open. I felt the need to swallow, but my tongue was dried out and my mouth felt empty of spit. Once again, there was an empty pillow beside me. I couldn't remember much after the last go-round with Mack, as I'd emptied the remainder of my tequila bottle, but I had the distinct memory that she'd complained about my snoring and had decided to go back to her place to spend the night.

As had become the norm, my head throbbed inside my skull. I wondered if it was the alcohol in general that had done it or if my body had decided it was allergic to tequila specifically. With one hand I rubbed my temples and blinked rapidly, trying to focus on the alarm clock on the other side of the bed. I squinted. Did that say ten?

Fuck. If I didn't get up soon, I'd miss breakfast in the dining room, and my stomach was already rumbling.

I heard tapping on the windowsill again. "*Rawck, let's go, let's go, let's go.*" I could hear the bird's feet tapping in time to his chant.

"Shut the fuck up!" I hollered. I was definitely going to put *buy a fucking gun* on my day's to-do list.

As Earnestine echoed my latest interjection, I rolled over onto my back. Fighting the throbbing in my head, I sat up and stared at her. She rocked forward and backward on her feet as she sang. I grabbed Mack's pillow and, rearing it back over my head, launched it at the window.

She ducked and it sailed over her head.

The fact that she hadn't been hit seemed to make her more determined to piss me off. She kept dancing. *"Shut the fuck up, shut the fuck up, shut the fuck up."*

I sucked in a deep breath and stared at her. Then without moving too quickly, I raised my pillow over my head. This was my last chance. I had to have perfect aim. Then in one quick movement, I launched it. It sailed over my head, across the room, and hit Earnestine square in the center of the body, bowling the parrot off my windowsill.

My eyes widened. "I did it!" I said, a dumb smile covering my face. And then instantly, the guilt hit. Had I seriously just killed a fucking bird? A beautiful green-and-blue parrot? One that actually *talked* and danced and would probably earn me a bundle if I recorded her and put her videos on YouTube or some shit like that?

I sighed. The thought made me realize that this was exactly what was happening with Pam. As much as I wanted her dead, there was no way my conscience would allow me to sign her death warrant. With guilt riding heavily on my heart, I stood up. I strode naked over to my window and looked out.

Beyond my cottage was a tropical jungle, and beyond the jungle was the ocean. It was far enough away that I had yet to attempt to walk there. Though, during particularly quiet evenings and when the wind blew just right, I could hear the faint whoosh of the ocean in the distance.

Looking down, I saw both of my pillows lying on the ground. Underneath one of the pillows, a bright blue feather stuck out. I wondered if the bird was dead beneath the pillow.

Fuck.

I'd killed the fucking bird.

What kind of godforsaken human being had I become? My mother would be so upset to know that I'd turned into a lustful, bird-killing drunk. The worst of the worst. The lowest of the low. The thought gnawed at my brain, and it turned my stomach to think that I'd killed a beautiful fucking bird, no matter how annoying.

I groaned and tugged on a pair of Calvin Klein underwear. In my normal life, back in the States, Hanes underwear had worked just fine for me. But here on the island, the only kind of underwear they sold in the upscale clothing boutique was Calvin Kleins, so I'd been forced to pay the outrageous prices for the small garments.

Opening my drawer, I discovered that I was out of clean shorts. So I rooted around in the pile of dirty clothes on the floor to find the least offensively dirty pair of shorts. I pulled on a pair of black Nike athletic shorts I'd worn to the beach a few days prior and plucked a bright red tank top that had the Red Cross insignia on the front along with the words "Orgasm Donor" from my top drawer. Slipping it over my head, I slid my feet into my flip-flops, plopped my fedora on my bed head of hair and pulled my shades down to cover what I could only assume were a pair of disgustingly bloodshot eyes.

Without even bothering to run a spot of toothpaste across my pearly whites, I walked out of my cottage and stood on my little covered front porch. I yawned, stretching my arms out wide. The weather was as it always was. Warm. Sunny. A little breezy. But perfect.

I strode around the back of my cottage to where my two pillows lay on the ground beneath my bedroom window. Unease squeezed the lower portion of my stomach into a tight ball. Squatting down, I moved each of the pillows carefully to discover the single blue feather alone on the ground beneath the pillows. The feather had been just that, only a feather. Earnestine was nowhere to be seen.

Finally, a bright spot! I wasn't a bird killer after all! Pleased, I let out a loud "Whew!"

Buoyed by the fact that I hadn't murdered Earnestine, I stood up, holding my pillows, and turned around. No sooner had my vision spun to face the side of my cottage than a loud thudding noise accompanied a sharp jolt of pain to the back of my head.

And that was when the lights went out in Paradise.

17

I WOKE UP FACEDOWN IN A PILE OF DROOL. THE GROUND BENEATH me rocked back and forth like a pendulum advancing time, causing my stomach to lurch and delivering the urge to purge whatever toxin had brought on my current state. But a throbbing in the back of my head stopped me from moving. I pried one eye open to discover that I lay in complete darkness. Had I slept through the entire day?

Fuck.

What the hell was going on? Why did my head hurt so bad? And where had the moonlight that usually seeped in through my open bedroom window gone?

I groaned as I rolled over onto my back, again fighting back the dire need to vomit as the ground continued to sway beneath me. I wondered why I wasn't on my bed. Had I passed out on the floor? Was that it? Had I drunk myself into a stupor, and I was now passed out on the floor next to my bed? Or in my cottage bathroom? Had I hit my head on the way down?

My fingers crawled out like spiders, radiating out from my hips across the hard surface beneath me. The floor was bumpy and rough; its sinewy fibers scratched against my backside where my shirt had ridden up. It felt like cheap motel carpet. Not that I had firsthand knowledge of what cheap motel carpet felt like against my backside or anything. No, this definitely wasn't my bedroom floor. I had hardwood floors in my cottage.

In the otherwise quiet room, I heard a faint, gentle slapping sound. It was rhythmic and steady. Slap, slap, slap. It moved in time with the rocking and swaying that I felt. Almost like I was on the water. But that wasn't possible. Was it? Was that the briny ocean air I smelled?

As I lay flat on my back, I tried to rouse my mind enough to focus. What was the last thing I remembered? I certainly didn't remember boarding a boat. I didn't even know anyone with a boat. So how could I be on the water? The last thing I remembered, through the pain in my skull, was waking up and getting dressed to go to breakfast. But I couldn't remember the actual breakfast. Had Al gone with me? I vaguely remembered leaving to go to breakfast. I'd stretched on my porch, and then what? I remembered walking around to the side of my cottage.

And then I remembered the bird in my window. Earnestine. I'd killed Earnestine! I'd walked around to the back of my cottage to retrieve my pillows and to see what had become of the parrot, and I'd stood up and ... I sucked in my breath. *I'd been hit in the head!*

Both eyes flashed open when the lightning bolt hit me. Was I dead? Was this what being dead felt like? Why did heaven sway, leaving me feeling nauseous?

And then the thought hit me. Maybe I wasn't in Heaven. Maybe all of my wicked ways had caught up to me. Maybe this was hell.

"Oh God," I groaned, my scratchy voice resonating in the dark. My hand went to my head, and I touched the lump on the back of my skull where I'd been hit. My hair was dry, no blood, but I definitely felt a stinging pain. Could dead people feel pain? Could they talk? Were there floors in hell? If there were floors, this was definitely the carpet for them.

I rolled onto my side and then into a sitting position. Slumped forward, I held my head between both palms. What the ever-living fuck was going on? I sat quietly, engulfed in my own thoughts about heaven and hell, when mindfulness finally kicked in. Heaven would be better than this. Hell would be worse. My rational mind told me I was still alive, but this was simply a holding cell I'd been placed in… a purgatory on earth, of sorts.

I had to figure out where I was. I managed to get to my knees and crawled around. The sandpaper-like carpet dug into my knees and shins as I crawled, the friction providing a heavy dose of carpet burn as I slid. With one outstretched arm, I felt the ground and the air in front of me like a blind man, waving my hand, just waiting to touch something, anything, and hoping I wouldn't crawl onto a nail or a rake.

It was my knee that slid against something first.

I froze and brought my hand to the object. Gingerly patting its shape, I felt the familiar soft brim and indented crown. It was my fedora! I put it on my head and only inches away discovered my sunglasses. Of course wherever I was, it was dark as the ocean floor, but I was still glad to find my sunglasses. At least I wouldn't have to go buy new ones wherever I was. I shoved the sunglasses into the pocket of my athletic shorts, put my hat on my head, and kept crawling.

By now, I was fairly confident that I was on a boat. The way the floor rocked beneath me, the gentle sound of water lapping against the hull, and the distinct marine scent meant I could be nowhere else.

I was on a boat.

Just fucking great.

I kept crawling and reaching until I came to a piece of furniture. Groping the squishy swath of cotton draped over the edge of a long, flexible surface told me I was next to a bed.

Putting both hands on top of it, I pulled myself up to a standing position and carefully walked around the bed, patting the top of it and wondering now if I was alone in the room.

"Hello?" I said quietly, careful not to be too loud lest whoever had put me on the boat should know that I'd woken up.

There was no answer.

Satisfied that I was alone, I stood a little taller and bravely took a step and a half towards what I assumed was a wall. I promptly took a nightstand to my thigh.

"Doh!" I breathed, bending over to rub the sharp pain out of my tender flesh. I was silently thankful for my height. If I'd been much shorter, the stand might have taken out another important piece of my anatomy. I felt around for a lamp but discovered nothing on the short piece of furniture.

I kept walking, arms extended, but more careful to feel around with my foot before stepping, and finally, my hand touched a wall. I slid my arm up and down, fingering the wall-papered panel, looking for a light switch or a door but coming up empty. I followed the wall around the perimeter of the room and then walked right into a hard, protruding sculpture hanging from a plaque on the wall.

I winced and rubbed my frontal lobe until the sharp pain subsided and was replaced, once again, with the dull throbbing I'd had before walking into it. With two hands, I felt the sculpture. It was cool and smooth. In the darkness, my hands quickly ran along the smooth, polished lines of a long animal muzzle with a protruding horn and a pair of ears.

Feeling around it, I kept going along the wall and seconds later discovered a light switch next to the edge of a doorjamb. With my spirit now buoyed by hope, my hand flicked on the light switch. But not so much as a flicker happened. Undeterred, my hand now slid down to the cool polished handle. I held my breath and slowly pressed down on it, but found it to be locked from the outside.

Fuck.

I was locked in a room on a boat.

Just fucking perfect.

But I wasn't about to roll over and give up, because the fact of the matter was I didn't have a choice. If I stayed where I was, whoever had put me in here, likely the people that had taken Pam, was coming back, and they certainly weren't coming back to take me out for a beer.

I had to get out of here now. I'd have to kick the fucking door down. I felt the surface with my hands, wondering how flimsy it might be. It was hard to tell. I took a step back and sucked in a deep breath, but as I prepared to charge, the feeling of déjà vu suddenly washed over me as a recent memory flashed before my eyes.

Hello? Bull in a china shop? Nicolette Dominion's sparkling, crystalline blue eyes flickered through my memory like an old movie. Only weeks prior, the feisty femme fatale had quietly stopped me from kicking down Cami Vergado's apartment door. She'd grabbed my arm right before I'd been ready to kick and told me that things could be handled with a much lighter touch. And then, in an ungodly sexy fashion, she'd pulled two bobby pins from her hair. *Step aside, sweetie.*

The memory raised the long black Grecian hairs on my legs. *Fuck*, that woman had been hot.

I'd watched as she'd used her mouth to bend the pins and then had gone about picking the lock. It had only taken her a minute or two to open Cami's door, and then she'd pressed the bobby pins into my hands. When she wasn't looking, I'd tucked the bobby pins into the inner hatband of my fedora as a memento of the second woman to have taken my virginity. And now I kind of wondered if that hadn't been fated to happen. Had fate known that I'd eventually succumb to this dilemma?

I popped the fedora off my head and felt around for the pins. And there they were, awaiting their extraction. I wondered if I could actually pick a lock in the depths of complete and utter darkness. Picking the lock in the light of day with Nico coaching me over my shoulder seemed just as dubious at this point. I wasn't a locksmith, nor was I a professional cat burglar.

But, I had to try.

I got down on my haunches and checked the bends in the pins. Feeling confident that that was how Nico had used them, I proceeded to feel the door handle for a keyhole. Surprisingly enough, the keyhole wasn't even a keyhole, but simply a small circle that one of the bobby pins slid easily into. I could feel the spring on the other side. It would literally be a matter of pressing the pin against the spring and turning the handle.

But I had to be prepared for whatever I saw on the outside. My adrenaline pulsed in my veins. I sucked in a deep breath and pressed the pin against the spring while simultaneously pulling down the door handle. I felt the lock click and I pulled the door open. A tiny sliver of blinding sunlight poured through the crack, forcing my eyes to shut and me to close the door. Settling back in my crouched position, I lifted my hat to replace the pins.

Back in the dark, I sucked in a deep breath and then let it out, slowly.

It was go time.

I pressed down on the door handle and pulled it towards me just a crack. My eyes were narrowed by the light. I'd no sooner pulled the door open a fraction of an inch than the force of a bear shoved it open all the way. As I rose, the door slammed against me and threw me backwards into the room, sending my hat flying.

18

BEFORE I EVEN HAD A CHANCE TO RECOVER FROM THE FORCE OF the door, a gorilla of a man hammered me across the head with a right hook, slamming me backwards onto the bed. The light that now poured into the previously pitch-black room shone around his head like a halo, casting a shadow across my attacker's face.

He jumped to the side of the bed and rained down another blow to my head, the bed beneath me cushioning the impact. I let out a yowl as his rock-hard knuckles struck my Brillo-y jaw. "Enjoy your little nap, sleeping beauty?"

I grimaced. "A pillow would've been nice." The words tasted metallic as I spat them out. Around me, the air carried a tinny sound, as if someone had rung a bell with my head inside of it.

He sneered at me, and as he reared back to deliver his fourth blow, my adrenaline kicked in and lifted the fog I'd been in. I raised my leg and shot a front kick into his chest, which caused his punch to come up short and gave me enough room to spring to my feet.

The big, burly man came at me fast, but I ducked into a

double-leg takedown thanks to my single year of high school wrestling. With him on the floor and me finally on top, I smiled as I blasted him in the face to give him a taste of his own medicine. He smiled back. His mouth was only spotted with teeth, but I was fairly confident the missing ones weren't of my doing.

He let me get off two more punches before he rolled me off him like a dented can of Bush's baked beans. But before I could get my six-foot-four-inch frame vertical, he was on his feet, his stealth and speed shocking me. He pulled my left arm into an armlock behind my back and grabbed a hold of my hair, holding me up on my tiptoes. Apparently *his* mother hadn't let him quit wrestling after the first year.

I knew my efforts to get away were now fruitless as he tiptoed me out of the room. So in one last act of defiance, I swept my fedora off the bed as we left the room and popped it back on my head.

Note to self: renew gym membership.

He forced me out into the corridor, where he grunted at me, "You got a date with the boss."

"The boss? Cliché much?" I adjusted my hat. "Unless you mean *the* Boss. In that case, wow, yeah, I'm in."

Mr. Big and Burly didn't even crack a smile. Instead, he released the grip he had on my hair and pulled a .45 Magnum he'd had holstered under his arm, pointing it at my skull.

"Right," I said, swallowing back the bile that had risen into my throat.

As my eyes adjusted to daylight, I could finally look around. It seemed I was in the lower level of a fancy boat. Though by the sheer size and poshness of the lower level, I had a feeling that boat was an understatement. Perhaps yacht was more accurate.

My attacker's face was now visible too. He was square-jawed, with bulbous black eyes and a wide nose that was not properly centered. His face was scarred in numerous places, from what I could only assume was years of experience in bar brawls. He shoved me forward, keeping his gun trained on me.

That was when I heard a familiar tune, heavy on the violin, and then Macdonald Carey's somber voice delivering his signature line: *Like sands through the hourglass, so are the days of our lives...*

My breath hitched in my throat and my heart froze. That was Pam's favorite soap opera. She'd recorded it on the television in my apartment and had forced me to watch countless episodes with her. I glanced up the corridor. There were several closed doors, and one open one. The light was on behind the open door. I was sure the sound of the television was coming from in there.

Mr. Big and Burly pushed me towards the room. "That way," he grunted, giving me another shove with the heel of his army boot.

When we passed by the room, I peered inside, catching a glimpse of a petite blonde woman, chained to the bed with her hands and ankles bound. I was surprised when Big and Burly pulled me to a stop in front of her door.

"Pam?"

The woman's head swiveled, giving me a chance to see her face. Indeed it was Pam, but she barely looked like the woman I'd laid eyes on the day before. Now her face was battered and bruised. Her right eye was swollen shut. I was sure it would be black by morning time. My heart sank seeing her like that. No matter what our issues were, no matter what she'd done to me, Pam didn't deserve that.

Her left eye widened and her jaw dropped when she realized it was me. She sucked in her breath. "Danny!" she breathed. She tried to get up but fell backwards. That was when I realized her neck was chained to the bed too. "Oh my God, they got you too? Danny! I'm so sorry, I thought I was going with the hotel man. I didn't know it wasn't him!" Genuine tears streamed down her cheeks.

"Are you all right?" I asked, surprised that Big and Burly hadn't shoved me along.

"No, I'm not all right! Th-that man hit me!"

I glanced back at Mr. Big and Burly, seething at him. "This guy?"

"N-no, not him. A different guy."

I stared at her swollen face and swallowed hard, trying to shove down the rage I felt. "Who hit you, Pam?"

"That man that grabbed me. He had a ponytail." She sobbed. "Oh, Danny, they're gonna kill me and feed me to the sharks. I heard them talking."

My spine stiffened. "No, they won't, Pam. I won't let them."

She sobbed harder. "But, Danny! They want money! I told them you don't have much money, but they seemed sure."

"I'll figure something out, Pam," I promised. As much as I *hated* Pam, I hated seeing her chained up and battered even more. Pam might be a cheater, but she didn't deserve to be tortured. She had a family that would be devastated to lose her. And suddenly I felt a giant amount of guilt and remorse for being so cavalier with her life earlier. Maybe it was because I hadn't really believed the sincerity of these people, or maybe it was just me being childish about the woman who had caused me so much embarrassment and pain, but not once had I stopped to consider her family. Not once had I stopped to think about her mother or her brothers or the little sister that idolized Pam, and me for that matter. Cara would've been crushed to know how I hadn't come to her sister's rescue when I had the chance. No, she thought better of me than that. And I'd let her down. I'd let my parents down. And as much as I didn't really care about her, I'd let Pam down. What kind of a man had I become?

"Time's up," grunted the man with the gun behind me.

"Danny! Don't leave me! Please, Danny!" screamed Pam as Big and Burly shoved me down the hallway past her door.

"I'm not leaving you, Pam. All right? Don't worry. I'll figure something out. I'm gonna get us out of this."

"Dannnnnnny!"

19

I STUMBLED AS I WAS SHOVED FORWARD UP A FLIGHT OF SPIRAL stairs. At the top, I landed in the yacht's saloon. It was a large space with a sofa, a television, and a small round dinner table. Through the windows, I could see the horizon in all directions, and I discovered there wasn't a speck of green for as far as the eye could see in any direction. As far as I knew, Paradise Isle could be a thousand miles away.

Fuck.

Big and Burly kept his gun trained on me. "Take a right," he grunted.

I turned, and we walked through a short corridor into the yacht's galley kitchen.

In the galley, he gestured towards another flight of stairs with his gun.

"I didn't realize it was gonna be leg day," I said, stopping at the bottom of the stairs and looking up as my stomach began to grumble, reminding me that I hadn't had any break-fast. "Hey, man, we wouldn't happen to be having this conver-sation with your boss over breakfast, would we? I haven't had anything to eat this morning."

"Zip it, wiseass," barked the man.

I grinned. "I'll take that as a no?"

Big and Burly's gun shot out and cracked me against the side of my skull. "Upstairs. Now."

Rubbing my head and now seething as I walked up the stairs, I cursed the man under my breath. I took my time, nervous as to what I might discover at the top of the stairs. At the landing, I found the yacht's control room was to my left, and to my right, a man sat behind a polished mahogany desk, drumming his fingers on a desk calendar. Two square-shouldered sentries stood on either side of him.

"Well, hello, Daniel. Finally, we meet."

He was younger than I'd expected, perhaps only in his early thirties. He had a round face with chubby cheeks mostly hidden behind a thick, brown full beard that made it difficult to tell where his neck ended and his face began. He wore dark round wire-rimmed glasses and had flyaway brown hair that bristled on top as if it had been rubbed against a balloon. The little Harry Potter lookalike was stocky, leaning towards fat.

"Harry," I said quirking a smile. "It's a pleasure to finally meet you. I've read all your books." I took a step forward to shake the man's hand. "Okay, I lied, I only saw the movies, but you were excellent in them."

The narrow slit in the man's mustache and beard combo curved into a smile. "Such a sense of humor. That's good. Really, really good." He walked around his desk to lean his girthy butt up against the edge. "And do you know *why* that's good, Daniel?"

I shrugged. "Helps to pick up the ladies, that's for sure."

"Oh, I'm sure it helps. I mean, you managed to convince Ms. Calcara to marry you. And she is certainly one Grade A piece of meat."

I pursed my lips. Pam was *mine* to disrespect, not *his*. Hearing him refer to her as a piece of meat, heated my blood.

He seemed to notice my failed poker face. "Ohhhh," he

drawled. "So Daniel's not as over Ms. Calcara as he'd like us to believe, huh, Smitty?"

"Nope, guess not," grunted Big and Burly.

The testosterone in my blood boiled now. Joke time was over. I took a step forward to point threateningly at the squat man. "You better not lay another hand on her."

Big and Burly and the two men stationed on either side of the desk all lurched forward to protect their boss.

Harry Potter held up a hand to stop them, and they froze in place. "Yeah? All of a sudden I'm not allowed to lay a hand on her, but only yesterday you gave me permission to feed her to the sharks?" Harry shook his head, chiding me. "Tsk, tsk, tsk. No, the reason that it's so *lucky* that you've got a sense of humor is because you're gonna need it."

"Am I?"

"You certainly are. Because here's what's about to happen. Look out there." He pointed out his office window, which looked out over the starboard side of the boat. "You see that little dot out there?"

I squinted, following his pointed finger. The blinding sun reflected off the water, making it difficult to see anything but its reflection. I could barely make out something floating in the waves. "Maybe."

"Okay, well, that tiny dot out there is a boat. Boat might even be an exaggeration. It's little more than a piece of aluminum, really. But it's my gift to you."

"Okay?" I asked, tipping my head sideways, wondering where he was going with this.

"What's going to happen is, in about one minute, I'm going to have Smitty here escort you off this yacht and into the ocean."

Like, *in the ocean*? I sucked on my split bottom lip, hoping the bleeding had stopped while my heart shot up into my throat. Pam and I had seen *Open Water* together, and it'd scared the shit out of both of us. Of course I'd never *admitted* to her that I was as freaked out as she was, but I'd had just as many nightmares as she'd had. Perhaps this was my penance for telling the kidnapper that he had my permission to feed Pam to the sharks. I swallowed hard but remained silent.

Harry lifted one of his dark brows. "Are you listening?"

I let out a breath but nodded.

"Okay. So, the fellas and I are letting you off here, and you're going to do one of two things. Either you're going to die—which, as a side note, is completely fine with me. You haven't exactly been the model negotiator."

Shifting my stance, I rolled my eyes. "Get on with it."

"Right. Or, two, you're going to swim to that boat out there. Of course, if it were *me*, I'd choose the latter."

"If it were *you*, you'd sink to the bottom of the ocean like a fucking tub of mashed potatoes."

Harry's eyes pinched together. That one had stung. "As I was saying… if you actually make it to the boat, you're going to board it, and then you'll find your way back to Paradise Isle. When you get there, you're going to wire seven million dollars into this account." He took two steps towards me and handed me a card with some numbers written on it. "And don't worry, the account is untraceable. Then, once I've successfully received the deposit, I will drop the lovely Ms. Calcara off at the nearest port of entry and she can jet away to safety."

I puffed air out my nose. "Like I'd believe for a second that you'd just let her go?"

"Oh, Drunk, you've got my word. You were right about Ms. Calcara. She's been quite the demanding one. A little whiny for my taste. Perhaps that's why you decided not to marry her, huh?" He looked at me as if waiting for an answer.

Instead I shook my head. "Nah, let me tell *you* what's *not* going to happen. I'm not wiring you a goddamned penny." I flicked the card he'd handed me into a spiral in the air before continuing, "While I go about rounding up *cash*, you're going to keep your filthy mitts off of Pam. Got it?"

Harry stared at me. The slit in his mustache and beard duo was slightly wider than it had been previously. I could tell he didn't like me changing the plan, but I could also tell that he was listening.

"We'll do the money transfer the old-fashioned way. I hand you a suitcase of cash and you hand me Pam. That's my last and final offer."

The man chortled into his hand. "*Your* last and final offer? As if you really think you have a leg to stand on here, Daniel?"

I shrugged. I might be scared of sharks, but I was prepared to swim with the fishes. I'd earned my swimming merit badge in the Scouts. I could tread water and wait for a boat to find me. Or I could swim to that little boat out there. If they expected me to paddle back to Paradise Isle, we couldn't be too far off its shores. And if ultimately I died, at least I died with seven million dollars in my bank account. My parents would be set for life with that kind of money.

"Your call. Take it or leave it."

Harry Potter glanced over at Smitty, who lifted a shoulder. Harry frowned at me. "Fine. We'll figure something out. I'll call your cell phone in twenty-four hours. I assume you'll be back to your place by then. But you sure as hell better knock off the smart-ass routine."

"I thought you said I was going to need my sense of humor."

"Well, I..." He frowned again. "Just shut the hell up." He pointed at me then, a bastardly sneer creeping across his face. "Throw him overboard."

I glanced over at Smitty, who was already coming towards me, his weapon aimed for any of the myriad vital organs and veins I held in my torso. The two nameless guards stood rigidly by the desk with their beefy arms crossed across their chest, feet shoulder-width apart. I hated the idea of leaving Pam alone with these bumblefucks, but I wasn't the one with the gun.

"Oh! Before you leave, Drunk." Harry held up a finger as if he were stopping me from leaving of my own volition. "A couple more things. I'm going to need you to play by the rules until we've made our exchange. First of all, no cops. Absolutely no authorities of any kind. Second, you may not contact the media. In fact, you may not speak about this to anyone. Got it?"

I fought back a smile. "Why? You shy? I mean, with looks like those, you really shouldn't be."

He puffed air out his nose. "Once again—the smart-ass routine is gone."

"Is that one of the rules too?"

Harry nodded. "It is."

I stubbed my toe into the deck, swiveling it like a little kid. "Aww, shucks."

"And finally, because we're dealing with cash, there will be no funny business."

"Yeah? What constitutes funny business in your book?"

"No fake bills, no tracking devices, no dye packs. I want the money in US dollars, and if you screw any of that up, Pam's wearing concrete heels straight to the bottom of the Atlantic. Got it?"

I stared hard at Harry then. Memorizing every little detail of his face. I was going to make this man pay. I didn't know how, but I was going to do everything in my power to make it happen.

He pointed to the exterior railing that ran around the hull of the boat. "Now. Walk the plank." He squinted one eye shut and added an "Arrr" for good measure.

Big and Burly spun me around and shoved a gun between my shoulder blades. I glanced at Harry over my shoulder as I walked towards the ship's deck. "You've been waiting your whole life to say that, haven't you?"

Harry grinned. "I have, as a matter of fact. I'll be in touch, Daniel."

20

I WAS LUCKY ENOUGH TO HIT THE WATER FEET FIRST, BUT THE impact knocked my hat off. So the first thing I did after resurfacing was to swim after my hat and then to dig my glasses out of my pocket and put them on my face. I already had a splitting headache. The culprit, of course, could have been one of many things: tension was high on the list; perhaps another blasted hangover; lack of food and caffeine; quite possibly the concussion I'd likely suffered after being lambasted in the head in the back of my cottage earlier that morning; and then there was also the beating I'd taken in the unicorn stateroom. I certainly didn't need the blinding sun to exacerbate my already-throbbing skull.

And now here I was, treading water in the middle of the Atlantic Ocean. Harry Potter's yacht had already taken off, heading for deeper waters, I assumed. I'd watched it go, hoping to find any notable clues about the true identity of Harry or his yacht. But it was simply a large white yacht with no visible lettering, at least not on the stern. Nothing gave me even the slightest inkling as to who Harry Potter might have truly been or where he'd come from.

The little johnboat they'd left for me was dozens and dozens of yards away. I only knew the general direction based on the proximity to the yacht's hull and the sun's position. I couldn't see it from where I bobbed, spitting salty water out of my mouth and feeling the biting sting it caused my split lip.

While I knew I was a decent swimmer, anxiety had already set in. Despite the opinion of Bruce of the *Finding Nemo* crew, sharks most definitely *weren't* friends. So before I took off on my swim, I had to pause, taking several deep breaths to calm myself. And then the pep talk came.

You got this, Danny.

It's like what? A football field? Maybe two? No sweat.

Sharks are probably out in the deep end of the ocean anyway. This has got to be the shallow end, the kiddie pool really. So get it together. You don't want Ma and Pops to have to have an empty casket for your funeral, so you gotta make it to that boat.

Got it?

Swim.

So I'd taken off. Wishing I'd had time to eat brunch before I'd been hit over the head. I might have had more in me then. But I swam until my shoulders burned. I stopped several times to correct myself, especially once I was finally able to see the boat. I was thankful the water was warm and it was a calm day. If the water had been choppier, there was no way I would have been able to catch up to it, but I could definitely tell I was gaining on it.

After what felt like hours, I caught up to the small flat-bottomed boat. Thankfully, they'd left the mooring rope dangling over the edge, and I was able to use it to pull myself up into the boat. Drenched, fatigued, and incredibly hungry, I fell onto one of the three welded bench seats and took almost a full five minutes to catch my breath, let my pulse return to normal, and to soak up the warmth of the Caribbean sun before I explored the contents of the boat.

Boat exploration turned out to be brief. I looked to the front of the boat and saw nothing. I looked to the back of the boat and saw the same. My shoulders crumpled inward.

Fuck.

I was quite literally up shit creek without a paddle.

21

I WAVED AT CAPTAIN BUTCH CAMRON AND HIS CREW AS THEY motored off, leaving me off at the mouth of Angel's Bay. Cap'n Butch had taken me in as far as his fishing charter boat could make it without getting hung up on the coral reef, and I swam the rest of the way to the shore, back-floating much of the distance. Because by the time I'd been rescued by the four-man crew, night had begun to fall, and not only was I burnt to a golden crisp, but I was also beyond ravenous and almost completely dehydrated.

Cap'n Butch's first mate, Cale, a young twenty-something fellow with waist-long blond dreadlocks pulled back into a ponytail, had shared the extra lunch he'd packed: a bologna sandwich and a bag of Flamin' Hot Funyuns. In retrospect, I shouldn't have eaten the Funyuns, but at that point, I probably would have eaten a live cat if someone had put one in my lap. Cap'n Butch had also kindly given me two bottles of water, which I'd absorbed almost as soon as they'd been handed to me.

Despite that gourmet supper, by the time I made it back to the Seacoast Majestic's sandy shoreline, I was so starving I thought I might pass out. Barefoot, after having lost my flip-flops when I'd been sent overboard, I staggered up the beach to the swim-up pool bar, where I discovered both Mack and Al seated in front of Manny.

Mack was the first to lay eyes on me.

She'd swiveled around casually on her barstool, holding a peach-colored drink and haphazardly taking in the beach scene. That was when I came into view. Her eyes widened and she nearly choked on the sip she'd just taken.

"Drunk!" she squealed before leaping off the stool to throw her arms around my badly sunburned shoulders. "There you are!"

"Ouch!" I winced and peeled her arms off my shoulders. "Easy there."

"Oh my God, what happened to you?" Her brown eyes were big as she gave me a once-over, noting my ragged, soaked clothing, bruised and swollen face, and my sunburn.

"Ay, ay, ay, Drunk! You look like shit," said Manny, leaning over the bar.

"Where've you been? I've been looking for you every-where!" added Al, who also looked shocked to see me in my present condition.

Mack pulled out a barstool for me and scooted over so I could sit between her and Al. "Everyone's been looking for you. I wanted to call the cops, but Artie wouldn't let me."

"Gimme a tall water, Manny," I said before shooting Mack a pleading look. "And I'll take one of Trin's chicken bacon wraps too, if you don't mind."

She hopped off her barstool. "Yeah, yeah. Of course. I'll be right back. But don't start the story till I get back."

"Hey, and some fries!" I added, not making any promises about saving my story for her.

Manny, Al, and I watched as Mack strode around the pool to the snack bar on the other side. Trinity wasn't working, but I knew someone else would hook her up for me.

"So what the hell happened?" asked Al. "Everyone's been looking for you. You left your phone in your room. You didn't tell anyone you were leaving the resort property. We were all worried."

"I left my phone here because I didn't *know* I was leaving resort property," I barked, swallowing down the tall glass of water in two big gulps. I tapped my glass on the top of the counter and slid it to Manny. "I was hit over the head and taken."

"Get out!" Manny practically hollered.

My eyes widened and I ducked, as if there were spies everywhere. "Shhh," I hissed. "We gotta keep this on the down-low, or else they're gonna kill her."

"The guys that got Pam are the ones that got you?" asked Al.

I glanced up at Manny. While I didn't have a problem with Manny knowing what was going on, I wasn't sure that spreading the information was such a good idea.

"Al already filled me in," he admitted before refilling my glass.

"Sorry, kid," said Al. "I wasn't sure what to think when you went missing."

"It's fine. We just can't let this get out. All right?"

Al and Manny both gave nods but were silent and ready to hear my story.

"So, yeah, the guys that have Pam are the guys that got me. Motherfuckers. I was in the back of my house, picking up my pillows, and they hit me over the back of the head. Next thing I know, I'm on a fucking yacht."

"What were your pillows doing in the back of your house?" asked Al.

I gave him the side-eye. "Slightly irrelevant, considering the fact that I just walked outta the Atlantic Ocean, don't you think, Al?"

Al shrugged. "I was just curious. I mean, it matters why

you were in the back of your house."

I swiveled my barstool to look at him full-on. "Why in the hell does it matter why I was in the back of my house?"

"I mean, how'd these guys know you were gonna be in the back of your house? How'd they know they could nab you there?"

"Fuck if I know." I swallowed the remaining water in the glass and slid it forward again. "Hit me again, Manny."

"I've never seen you drink this much water, Drunk." Manny took the tall cylinder and refilled it once again. Ice clinked against the glass.

"I'm fucking dehydrated. I just about died!" I took another swig of water. "Now, can I finish my story before Mack gets back? I can't have her knowing all of this. She might tell some of the rest of the girls at the front desk, and then it's all fucking over. Pam'll be dead and it'll be all my fault."

"Finish, finish," said Al, rolling his gnarled hands, like he wasn't the one interrupting my story.

"Fine. So I wake up on a fucking yacht."

"A yacht?" cried Al. "What were you doing on a yacht?"

I gave him the side-eye again but didn't respond. "Some guy named Smitty is responsible for this mess," I said, pointing at my split lip and swollen face. "And I met the mastermind behind this whole fucking situation," I growled into my third glass of water. "Awkward-looking little punk ass."

"So what was the point of them grabbing you only to let you go?" asked Manny.

"I think they wanted me to see the condition that Pam's in so I'd take this more seriously," I said, my heart heavy. "They've got her chained up. That ponytailed guy that nabbed her put hands on her. Her face was all swollen and bruised. She looked like shit, and she was absolutely terrified."

Al nodded. "You gonna pay them now or what?"

I rubbed my still-throbbing head. "I don't know. I've had a lot of time to think about all of this, and there's got to be another way to rescue her without giving them the money."

"Another way? Drunk! Haven't you learned your lesson by now? The money's not worth it! Pam's life is at stake."

"I think I can save both," I said. "I just have to figure out how. I mean, at least now I know where they're holding her. I feel like I've got more to go on now."

Mack reappeared with a chicken wrap basket and fries. "Alora gave you a double scoop of fries and said she's happy you're back." She wrinkled her brow at me. "Did you and her ever have a thing?"

I chuckled. "No, I can honestly say we haven't had a thing together." Taking the basket, I shoved four fries into my mouth. "Mmmm, thanks, Mack. I needed this so bad."

"So are you going to tell me where you've been all day?"

"Where I've been all day?" I shot a glance at Al and Manny and then looked at Mack again. "Oh, I just went to visit a few friends, that's all."

"A few friends? Friends did this to you?"

"You know, sometimes friends play rough," I said with a shrug.

Mack's face glowed red beneath the dimming light. She put her hands on her hips. "Tell me the truth, Drunk. Did you really go to see another woman?"

I let out a chuckle. If *only* that was who I'd been to see. "Nah, Mack. There's no other woman. But it's a long story, and I'm fucking exhausted and my body hurts like hell. I just wanna go crawl into bed. Let's save the story for another day."

Mack smiled sweetly. "Okay, well, how about I take you back to your cottage?" She cozied up to my side. "I'll nurse your wounds."

Every fiber of my body ached, from my hair follicles on the

top of my head all the way down to the hair on my big toe. Being nursed back to health sounded good and all, but all I really wanted to do was to sleep and figure out how I was going to save both Pam and my seven million dollars. I gave Mack a half-grin. "How 'bout a rain check on that offer?"

22

I awoke the next morning stiff as hell in all the wrong places and keenly aware that someone was staring at me. I whole-body flinched, my legs and arms jerking upwards and my eyes flickering open, ready to take on whoever had come to bean me over the head and abduct me for the second time in as many days.

"*No morning kisses, no morning kisses, rawck!*" cracked Earnestine, staring down at me from the headboard of my bed. She flapped her wings and walked along the top edge of my bed, bobbing her head to music only she could hear.

I stared up at the bird, my heart beating wildly in my chest. "Shit!" I screamed at the bird. "You fucking scared me!"

"*Shit, shit, shit,*" she chanted while jumping up and down at the peak of the curved headboard.

Damn, the bird had attitude.

Women!

Knowing I had a big day ahead of me, and for once not hungover, I gingerly eased my way out of bed and headed for the shower. I figured a nice cool shower and a handful of ibuprofen ought to ease some of the aches and pains Smitty and the day of swimming, dehydration, and sunburn had caused, and I was right. The shower was exactly what I needed to feel remotely human again.

When I was done, I walked, dripping wet, into my bedroom, only to remember that I had no clean clothing left to put on. But after a careful exploration of every drawer, I discovered a pair of lime-green-and-blue swim trunks in the bottom drawer. I sighed. They'd have to work.

The bathroom mirror revealed the damage the day before had inflicted on me. Though my hat had taken a beating and was now slightly discolored courtesy of the saltwater bath we'd both taken, I was thankful I'd been able to save it, as it had protected my face from the blisters my shoulders now sported. I fingered my lips. They were both chapped, split and swollen, and they hurt to move. I also had some bruising along my jawline, but I managed to shave anyway.

Because my hat was damp, discolored, misshapen, and unwearable for now, I ran product through my dark, wavy hair. It had been weeks since I'd needed to style it, and I realized I was badly in need of a haircut. I stepped back to take in the overall package before leaving the bathroom. Despite the myriad of problems the mirror reflected, my birth defect of a big nose included, I didn't look quite as horrible as I felt. My body looked far better in Caribbean lobster red than it did in Midwest winter white. My face, though distorted by a beating, was still what many women would call handsome, and I personally felt my new bruises and scars only added to my ruggedness. For the mission I had planned for the day, I needed to look my best.

I spritzed on a little cologne. My brows knitted together and my mouth formed an O as the woodsy scent stung the sunburned skin on my bare chest. I patted it lightly as I strode into the kitchen. There I picked up my phone and dialed. It rang twice before Al's codgerly old voice picked up on the other end.

"Yeah?"

"Meet me for breakfast?"

"I already had oatmeal."

"It's only fucking eight o'clock."

"Yeah, well, I've been up since four thirty."

"Holy shit."

"Sucks to get old."

I sighed. "I think I'll pass on that, then."

"On breakfast?"

"On getting old."

"Oh." Al was silent then.

"So you'll meet me for breakfast?"

"I'll be there in ten."

BAREFOOT AND SHIRTLESS, I beat Al to the lobby. I stopped into Angelita's Bay Boutique, the upscale clothing store on site, and spent all of three minutes picking out some new clothes. Until the Pam situation was resolved, there was no way I was finding time to do laundry. So, I plucked one tank top of every style from each rack until I'd hit ten. I put three new packages of underwear on the counter, and six new pairs of shorts. Unfortunately for me, the store only had two pairs of athletic shorts. The rest were Bermuda-style shorts, which I detested more than I detested mandals with Velcro. But I didn't have a lot of options.

And since today was an important day, I actually changed out of my swim trunks and into one of the Bermuda shorts, a pink pair that clung to my butt. I let Tish, the fifty-seven-year-old sales clerk with the blonde bird's nest of hair, pick out a shirt to match. Which was how I ended up wearing a short-sleeved linen shirt printed with black pelicans. She also tried to sell me a pair of leather mandals, with said Velcro, but I opted for a pair of tan loafers instead. I figured if I had to do anymore impromptu transatlantic swimming, those had a better chance of staying on my feet, as opposed to another pair of flip-flops. I did, however, buy a new pair of flip-flops because they said beach casual much louder than the boat shoes, and I'd actually grown to love letting my hairy toe flag fly.

With my boutique shopping sack slung over one shoulder, I leaned back against a pillar in the lobby. I propped one foot up on the wall behind me and tipped my head forward. I lowered my shades to the bridge of my nose and stared all "male-modelish" at the doorway, waiting for Al to arrive.

I watched as he nodded hello to Mariposa, Mack, and Alicia at the front desk.

"Good morning, Mr. Becker," I heard Mari call out to him.

"Good morning, Mari. You seen Drunk?"

Mari pointed towards the boutique. She'd seen me go in but apparently hadn't seen me come out. "I think he's in Angelita's."

He didn't even slow down as he passed me on his way to Angelita's. I cleared my throat. "Uh-hum."

Al kept walking.

"Uh-hum!" I barked louder, shifting around the pillar, so he'd still be able to see me from the other side.

Al kept walking.

"Al!" I finally hollered.

Stoop-shouldered, Al stopped walking and waddled around in a half-circle until he faced me. "There you are. Why are you leaning like that? You look ridiculous."

"Like my new threads?"

"Your new what?"

I straightened to my full height. "My new clothes, Al. Geez. Move into the twenty-first century, man."

Al looked me up and down, his puffy white eyebrows raised. "Ohh. That shirt's much better than the shirts you usually wear."

"Yeah? I look good?"

"I didn't say that."

"Of course you didn't." What had I been thinking? I shook my head, a grin slowly spreading across my face. I appreciated the fact that Al told it like it was and was stingy with his compliments. That meant when he actually did say something nice, you knew he meant it.

Al started towards the dining room and then beckoned me to follow him. "Come on, I'm hungry."

"You said you already ate."

"I haven't eaten second breakfast yet."

"Right." I tugged my sunglasses off my face, shoved them in my pocket, and caught up to him.

He turned to me, holding a finger up. "Hey, before I forget. Evie's worried about you."

I grinned. I loved Mrs. Al like a second mother. "Aww, Evie's worried about me? How sweet is that?"

"I told her you'd barely eaten anything yesterday. She said she wants you to come over for lunch, and she'll cook you a good, hearty meal."

My eyes perked up as we passed the seating hostess, giving her a little head nod. "Yeah? What kind of good, hearty meal?"

"Midwest style. Fried chicken, mashed potatoes and gravy, and corn on the cob."

I stopped walking and looked down at Al. "Well, what the hell are we going to second breakfast for? Can't we go eat that right now?"

Al swatted at me. "Funny. But no. She just ran into town to do the shopping. Are you in?"

I nodded emphatically. "Definitely! Definitely I'm in."

"Great. Now, did you give the situation any thought last night? We got a plan for today?"

I nodded. "Yeah, after breakfast, we're going on a recruiting mission."

"Speak English?" Al said, cupping his ear.

"We're gonna go get a little help from a friend," I said loudly.

"Yeah? Who's that?"

I grinned mischievously. "Oh, you'll see."

THE PARADISE ISLE ROYAL POLICE FORCE was located in a large white two-story stucco building with arched doorways and red clay roof tiles. It looked more like an apartment building or a hotel than a police station, but the multitude of police cruisers out front gave its contents away.

"You really think this is a good idea?" asked Al as we walked up the front sidewalk.

"It's my only idea. I barely know anyone on this island. I have no resources. I barely even have a sense of direction. So, yeah, I'm hoping it's a good idea."

"I thought you said the kidnapper said no cops."

I shrugged. "What he doesn't know won't hurt him. Come on."

I held the door for Al, and the two of us were soon face-to-face with Jefferson, the young man that worked the front counter. Jefferson looked up at us and smiled, his pudgy cheeks dimpling. One of his eyes met mine while his other eye watched down the hallway. "May I help you?"

"We're here to speak with Officer Cruz."

Jefferson looked surprised. "Officer Cruz?"

I shot a side glance at Al but nodded. "She still works here, correct?"

"Yes, of course. I'll have her step out to see you."

"Thanks."

Al and I stepped back and with folded arms, I gave the bulletin board on the wall a once-over. There were wanted posters, missing dog posters, missing children posters, and missing bike posters. I even saw a poster advertising a missing rooster.

"Drunk?" I spun around to see Officer Francesca Cruz looking at me with her hands boosted on her hips and a smile of surprise lighting up her face. Officer Cruz stood about five foot five. Her athletic build filled out her Paradise Isle RPD uniform in all the right places. Her dark brown shoulder-length hair was pulled back into a sleek ponytail. She was a sight for sore eyes. "What are you doing here?"

"Officer Cruz, it's good to see you!" I gestured towards Al. "You remember Al?"

"Of course I do. How've you been, Al?"

Al grinned. "Tired, but good."

She got a little closer to me, narrowing her eyes as she moved. "What happened to your face?"

I fingered my battle wounds lightly. "Oh, I ran into a wall."

"With your jaw?"

"And I fell down some stairs," I added flippantly.

She shook her head. "What are you guys doing here?"

"We came to take you to coffee," I said, glancing back at Jefferson, who had one ear trained on us like a hawk.

She rocked back on her heels, her thumbs caught inside her belt loops. "I don't drink coffee."

"Well, then, we came to take you to lunch."

"It's like nine thirty, Drunk." She quirked a grin when I slumped forward.

Al patted me on the arm as if to say "I got this." "We came to take you to ice cream. Go tell your boss you're taking a break. We need to speak with you."

Francesca's dark eyes swiveled from Al to me and then back to Al again. I could tell that something in our eyes told her we were serious. She nodded. "Okay. Gimme a minute. I'll meet you outside."

23

Francesca insisted on taking us to her favorite ice cream shop, The Hairy Coconut, which was literally a hop, skip, and a jump away from the Paradise Isle RPD. It was located on the Paradise Isle boardwalk, just one of the many kitschy little shops nestled amongst groves of palm trees that shaded the sidewalk which slowly wound its way between the natural coastline and the many local pubs, restaurants, shops, and art galleries. A live Caribbean band's music carried for blocks, and where it dropped off, music was piped in over speakers mounted in the trees. The soft morning breeze and the shade of the palm trees dispelled the heat, allowing many to enjoy their breakfast or early ice cream treats al fresco.

With my rocky road waffle cone in one hand and a cup of water in the other, I sat down at the table across from Al and Francesca. Al quietly spooned his chocolate sundae, while Francesca worked on her double scoop while staring at me.

I lifted a brow and glanced across the table at her. "What are you staring at?"

She smiled, her eyes flickering back down to her ice cream. "Sorry. It's just that you're so red! You look like a lobster!"

I straightened my elbow and looked down at my arm. "Oh,

yeah. I fell asleep on the beach," I said with a nod. I really didn't feel like getting into all of the details.

She winced. "Oooh, that's dangerous on this island."

"Tell me about it."

She touched my skin lightly. "Does it hurt?"

"It doesn't tickle." I took a quick bite of my ice cream and then nodded towards hers. "So what kind of ice cream did you get?"

She looked at her cone. "Mmm, I got two different kinds. The top scoop is Oreo cheesecake, and the bottom is nutty coconut."

I let out an inadvertent gag. "Ugh. Are you serious? Nutty coconut?"

She nodded. "Yeah, why?"

My whole face twitched. One eyebrow went up, and I made the face of someone who'd just bitten into a sour lime.

Al chuckled. "Drunk has a coconut aversion."

"Oh yeah? Paradise Isle is a bad place to have a coconut aversion," said Francesca through continued licks of her cone. "Everything here has coconut in it. It's like an island staple."

"Oh, trust me, I'll manage to avoid it. Even if I have to live off tequila alone."

Al nodded. "And trust me, he's trying."

Francesca leaned an elbow on the table and settled her chin into her palm. She looked at me with interest. "So, I'll be honest. I was shocked to see you at the station. I didn't think you'd still be on the island. I assumed after everything, you'd have gone back to the States by now."

Officer Cruz had offered her assistance when I'd needed help proving my innocence in the murder case I'd helped solve a few weeks back. Working together had been a win-win situation. I'd netted seven million dollars, and she'd gotten a notch on her belt by collaring the crook. We'd hoped it had helped her off the bottom of the totem pole at the PIRPF.

"Drunk's working at the Seacoast Majestic now," said Al.

Francesca turned to me, her eyes bright. "No kidding? You're living on the island now? Full-time?"

I lifted a shoulder. "For now anyway."

"You don't have to go back to the police department in Missouri?"

"Nah," I said, swatting at the air. "They don't really need me there."

"What does Artie have you doing at the resort?"

I straightened my shirt and sat up proudly. "You happen to be looking at the new head of resort security," I said, waggling my head.

She nodded knowingly. "Ahh, I get it." The table was silent for a moment until she glanced at each of us in turn. "So, I don't understand. It sounds like everything should be going good. But you fellas seemed tense earlier. What's going on?"

The ups and downs of the last couple of days weighed heavily on my shoulders. I let out a heavy sigh and allowed my body to sag slightly. "You're right. There is something going on."

Her head bobbed. "I knew it. What's up?"

I glanced over at Al and then back at Francesca. "Well, you knew why I came to the island in the first place, right?"

"Yeah. Pretty sure," she said, pursing her lips. "You got left at the altar?" She reached across the table and put a hand gently on my arm. "I'm so sorry."

I winced and pulled my arm away. "I didn't get…" Al's chuckle made me shoot a contemptuous glare in his direction. "I didn't get left at the altar, thank you. I got cheated on the night before the wedding. There's a difference."

"What's the difference?" asked Al.

"The difference is *I left her*!" I said, raising my voice.

Francesca shook her head. "Okay, so what's this all got to do with me?"

"His ex came to see him this week," said Al.

Francesca's big brown eyes widened. "No kidding?"

"Her name is Pam Calcara," I said. "She flew out here three days ago."

"To see you?"

"She wanted to see if we could work things out."

"Yeah? Did you?"

I frowned. "Not even close. I shut her down and then promptly asked the resort's concierge to make sure she got on a plane back to America. But the problem is, she never got on the plane."

Francesca's brow wrinkled. "Okay? So she's still bumming around the island? I mean, I get how that might bother you. But, Drunk, that's hardly against the law…"

I shook my head. "That's not it." I glanced around the open-air seating, my eyes flitting this way and that to make sure no one was listening, then I leaned across the table. "If I tell you what happened, I'm going to need you to promise me that this doesn't leave this table. It's very important that you don't tell anyone else."

"Why not?"

"It just is. Can I count on you to keep it between us?"

"Drunk…"

I reached my hand across the table and touched hers. "Please. Officer Cruz. *Francesca*. I need help, and you're the only one I feel comfortable coming to."

She looked down at the hand I'd placed on hers and then quietly pulled it away. "I mean, if you've done something illegal, if you've *hurt* anyone, I have to…"

"I didn't do anything illegal. I swear. *I* wasn't the one that hurt Pam."

"So then what's going on?"

"Promise me you'll keep it between us."

She sighed. "Okay, as long as you didn't do anything illegal, then I promise."

I nodded. "Thank you. Okay, well, the thing is… my ex was kidnapped."

"Kidnapped!" Francesca's brows shot up. "By who?"

"I don't know their names, but I have seen their faces."

"You saw them take her?"

"Sort of. I've got video footage of her leaving the resort with this one guy. We're pretty sure she didn't know him. But the deal is they're demanding seven million dollars ransom for me to get her back. I didn't believe them at first, and to be honest, I was a little salty about the breakup, and I didn't really care if they returned her or not."

"A *little* salty?" said Al, with a chuckle.

"Fine, a lot salty. *Maybe* I told them they could feed her to the sharks for all I cared…"

"Drunk!" breathed Francesca. "You said that in response to a ransom demand?"

I let my head drop, feeling guilty once again for my cavalier attitude. "Yes, I know, I know. I regret it now. Now that I've seen her captured firsthand."

"You saw her captured firsthand?"

"Well, after not responding particularly well to their threats, yesterday morning they hit me over the head and abducted me from my house. They took me to see Pam." I felt my throat constrict as I once again pictured her bruised and battered face. I swallowed hard. "They beat her."

Francesca frowned. "I'm so sorry, Drunk." She pointed to my lip then. "So that's what really happened to your face?"

I nodded. "I met Smitty. He's the muscle of the operation. Know anyone by that name?"

Francesca thought about it for a second before tipping her head sideways. "Mmm, I don't think so. I mean, I can do some digging. Do you know where they're holding her?"

"On a yacht. That's all I know. They dropped me off somewhere off the coast of the island, and I had to swim for my life. If it hadn't been for learning to swim in the Scouts, I'm not sure I would've made it."

A smirk replaced Francesca's concern over the situation. "You were a Boy Scout?"

I tipped my head forward. "Yes, ma'am."

"So were my brothers. At least the oldest ones were. When we lived in the States."

I took a sip from the water I'd ordered to go with my ice cream. My mouth was parched once again. I had a feeling it was going to take a while to get over the dehydration I'd suffered the day before. Perhaps I'd been dehydrated even before I'd been abducted. "Here's the thing, Francesca. I need to figure out how to save Pam. I can't just let her die."

"Well, we can talk to Sergeant Gibson. I'm sure he—"

I held up a hand to stop her from going any further. "Ehhh," I buzzed like the big red Xs on *Family Feud*. "No. The guy said no cops. No media. No funny business."

Francesca looked perplexed. "I don't get it, Drunk. They're asking for seven million dollars? Why do they think you can get your hands on seven million dollars?"

"Because he *has* seven million dollars," said Al. "Probably by now he's got *more* than seven million dollars. The first-quarter markets have been killer, and I picked some amazingly high-yield funds for him to invest in. He's probably sitting on an extra two fifty by now, maybe more."

Her head swiveled to stare at me. "What? Where'd you come into that kind of money, Drunk? Is this the real reason you don't want me to go to my boss? Are you into something shady down here?"

I shook my head. "No, no, no. Look. After that whole thing went down with recovering those cold-storage keys, my *team of professionals*"—by which I meant Al's geriatric squad—"was unable to locate the owner of the last key. And since Jimmy gave it to *me*, I was informed that it belonged to me."

"Drunk, I'm not sure that's how that works... Jimmy was a criminal! That money was stolen."

I pursed my lips. "It is what it is. Finders keepers, losers weepers. Anyway, it's over now. I cashed out the cryptocurrency two months ago when the Bitcoin market hit an upswing. And I might have to give it to this kidnapper now. But I'd like to avoid that if all possible. I just don't know how."

"So, what do you want me to do?"

"I need you to help me figure out how to get her back!"

"Without spending the seven mil? Is that it?"

"Look, Frankie, it's not about the money entirely—"

"Francesca."

"Right. I'm sorry. Francesca, it's not about the money entirely. I mean, yes, I'd like to keep it, but what if I hand them this suitcase of money and they kill Pam anyway? What then?"

She nodded. "Yeah, there's always a risk of that happening. Have they set up the exchange yet?"

"No, not yet. Harry said he'd call me in twenty-four hours. It was sometime after lunchtime when they dropped me overboard, so we have a few hours until he's supposed to call to make arrangements. I'm supposed to be getting the money together."

"Harry? You know the guy's name?"

I cracked a smile. "Oh. No, Harry's just the nickname I gave the guy. He kind of looks like Harry Potter. He's got the same glasses. Dark hair, you know?"

"You didn't call him that to his face, though."

"Oh, no. I did. I told him I'd seen all his movies." Remembering the look on the man's face when I'd said that almost made me giggle like a twelve-year-old girl at a sleepover.

"Drunk! You know, it's probably not such a wise idea to crack jokes at the kidnapper's expense."

I wagged a finger in the air. "You know, Harry said something about that. I'm pretty sure he said that me cracking jokes is against the rules."

"What rules?"

"He gave me a list of rules. No cops. No media. No dye packs. No fake cash. No tracking devices. No funny business."

I ticked them off my fingers as I recalled them all. "And no jokes."

Francesca leaned back in her seat. "And so what exactly do you expect me to do to help you if I can't go to Sergeant Gibson?"

"I don't know. Back in the States, if something like this happened, I'd go to my pal Mikey. He's a detective. He always knows what to do."

"But you're a cop, too, Drunk," said Francesca.

"Correction: I *was* a cop. *In the States*. Plus I was barely even off probation. So it's not like I had that shit on lockdown even when I was *there*! And then there's the fact that I have absolutely no connections down here except you. Your whole force seems to have it in for me. So even if Harry had given me his blessing to call the cops, I'm not sure that it would have been such a good idea. They might've tried to pin the whole thing on me in some way."

Francesca sighed. "I really don't know what I can do to help."

"I've got security footage of the person who took Pam. I took a screenshot of his back. He's got a pretty specific tattoo. Plus I have a make and model of the car. You could take a look at it for me?" I pulled the folded paper I'd printed out earlier from my shirt pocket and slid it across the table to Francesca.

She sighed and looked down at it. "That's it? That's all you want me to do? Just do some digging on this guy?"

"And I was hoping maybe you'd come back to the resort with me. Be there when this guy calls. Maybe between the three of us, we'll figure out a solution."

"I can't just leave work, Drunk."

"What were you doing when we got there? Working a high-pressure case?"

"Not exactly," she said, suddenly finding the waffle-weave pattern in the iron patio table interesting.

"What were you doing?"

Her cheeks flushed red as she slowly lifted her eyes from the table to meet mine. "I was opening and sorting the sergeant's mail for him."

My eyes widened. "Woooow. Wow. That's some heavy-duty shit right there." I turned to look at Al and pushed my chair back from the table. "Come on, Al. We really should get Francesca back to the station so she can get back to work on her big assignment."

"Drunk..." sighed Francesca.

"No, I mean, I certainly wouldn't want to ask you to work an *abduction* and *ransom* case over opening the boss's mail."

Al furrowed his brows. "They didn't give you a little more responsibility after you helped nab Jimmy's killer?"

"Actually, I got in trouble for not calling for backup sooner," she admitted glumly. "So it's not that I don't *want* to get involved in a big case, it's just that I don't want to lose my job doing it."

"Fine. Sergeant Gibson never has to know!" I promised.

She glanced up at Al.

"I certainly wouldn't tell anyone you helped," he said.

"Neither would I."

Francesca finally let out a heavy sigh and then stood up. "Oh, fine. But I'm in charge of this case from here on out."

I grinned. "Totally fine with that. Nothing turns me on more than taking orders from a woman!"

"Drunk!" exclaimed Francesca. "If we're going to work together, you certainly can't say things like that."

I saluted her. "Sure thing, boss. Whatever you say."

Francesca made a face. "Yeah, I'll believe it when I see it."

24

"You got any Tums?" asked Al as soon as I opened the door to my cottage.

I reached inside and turned the light on. "In the bathroom."

Without saying a word, Al shuffled off across my living room.

I furtively glanced around the room, wishing I'd had the foresight to have picked up a little more, but I'd been in a hurry. I opened my front door a little wider and gave a deep bow. "Welcome to my castle, m'lady."

Francesca Cruz stepped into my cottage and glanced around at my bamboo and rattan furnishings. The place had come furnished, which I was eternally grateful for, because I could go years in an apartment with the only furnishings being a TV and a mattress in the living room.

I rushed about, picking up empty liquor bottles and tumblers from the end tables and the floor.

"Did you just have a party?" she asked, her brows lifted.

"Party? Oh, no. I just..." I gave it a split-second thought. "Oh, *party*! Yeah, I mean, if you can call it that. I had a few friends over, you know. They're big drinkers."

Her head bobbed as she walked around. "This is a cute place. I didn't even know these cottages were back here."

"Yeah, Artie lives next door." I pointed out the window in my living room. "That's his place. He's got a pool. He lets me use it whenever I want. So that's a nice perk."

"Who lives in the one on the other side of you?"

"As far as I know, that one's empty right now."

She strolled around the living room as Al reappeared, rubbing his stomach.

"What's the matter, Al? Got a tummy ache?" I plumped out my bottom lip teasingly.

"Indigestion."

Francesca disappeared down the hallway.

"It's probably just the stress of the situation," I suggested.

He nodded. "Probably."

"Hey, who's this?" Francesca's muted voice carried down the hallway.

I found her standing in my bedroom door. "Oh, that's Earnestine."

I was just about to rush at the bird, arms flapping, to shoo her out my window, when Francesca cooed at her. "Oh! What a pretty bird!"

Earnestine flew across the room to land on Francesca's arm. *"Pretty bird, pretty bird!"* she mimicked.

"She talks!" said Francesca, her whole face lighting up with excitement. "Amazing! What a sweetheart."

I wrinkled my nose. "She's not such a sweetheart at the crack of dawn. She's worse than an alarm clock."

"She wakes you up in the morning?" She said it like it was an impressive feat.

"Well, yeah, but trust me. No one wants to be woken up by an obnoxious parrot. It's like nails on a chalkboard after a long night of dri… after a long night at work."

"What else does she say?" Francesca carried her past me to the living room.

"No! I..." I really didn't want Earnestine in my living room. She'd already taken over my bedroom, and I didn't really need the feathery old gal taking over my living room too. But Francesca kept walking, a silly smile plastered on her face, like a kid, playing with a new toy on Christmas morning.

She ran her petite fingers down the bird's head and backside. "Hi, Earnestine," she said, her voice taking on a babylike quality. "I'm Francesca. You're gorgeous."

"*Pretty bird, pretty bird,*" crowed Earnestine.

"Yes!" Francesca laughed.

I couldn't take my eyes off of her easy smile. "You've got a great smile."

Behind her, Al lifted his puffy white brows as he quietly slid into a barstool at my kitchen counter.

Francesca pulled her eyes off of the bird to look at me intently. "Have you forgotten already? You're not supposed to say things like that."

"Like what? It was just a compliment!"

Francesca sighed and reached out to hand me Earnestine. "What time is your guy supposed to call?"

"Any minute," I assured her. "You wanna sit down?"

"Sure," she said.

As she got comfortable, I ran Earnestine back to my bedroom and tossed her out the window. "Now off you go," I hissed.

I turned my back on her, slamming my bedroom door behind me.

"Francesca, can I get you something to drink?"

"I'd take a bottle of water if you've got one," she said. She pointed at a picture on my end table. "These your folks?"

I stared at the old couple on my end table. The white-haired woman had her arms looped around the white-haired man's neck like he was giving her a piggyback ride. I was pretty sure my mother had never looped her arms around

Pops' neck ever in her life. I chuckled. "I'm pretty sure that picture came with the frame."

"Yeah? And you're just leaving it up?"

I handed her a bottle of water. "Honestly, I'm not really one for home decor."

"Drunk's idea of decorating is lining up empty tequila bottles," said Al.

I shot him a look and then forced a smile. I strode over to Al and patted him over emphatically on the shoulder. "Al's a funny guy, isn't he?" I gave him a little squeeze. "Can I get *you* something, Al? A water, a sandwich, a muzzle perhaps?"

Francesca laughed. "It's all right, Drunk. I get it. Your fiancée just left you. So you're living the bachelor life right now. There's nothing wrong with that."

"My fiancée left m—" My mouth gaped. "*I left her*. But, yes, I do happen to be enjoying the bachelor life again."

She chuckled softly. "I've got six brothers. I completely understand the need for boys to be boys."

"You've got *six* brothers? Geez. My parents decided that life was perfect after having me, so they stopped there. Well, either that or they decided they didn't want to risk having another one just like me." I smirked. "Either way… I grew up an only child."

"Well, that explains a lot," mumbled Francesca under her breath, but just loud enough for me to hear her.

I pretended that I didn't. "So what's it like having six brothers?"

"Busy," she admitted with a nod. "My brothers were involved in lots of stuff."

"You said you moved to the island when you were in grade school, right?"

"Yeah, but I was the youngest. Some of my brothers had already graduated high school when we moved, but they all moved too. It's kind of a long story."

I plopped down into the sofa next to her. "Well, I don't

know about the two of you, but I happen to be waiting for a call. I've got all the time in the world."

She giggled and opened her mouth to speak, but my phone rang. *From my mouth to God's ear*, I thought. I leaned over the coffee table and looked down at my cell phone. "Restricted," I said. "It's him."

Francesca's face sobered almost instantly. She sat up higher and leaned forward to retrieve the small notepad and pen she'd dropped onto my coffee table. "Put him on speaker-phone," she instructed. "I'll take notes."

I sucked in a deep breath to calm the adrenaline that had suddenly shot through my veins. Slowly, I let it out and answered the phone. "Drunk here."

"Ahhh, so you *did* make it back. Impressive."

"You thought I didn't know how to swim?"

"I figured you had a fifty-fifty shot. But I'm sure you had a little motivation to make it."

"Yeah," I grunted. "And, hey, thanks for the paddles. That was sweet of you to include them."

"My pleasure." I could almost picture his shit-eating grin. I'd have to be sure to wipe that off his face next time I saw him. "I needed to make sure we had time to sail away."

I grunted. "So, what's the plan?"

"Have you gotten the money together yet?"

I glanced over at Francesca, who was now standing next to Al in the kitchen. She shook her head.

"Are you kidding?" I asked. "I literally just woke up. After all of that swimming and then waiting for someone to see me and bring me back to shore... let's just say I was *beat*."

"Well, clock's ticking. You better get on it. We're meeting in two days."

"Two days!" I bellowed. "You think I can get seven million dollars to fit in a suitcase in two days?"

"Oh, I'm sure you'll figure out a way." Even if I had really planned to hand over seven million dollars, I wasn't sure that

I'd be able to get it together in that short amount of time. I didn't think banks acted that fast, especially international banks that I didn't hold an account with. "And if not, there's always my original plan. You can just wire me the money."

"I'll get it together."

"Good. Okay, are you familiar with Gull Island?"

"I've heard of it."

"It's a very small uninhabited island off the southern coast of Paradise Isle."

"I said I'd heard of it," I repeated gruffly. Even though I didn't know anything about it, he didn't need to know that.

"Okay, well, in two days, we'll meet there. I'll call you when the time nears and give you a time and further directions. Got it?"

"I mean, there's really not much to get," I deadpanned.

"No jokes, remember?"

"Who's joking?"

"All right. Get going on getting my cash!"

25

"Mmm! Evie, I haven't had fried chicken this good since... well, since whenever it was the last time my mom made it," I said, through a mouthful of Evie's greasy but perfectly crispy fried chicken.

A smile of satisfaction poured across Evelyn Becker's face. I could see that she was pleased to have both filled my stomach and gotten an opportunity to mother someone. And I certainly wasn't complaining. As a self-proclaimed momma's boy, I appreciated being mothered. I liked everything mothers provided. Food. Clean clothes. A tidy house. Fresh bedsheets. And even haircuts.

So when I'd called home to tell my folks that I was staying on Paradise Isle to accept the head of resort security position, my pops had piped in on the conversation, "Good, it's about time you got off your mother's tit." Pops was about as subtle as a brick to the head, but I was used to it.

Seated out on their cottage's small beachfront porch, Evie clasped her hands together in front of herself. "I'm so glad you like it. And I'm so thrilled I finally got to meet Officer Cruz!" She turned to smile at Francesca. "Al told me all about how you helped them with that horrible shooting situation in the airport. Don't your parents worry about you being a police officer?"

A quiet smile turned the corners of Francesca's mouth. "My mother worries, yes. I lost my father when I was a kid. I have older brothers, though, and yes, they all worry. *A lot.*" She said it like it was a source of contention amongst her family.

Evie gave her a sad face. "I'm so sorry about your father, dear."

"Thank you. It was a long time ago." Francesca's long eyelashes swung down towards her plate. It was obvious she didn't like to talk about it.

"Francesca is from the US originally," I said before taking a big spoonful of mashed potatoes covered in Evie's savory chicken gravy.

Evie looked surprised. "Oh, are you? I guess I just assumed you were from the island. What part of the US?"

"Florida," she said before adding, "Boca."

"Oh, Boca Raton is lovely." Evie glanced over at her husband. "Al and I visited Boca Raton for a conference in... what was it, Al? Sixty-six?"

Al didn't even look up from his supper. "Sixty-nine. It was right after Jim was born. Remember? We left the kids with your mother."

Evie's eyes brightened. "Oh, yes. You're right! Jim's our youngest. He was kind of our surprise baby. I never left any of the other children when they were born, but sometimes you get to the end of the line and, well... you just need a break."

Francesca smiled at her. "Oh, you sound just like my mother. She used to tell me that all the time. She'd say, 'Having six boys will be the end of me.' Then she'd send my brothers to visit my aunt and uncle so we could have girl time and she could catch her breath."

Evie smiled sweetly. "Ahh, I'd like to meet your mother. I bet we could swap some stories!"

"I think you sure could," Francesca said through a chuckle.

"Do you have any children, dear?"

I heard Francesca's breath catch, and suddenly all the air felt like it had been sucked out of the room. I tried to look at her without it being obvious. She didn't wear a wedding ring, but I'd never actually asked her if she was single.

Francesca looked up and gave Evie a tight smile. "No, I don't have any children. I've never been married."

"Oh, well, a woman as beautiful as yourself shouldn't have a difficult time finding suitors."

Francesca lifted her brows. "Oh, you'd be surprised by the types of men that approach me," she chuckled. "No, there's a reason I'm single. The right man just hasn't come along yet."

Evelyn Becker turned her blisteringly blue eyes on me then. "Well, I sure know someone who's single. Don't you, Terrence?"

Hearing my middle name come out of Evie's mouth reminded me of my mother. I rubbed the bristle that had already started to regrow on my chin and quirked a grin. "Yeah—you know, I hear Gary Wheelan's on the prowl."

Evie swatted the linen napkin across the table at me. "Oh, Terrence. You're such a little jokester."

"So I've been told."

While I thought Francesca Cruz was one of the most deliciously appetizing women I'd met on the island, I knew better than to start something with her that I couldn't finish. Because after the clusterfuck of a relationship I'd just gotten out of, there was no way I was interested in another one. All I could handle for the time being, and possibly forever, was casual, no-strings-attached sex.

I shifted uncomfortably in my seat. "Evie, you didn't happen to make any pie to go with this amazing meal, did you?"

Evie's eyes widened. She squealed and pushed herself back on her chair. "You know me so well, Terrence. Of course I did! I made you your favorite chocolate pie."

I grinned at her. "I knew it!"

"Are you ready for a slice?"

I looked down at my plate. I had a lot more chicken I wanted to eat, but I also wanted to chat with Francesca about the case without Evie listening in. "I'm ready whenever you are."

Evie stood up and walked towards the sliding French doors. "I'll be back in a jiff."

When she was inside the house with the door shut behind her, I turned to look at Francesca. "So, now that you've had a chance to hear the kidnapper for yourself and had a little time to think on the situation, do you have any great ideas?"

Francesca put down her fork, almost like she was also thankful to have steered the conversation back to a *safe* topic and off her dating life. "Yes, as a matter of fact. I do have an idea. Two of my brothers work at the King's Bay Marina, which is on the other end of the island, and three of my brothers run a charter fishing service. I'm pretty sure between all of them I can get us access to a boat. I'd say first thing tomorrow morning, we ride out to Gull Island, scope it out. See what kind of trap we could set. Maybe I could even get a few of my brothers to help us out."

I leaned back in my seat to picture the takedown. We'd have all of Francesca's brothers lying in wait on the island. Old Smitty and Harry would show up with Pam, her arms tied behind her back. They'd be armed, of course, but so would Francesca's brothers. They'd shoot, Smitty and Harry would fall to the sand, Pam would be free, and I'd still have seven million dollars in my bank account. I smiled. "Perfect."

She grinned. "Yeah? You like that idea?"

I nodded. "I do. What do you think, Al?"

Al moved his fork across his plate but didn't look up. "I think the kidnapper's gonna think of that."

I swatted a hand at the air. "Nah, he's not gonna think of that. He's practically a kid!"

"I thought you said he was in his thirties."

"Or twenties." I shrugged.

"You're in your thirties and you thought of it. I'm sure he's seen the same movies you have," said Al.

"Al could be right," said Francesca. "If he's got eyes on the island and we go out there during the daylight, he's gonna see us and know we're laying a trap."

"Fine, then let's go out tonight. As soon as it's dark."

"I'm not sure I can get a boat rounded up that quickly. I'll have to talk to my brothers."

"And you'll have to change out of that uniform. Because if they do have eyes on us, and they see you in that uniform, then they'll know I talked to the cops."

Francesca nodded. "Well, obviously. But for now, I should get back to work. I could explain away a short absence, but not the rest of the day. I'll look into that picture you gave me and see if I can't get a lead on the car that picked Pam up. I'll also call my brothers on the way back to work and see if I can set something up for tonight."

I rubbed my hands together excitedly. "Perfect. I owe you big-time."

She nodded. "Yeah, you do." She pointed her finger at me. "And don't think I won't collect."

I held my hands up defensively. "Hey, I hope that you will! So, what should I do in the meantime?"

"I think you should get your butt over to the bank and see what it'll take to get your hands on that cash."

My mouth gaped open. "What? Why? We've got a surefire plan!"

Francesca frowned. "Drunk! It's hardly surefire. It's *something*, that's all that it is. But regardless, if things go south, as some ransom situations do, you might need to actually hand over the money in order to save her."

I let my head drop. That was not the advice I wanted to hear.

"You can't be serious?"

"Drunk…" began Al.

I held a hand up to stop him. "Yeah, I know. Fine. Al and I will run to the bank after lunch."

Francesca nodded. "All right, then I'll be in touch when I've gotten us a boat."

26

After lunch, the first order of business had been visiting the Paradise Isle Royal Bank, located, oddly enough, in a gated estate on the western edge of the island. After I was able to provide proof of funds, they said they'd have the money available for me within two days' time.

Thrilled to have that task at least knocked off my honey-do list, though disheartened at the prospect of having to part with the funds, Al and I met hours later at the address Francesca had given us.

I knocked on the door and then stuck my finger out to cover the little round peephole.

Al swatted my hand away from the door. "Knock it off. She shouldn't open the door without knowing who it is. That's dangerous."

"She just texted to tell us we could come over," I said, reapplying my thumb to the small glass circle. "She knows who it is."

"What are ya? Six years old? Knock it off." More hand swatting.

I stared down at Al. He was so short that from my vantage point I could easily play connect the liver spots on his bare scalp. "I'm just having a little fun. What's the big deal?" Without turning my head from his, I reapplied my thumb to the door's peephole, just as Francesca opened the door. My thumb hung in the air.

"Hey. What's with the thumb?"

Al crooked his own thumb in my direction. "He's an idiot." Then he shuffled inside her apartment.

Francesca's brows lifted as he walked past her. "Ah. I see. Come on in." The woman was barefoot and towel-drying her wet hair. She wore a clingy army-green tank top tucked into a pair of cutoff blue jean shorts. It was the first time I'd seen her out of uniform and with her hair out of its ponytail. Seeing her that way almost made her seem like a different person entirely. Her wet hair on her shoulders, framing her face, made for an especially alluring sight. I had to fight like hell not to stare at her nipples, which strained against her bra and the damp fabric of her tank top. I couldn't comprehend how she'd yet to find suitable male companionship looking like that.

I walked through the open doorway. "Thanks," I said, keeping my eyes scanning the top of her head. "Nice place."

"Eh, it'll do. I don't make a lot. This is the best I can afford on a lowly cop's salary."

"No, I like it," I said. Even though the building had been in a crappy part of town and the steps up to the apartment were covered in shabby carpet and peeling layers of paint, her individual apartment looked nice. I had to guess that she'd done some work to it, as the grey walls looked like they had a fresh coat of paint on them, the doors, doorjambs, and all the wood moldings looked like they'd been refinished, and the light fixtures didn't look like they'd been purchased in the dark ages. She had pictures covering almost every square inch of the place. I inhaled deeply; it smelled like vanilla and citrus.

"It smells really good in here."

She grinned. "Thanks, I sort of have an affinity for melts."

"Melts?"

"Yeah, you know, those little scented wax melts." She pointed at an antique armoire in the corner. "That whole cabinet is filled with melts."

I nodded. I was pretty sure my mother had a friend who sold that stuff back in the States. "Oh, yeah. What is it? Smells like vanilla and citrus."

"Close, it's… lemon vanilla cake."

"I like it."

She gestured towards the living room as she rubbed a towel against her hair with the other hand. "Make yourself at home. I just got out of the shower. I need to finish getting ready."

Al stood before a wall of pictures. "This your family?"

She nodded before disappearing into her bathroom. "Yeah. Those are all my brothers and my nieces and nephews. That's my mom in the middle."

I stared over Al's head at the wall of pictures. She had an enormous family. I didn't even know what it would be like to have so many relatives. Both of my parents had siblings, but they lived far away and we didn't see them very often, so I really hadn't grown up with any cousins, and as I was sibling-less, I hadn't ever had nieces or nephews either.

"Wow, you have a ton of family members!" I shouted.

"Yeah, I know. They're a lot of fun," she hollered back. She appeared back in the living room with her wet hair now knotted in a bun on the top of her head. It pulled at the skin next to her eyes, sharpening her high cheekbones and giving her an even more ethnic look.

I sucked on my bottom lip. *Wow.* The woman was flawless.

"This one's your mother?" asked Al, pointing at a picture vaguely in the center of the wall. It was a black-and-white snapshot of a wrinkled woman with a broad smile on her face. If she'd looked like Francesca at any point in her life, it was now hidden behind years and years of age lines.

"Yes, that's my mother. That's my favorite picture of her. She looks so… *happy*."

"What's her name?" I asked.

"Guadalupe. Everyone just calls her Lupe."

"You said she lives on the island?" asked Al, turning to look at her.

"Yeah. She lives with my oldest brother, Solo, his wife, Marina, and their children." She pointed at a group picture on the wall of a brooding, tall, broad-shouldered man with a wife who was short enough to fit under his armpit and to easily be confused with one of the children. There were a handful of kids, all of them dressed in similar colors of peach and aqua, like they'd just come from a family outing.

"Beautiful family," said Al. "Very beautiful. Makes me miss my own."

"I'm certainly lucky," she agreed. "All right, we need to get moving. Just let me get on some shoes and we'll go."

There was a knock at the door.

I turned towards Francesca. "You expecting someone?"

"Oh, that's just Hugo," she said casually, walking towards the door.

"Hugo?" I straightened and my voice deepened inadvertently. "I thought you said you were single."

"I am." She chuckled before opening the door to let the largest dog I'd ever seen come running into her apartment.

"Hey, buddy," she cooed as he zipped past her to stand directly in front of me, barking wildly.

I looked down at the enormous dog that stood nearly chest-high to me. His face was close enough to mine that I could taste the fish that he'd eaten for lunch. "I take it this is Hugo?" I shouted over his barking.

"Yes, this is Hugo." She took a hold of the leash he'd pulled out of the hands of the woman in the doorway and drug him over to her side. "Relax, Hugo, this is a friend. Relax." She patted him gently.

I stared wide-eyed at the lanky dog. He was tan with a black face, pointy ears, and long jowls. "What kind of dog is he?"

"Great Dane," said Al, shuffling over to Hugo's side.

Immediately, Hugo relaxed, allowing Al to pet him and scratch him behind the ears. Taking a cue from Al, and wanting Hugo to not want to eat me, I tried to walk over and scratch his ears too. Immediately Hugo began barking wildly at me again.

I took a step back. "I don't think he likes me."

Francesca smiled. "Probably because you're so big. Hugo's kind of a gentle giant. He's easily intimidated. I got him to be my guard dog, but I usually end up guarding him."

I grimaced and pointed a finger at the small pony. "So you're saying that *he* is intimidated by *me*?"

She nodded. "Yeah. Crazy, huh?"

"Yeah."

She looked at the young woman standing in the doorway. She was blonde and tanned, wearing spandex shorts, sneakers, and only a sports bra for a shirt. Earbuds dangled around her neck. "This is Courtney. She does doggy daycare and watches Hugo while I'm at work."

"Hey," said Courtney, giving Al and me a little wave. She gestured towards the hallway. "I live next door to Frankie, so I usually walk Hugo home from daycare when I get off work." She turned her attention to Francesca. "So... he didn't eat all of his supper. Abby was at daycare today, so he played hard. You know how he feels about her. I have a feeling he's going to sleep well for you tonight."

Francesca ran a hand down along Hugo's neck. "Hugo! Did you play with Abby today?"

At the mere mention of Abby's name, Hugo's tail went wild, nearly taking out Courtney, who stood behind him in the doorway.

Holding her hands out in front of herself, Courtney

laughed while backing up towards the hallway. "Chill, kid. Chill. Geez!"

"Well, I'm glad he had a hard day, because I'm going out here shortly, and he's staying home alone. Thanks for bringing him home."

Courtney's eyes widened and she let her gaze linger on me for a noticeably long moment. "Yeah? Hot date?"

Francesca rolled her eyes and began closing the door on her neighbor. "Thank you, Courtney. Have a nice evening."

Courtney's fingers fluttered a goodbye at me and Al. "Bye, guys. It was nice to meet you."

Al wiggled his fingers back. "Bye," he sang in the same little tone.

With the door now shut, Francesca shook her head. "Sorry about Courtney."

"No problem. Are you ready?" I eyed Hugo. He was still at Francesca's side, but staring at me suspiciously.

"Almost, I just need to put some shoes on. I'll be right back." She walked away from Hugo and he literally froze in his spot, staring at me, his body stiff, his ears at full attention.

I held a friendly hand out to him, and he barked at me. My hand snapped back to my side.

"Hugo!" called out Francesca.

I let out a nervous laugh. "How about Al and I meet you downstairs?"

27

It was dark when we pulled up to the King's Bay Marina in Francesca's white 1986 Suzuki Samurai. Francesca had refused to let me drive the fun-looking little stick shift, and Al was too old to crawl in the back, so I'd had to fold my stork-like legs in half to fit into the small backseat. I rode with my knees up by my chin, so by the time we unloaded in the harbor parking lot, my body was stiff from the ride.

Piling out, we paused in the parking lot next to the vehicle. Francesca stuck her head into the backseat, looking for something, while I bent over, trying to rub some life back into my now numb legs. When I straightened, a flash of Francesca's backside made my head inadvertently tip to the side.

Damn.

There was no denying, the woman had a killer ass.

Al caught my slack-jawed stare and elbowed me in the ribs, shooting me the stink eye.

"What!" I mouthed, feigning indignation.

He gave me a warning glare just as Francesca emerged from the backseat. I caught the scant outline of a handgun in the dark before it made its way into a holster under her shirt.

"You're bringing a gun to a boat ride?" I asked.

"You can never be too safe," she said, her voice dead serious. She strode around to the back of her vehicle and swung the back door open. She pulled out a duffle bag and slung it over one shoulder before slamming the door shut again.

"What's in there?"

She patted the tote. "Basic necessities. Flashlight, rope, radio, batteries. Stuff like that."

"You do this kind of stuff a lot?"

She smiled. "Drunk, I'm a cop. I'm always prepared. You're a cop, aren't you the same way?"

"I *was* a cop, and honestly, *no*, I wasn't like that at all."

"Probably part of the reason you had a hard time making it off probation," said Al.

"Ouch," I said, rubbing the sting from my shoulder. "You give your own kids this much tough love?"

"Not as much. Of course, I raised *them* to have a good work ethic."

I winced. "Geez, Al. The hits just keep coming."

Francesca chuckled. "You two are funny. Come on. Solo and the boys are in the marina office. They're waiting for us."

"Solo and the boys?" I asked as Al and I took up a spot on either side of her.

"Yeah, five of my brothers are here. Solo's the oldest. He and Beto work here at the marina. My brother Miguel runs his own charter boat fishing company. Rico and Diego work for him."

"Didn't you say you had six brothers? What about the sixth?" I shot her a cheesy grin. "Does he own a fish cleaning company?"

She shook her head without bothering to smile. "No, Jaime's a model."

"Oh."

"This way," she said, pointing up the wooden walkway towards a small shack-like building where the lights inside glowed brightly, illuminating the night sky around the building. The air was eerily calm as muted Latin music rolled down the gangway. The water in the harbor was glassy with the moon and the marina lights reflecting off its inky black surface. The vague silhouette of ships still out to sea looked like an oil painting hanging in the night sky.

"Nice evening for a boat ride," said Al, reading my thoughts.

"What did Evie say about you riding along with us tonight?" I asked.

"She said not to fall overboard."

"Good advice."

Al nodded. "I thought so."

Francesca tipped her head sideways. "Now how is that you two know each other again?"

"Al and I were on the same flight here from Atlanta," I explained. "We rode the shuttle to the resort together, but we actually *met* at the resort's swim-up bar."

"It was love at first sight," said Al with a hint of a chuckle. "Drunk couldn't keep his hands off me after that."

"Evie jealous?" I asked.

"Not really. She said I could do worse."

I laughed. I knew Evie loved me.

Francesca stopped at the harbor office door. Without bothering to knock, she pushed open the door and barged inside, where we discovered five burly, dark-haired, dark-skinned men sharing a beer and laughing like they had nothing better to do than to enjoy life. They all stopped talking the minute the door opened and turned their heads. When they saw it was Francesca, they all raised their beers and cheered. "Ayyyy!"

"Panchita!" cheered a couple of them in unison.

Francesca's face lit up. "Hey, guys. Thanks for helping us out."

"No problem, anything for our kid sis," said one of the men. Despite the fact that he was the shortest of the brothers, he still clocked in at least five inches taller than Al.

"Thanks, Rico," said Francesca. Then she turned to let Al and me in. "Guys, these are friends of mine. This is Al."

"Al Becker," said Al, extending a hand to each of the men in turn.

"Hey, Al," said one of the men.

"And this is Drunk. He was a cop in the States."

"What kind of name is Drunk?" said the one I recognized from the pictures as her oldest brother, Solo. His voice was deep and commanding and immediately drew silence from his brothers.

"A family name," I said with a shrug.

"Yeah? I never met another Drunk before," he said somberly.

"Oh yeah? I've met lots of Drunks," I laughed at my old standby joke.

Solo didn't seem to think it was funny. He glanced over at his sister. "Where did you meet these guys, Francesca?"

"Drunk was the one I was telling you about. The one that helped me collar those guys at the airport several weeks ago."

Rico lifted his eyebrows. "That was you, man?"

I nodded. "Yup."

"Officer Cruz really helped us out," said Al, beaming at Francesca. "You all should be very proud of her."

One of her brothers patted her on the shoulder. "Oh, we're proud of her. We just don't really like what it is that she does for a living."

I made a face. "Why? It's not like she's a stripper or something."

All the steely-faced men stared at me.

I shifted in my boat shoes awkwardly. "I mean, she's a cop. That's pretty respectable…"

Finally, one of the guys stepped forward. "You got something against strippers?"

I held up my palms and lowered my head, tipping it

slightly. "Hey, don't get me wrong. I got nothing against strippers. Most cost-effective therapy out there."

"Cuz my wife's a stripper, yo."

The air left the room, leaving a stale, hollow sound in its wake.

My eyebrows peaked and my body froze. I let out a long low, "Ohhh. Ahhh, man, you know…"

Francesca rolled her eyes and shoved the guy out of the way. "D, shut it." She looked at me. "Don't pay him any attention, Drunk. Diego's not even married."

"Hey, man, I could be married to a stripper," he said, patting his puffed-out chest.

I cracked a smile. "You had me," I said, wagging my finger at Diego. My eyes scanned the room as all the brothers guffawed, except Solo. He still stood staring at me like I was an unwanted intruder creeping on his sister.

Francesca held both hands up to settle her brothers down and get us back on task. "Okay, okay. Al, Drunk, I'll give you the formal introduction once, so listen closely." She drew in a deep breath. "That one is Solomon Junior, Solo for short. He's the oldest and runs the harbor here."

She pointed to a round, pudgy-faced man next. He was the widest of the group, with enormous shoulders, arms the size of my thighs, and a potbelly that hung over the belt of his dirty work jeans. "The next oldest is Miguel. He's the one whose boat we're using tonight."

"Thanks for that," said Al.

"Oh, yeah, thanks," I added, feeling once again awkward.

Miguel gave us a two-fingered salute.

"Next oldest is Diego. He works for Miguel."

"Works *with* Miguel," corrected Diego.

Miguel looked at his brother with one brow lifted. "You pay for the boats?"

Diego snorted.

"You put fuel in 'em? You cut the paychecks?"

"As a matter of fact, I *do* put fuel in the boats."

"You *pay* for that fuel?"

"No?"

Miguel nodded as if he was justified. "All right, then. You work for *me*."

Francesca sighed and moved on to the next brother. "This is Roberto."

"You can call me Beto," said Roberto, holding out a hand to shake mine and Al's again. Roberto was almost as tall as Solo, but not quite. He was the lightest-skinned of the men. He wore khaki pants, loafers, and a white polo. "I work *for* Solo here at the harbor."

"Beto does the books," explained Francesca, though she hadn't needed to. By his clean apparel and less sun-damaged skin, it was obvious he wasn't working outside day in and day out like his brothers.

"And last but not least, this is Rico. He also works *with* Miguel and Diego."

I stared at the lot of them, four of them laughing and joking, one stone-cold serious, Latin music still playing in the background. I couldn't imagine growing up in a family like Francesca's. I imagined it had been loud and boisterous and more than a little crazy. I'd grown up in mostly silence. The only time it was ever loud in my house was during football and basketball season, so it was difficult to relate.

"Well, it's really good of you all to help Drunk and me out like this." Al pulled a handkerchief from his pocket and rubbed the back of his neck. "Drunk's found himself in a bit of a predicament again, I'm afraid."

All eyes turned to me.

Unsure what Francesca had told her brothers about the situation I was in, I glanced over at her, seeking any assistance she might feel like providing, which, by the look on her face was absolutely none.

All right.

Go time.

I cleared my throat and shifted my weight to my other foot. "Yeah, so a quick bit of background on me. I came to Paradise Isle on my honeymoon," I began.

Solo stepped forward then, holding up a hand to stop me, his eyes narrowed into slits. "Wait, you're married?"

Francesca got between us. "Solo!" she chastised. "Let him finish, all right?"

I took a deep breath as Solo slid up onto the top of his desk. Folding his arms over his chest, he nodded at me. "Fine, go ahead. It's not like we all have things to do and places to be."

"Solo!" she barked.

He pressed his lips together as if to say, *I'll be quiet.* He reached over and turned off the radio. The room fell silent.

"Right, so anyway, to answer your question, *no*, I'm not married." I swallowed hard. I really didn't want to share the next part, especially with Francesca's brothers. But I knew for them to have any kind of buy-in into my situation, they were going to have to really understand my plight. "The night before my wedding, I caught my fiancée in bed with her ex-boyfriend."

All the men in the room winced, except Solo. He sat expressionless.

"Oooh, man!" cried Rico. "That's gotta burn."

"Yeah." I nodded, letting out a heavy sigh. "Definitely. So, anyway, I ended up flying out for my honeymoon by myself. That was almost two months ago. That was when I first met Francesca. She was very helpful with everything that went down. Like Al said, you should all be very proud of her."

"So, what's the problem now?" asked Miguel.

"Okay, well, my ex-fiancée, Pam, showed up a few days ago. Of course she had her excuses, but ultimately she just wanted to get back together."

Several of Francesca's brothers made pained faces, as if they'd been in my shoes before.

"Yeah, so, I was upset that she'd followed me out here. I told her to leave. I even made arrangements for our resort concierge to drive her to the airport for her flight out. But then I found out she didn't make the flight, and lo and behold, I discover that she'd managed to go and get herself kidnapped."

All eyes shot open then. Even Solo's. It was as if he hadn't been able to stop it.

"No way, man. Is she okay?" asked Rico.

"Is she still alive?" asked Beto.

"Yeah, as of yesterday, she was still alive. The same guys that took Pam got their hands on me yesterday. Hit me over the head and next thing I know I'm waking up locked in a room on a yacht."

"A yacht!" said Rico.

I nodded. "That's where they're holding her."

"Can you describe it? The yacht?" asked Solo. "Maybe we've seen it in our waters."

I shrugged. "I mean, it was white. And long. I couldn't tell you how long. It had windows. And maybe three levels... more?"

"Did it have a flybridge, an open bridge with a hard top, a skylounge, maybe? Like, can you give us a little something to go on?"

I balked. The man wasn't speaking my language. I rubbed a hand against the back of my neck. "Honestly, I didn't get much of a tour of the inside. I only saw it as it sailed away, leaving me to swim back to the island."

"Oooh," sighed Diego. "They made you swim back?"

"Yeah, pretty much." I lifted the sleeve of my shirt to show them my blistered shoulders. "Hence the sunburn. Let's just say yesterday wasn't that great of a day."

The men all nodded their sympathies.

"So, anyway, these guys, they want money. And, you know, I'll be honest. When they first called to ask for the ransom money, I was a jerk. You know? I didn't care what happened to my ex. She did me wrong. I wasn't in the mindset of helping her." I tried to gauge the guys' reactions. Were they able to see my side of things? Or did they think I was a horrible guy for not rushing to my ex's aid? Their faces weren't very telling. A bead of sweat ran down the back of my neck and between my shoulder blades. "But when I saw her on the yacht, and I saw that they'd knocked her around, I realized that her life really was in danger. It still is. So I'd like to try and rescue her. I know they want money, but what if I get the money together, give it to them, and then they kill her anyway? I just feel like I don't have a lot of options."

When I was done talking, I looked around the room. It had fallen completely silent. No one moved, no one said a word. They only exchanged uneasy glances. It was as if they felt bad for me but weren't sure if they wanted to get involved.

After what seemed like minutes, Solo finally slid off the desk and onto his feet. He let out a heavy sigh. "How can we help?"

Without missing a beat, Francesca spoke. "The kidnapper called today while I was with Drunk and Al. He wants to do the ransom and hostage exchange on Gull Island in two days."

"Gull Island? Why? There's nothing on Gull Island," said Rico. "Just tall grass and piles of bird caca."

"Yeah, so, I was thinking. Maybe if we got out there now, we could set up some kind of sting," said Francesca. "You know? Then we'd be able to grab them while they're setting things up."

"Sounds dangerous," said Solo, shaking his head. "No. We're not doing anything that puts your life in danger."

Francesca put both hands on her hips. "Solo. Stop. I'm a cop. I'm not some kind of weakling. I can take care of myself."

Still, he shook his head. "Absolutely not. And as the head of the family, I forbid it."

Francesca furrowed her brows. "*¿Qué dijiste?*" She took a

step towards him and cocked her head slightly. "Did you just say you *forbid* it?" she rattled off in Spanish.

He stood up taller. "*Eso es cierto.*"

She let out a snort. "*¡Estás loco, Solomon!* Just because you're the oldest doesn't mean I have to do anything you say. I came to you for help. I thought maybe you could provide us a ride out there. I didn't come here to ask your permission or for you to interfere in my business."

She turned around and strode towards the door. Her jaw was set and her face flushed. "Come on, Al, come on, Drunk, let's go. We'll find someone else with a boat that isn't such a *chauvinist*, that can take us to Gull Island."

Francesca was already out the door when Solo's shoulders slumped forward. All his brothers looked at him silently. It was obvious that he was regarded as the boss of the family.

"Panchita, wait!" he hollered, holding up a hand.

All eyes turned towards the doorway.

It remained empty for several seconds.

Finally, we heard the sound of Francesca's sneakers on the boardwalk. She stepped back inside the harbor office doorway. "*¿Qué?*"

"You know it will kill Mami if something happens to you."

"Nothing's going to happen to me, Solo. You'll all be there. Drunk's a cop. These guys aren't even going to be there tonight. We're just scoping it out. See if we can't think up a plan to trap them."

Solo let out a weighted sigh. "Fine. We'll take you, but only because you're going to let us protect you if something happens."

Francesca smiled. "Nothing's going to happen, big bro! I promise!"

28

MIGUEL MANEUVERED THE TWENTY-NINE-FOOT BLACKFIN sportfishing boat from the pier as the rest of the group all gave a wave to Beto, who had stayed behind on the wharf. He unfolded his arms and gave us a solemn nod before turning to head back into the marina offices.

Seated on the edge of the flybridge with his legs dangling over the ladder, Rico cranked backwards to look at his brother as we motored away. "Solo, you really should lay off Beto. He's turning into an old man."

"There's nothing wrong with having priorities," Solo said to his brother. "You'd all do well to take a lesson from Beto."

"It's not about his priorities," Rico argued. "I mean, I get that he's got a good job, but it's late. He should be allowed to take a little time off. You know, roll up his pant legs and get his shoes wet or something."

"I didn't tell him he had to work. Beto chose to stay behind because he's dedicated to his job and he has mouths to feed. Someday you'll understand."

Rico shrugged and climbed down the stairs as Miguel, steering from the captain's station on the flybridge, motored us through the narrow mouth of the channel.

As we picked up speed, the warm night air caressed my cheeks. Seated on the upper flybridge, I leaned against the back of the settee. Al and Francesca flanked either side of me while Solo sat in one of the swiveling helm chairs directly across from us. Miguel sat between us in the other. Both Diego and Rico stood in the lower-level cockpit.

"Hey, man, I sure appreciate your help," I said, looking at Miguel. My eyes shifted as they inadvertently met Solo's. "You know, you guys letting us use your boat to get out there and all."

Solo crossed his arms over his chest and before Miguel could respond, he butted in. "What's the plan when we get there?"

I cleared my throat and crossed my leg over my knee, leaning forward slightly. I was supposed to have a plan in order to make a plan? I didn't know a single thing about Gull Island. I'd never been there before. I'd never seen it on a map. So how could I possibly be expected to have a plan? "Oh, the plan?" I cleared my throat.

Solo's mouth tightened. He cocked a brow as he glanced over at his sister. "You do have a plan, don't you?"

"Of course we do, Solo," said Francesca. The moonlight glowed behind her head, making her dark hair look almost golden, angelic. "Our plan is to get out there, scope the place, see what kinds of traps we might be able to lay. We don't want to go into the ransom drop blind. This is really just a scouting expedition so we can come up with the plan."

He glanced over at me again.

I shrugged, cocking my thumb sideways towards his sister as if to say, *What she said.*

Solo's eyes narrowed on me. "By failing to prepare, you're preparing to fail. Do you make it a habit of living life recklessly?"

"Not really. Back in the States, my life was pretty boring."

"Yeah?" said Miguel, taking his eyes off the water for the

first time. "But you're a cop in the States. That couldn't be too boring."

I shrugged. "Eh. I got a late start. I was barely off probation when I left."

"At your age you were barely off probation? That doesn't bode well for your character," grunted Solo.

My mouth went dry, but I couldn't help but agree with him. "You're probably right. It took me a while to figure out what I wanted to do for a living. I joined the police academy late in life, and even when I did, I didn't take it as seriously as I should have."

"Would you do things differently now?" he asked.

"Solo!" chastised Francesca. "Stop bothering Drunk with silly questions."

"It's not a silly question, Panchita. You're putting *your* neck and *your* career on the line to help this guy who doesn't even take his own life or career seriously." Solo's eyes lowered, and a deep groove formed between his eyes. "Sometimes these kinds of experiences add character to a man. I just wondered if he'd go back and do things differently now that he's had these things happen to him."

Solo's questions made me wonder. *Would* I do things differently now if given the chance over again? Would I have started my career earlier? Would I have tried harder at the academy? Would I have tried harder to get off probation? Maybe if I'd been more concerned about my career, I wouldn't have had time to fall for Pam's feigned innocence back then. I shrugged. "Maybe. I really don't know."

We hit a wave and the boat rocked forward, sending a fine mist of saltwater spraying against my back and reminding me of the mission that we were on. The fact remained, I didn't have the luxury to do things differently. Now, I only had my wits about me, the people in this boat, and the shirt on my back. That was it. I had to do the best with what I had.

Al gave me a little pat on my knee. "I'll tell you this, fellas.

Drunk might not have come to the island with the right mind-set, but he's certainly doing his best to resolve this situation. His heart is in the right place and that's what matters."

"Thanks, Al," I said, even though I wasn't sure that my heart actually *was* in the right place.

Solo's hard look made me curious as to what he was thinking. Then, without notice, he quietly stood up and climbed down the stairs to the cockpit. Apparently it was his not-so-subtle way of telling us he was done with the conversation.

I glanced over at Francesca.

She rolled her eyes and drew up one golden-tanned knee. She swiveled slightly into the wind, turning her back to me. She reached back and pulled the tie from her hair. The wind caught hold of her damp tresses, tossing them backwards.

I closed my eyes and inhaled. Her hair smelled sweet, like milk and honey. The combination of the beautiful night and her scent was intoxicating. And in that moment, I wished we were on the boat under different circumstances and not surrounded by her brothers.

Seconds later, Diego climbed the stairs and took Solo's spot next to Miguel.

The ride was silent for a while until finally, Francesca turned to face her brothers again. "Guys, I really like the new boat."

Miguel gave Francesca a sideways glance. "Yeah? I got it off this old-timer who lost an arm in a boating accident a few months back. He gave me a sweet deal because he was sick of looking at it."

"It's much larger than the old fishing boat."

He nodded and hooked a thumb over his shoulder. "The cabin down there has a dinette *and* a head in it." He grinned from ear to ear.

"No more pissing off the side of the boat now," hollered Rico from the cockpit.

"Classy," said Francesca with a sly grin. "What about the other boat? You sell that one?"

"Nah, Diego's captaining that one now."

"Nice, D!" said Francesca.

Diego grinned from ear to ear. "Workin' my way up, you know. I'm gonna buy it from him when I've got enough money saved up. Then I'll be working *with* him instead of *for* him."

"And now you can have two charters out at once. That's gotta help with bringing in the work."

"For sure. Plus Rico's working on updating our website," said Miguel. "So now clients will be able to book one of our boats right there from their computer or their phone. It's gonna be slick. As soon as I can afford it, I wanna buy a third boat, so Rico can captain that one."

Francesca shook her head, pride beaming from her face. "You're gonna have a whole fleet someday. Cruz Brothers Charter Fleet," she said with a giggle.

With a wide smile, Miguel's head tipped forward. "I like the sound of that."

After another twenty minutes of small talk, Miguel pulled the boat up skillfully along the outer bank of a dark island. From a distance, it had looked like a shadowy blob, like a giant monster rising up out of the sea, but up close, I could now make out the shapes of natural rock formations. Other than that, the island appeared to be a barren wasteland.

Diego stood up. "Here we are. Gull Island." He rushed down the stairs, nearly jumping from the top deck.

"Not much to it," said Al, his voice almost entirely drowned out by the shouting of Francesca's brothers as they worked to help secure the boat meters off the coast.

"Agreed," said Miguel before going down next. "Panchita, you can help these two get out?"

"Of course," said Francesca.

Francesca and I both helped Al down the stairs to the cockpit, where she grabbed her duffle bag and tossed it over the transom onto the swim platform. Following her brothers, she swung her leg over the edge and then jumped into the waist-deep water. "We'll have to wade in. The boat can't get that close to the shore." She reached over and lifted her duffle bag over her head so it wouldn't get wet while she waded.

Al held a shaky hand out to me as he tried to lift a leg over the transom. "You'll have to lower me down, Drunk."

I took him by the elbow and tried to reel him back in. There was no way I was dropping an eighty-seven-year-old man into the Atlantic. I shook my head. "Not happening. You're staying here."

"Like hell." He tried to climb out of the boat himself. "I got great night vision. You're gonna need me out there."

I closed my eyes and sighed. "Dammit, Al, this is only gonna make things more difficult. There's nothing to see out there."

Al fingered the air. "Aha! You just proved my point." He stabbed the same finger into his chest. "*I* can see plenty."

I slapped my forehead and slid my hand down my face.

"Drunk, did you learn nothing the last time we worked together? We're in this as a team. Now if you don't help me out, I'll just fall overboard and *you* can explain to Evie why you made me do the one thing she told me I'm not allowed to do."

I closed my eyes.

Fuck.

"I can get my brothers to help him," Francesca offered, looking back over her shoulder at us. She turned around again and cupped a hand to call to the four men that had already disembarked and were halfway to the shoreline. "Hey, Solo!" she hollered. "Drunk needs your—"

"Shh!" I swatted the air. The last thing I needed was Francesca's brothers thinking I wasn't strong enough to lower a ninety-pound man into the water. "No, I'll do it. Don't we have a life jacket or something that he can put on, though? I'd feel better if I could tether him to me or something."

"Probably under those seats on the flybridge. Where we were sitting," she explained while pointing.

I glared at Al. "Not a move, got it, old man?"

"Yeah, yeah," he grumbled.

I glanced over my shoulder before heading back to get the lifejacket. Her brothers were already to the shoreline. I groaned.

Minutes later, with Al and me securely buckled into a life-jacket and the two of us tied together, we waded through the warm waist-deep water to the shoreline. Al was light, so the water tended to try and sweep him off his feet. I was thankful he'd allowed me to put him in a lifejacket.

As we neared the shoreline, water lapped at its sandy edges. Beneath the moonlight and with the help of Francesca shining her flashlight, we could immediately see the mountains of white that covered almost every square inch of the beach.

"Holy. Literal. Fucking. Shit," I breathed as we looked out upon the piles of bird crap.

"Language," barked Solo, shooting me a look of disgust. "My sister's present."

Francesca made a noise before backhanding her brother's arm. "Solo! Relax. I've heard way worse at the station." She moved her flashlight around the island.

Still tethered to me, Al walked forward on the beach until he hit the end of his rope. Unable to go any further, he padded around me in a semicircle, looking into the darkness. Finally, he looked up at me stiffly.

"There's nothing to see out here," he said as if giving me his official report.

I frowned. "I told you there wasn't shit out here."

"I know, but I'm from the 'Show Me' State."

"What the hell're you talking about? You're not from Missouri. You're from Nebraska."

"Well, I can see Missouri from Nebraska."

"You're a pain in my ass, Al."

Al cupped a hand to his ear. "Eh?"

I rolled my eyes.

"*I* see something," said Solo. He pointed towards the horizon. "There's a boat out there."

I followed his finger, squinting into the darkness. "I don't see anything."

"It's there. Trust me. Its lights are off."

Everyone else's eyes tried to see what Solo saw.

Finally, I gave up trying to spot Solo's ghost ship. "All right, well, listen, we need to come up with a plan."

"Mm-hmm," growled Solo.

Gritting my teeth, I ran a hand through my hair. I needed to figure something out quickly. The shadowy outline of a wall rising up in the distance caught my eye. "Francesca, throw some light over there, will ya?"

She turned her big beam of light onto a wall of rocks on the west side of the island. The ocean rubbed up against the side of it, creating white rolls of foam.

"Well, maybe we could put a couple guys behind that rock line over there."

"A couple guys?" said Solo, looking surprised. "You got an army on your side or something?"

Immediately my error became evident to my own ears. I'd mistakenly assumed Francesca's brothers would help us with the sting when the time came. "Oh, well, I…"

Suddenly my phone rang.

Saved by the ringtone, I thought as I dug my phone out of my shirt pocket. Without even looking at the screen, I answered it. "Drunk here."

"Daniel! We speak again." The familiar menacing voice resonated like a bomb in my ears.

My head dropped. *Out of the frying pan and into the fire.*

"Harry, it's not been long enough," I quipped, instantly regretting I'd even answered. "What can you do for me?"

"Daniel, listen, I feel like I've been a fairly patient man. Many others in my shoes wouldn't have been *nearly* this patient. But now I think we have a few things we need to discuss. It looks like you decided not to play by the rules," he drawled into the phone.

My heart froze in my chest and my mouth went dry. Any unease I'd had about Francesca's brothers giving me a hard time immediately dissipated. I had bigger problems. "The rules?" I swallowed hard and sent a furtive glance up to the group of people I'd had a major hand in gathering on the island. They all stared back at me expectantly. "I suppose you mean the jokes. Well, you're absolutely right. You have my apologies. Old habits die hard, you know. I'll do my best to knock it off." I stuck a finger in my other ear to block out the sound of the surf breaking against the rocks. "Hey, while I gotcha on the phone. I went to the bank today to start the process of getting your money." I hoped he'd be excited to hear that and would let me go about my business.

"Well, that's good to hear. And quite honestly, if I hadn't heard that, things might have gone badly for you this evening."

I turned around, giving Francesca and her brothers my back. "I'm glad to hear that you're pleased," I said, my body rigidly anticipating the purpose of the phone call. "So, if that's all you needed, I'll let you—"

"Not so fast, Daniel. The *reason* I say that, is because if you *weren't* working on getting me my money, I might've been tempted just to end this all right now."

"End it?"

"That's right. Call the whole thing off."

I furrowed my brows. "Excuse me?"

"Because it would only take a second to erase this entire problem, right off the face of the earth."

My voice caught in the back of my throat. I coughed a little. "Erase the problem? Are you talking about hurting Pam? Because I—"

"No, I wasn't talking about hurting *Pam*, Daniel."

"Drunk, what's going on? What's he saying?" asked Al, hobbling around me so he could look me in the eye.

I held a finger up and mouthed a shhh.

Harry continued, "Because like I said earlier, you aren't playing by the rules I laid out for you."

I winced. Had he seen me going to the police station to get Francesca earlier?

Fuck.

"I don't know what you're—"

"Don't mess with me, Daniel. I told you specifically no funny business."

"Funny business?" My voice might have risen an octave.

"You know, I had a feeling you might try and pull something," said Harry. "I'm just a little surprised you'd be so *obvious* about it."

"Excuse me?"

"I mean, I've given you chance after chance to make this a simple process, but you just can't do what you're supposed to do, can you?"

"Well, I—"

"But not to worry. I've come to the conclusion that there's a *reason* all of this is happening."

"A reason?"

"The stakes just aren't high enough," said the man on the other end.

"Oh no, the stakes are plenty high, thank you," I said, nervously turning to look at Francesca and her brothers standing in front of me.

"The problem is, you honestly think I won't kill Pam."

I shook my head, my heart now beating wildly in my chest. "Oh, no. Trust me, I believe you."

"But I don't think you do."

"I do, I do. I swear."

"Perhaps what you need is a little reminder about who's running the show?"

My eyes widened, and I suddenly wondered if he knew *exactly* what I was up to. Did he have eyes on us somehow? I waved a hand at the group behind me, motioning for them all to get down. I pulled the phone from my face for a second. "Everyone, get down!" I hissed while unclipping Al's lifejacket from my own. "I think he can see us!"

I heard the men behind me cursing as they fell to the guano-covered beach. Francesca and Solo came to grab Al, and the two of them got him to the ground too.

As I returned the phone to my ear, I glanced around the island, looking for any signs of Harry and his men. Or maybe Solo actually *had* seen a ship. But if it was there, I couldn't see it. It was completely dark. I could barely see anything! How could he see us? Were there sharp shooters hiding out on the island?

I shook my head. "I promise you, I do not need any reminders. You are in charge. It's obvious," I said, for the first time actively nervous about what he might do.

"It's good to hear that you're taking me seriously now. But *that's not enough*. Now you need to fear me." The phone clicked.

I looked at the group. "We gotta get out of here. I think he knows we're here and he's not happy! Hurry, we need to get to the boat and get off this island before something happens!"

Solo was the first one up. He lifted Al to his feet. I ran over to him and hooked an arm through his elbow, scooping him up like my new bride. I took off running for the shoreline with the rest of the crew keeping pace behind me.

I'd no sooner gotten the bottoms of my feet wet than Solo came to a halt and yelled, "Look!"

From off in the distance, a bright starburst of light streaked across the water like a shooting star and headed right towards our boat, leaving a whistling sound in its wake. Then in a brilliant burst of light, a fiery explosion threw us all back into the sand. Miguel's new fishing boat burst into a million pieces, the blast lighting up the night sky, warming our faces from its heat and throwing a hailstorm of shrapnel flying around us.

I flipped Al over into the wet sand, covering him with my body as pieces of the boat that had been launched into the sky came crashing back to the ground. Glancing sideways, I noticed Solo had done the same with Francesca. The rest of the men crawled away trying to get as far inland as possible.

When the raining debris finally stopped, Solo looked over at me, his face set in a stony grimace, his angry growl stopping time. "You owe my brother a boat."

29

THE NEXT MORNING, AGAINST HER BROTHERS' WISHES, FRANCESCA agreed to meet Al and me for breakfast in the resort's main dining hall at nine. It had been a long, agonizing evening dealing with a horde of angry Cruz brothers while waiting for Beto to grab Miguel's spare boat and drive it out to Gull Island to rescue us. Despite that, I woke up surprisingly refreshed, possibly because I hadn't put any alcohol into my system for two nights in a row. So I was pleasantly surprised to wake up that morning with a renewed sense of energy, ready to come up with a new plan to save Pam.

The lobby's sliding glass doors parted and I walked in, giving a nod to Mariposa. "Good morning, Mari."

Mari glared at me, her dark eyes trailing me as I walked.

I nodded at the other girl behind the counter. "Morning, Alicia." Alicia gave me a hard stare as well. Talk about a hostile work environment. And here *I* was the one getting in trouble?

"Say good morning to Mack for me, will you?" I said as I breezed past the counter.

"Maclynn didn't show up for work this morning," said Mari. "No doubt your fault once again. This is the third time this week that she's been late. No call, no show. Third warning is a fireable offense."

I came to a screeching halt and turned around. At this point, I was pretty sure I'd be blamed if the sun didn't rise in the morning, but I felt the need to defend myself nonetheless. "Sorry, Mari. I can't take credit for this one. Mack wasn't even with me last night."

"Dumped her already, huh?" smiled Alicia, a hand on her hip.

I made a face. "She just wasn't with me, okay. What time was she supposed to be here?"

"Eight o'clock, same as always," said Mari.

I glanced down at my watch. It was a quarter to nine. "She probably just overslept. I'll give her a call."

Mari's hard stare bristled the hair on my arms.

"What!" I snapped, lifting my brows and throwing both hands up defensively. "It's not my fault, I swear. I'll admit, the other two times were probably my fault. But today's not my fault."

I walked away. Pulling my phone out of my shirt pocket, I dialed Mack's number. It rang at least a dozen times and then told me that her voice mailbox hadn't been set up yet. I'd had three missed calls from Mack the night before but hadn't bothered to return any of them because of the Gull Island fiasco. And by the time I'd been properly chewed out by *each* of Francesca's brothers and gotten home, it was late, and I'd been too exhausted to entertain.

Even though I loathed texting, I fired off a quick text.

G'morning, Mack. Sleep okay? You better get to work. Mari's in a mood. She said she's gonna fire you if you don't show up soon. I'll call you later.

"Drunk!" called Francesca from the lobby's doors.

I turned to find Officer Francesca Cruz dressed in street clothes once again. She wore short black shorts with frayed hems, a grey tank top, and an open black-and-grey plaid shirt with cutoff sleeves. Her shiny black hair still looked slightly damp and hung down straight past her shoulders. She certainly didn't look like a cop. She looked like just a regular resort guest. A very *sexy* resort guest.

I smiled at her, ignoring the look of disdain I earned from both Alicia and Mari for doing so. "Hey! Good morning, gorgeous." And then, just to get Alicia and Mari back for being so hostile, I slung an arm over Francesca's shoulder and kissed her on the temple. "Thanks for coming."

Walking side by side towards the dining room, Francesca promptly shot me a look of surprise and returned my arm to my side with a sweep of her hand across her shoulder. "You know my brothers are pretty pissed at you."

I winced. "Yeah. I know they are. And each and every one of them told me just how mad they really were. I didn't think they were holding back." I grinned at her. "But don't worry, I'm sure insurance will cover the boat."

"You better hope it does."

I waggled my eyebrows at her. "But if we can figure out how to get Pam back without giving the kidnappers the money, then I'd be able to buy them a new boat. Maybe I'll even throw in an extra one just for their trouble. Think that'll make them like me again?"

"Drunk!" she breathed. "You can't be serious! After what went down last night, you *still* want to try and get Pam back without handing over the cash? Are you crazy?"

I shrugged. "I hate the idea of parting with that kind of money. It's my safety net."

"You saw what they did last night! They're gonna kill her if you don't give it up!"

I put a hand back on her shoulder and gave it a little squeeze. "Relax. We're gonna figure something out." I pointed to a table where Al already sat, sipping on a cup of coffee while reading the newspaper. "Hey, Al."

Al folded the paper and waved it in the air as a hello.

"Good morning," he said to both of us. Then he turned his attention to our guest. "Francesca, you look radiant as always."

"Good morning, Al. How're the arms?" she asked, taking the seat I pulled out for her at the table.

Al examined the sides of his forearms. Some of the shrapnel from the night before had struck him before I'd gotten him rolled over, leaving him with some cuts and bruises and one long strip of red, raw flesh that was now covered with a glossy coating. "Eh, Evie cleaned me up. No worries. I'll live."

"What'd she have to say about the events of the evening?" I asked, fearing Evie's wrath.

"She said I'm not allowed to play with you off resort property anymore," grunted Al.

"I figured that's what she'd say. I can't say I don't disagree with her."

"Your opinion doesn't count," he snapped. "If I'd listened to you and stayed on that boat last night, I'd have been blown into a million pieces."

I rolled my eyes, nodding. I'd heard it a million times on the way home from the boat trip. "You're a broken record, Al. You need some new material."

"We're a team, Drunk. You can't discount a member of your team."

"One of these times, you're really gonna get hurt," I said. "And then what?"

Al shrugged. "And then I'll have a good story to tell."

"If you survive."

"If I don't, then I don't. I'm eighty-seven years old. I don't expect to live forever. I just gotta figure out how to convince Evie that it's safe for me to hang out with you again."

Francesca nodded as she grimaced. "My brothers aren't very excited for me to hang out with you again either."

My mouth gaped. "I think I missed the part where this

became all my fault! Guys, I didn't tell the bad guys to kidnap Pam and hold her for ransom! And I didn't tell the bad guys to blow up your brother's boat!"

"You could've just made it easy and given them the money when they first asked for it," said Al.

"I mean, yeah, there's that. But you both know the United States doesn't negotiate with terrorists, and I'm a US citizen," I argued weakly.

Al's watery eyes swung up to meet mine in shock. He shook his head and swung his hand across the table, chopping the air decisively. "No. Now, after all of that, someone could've been killed. *Pam* could've been killed. She could be dead right now. I'm not going to allow you to play with her life like this. Now, enough is enough. When the kidnappers call back, you will set up a time and place to exchange Pam for the money. And that's that."

"You're beautiful when you're angry."

Al swatted my hands away. "Enough with the jokes! I'm being serious!"

I sighed. I knew he was being serious. "Fine. I'll give 'em the money," I whispered, keeping my fingers crossed beneath the table. "As soon as they call again, we'll get the drop set up."

Al reached across the table and patted me on the shoulder. "Attaboy. I take it you haven't heard from them yet?"

"No, but I'm sure I'll get a call sometime this morning. Harry's definitely going to wanna gloat about blowing up the boat."

"I wish you had a real name for this guy so I could track him down. My brothers wanna kick the ever-living crap outta him."

"Oh, trust me, I'd like to do the same," I said, wishing I really did have a name. Not that he would have given me a *real* name.

It wasn't until we'd finished eating breakfast when the call we'd been waiting for finally came through. Once again the number showed as restricted.

"Drunk here," I said, reaching across the table to steal one of the pens Francesca had brought with her.

"Do you fear me now, Daniel?"

"I'm sorry, who am I speaking to?"

"Didn't I say no more games, Daniel? You know damned good and well who you're talking to," said the voice on the other end of the phone. I could hear the anger seething in his words.

"I'm not trying to play any more games," I said honestly. "I was just asking who I was speaking to. You never did tell me your name."

"My name?" he sounded surprised.

"*Sí, tu nombre.*"

He was quiet for a moment. When he came back on he sounded a little calmer. "How about you just call me Dexter?"

"Dexter?" I nearly choked as I swallowed a ball of spit. "Like the psychotic character on the TV show?"

"If that's what trips your wire, then yes, like the psychotic character on that TV show."

I rubbed the scruff that had grown back on my chin and narrowed my eyes. "Is that your *real* name, or can you just kinda see yourself in him?"

The man on the phone sighed. "Let's just say I appreciate his coolness under pressure."

"So Dexter isn't your real name, then?" I pressed.

"Daniel. Do you really think I'd give you my real name so you can go do your little digging and hunt me down after this is all said and done?"

"Well, my mother always says it doesn't hurt to ask questions."

"Aww, isn't that sweet," he purred. "All right, now, enough about *your mother*, let's talk about the current state of events, shall we? Thanks to your little *excursion* last night, plans have now changed."

Even though he couldn't see it, I wagged my finger in the air. "Oh yeah, speaking of last night. You owe my friend a boat, by the way."

"No, I think *you* owe your friend a boat. It's not my fault *his* boat got in the way of *my* missile. But, now that you know I'm serious about my threats, are you ready to listen?"

I sighed into the phone. "Do I have a choice?"

"We always have a choice, Daniel."

I groaned. "Fine, what's up?"

"Tomorrow at precisely eight o'clock p.m., I will call you and we will set up the drop location. You'll need to be ready to move quickly. You need to be alone, and if I see that anyone is following you, Pam dies. In the meantime, you should have the cash ready to go. Once again, no funny business. No dye packs, tracking devices, nothing. Got it?"

"Yeah," I whispered.

"And, Daniel, I saved my last missile for you."

"That's very kind of you, but you really didn't need to."

"Mess up again and it's all yours."

I swallowed hard.

Al pointed at me then. "Ask about Pam," he whispered.

"But how do I know that Pam's even still alive?"

"Oh, I can assure you. She is."

"Forgive me if I don't trust a guy named Dexter."

There was a pause before I heard a sigh. "Just a second."

There was a shuffling sound on the other end of the phone. Seconds passed, and then all of a sudden I heard a squeal and then a thud. *"Danny?"* said Pam into the phone. "I-is that you?"

"Pam, are you all right?" Her terror filled voice sped up the adrenaline in my veins.

"No, I-I'm scared. They're gonna kill me!"

"Pam, where are you?" I shouted into the phone. "Are you still on the yacht?"

"Tsk, tsk, tsk," chided Dexter. "That would be against the rules, Daniel. And remember. From now on, you're playing by my rules or I'll call this whole thing off, and I think you know what that means for Pam."

"You better not lay another finger on her," I spat into the phone. "Or I'll lay a finger on you."

"Mmmm, sure you will, Daniel. All right. Be ready tomorrow night. Eight o'clock is go time."

30

THE NEXT EVENING, I SAT IN THE BACKSEAT OF FRANCESCA'S Samurai, smashed between a one-hundred-and-seventy-five-pound Great Dane and the window. Hugo glared at me as I rocked from side to side to keep the blood moving in my legs and butt. "He's staring at me," I whined.

"Because you're rocking," said Francesca. "Quit rocking."

"I'm trying to stay out of his line of drool."

She reached across Al's lap and opened the glove compartment. Pulling out a hand towel, she flung it over her shoulder. "Here. I always keep a slobber rag handy."

Curling my lip, I took the rag from her. "Thanks." I blotted awkwardly at Hugo's drippy jowls. I'd never really considered myself a dog person. Some of my buddies had dogs, but I'd never known quite how to be around a dog. They made me nervous the way they stared at me and quietly begged to get bites of my sandwiches or my fries. I'd never been fond of sharing my food. "Here ya go, buddy, let's get you cleaned up, huh?"

Hugo groaned at me like I was annoying him, but I persevered. I was just thankful that he'd gotten over his wanting-to-eat-me phase. His groan at least meant we were now on speaking terms.

It was a warm, humid evening. A breeze blew through the dimly lit vehicle, bringing with it a cacophony of nature's finest instruments: the tree frogs, coquis, geckos, and crickets. The powerfully sweet perfume of night-blooming jasmine counteracted the random air biscuits Hugo seemed to think appropriate to float in the packed vehicle.

"It's after eight. Why hasn't he called yet?" I let my head fall backwards against the headrest.

"Be patient," said Al. "He'll call."

"What if he killed her already?" The thought had been on my mind since I'd woken up that morning. The closer and closer it had gotten to *go time*, the more I'd worried about the plan I'd concocted. Was I doing the right thing? Would Dexter live up to his end of the deal? Would we actually get Pam back alive?

Francesca shook her head. "He wouldn't have done that. He's not that stupid."

My eyes widened as I hugged the duffle bag of greenbacks to my chest. "Oh, yes, he is. He's stupid *and* psychotic. It's a dangerous combination."

"I agree with that statement, which is why we downloaded that app to your phone. Al and I will be listening to everything you say, so if anything happens, you just say the magic word and we'll be there."

I dropped the phone into the front pocket of my shirt and smirked. "What should the magic word be? Abracadabra?"

Al swung his hand backwards. "Lay off the jokes, kid. You have to take this seriously. They could've killed all of us when that boat exploded. Pam's life is in jeopardy. Now that you're really gonna hand over the seven million dollars, it's not the time to let your mouth get you into trouble."

Al had gone with me earlier in the morning to withdraw the cash from the island bank. He'd helped me make sure that it was all there, and then we'd put the stacks of cash inside the biggest duffle bag we could find. That very duffle bag now sat on my lap, heavy with its unspent riches.

Francesca turned around in her seat so she could face me. "Let's not get complicated, all right? The magic word is *help*, Drunk. Easy as that. Can you remember it?"

"How could I forget? That's about the most unimaginative magic word I've heard in my life. *Help*. That's like asking Dexter, 'Can you excuse me for a moment while I alert the cops that I'm in need of assistance?'"

She frowned. "You got a better word?"

"Of course I do. Anything is better than *help*."

"Okay, go ahead. We'll use your word as the magic word."

I nodded and my lips plumped out in front of my face as I searched for a word. "Hmm, how about Aloysius?" I said, tossing out the first thing that popped into my head.

"Aloysius?" she repeated, her lip curled.

"Mm-hmm. It's a name. You know, like Rumpelstiltskin."

"Why in the world would Aloysius be the magic word?" barked Al.

Even Hugo looked at me like I was daft.

I shrugged and looked out the window. "I don't know. It's catchy. If I ever have a son, I might name him Aloysius. Aloysius Drunk. Doesn't that sound kind of smooth?"

Al waved a hand in the air. "No, no, no. If you have a son, his name has to be Daniel Drunk the third. I don't think you have a choice in that matter. It's what you do when you're a junior."

Francesca curled a lock of hair around her finger as she looked in her rearview mirror at me. "You're a junior too? Like Solo?"

"Yeah." I curled my lip.

"Did people call you Junior when you were a kid?" she asked.

"Only my Pops calls me Junior."

"What does your mom call you?"

"Terrence. Evie calls me Terrence too."

"I thought I heard Evelyn call you Terrence the other day at lunch. I wondered what that was about."

"It's my middle name," I admitted. "Mom calls my pops Danny, so she's always called me by my middle name."

Francesca nodded and turned to look out the window. "Sounds about right."

"I was Terrence in elementary school, but when I started over in middle school, I started just going by Drunk. I had a couple of holdout teachers who insisted on calling me Daniel, but for the most part, everyone I've ever known since has called me Drunk. Sometimes I even forget my name's Daniel," I said.

I glanced over at Hugo and then shoved past him, planting my elbows into the backs of the two headrests. I stuck my head into the front seat so it hovered over the center console. "Your dog walker called you Frankie the other day. So, now that we're getting to know each other on a more personal level, can I start calling you Frankie now?"

Francesca made a face and looked over at me. "What are you talking about? We barely know anything about each other."

"Are you kidding?" I balked. "I know tons of things about you now."

She tipped her head sideways, skepticism written all over her face. "Name five things you know about me."

"Five things?" I scoffed. "I'll name ten. I know where you live. I know you like vanilla-and-citrus-smelling wax melts." I ticked my fingers as I named things. "I know you have six brothers. I know at least five of them hate me. I know you lived in Florida."

"Boca Raton," added Al, holding up one gnarly, age-stunted finger.

"Yeah, Boca Raton. I know you're a police officer but

none of your family likes that fact. You drive a 1986 Suzuki Samurai that you are extremely proud of and won't let anyone else drive. You're bullheaded. You're fucking gorgeous. Your mom's name is Guadalupe, and your father passed away when you were in elementary school." I held up my hands, my fingers all sprawled out. "Ha, that's eleven."

Francesca groaned. She knew I'd won. "There are only a handful of people who call me Frankie," she admitted. "My brothers all call me Panchita. Everyone at work calls me Officer Cruz. I don't even think most of the people at the station know my first name." A soft smile covered her face. "And I really don't have a big group of friends, I keep to myself a lot. I'm so busy between work, family, and Hugo that I haven't had a lot of time for friends."

"So are you saying you'd rather I called you Francesca?" I asked. I'd been staring at her as she spoke, captivated by the delicate little ridge above her top lip and by the way her plump bottom lip moved. Her mouth was positively edible.

She sighed and leaned her head back against her seat. "Well, can I call you Danny? It sounds weird calling you Drunk."

I grinned down at her. "You can call me whatever tickles your fancy, sweetheart."

A choking sound in the passenger seat made me turn to see Al with his tongue out, pretending to choke. "Anyone have a spoon they can gag me with?" he muttered.

Francesca smiled.

Hugo let out a low bark.

"Oh geez, there's that German humor again," I said, rolling my eyes. "Whatsamatter, Al? All outta pies?"

"You should talk," he snapped back. "Your mother's the only one who thinks you're funny."

As Francesca covered her mouth to laugh, my phone rang.

A muted pallor fell over the vehicle, dissipating the easy

camaraderie we'd all just fallen into. Even Hugo's eyes looked wide.

I swallowed hard, my stomach instantly rolling into a doughy ball that kneaded itself repeatedly without my consent.

Francesca gestured at me, extending the pinky and thumb on one hand and holding it up to her ear.

I nodded and then slid the little green icon sideways. "Drunk here."

"Well, so good to speak to you again, Daniel. How are things going?"

"Mmm, could be better, I suppose," I said dryly.

"Yes, I suppose they could be. But, now it's finally time to begin our little adventure. Are you ready for your instructions?"

"First I want to speak with Pam."

"Do you have my money?"

"I want to speak to Pam," I said, my tone harsher this time.

"*Do you have my money?*"

"Yes, you motherfucker. I have your money. Now lemme talk to Pam."

Seconds later, Pam's voice cut the silence in the SUV. "Danny?" she called out.

"I'm here, Pam."

"Danny, they said they're gonna let me go tonight if you bring them the money. Did you get the money?"

"Yeah, Pam. I did. I've got it right here. Hang tight, we're gonna get you outta there very soon."

"Oh, Danny! Th—"

Pam's voice suddenly disappeared.

"*Pam?*" I shouted into the phone.

"Pam had to go get ready for her big appearance this evening," said Dexter, replacing her on the phone.

"So, here's the plan. Are you familiar with Tiburon Point?"

"Tiburon Point?" I repeated aloud in the car.

Francesca nodded. She knew the place.

"Yes, somewhat familiar with it," I lied.

"All right, well, what I need you to do is to drive out there and await my next phone call. As a reminder, I've got surveillance on the area and you'll be watched at all times. If I so much as suspect that you're working with island authorities, another gang of good ole boys, or anyone else, not only will Pam be killed, but I'll let you have that missile I saved for you. Read me?"

"Loud and clear."

"All right, it shouldn't take you more than twenty minutes to get there from the resort."

My body froze. We weren't at the resort. We were parked in a parking lot near a little ocean inlet. We'd hoped that if we weren't at the resort when he called, he wouldn't be able to follow us from there. I glanced over at Francesca. Could we make it in twenty minutes from where we were?

Thirty minutes, she mouthed holding up three fingers on one hand and making a zero with the other hand.

"Yeah, hey, listen, Dex, I'm gonna need at least thirty. I mighta had the chefs at the resort fix my steak a little too rare this evening. I've got a really bad case of the meat shits right about now. I'm gonna need at least another ten on the john before I head out."

"Perhaps tomorrow you'll need to do a spray and wash on your seats, then. Because if you're not in the Tiburon Point visitor's center parking lot in twenty minutes when I call, the deal is off and Pam is dead."

With that, the phone went dead.

"Shit," I said, bobbing my head. "Can we make it?"

Francesca shrugged. "We can sure try. You better go."

I nodded and looked at Hugo as Francesca slid out of her door so she could fold down her front seat to let me out. "It's been real, buddy. We should hang out again sometime." I gave him a pat before climbing out the back of Francesca's SUV. I tossed the duffle bag into the front seat of the little white resort car that Artie had let me borrow for the evening and then slid behind the wheel. I rolled down the window and shouted over to them. "I have no idea where I'm going."

"I'll lead you. When we get near it, I'm going to have to break away so we aren't seen coming in together. Just follow the signs from there and it'll lead you to the point."

I nodded. "Thanks, Francesca. Hey, do me a favor and take good care of Al for me, all right? I can't have anything happening to him on my watch. He had to sneak away the way it was."

"Nothing's going to happen to him. You've got my word. Now let's go! Otherwise we won't make it on time."

I pointed at Al. "You keep her safe too. Got it, partner?"

"Don't worry about us," shouted Al, waving a hand in my direction. "Worry about your own ass. Got it, kid?"

I nodded.

Before I'd even started the car, Francesca tore out of her parking spot, her taillights glowing in the increasingly dark night air. And then she was gone.

I raced after her, but she was more accustomed to driving on the wrong side of the road than I was. She'd learned to drive that way, having moved to the island in grade school. But for me, it felt like I had two left feet, making turns around corners seemingly backwards. Francesca raced down alleyways and took every shortcut she knew, but then she hit Walker's Road, the main drag, a four-lane road that spanned the entire island from one end to the other. Having driven around the island once or twice since I'd been there, I knew it was the only way to get from where we were to the other side of the island, where I assumed Tiburon Point was located. She zipped in and out of traffic like a seasoned professional, while I fought like hell not to crash.

My eyes kept glancing at the time on the dash. We had six

minutes to get there, and I didn't know how far away *there* was.

When Walker's Road narrowed to two lanes, Francesca took a sharp turn onto a dirt road. I cranked the wheel hard to follow her, my wheels skidding out behind me. Then suddenly there were cherry lights in my rearview.

Fuck.

"Francesca, I'm getting pulled over," I said aloud, hoping she could hear me through the app we'd installed on both of our phones.

I pulled over to the side of the road. My hands tapped the steering wheel as I waited impatiently for the cop to make his way to my window.

"I'm sorry," I said immediately to the young black officer who approached my car. "I know, I probably looked like I was driving erratically, but there was a bee in the car." The lie was one of the dumber ones I'd heard as a rookie cop, but it was one I thought I could sell.

"A bee?" The man was maybe all of twenty-three or twenty-four. His hair was cut short around the sides and back and was curly on top. "Have you been drinking, sir?"

"I swear, I haven't had a drop of alcohol. There was a bee in the car. I pulled off the road because it was threatening to sting me! And I'm allergic to bees." I swatted the air in front of me, pretending to shoo something out the window. "There he went! Watch out!"

The officer ducked and pivoted backwards on one foot. There were no streetlights where we were and the moon was hidden by a grove of palm trees in the distance. Only the glow of his headlights on my bumper cast any light on the darkened road, and yet it was dark enough that I was sure he couldn't tell whether a pterodactyl had just flown past his nose or not.

I pointed at his shoulder. "Oh my God, stay still, it's on your shoulder now!"

He hopped backwards, swiping a hand across his shoulder. "Did I get it?"

"Mayday, mayday. Rumpelstiltskin, Rumpelstiltskin!" I shouted into my chest.

The officer heard me yelling and strode back over to the car quickly. "Sir, I'm going to need you to step out of the vehicle."

"But I'm in a hurry."

"Sir, out of the car." His voice told me he meant business now.

The headlights of Francesca's SUV came barreling out of the darkness. She sidled up next to us. With one elbow leaned out the side of the car, Francesca smiled at the uniformed officer, her hair blowing against the breeze. "Ross? Is that you?"

The young cop turned to look at Francesca, his eyes narrowed. "Officer Cruz?"

"Yeah? You got an issue you need help with here?"

His eyes widened, and he turned to look at me and then back at her. I could tell she'd flustered him.

I hear ya, buddy. She has that effect on people, I thought.

"Oh, well, he was driving erratically," he said.

I leaned over the steering wheel to yell out my window at Francesca. "It was a bee, Officer Cruz. I had a bee in the car. Picked it up at that last stoplight."

Francesca nodded. "Oh man, I picked up a bee through that intersection back there too! I think someone must have been moving a bee hive or something."

"And I'm allergic," I added for emphasis.

She shook her head, her eyes wide with concern. "Oh, wow. Are you all right, sir? Did you get stung?"

I raked my fingernails across my neck. "I'm not sure. My throat does feel a little itchy."

Francesca shook her head. "Ross, you better let this man go. If he winds up with an allergic reaction and doesn't get to a medical professional immediately, it would be on the department, and you know Sergeant Gibson wouldn't like that."

"B-but he kind of appears to have been drinking…"

"He hasn't. Can't you see the whites of his eyes? They're fine. He's as sober as a priest on Sunday. Let him go."

Officer Ross to turned to look at me then. I could tell he really didn't want to let me go, but he also seemed to want to do what Francesca wanted him to do. Maybe she wasn't as low on the totem pole as she thought she was. He nodded at me. "I hope you didn't get stung."

I shot Francesca a wink. "Sure thing, Officer Ross, thanks for your concern." I peeled out of the parking lot. The whole incident had eaten up three of my precious minutes. I had two to spare and still no idea where I was going.

I gunned the engine and took off. My tires spat out gravel dust as I roared down the road. My headlights illuminated a sign that read *Tiburon Point and Turtle Bay 3 km.*

I pressed on the gas. "What in the hell does three kilometers convert to in miles?" I said aloud, trying like hell to remember something I'd learned in high school. I plowed through a patch of chickens dawdling in the dirt and then nearly rear-ended a slow-moving truck that seemed to think he owned the road. Honking at him, I swerved just as my phone rang.

I stared down at it, my heart frozen in terror. The number said restricted.

It was him.

I swallowed hard as I followed the natural curve of the road, my tires skidding out behind me. Letting it ring a few more times, I finally answered it. My pulse beat loudly in my ears.

"Hello?"

"You're late."

"I'm almost there."

"Almost isn't good enough." The line went dead.

I slammed the palm of my hand into the steering wheel. "Fuck!" I screamed into the empty car. "Shit!"

The car broke through the trees and into a clearing, and from there I could see the bay and a long piece of the island that stuck out into the water. It had to be Tiburon Point. I pulled to a screeching halt in the outer perimeter of the parking lot, and my head fell backwards against the headrest. Had I seriously just missed the deadline by a few seconds? Had I just fucking gotten Pam killed?

Fuck!

My phone rang again.

Hope sprang back into my body. My hand trembled as I picked up the phone and stared down at it. It was him.

My voice was hoarse when I answered it now. "Yeah?"

"What took you so long?" he growled.

"I got pulled over by a fucking cop."

"A cop?" There was a pause. "Did he follow you?"

"No. I'm sure he didn't."

"You got the money?"

"Of course I do. I wouldn't have come without it," I said, my heart ramming itself wildly against my chest.

"Good. Then it's time to get started."

31

"P<small>ARK NEXT TO THE VISITOR'S WELCOME SIGN,</small>" <small>COMMANDED</small> Dexter.

I moved the car as he asked and shut off the engine. "Done. Now what?"

"Now, get out of your car. Leave any weapons you might've brought behind."

I hooked an arm through the duffle bag's straps, hoisted it onto a shoulder, and climbed out of the car and into the darkness with my cell pressed up against my ear. "Now what?"

"Now, I want you to walk up to the northernmost edge of Tiburon Point. There will be a boat waiting for you there. When you get to it, get inside and motor out a little ways. You'll see another boat not far off the shoreline with a spotlight in it. That's where you're headed. Inside the second boat, you'll find Pam and a friend of mine waiting for you. Leave the cash in your boat, and switch boats with my friend. You keep the girl, we keep the cash. It's as simple as that."

"Okay. I got it. Anything else?"

"Yeah, no funny business. Don't screw this up. Comprende?"

"Yeah."

"I got eyes on you, Daniel. You screw this up and Pam takes a fucking bullet to the skull."

"I said I understand!"

"Okay, then this will all be over in a few minutes. It's been a pleasure doing business with you, Daniel."

"Yeah, fuck off."

The last thing I heard before the phone went dead was the nauseating sound of Dexter's laughter. I double-checked the eavesdropping app on my phone, and once I was sure that Dexter's call hadn't disrupted anything, I took off.

Following the shoreline on foot, I narrated my actions for Francesca and Al. "I'm heading up to the tip of the point. There's going to be a boat waiting for me. I'm to motor out until I see another boat with a spotlight. Pam and one of Dexter's goonies will be inside. I'm supposed to take their boat with Pam in it, and they're taking mine with the cash."

Since the exchange was happening in the middle of the ocean and it was dark, I knew there was no way Francesca was going to be able to get her sights set on Dexter's guy, but at the very least they could provide a quick getaway when the deed was done. "When I get back to the shoreline, be ready for me in case we gotta dash. Maybe you should put Al in Artie's car. Send him back to the resort before anything bad goes down." The moon provided enough light for me to see where I was walking, and up ahead I could clearly see a small speedboat moored to a tree and idling along the shoreline.

I jogged up ahead to the boat, tossed the duffle bag inside, and untied the line. With my adrenaline pumping, I jumped into the boat and drove away. It didn't take long before I saw the solitary strobe light glaring at me beneath a dark sky. As I drove, it occurred to me that perhaps Dexter might've shopped for the boat Pam now waited in in the same place he'd found that little johnboat I'd been forced to take a few days prior. If that was the case, and if I gave Dexter's chump the boat I now drove, he'd be able to motor away with the cash while Pam and I sat out all night, paddleless and with our thumbs up our asses waiting for the sun to rise so we could find a passing charter boat again. Which, of course, was Dexter's plan for making it impossible for me to chase him and the money and gave him plenty of time to get out of local waters.

Sure that I wasn't about to let that happen again, I formulated a plan as I drove. "Guys, I don't know if you can hear me all the way out here or not, but there's been a change of plan. I'm keeping the boat I'm in. There's a high probability that Dexter's not gonna like the new plan, so I'm definitely gonna need a car to pick me up at the shoreline, because I'm about to be in an almighty hurry."

I barely heard the sound of the ocean moving around me as my own blood pumped hard through my ears. My plan had to work. I had to get out of there before Dexter's goon figured out the truth.

The strobe light moved closer and closer until finally, I could see the shadowy outline of two figures on a small boat. It was indeed almost identical to the little boat I'd taken several days prior. One of the figures stood, waving me in. In the dark I could only make out his shape, a tall thin man with a ponytail sticking out the back of his cap. It was the man that had abducted Pam in the first place. My eyes slid back to see the second figure. She had a bag over her head and appeared to have her arms and legs bound as she sat silently. I could only hope that she was all right.

"Toss me your line," said the ponytailed man.

After getting a little closer, I did as instructed. That was when I noticed he held a rifle in his hands. Holding it, he bent over to tie the two boats together. I took the opportunity to grab the bag of money from the floor, and the second he stood upright, I tossed it over to him.

He looked down at it curiously. "No, the money stays in that boat." He tossed the bag back to me.

"No, I'm sure your boss said to put it in your boat."

Feigning confusion, I tossed the bag back to him like we were playing a game of hot potato. "You're welcome to make sure it's all there."

A look of befuddlement passed across his face as he unzipped the bag and peered inside. While he was busy inspecting the contents, I climbed over into his boat and walked to the back of the boat where I hooked an arm under Pam's elbow to stand her up.

"Don't worry, Pam. I got you," I whispered into her ear. I moved her towards the edge of the boat. A muffled scream came from the back of her throat, like her mouth was gagged beneath the bag she had over her head.

He looked up at me, his bottom lip filled with a wad of chew. "What the hell're you doing?"

I pointed to Pam. "Getting the girl."

The ponytailed man frowned. The duffle bag was slung over one shoulder now, and his rifle was aimed at me. "This ain't the plan," he snarled before spitting over his shoulder into the Caribbean Sea. "The boss woulda told me if we were changing the plan. You're supposed to take this boat. I take that boat."

I rubbed a hand against my chin and tipped my head to the side. "You sure? I swear he said I take the boat I road in on and you take the johnboat."

The guy nodded. "Yeah, I'm sure of it. This boat ain't got no motor on it."

I lifted my head, then turned slightly, looking over my shoulder as if to check the motor status for myself. As I did, my hand balled into a fist. "Huh, so you're right." I turned back around in a flash, letting my weight shift forward, and plowed my fist into the scrawny man's face, catching him off guard. The long-nosed barrel of the gun swung towards the boat's hull as he toppled backwards. His leg caught on one of the welded bench seats in the little johnboat, and the weight of the duffle bag on his shoulder pulled him backwards towards the water. I wasted no time in launching myself at him again, and I gave him a steady shove. He, the rifle, and the duffle bag fell into the water with a splash.

Pam's muffled screams drew me back to her.

"Shhh," I hissed. "Do you trust me?"

Her head bobbed.

"Good." With that, I reached over, drew the little speedboat closer to me and gave Pam a shove. She toppled over headfirst into it. "Sorry about that," I yelled as I heard the resulting thumping sound, followed by a choked scream.

The ponytailed man's head reappeared in the inky water. He struggled to keep the money hanging from his shoulder while keeping himself afloat. But the bag was now soaked and obviously had become even heavier than it already was. He splashed around, trying to get a hand on the motorboat. I reached down and used the line I'd thrown him to pull the boat backwards and out of his reach.

"You piece-of-shit motherfucker!" he sputtered as he fought to get a hand on the johnboat.

"Better not let that money sink to the bottom of the Atlantic," I chided. "Boss'll be real pissed if he has to hire a diving team to go after it. Might make quite the spectacle."

As I secured the two boats together down by the stern, ponytail man finally managed to get ahold of the johnboat's hull. I used my long legs to step from one boat to the other and then gave the johnboat, along with the man, a shove. Ponytail man cursed wildly at me while I rushed to the helm of my speedboat and slid into the captain's chair.

"Later, gator," I said, pressing against the throttle and giving a nod to the man as he fought to get the soaked bag of money out of the water and into the boat. "Hang on tight, Pam," I hollered back as she lay helplessly in a heap on the bottom of my boat, her butt sticking up in the air. With one hand on the steering wheel and the other on the throttle, I maneuvered us back towards the shoreline. A fine mist of water sprayed the air as I picked up speed. Excitement bubbled up in my chest. I'd done it! I'd gotten Pam!

And then, seemingly out of nowhere, there were headlights behind me. Shots flew over my head, whizzing past me and sending up sprays of water.

Oh shit.

"Francesca, I got problems," I said, bowing down low and speaking into the phone in my shirt pocket. "Rumpelstiltskin, Rumpelstiltskin! I'm running this baby as far inland as I can get it, be prepared. Have the car waiting for me!"

While I picked up speed, the boat behind me closed the distance between us faster than I would've liked. Bullets continued to fly, but thankfully, they didn't seem to be able to shoot for shit. I ducked my head low beneath the steering wheel and buried the throttle. The boat planed on top of the water and exploded through the mouth of Turtle Bay. Behind me, Pam wriggled around, trying to sit upright. "Stay down, Pam. They're shooting at us. We're almost there!"

The boat lurched when the hull hit the edge of the reef, sending Pam toppling forward again and me slamming against the wheel. When it came to a stop, the boat listed hard to the port side. I rushed to the back, grabbed Pam around the waist and pulled her over to the edge of the boat. Jumping overboard into the shallow water, I tugged Pam towards me, scooping her up in my arms. I struggled to get her over the gunwale and into my arms. "Damn, Pam. What've they been feeding you on that yacht?"

Noises gurgled from her throat. But there wasn't time to waste waiting for an answer as shots continued to fly.

When I finally managed to get her off the boat, I did the best I could to run across the jagged bed of rock, shells, and sand just below the water's surface with Pam weighing down my escape. And as I neared the beach area, I could see both Francesca's Suzuki waiting for me and the Seacoast Majestic's white car backed up to the beach with the back doors wide open.

Francesca yelled at me from her window, "Get in the car!"

Al's hand was out the window of the resort car, waving me forward. "Come on, come on!" I could hear him yelling.

The boat that had been chasing me hadn't run aground. Instead, they continued shooting at me from their boat, continuing to miss in the darkness.

I dumped Pam as far into the backseat as I could get her and then crawled in behind her. Slamming the door, I hollered at Al. "Go, go, go!"

Al stepped on the gas, sending Pam and me rolling backwards against the seat. Still gagged and bound, Pam squealed the whole time. Francesca's lights trailed behind us.

When our tires hit the dirt road that would lead us back to the main drag, I slammed a hand into the headrest. "Hell yeah! We did it, Al!"

"Damn straight we did! Good job, kid!"

I shook my head as I watched the rearview to make sure that Dexter didn't have any guys following behind Francesca. When the coast looked clear, I turned around. I met Al's eyes in his rearview mirror. My heart still pounded wildly. "Oh my God, I can't believe it. We did it, Al. We saved Pam *and* kept the money!"

Al's eyes widened. His head snapped sideways. "What?!"

The car began to slow.

I glanced over my shoulder. "What are you doing? Go, go, go! Before they figure out what was really in the bag!"

"What was really in the bag!" repeated Al, stepping on the gas again. "Whaddaya mean, what was really in the bag?"

I shrugged. "It wasn't all money in there."

He stared at me through the rearview mirror. "What the hell are you talking about! I helped you count it all. The money was in there!"

"There was a little money," I admitted. "I put some real bundles of money on top for show. The rest was just bundled paper wrapped with real bills. They're only walking away with maybe a hundred thousand tops. Basically, they got a portion of the interest the seven million earned me." I smiled proudly. I'd managed to pull one over on old Dexter, and boy did it feel *good*.

"Well where'd the rest of the money go?"

I grinned. "I hid it."

"You *hid* it? Where? In your house?"

I laughed. "I'm not that stupid. No, trust me. It's safe."

Al shook his head. "I can't believe this, Drunk!" he hollered. "Are you insane! That could've gone belly up! You were gambling with Pam's life!"

I shrugged as I looked over at Pam, who was now really screaming behind the gag. I kind of didn't want to take it out of her mouth. She sounded pissed, and I really didn't wanna hear it. I'd saved her life, hadn't I? "Yeah, well, I couldn't be sure that she'd actually *be* there! The last thing I wanted to do was hand over seven million dollars, only to find out that she wasn't even at the drop anyway! And look! It worked!"

Pam continued to shift about in her seat, squealing and making a ruckus.

"Oh for goodness' sake, Drunk! Get that bag off the poor woman's head! She probably can't breathe!"

I sighed, wishing I could just drop her off at the airport like that. "Oh, fine, if I must." I pulled her into a better position and untied the rope that they'd secured the bag with. Then, with one tug, I pulled the bag from her head. My eyes widened as I saw what sat before me. "Oh my God. Mack?"

32

"Mmmrrrhhh," screamed Mack through her gagged mouth.

"Mack?" Al turned around in his seat and the car jerked sideways.

"Al! Keep it on the road!"

"But that's Mack!" he screeched.

"I know! I can see her!" I hollered back. My heart thumped wildly in my chest as I unwrapped the tape from her head and pulled the rag from her mouth. "Oh my God, Mack! How did you get out there?!"

"They fucking took me!" she screamed. "They fucking picked me up on my way home from work and took me! Have you not been looking for me?!"

I winced. I'd been a little too busy trying to figure out how to save my ex-fiancée and getting together seven million dollars to worry about what my current fling was up to. And then I remembered Mari's complaint that Mack had been late to work. No call, no show. I hung my head. *Shit, I should've known.* "I mean, I texted you, warning you that Mari was going to fire you if you didn't show up."

Mack rolled her eyes. "Oh, just fucking great. Now I'm

gonna lose my job over all of your bullshit? They've got your ex, you know."

"Yeah, I'm aware," I snapped. "I've been busy trying to get her back."

"I can't believe you didn't tell me what was going on!" She held her zip-tied wrists up to me. "Can you please cut these off me?"

I leaned forward into the front seat. "You got a pocket knife or anything?"

Al shook his head. "I carried a pocket knife for seventy years," he said. "Moved to Paradise Isle and decided I wouldn't have a need for it anymore."

"Sorry, Mack. We'll get it off when we get back to my place."

"Mack, I don't understand. If you're here, then where's Pam?" asked Al, watching her through the rearview.

Mack shook her head, her curly brown hair bouncing around her shoulders. "She's back on their yacht. That's where they've been holding me—with her. They said they were keeping her just to make sure you didn't pull any tricks tonight. And now look what you did, Drunk! You probably ruined it for Pam. I'm positive they'll kill her now. That one guy was pretty pissed at you."

"Do you know their names?" I asked. "The guys on the boat. Could you hear any of their conversations?"

Mack frowned. "No, they mostly kept us on a different side of the yacht than them. I have no idea who they were." The severity of the situation finally sank into her brain, and she started to cry. "Drunk, I was so scared! They threatened to kill me!"

I put an arm over her shoulder as she sobbed. I felt horrible. Now I'd gotten Mack dragged into this. "I'm so sorry, Mack. I had no idea they'd even *know* about you and me. But I suppose everyone around the resort knew about us. Did they hurt you at all?"

"One of them hit me across the face. Felt like my eye was going to pop it hurt so bad." She closed an eye and pointed to her face. "Can you see anything?"

I examined Mack's tear-stained face. There was definitely a lump there, but it was hard to see any redness or bruising in the darkness. "You'll probably have a shiner in the morning."

She shook her head as the tears began to subside. "The other girl was beat up way worse, though. She looked like hell. And they still have her, Drunk. When that guy finds out you didn't give him all the money, he's gonna lose it on her. You should've just given them the money."

Mack's words tugged on my conscience. I'd only been doing what I thought was best. "I understand, but my gut told me they were gonna pull something on me tonight. And look! I was right. They weren't even gonna give Pam up!"

"Maybe they would've let her go after they were sure you'd given them the seven million," suggested Al. "I can't believe you pulled a fast one on them, and on me! And you didn't even tell me! And I'm your partner!"

"But I was right!"

Al shook his head. "You don't know that you were right, kid. We haven't gotten Pam back yet, and you just jeopardized everything!"

"I agree with Al one hundred percent," added Mack.

I refused to meet their eyes then. Had I seriously just ruined everything? *Again?* I sat in silence, refusing to speak, as Al drove us all the way to my cottage at the Seacoast Majestic. Francesca and Hugo pulled in behind us next to Al's golf cart.

When the car came to a stop, I climbed out first and then reached back in and pulled Mack out and helped her to her feet. I kept one hand under her arm so she wouldn't tip over.

Francesca hung her head. "I heard everything," she said. "It wasn't Pam on the boat."

"Yup," I said. "It was my friend Mack."

"Who're they?" asked Mack, looking Francesca and Hugo up and down with annoyance.

"Friends of mine," I said.

Mack furrowed her brows angrily. "I've been gone a *day* and you've already moved on? Nice, Drunk! While I'm getting punched, you're over here getting busy with… with… her."

Francesca held up a hand. "It's really not like that—"

But Mack wasn't done. "Wow, you know, Mari's right. You really are a manwhore." She shook her head. "She warned me. I shoulda listened."

"Thanks," I growled.

Hugo let out an annoyed bark, almost as if he were trying to tell me he was on my side.

"We're not *that* kind of friends," said Francesca, obviously frustrated. She furrowed her brow as she addressed me next. "Boy, Danny, where do you find these girls?"

"They find me," I groaned. "Come on, let's get you inside and get these zip ties off of you."

I carried Mack inside my cottage and went about cutting off her ties.

"So you really didn't give them the money?" asked Francesca.

I shook my head. "Nope. After Al and I stopped at the bank, I spent the rest of the day making fake money bundles. I figured it would be a night drop and they'd only look at what was on top, and by the time they got all the way down to the bottom, I assumed I'd have Pam and we'd be long gone."

Al's hands flared out on either side of himself. "What kind of idiotic, dumb, stupid, idiotic—"

"You're repeating yourself again," I cut in.

"Drunk!" he bellowed. "I told you! There's a time for fun and games and there's a time to take care of business! Today you were supposed to take care of business."

I shook my head. I was already feeling pretty bad about the

situation. Al was only making me feel worse. "I'm sorry. I don't know what I was thinking—"

"You weren't thinking!" he railed. "You were being selfish and greedy and gambling with Pam's life! You were gambling with our lives too. They could have killed us all, you know."

I sighed. That was the last thing I wanted. "Yeah, you're right."

"When they figure out that was a bag full of fake money, it's over," snapped Al. "You're giving them the real cash. That money wasn't even yours to begin with."

"But finders keepers—" I began weakly.

"Al's right," cut in Francesca. "That money wasn't even yours to begin with. Finders keepers or not. I think now, it's just better to give them what they want to let Pam go. They don't want blood on their hands. Otherwise, I think they would've killed her by now. I mean, look, they had Mack. They could've killed Pam and ransomed Mack, but they didn't. But I have to agree with these two. I think if you would've just given them the real money, she'd be cut loose by now."

I glanced over at Mack. She'd been the one on the boat with them, after all. "You really think they're right, Mack?"

Mack shifted her weight. With her hands on her hips, she nodded vehemently. "Are you stupid? Of course I think they're right! It's what I've been saying!"

I let my head drop into my hands, and I scrubbed my face with the pads of my fingers. "Ugh, fine. Maybe I was just being selfish. You're all right. I'm wrong. All right? When Dexter calls back, I'll make a deal for sure. I'll get Pam back. I swear. No more funny business."

Mack puffed air out her nose. "If she's even still alive. That guy… Dexter? Was that his name? He seemed pretty pissed at you. I'm shocked she's made it this long. Why is it you haven't gotten the police involved in this?"

"They told him not to," said Al. "Said they'd kill her if he did."

My phone rang again. I didn't have the heart to answer it. "Someone else answer it," I said, tossing it onto the kitchen counter.

Al strode over to it and picked it up. He looked at the number on the screen. "Restricted. It's him." He held the phone out to me. "Answer the phone, kid."

I glanced up at Al. His watery eyes told me he wasn't fooling around. He'd had just about enough of the situation. With my heart lodged in my throat, I sighed and answered the phone. "Yeah?"

"Are you *fucking kidding me*! You really don't think I'll kill her, do you?!"

"I had a feeling you were taking me for a ride," I bellowed into the phone. "And look! I was right! You kidnapped Mack!"

"Yeah, well, I had to keep Pam for insurance. Just in case you tried something. And whaddaya know, I was right! I got a tiny fraction of the money. Now I really get to kill her!"

"If you kill her, you'll never get the rest of the money," I interjected. "Listen, I promise. No more games. No more wise-cracks. The money's yours. Just tell me when and where."

"I can't trust you to deliver anymore, now can I, Daniel?"

"You can trust me! I promise. No more screwups. All right? I-I'll meet you anywhere you want. I'll go out right now and bring you the money."

"It's too late for that. Too. Fucking. Late." The phone went dead.

I dropped the phone on the counter. "Shit," I breathed. "Fucking shit. He's gonna kill her."

Al's face went pale. He shook his head. Then he wagged his gnarly old finger at me. "I told you. Didn't I tell you?"

"I know, Al! I know!" My ears were ringing now. The tension that had me knotted up on the inside was now playing havoc with my head.

Mack took a step towards me, one hand on her hip and the other pointed in my direction. "Listen, Drunk. You and I had a good thing going for a minute there, but this shit you're into is fifty shades of fucked up. I don't want any part of it. I just wanna go home, take a shower, ice my eye, and forget those asshats ever laid a hand on me."

I sighed. "I'm so sorry, Mack. I really am. I had no idea they'd..." I tried to put my arms around her, but she took a step back and held up her hands defensively as if to say *don't touch me*. I nodded. "I'll take you home."

"No way. I'll drive myself home," she snapped.

"Your car's here at the resort?" I asked.

"It's in the employee parking lot down by the security shack. They nabbed me after work."

"You can't walk all the way over there by yourself," said Al. "They could be out there and nab you again!"

"Oh, don't worry. I'll be prepared this time."

"Come on, Mack. Just lemme give you a ride," I begged. The last thing I needed was her getting stolen again. Then I'd have two women to figure out how to get back.

"Don't touch me, Drunk," she said, snatching her hands away from me. "If you would've just given them the fucking money, all of this would've been over."

"Not for Pam!" I argued. I was beginning to get tired of hearing that it was all my fault.

"I'm walking," said Mack, heading for the door.

Al shook his head. "Oh, no, you're not, young lady. Not on my watch." Al dug in his pocket and pulled out the keys to his golf cart. "It's getting late anyway, and there's nothing else we can do about this tonight. I should be getting home to Evie. My ride's out front. I'll drive you to your car."

Mack's ferocious stare turned on Al. She considered him for a brief moment before her look softened slightly. "Oh, fine. Come on. I wanna get home. I need to get up early so I can check the want ads for a new job!"

"Al and I'll talk to Mari in the morning," I promised. "We'll do our best to get you your job back."

"If it means working with you again, I'm not sure I want it back," she said, her face screwed up in a pout.

I sighed.

Al gave us a little wave as he followed Mack out to the porch. "Call me in the morning."

"Goodnight, Al, and thanks," I said before he left. "I owe you one."

"I'm keeping count. You owe me half a dozen," he said. "And don't forget it."

"I won't. Trust me."

33

THE SECOND THAT AL WAS GONE, I WALKED OVER TO THE cushioned rattan sofa in my living room and fell backwards onto it. My long legs hung over the end. I leaned my head backwards and covered my face with my hands. "Uhhhh. Fuck!" I bellowed into my palms.

I heard the shuffling of feet and felt what I assumed was Francesca staring down at me. I peeked between my fingers only to see Hugo's long narrow face only inches from mine. He tipped his head sideways curiously.

"Hey, Hugo," I said, now feeling oddly guilty about having cursed in front of the dog, like he was a little kid or something.

Hugo let out a little whine from the back of his throat.

Francesca padded over to me then. She lifted my legs up off the end of the couch and slid in under them. She patted me quietly. "I'm sorry about Pam, Danny."

I groaned. "You know, the truth is you shouldn't be. Because hell, *I'm* not even sorry. How bad is that?"

"What do you mean?"

I sighed and then scooted up on the sofa so that my back was against the armrest. "I think the cold, hard ugly truth is, I'm not sorry. Pam screwed me over so bad. So bad," I added under my breath. "And so while I've tried really, really hard to do the right thing, I think ultimately, the fact that I haven't been willing to give up the money tells me that I'm incapable of doing the right thing."

Her head shook. "No, you're not…"

"I am!" I shouted, running my hands through my hair like a crazed lunatic. "I am! I'm an asshole! I'm a jerk! When those kidnappers first called, my gut reaction was to tell them they could go ahead and *kill* her. Who says shit like that?"

Francesca lifted her brows. I could see the unspoken truth behind her eyes. *Bad people say shit like that.* That's what she was thinking. I saw it. "I mean, that was just your broken heart talking."

"Pfffh," I muttered. "I don't have a heart. People with hearts don't tell kidnappers to kill their exes."

She smiled softly at me. "I'm sure if other people were given the same opportunity that you were given, they might've chosen to do the same thing."

"Maybe a crazy person would've! Not someone with a rational brain!"

"But you're rational now! You regret saying that now."

"Do I?" I asked, tipping my head to the side. "Do I really? I mean, look, I tried *yet again* to keep the money. I put money ahead of a woman's life."

"Yeah, but that was because you believed they weren't going to turn her over to you. And look, you were right. They didn't give her to you. You probably did the right thing."

My head fell into my hands again. "But what if I just did it because I was selfish? Because I thought I could maybe save Pam *and* keep the money."

"Is that why you did it?"

I shrugged. I really didn't know the answer to that question. I'd rationalized it all in my brain before I'd done it. I'd told myself that I was only doing it to protect Pam. But now that she might actually die, I wondered if I'd really only done it to keep the money.

"I don't know," I finally whispered before admitting, "I really don't want her to die."

"Okay, well, that's a start. That means you're not as cold-blooded as you're giving yourself credit for."

"Then why didn't I just do what they told me to do? Why did I have to play games?"

"Because you're a cop," suggested Francesca. "Look, Danny. You might not have been the greatest cop back home, but even bad cops have to have a certain level of *trust your gut* in them. You trusted your gut. That's it. Quit being so hard on yourself."

"But what if I just got her killed?"

Francesca opened her mouth, but whatever words she had to say seemed dammed up in the back of her throat. Finally, she shook her head. "I don't know, Danny... I just don't know."

For the first time in months, maybe even years, a tear rolled down my cheek. It caught me off guard at first. Like, I wondered if my ceiling was leaking or something. I looked up. And that was when another tear came and I realized the leak had come from my eyes. Was I seriously going to *cry* right now? In front of *Francesca*? Over *Pam*?

Knock it off, you fucking idiot!

Francesca rubbed my leg. "I'm sorry, Danny."

I let out a chortled half-laugh as I wiped away the tears. "I don't even know why I'm crying right now. I hated the woman."

"You didn't hate her," said Francesca. "If you hated her, you wouldn't have proposed to her. I think the truth is, it's not hate that you're feeling."

I ground the heels of my hands into my eyes and then looked up at her. "No, I'm pretty confident this is hate. I've never actually felt this before, you know. I usually get along with everyone. But this—this *emotion* I'm feeling is pretty intense. It's definitely hate."

She smiled gently. "Maybe it feels like hate right now. But from the outside looking in, I don't see hate. I see *hurt*."

"Puh," I spat. "No, not even. I'm not hurt. I'm *mad*!"

"When it comes to Pam, what are you mad about exactly?"

I made a face. What kind of a question was that? Where should I start? "Well, I'm mad because I wasted my time on her. I was ready to settle down, start a family, you know, find my person, and all that stuff."

"And you thought you had found it in Pam?"

I shrugged. "Obviously I didn't."

"But you *thought* you did," said Francesca. "That's why you were getting married. And then she made a mistake."

"A huge *fucking* mistake."

Francesca nodded. "Yes, a huge *fucking* mistake. But that doesn't change the fact that you *loved* her enough to want to marry her. Love doesn't just go away sometimes, Danny. And I think that's the problem here. How have you dealt with breakups in the past?"

"Breakups in the past?" I said blankly.

"Yeah, like in past relationships."

"I haven't had past relationships. Pam was my first real relationship."

"You're kidding."

I shook my head. "Not kidding. I've always been kind of a playboy. The truth is, women have always had a hard time taking me seriously."

"Well, no wonder. You make jokes out of everything!"

"Not *everything*. I mean, yeah, I might joke around when I'm tense or uncomfortable, but I can be serious too."

Francesca eyed me.

"What?" I smiled, staring back at her. "I can!"

"In the short amount of time that I've known you, I've rarely seen the serious side of you," she countered.

I looked away and shrugged. "Yeah, I suppose it doesn't come out often. But you know, when I was in my twenties and dating, that was fine. Because for the longest time I was never looking for anything serious. Until I was about thirty-two. That was kind of when I turned a corner, and I decided I wanted to meet someone. I met Pam at church, believe it or not."

Francesca's jaw dropped. "*You* go to church? Get outta here."

I laughed. "Thirteen years of Catholic school," I said, bobbing my head. "Yours truly was even an altar boy."

"I would've never guessed."

I shrugged. "I might have let some of that fall by the wayside after I left home. I'm not a very good Catholic."

"So Pam really was your first love?" asked Francesca, nodding. "Well, no wonder you're feeling like this. Losing your first love is hard."

I turned to her then, curious how she seemed to know this. "You sure seem to know what you're talking about. Was losing your first love hard?"

Francesca waved a hand at me dismissively. "We're not going there, Danny. This is about you, not me."

I sighed. I was tired of talking about me and Pam and the emotions I was feeling. It seemed like that was all I'd been doing since she had shown up on the island.

Francesca pushed my legs off her, forcing me to sit up on the sofa next to her. "Look, as an outsider, I've had a chance to kind of see some of the signs your exhibiting."

I quirked a brow. "Signs?"

She nodded and gestured towards my coffee table, where empty bottles of liquor and sticky tumblers were sprawled around. "Did you drink this much before you and Pam broke up?"

"No, I'd given up drinking when I decided to look for love. But I drank before we met."

"*This* much?"

"Maybe not this much."

She grinned like she'd expected that answer. "As far as I've been able to see, you seem to be having a good time with the ladies," she said. "Were you this, uh-hum"—she cleared her throat—"*loose* before Pam?"

I grinned and waggled my eyebrows at her. "Maybe."

"Danny!" she said with a laugh. Her elbow flared out and poked into my side.

I rubbed my ribs, pretending that it had hurt. "Okay, fine, maybe not to this extent."

"Right. See, what you're doing is, you're using alcohol and women to fill the gaping hole that Pam left in your heart when you broke up. That's not *hate*, Danny, that's *hurt*. She *hurt* you."

I lowered my head. "And you think that makes a difference?"

"When people are hurting, they do dumb things. Sometimes they want to lash out and hurt the people who have hurt them. I don't think you're a bad guy, Danny. I think if all of this kidnapping and ransom stuff had happened *before* the breakup, there wouldn't have even been a question about the money. If you'd had it, you would've given it all up for the woman you loved. Am I right?"

"Yeah," I whispered hoarsely. "Of course I would have."

"Exactly! That's because the *true* Danny Drunk, the one inside, is a *good person*. He's not money-hungry and greedy. He doesn't put his needs in front of the person that he loves. He's just gone off the tracks a little, in more ways than one," she added, her eyes skirting my messy house. "But that's only because he was burned and he's hurting right now. You've got to figure out a way to forgive her. That's the key, Danny. You *have* to forgive Pam."

"I don't know if I can."

"You have to. It's the only way you're going to move on with your life. It's the only way you'll ever find love again. It's the only way you'll be able to put this whole situation behind you. You have to forgive her for making a mistake. That doesn't mean you have to take her back, but you have to recognize the fact that she's human and she made a mistake. I'm sure she regrets it. That's probably why she came out here. To tell you she regrets it."

My head bobbed up and down.

"See! You might not have seen it this way, Danny, but she was trying to give you a gift."

I looked up at Francesca sharply. "A gift? What are you talking about? She was only trying to get me to forgive her so we could get back together."

"Maybe. But the *gift* that she was giving you was the ability to find closure. The way I've heard the story, you took off after you found her in bed with her ex. I bet the two of you didn't even have a chance to discuss it. I bet you didn't even take the time to tell her how you felt, did you?"

"Hell no. I hightailed it out of there."

"Right! So here you are, still dealing with this *hurt* over what she did to you, and then she goes and gets *kidnapped*. The normal you, the rational, level-headed, big-hearted Danny Drunk, wasn't around. The *hurt* version of you was what was here, and that's why things have played out the way they have. You have to figure out how to forgive Pam, and you have to get the closure you need to move on."

I turned my head to look at her. She had such a beautiful face, and it was more relaxed than I'd seen it before. She made it all sound so easy. "How am I supposed to just forgive Pam for what she did? She took away the future we'd been so excited to build together. She wasted my time, the time I could have used to find the *right* person."

"You know, Danny, if you're at all a religious guy, like you say you were brought up to be, then you have to have some kind of sense of the bigger picture. You have to believe that everything in life happens for a reason."

My brows shot up. She couldn't be serious. After everything that was going down! "What reason could there possibly have been for all of this to have happened?"

Her head shook softly. "I don't know. Maybe all of this happened so that you would come to the island. And maybe Pam was kidnapped so that you could figure out how to forgive and to get the closure you need so you can quit being such an island bum. We have enough island bums. We don't need another one," she chuckled. "Maybe ultimately you were led here to meet the woman you were destined to spend your life with."

I turned to look at her then. Her face was only inches from mine. Her big brown eyes looked up at me with such sweet tenderness that the sudden desire to kiss her came at me hard. My heart raced in my chest. I could read the signs, and in that moment, I felt like even *she* wanted me to kiss her.

My jaw clenched tightly. Because as much as I *wanted* to kiss her, I knew I wasn't ready for that. She had to know I wasn't. I was a broken man, and before I could even consider thinking about Francesca in that way, I had to fix myself.

I reached a hand out and cupped the side of her face. I pulled her to me and did the only safe thing I could do that would even remotely quench my thirst to taste her skin. I pulled her to me and kissed her on the forehead.

I let my lips linger. Mostly because I didn't want her to see how much I would have preferred to be kissing her lips. And also because I was scared that if I did let her go, I might act on that temptation. But I couldn't. I couldn't jump into any kind of a relationship with Francesca Cruz. She was too good for me. She didn't deserve a mess of a guy like me. She deserved something better. *Much better.* And if I was ever going to start something up with her, I'd have to prove to *myself* that I could be someone she deserved. And at this moment, I wasn't that guy.

I whispered into her forehead. "Maybe you're right, Francesca."

My hand dropped and she pulled her head back. Our eyes met, and I knew she knew how I felt. She knew it was a wrong time, wrong place kind of thing. We were trying to recover my ex from the clutches of an evil man. And I had a lot of work to do on myself. She got it.

"It's getting late," she whispered back, tearing her eyes from mine.

"Yeah," I said. "We need to get an early start tomorrow if we're going to figure out how to get Pam back."

"Okay." She nodded. She stood up and walked over to Hugo, who was snoring softly on a blanket he'd found on the floor. "Come on, Hugo. We better get going. It's late."

Hugo didn't budge.

"Oh man, he's out like a light," I said. "Why don't you two just stay here tonight?"

"Danny, I—"

I held up a hand. "I'll sleep on the sofa. You and Hugo can have my bed. Just don't let him drool on my pillow, please."

"Danny! Your legs hang over your sofa! I can't make you sleep here."

I grinned. "Oh, trust me. I've fallen asleep on this sofa many times since I've moved into this cottage. It's comfy, and I don't mind a bit." I lied about the comfy part, but if it meant Francesca didn't have to drive home, I was happy to sleep on the sofa.

She looked down at her dog, who pawed at the air in his sleep. "He does look comfortable."

I stood up and took her by the hand. "Just let him stay there. Come on."

I led her to my bedroom and opened the door. "The most comfortable bed on the island," I promised with a wide grin.

"And as you can tell by the fact that the bed is fixed, house-keeping was here today. You get fresh sheets and everything."

"Yeah?"

"Definitely."

"You're sure you don't mind?"

I shook my head. "I'm absolutely positive I don't mind."

"Okay." Standing up on her tippy-toes, she extended her neck to plant a kiss on my cheek. "Thanks."

The feel of her lips on my cheek made my body tingle. It was going to be a rough night sleeping alone on the sofa after that simple little gesture. I squeezed her hand before letting it go. "G'night, Francesca."

"G'night, Danny."

I turned to leave.

"Oh, Danny?"

I stopped and turned to look at her. "Yeah?"

"You can call me Frankie if you want."

My head bobbed. "G'night, Frankie."

"G'night, Danny."

34

I WOKE UP EARLY THE NEXT MORNING TO MY PHONE RINGING.

My eyes flashed open. My body jerked to attention and, forgetting where I was, I rolled off the narrow sofa and onto the floor with a thud. Hugo, who was lying across the room in a ball, looked up at me and yawned.

I scrambled to grab the phone as it rang again. It had to be the kidnapper calling back!

"Drunk here," I croaked.

"Terrence?" The sound of a sweet old lady's voice caught me off guard.

"Evie?" I said, rubbing a hand against my scalp and suddenly wondering what time it was. Only a slim sliver of light came in from beneath my living room's shades. "Is everything okay?"

"I hope so. Did Al stay over there last night?"

"Al?" I lifted myself up off the floor and plopped down on the sofa again. This time in a seated position. "No. Why?"

"Well, I'm not sure exactly," said Evie. "He's not here. Maybe he's just gone to breakfast early. But he usually leaves me a little note if he leaves before I've woken."

I frowned. "But you saw him come home last night?"

"I didn't. That's the thing. I was reading in bed, waiting up for him, and I guess I fell asleep. His side of the bed is made, and it seems odd that he'd straighten it before I was awake. But if he came in last night after I'd fallen asleep, it's possible he decided to watch television in the living room so as not to awaken me. Sometimes he falls asleep in his chair, and if I don't wake him, he doesn't come to bed. But then it occurred to me that perhaps if it had gotten late, he'd decided to stay at your place last night. Of course I would have appreciated a call if he'd—"

"Evie, Al didn't stay with me." Panic crept up into my chest and grabbed hold of my heart tightly.

"Oh dear…" she began. I could hear the worry in her voice. "He hasn't answered his phone either."

I had to keep it together. Evie couldn't know that I was now just as concerned as she was. "Don't worry, Evie. He probably just doesn't have his hearing aids in. I'll go check the dining room and the lobby. I'll check with Artie too. I'm sure he's fine. No worries. Okay?"

"It's hard not to worry. He's all I've got!"

"I know he is. And I won't let anything happen to him. Let me run out and do a little digging, okay?"

"Yes. Thank you, Terrence. Call me the second you find him. Please?"

"Don't worry, I will. I promise."

I hung up the phone and tried to center my thoughts. Al had left last night after volunteering to take Mack home. I wondered if Mack had made it home. I flipped through my contacts and found Mack's number and dialed. It rang and rang, and then the message that said the user's voicemail hadn't been set up yet picked up again.

Ugh. She wouldn't answer for me anyway. She was too pissed at me because I'd almost gotten her killed the night before. *Women.*

I needed to go look for Al.

I slid my feet back into my boat shoes and strode towards my bedroom. I gave a little knock on the door before opening it and peering inside. Francesca was curled up in my quilt. Her dark hair was sprawled out across my pillow. I snuck over to the bedside. I hated to wake her up, but this could be a serious emergency.

"Frankie," I whispered.

She didn't move.

I sat down on the edge of the bed and touched her shoulder. Her skin was warm and soft. "Frankie," I whispered again.

"Hmmm?"

"Time to wake up. We have a bit of an emergency situation on our hands."

She practically sprang out of bed. "Did Hugo poop on your floor?" she asked, her hair wild. "Don't worry, I'll clean it up."

"Well, good morning to you too," I said, flashing her a smile.

Her eyes blinked sleepily. She inhaled a deep breath and then smiled back at me, her head cocked sideways now. "Good morning, Danny. Did Hugo poop on your floor?"

"No, as of now, my floor's safe. But Al isn't. Evie just called. She doesn't think Al made it home last night."

Francesca's eyes widened. "What!"

"I need to go look for him."

She immediately went for her shoes. "Correction, *we* need to go look for him."

35

"Thanks, Artie," I said before hanging up the phone. I turned to Francesca, who was in the driver's seat of her vehicle. "Artie said Al's not in the dining room, the gift shop, or the men's room in the lobby. He just went and checked for me."

"Well, we know Al was driving Mack back to her car, and then he was supposed to head home after that," she said, turning down the driveway that would lead us to the employee parking lot. "We'll start by checking to see if Mack's car is still there."

I manually rolled down Francesca's window and leaned into the fresh island breeze. I needed the air to clear my head and calm me down, as I was already feeling panic's tight grip twisting the pit of my stomach. "Shit, Frankie. What if they got Al?"

Turning to look at me, she shook her head. "There's just no way. Why would they take him?"

"I don't know. Maybe they were trying to grab Mack again and they got Al somehow."

She hooked a right when we hit the parking lot. "Let's not go jumping to conclusions."

I sucked in my breath when I saw Al's pride and joy sitting there. "Oh my God," I whispered, pointing to the sleek black golf cart. "That's Al's."

Francesca shook her head. "That can't be good." She pulled her vehicle up to a stop next to the golf cart. There wasn't a single trace of Al inside. She looked around the lot. "Do you see Mack's car?"

I motioned up ahead. "Drive around. I'll scope it out."

"What's she drive?"

"It's a little silver Honda. Four-door."

The parking lot was small. Cars were parked around the perimeter of the lot, with two rows of cars nose to nose in the center. It took us all of thirty seconds to inspect the lot and discover that Mack's car wasn't there.

"So now what?" I asked, throwing my hands up.

"We speak to the guard shack. See what they know."

"The staff switches over at six a.m." I explained. "They're not gonna know what happened last night."

"You got any cameras on the entrance?"

"I've got eyes on the entrance and the guard shack, but not on the employee parking lot."

She shook her head. "You're gonna want to get working on that."

"I know. It's on my to-do list. I've been a little slow getting things done." I shook my head. After everything Francesca and I had spoken about last night, I knew now that not only had I let the hurt I felt over Pam's betrayal affect my personal life, I'd also let it affect my professional life. I'd put only the bare minimum into my job as head of resort security. All of that was coming to an end here and now.

"Let's speak to the guards, and if they don't have anything, we'll go check out the security cameras," said Francesca.

"You read my mind."

Francesca pulled her vehicle over to the guard shack, and Caleb Wilson, the dayshift guard stepped out.

"Good morning, Drunk." He tipped his hat at me. Caleb was a fairly serious man. He was clean-shaven, with a wide nose and dark, squinty eyes. "Is there something I can help you with this morning?"

"Yeah, Caleb. This is my friend Francesca."

He nodded at her.

"We're trying to figure out what happened to the owner of that black golf cart parked in the employee lot. Do you know where he went?"

Caleb shook his head. "No, the cart was there when I got here. I asked Davis, the night guard, about it. He was surprised to see it there. He said he hadn't even noticed someone drive it in."

"Did he mention if there was any kind of security issues last night in the employee parking lot?"

"He said it was a quiet night," said Caleb. "Is there something I should know?"

I frowned. "No. Not yet. But I'm looking for Al Becker. He's the owner of the golf cart. If you hear anything about his whereabouts, I'd appreciate a call."

Caleb gave a tight smile. "Sure thing."

"Thanks."

Francesca put the vehicle in motion, and we took off.

"Let's head to my office and we'll have a peek at the security footage of the guard shack last night."

"Got it."

FRANCESCA TOOK the seat next to me as I pulled up the footage.

"I don't even know what time it was when Al and Mack left last night, do you?"

Francesca shook her head. "No, but the guard shack can't have that much action, can it? We were at Tiburon Point at around eight thirty. It had to have been at least nine thirty when we got back. Start then and just see who comes and goes from there."

I nodded and fast-forwarded to the parts we were looking for.

We spent the next twenty minutes fast-forwarding through footage and pausing every time a car passed through. There were several cabs that passed through the gates, but they were all innocuous-looking island cabs. We watched several resort employees leave for the evening, and then we saw Mack's car drive away.

"Rewind that," instructed Francesca.

I rewound it, and we watched it three more times. It was clear that it was Mack driving, and there was no one else in the car. She hadn't been abducted again.

I slammed my hand down on the desk. "Dammit!" On my feet now, I paced the room. "What the hell happened to him? Old men just don't up and disappear!"

"Calm down. We're not going to find Al if we lose our heads."

"I don't even know where to look, though!"

"We'll figure something out," she promised, though I could tell by the look on her face that even she wasn't so sure. "I think we need to speak with Mack. She was likely the last person to see him before he disappeared. Maybe she saw something before she left."

"I already tried calling her. She doesn't answer her phone."

Frankie winced. "Yeah, she was pretty upset when she left last night."

"Maybe we—"

My phone rang then. I felt it vibrating in my pocket and closed my eyes. It could be a handful of people. It could be Artie calling to tell me that Al had been there all along. It could be Caleb at the guard shack telling me that he'd called Davis and they knew what had happened to Al. It could be Evie calling for a status update. And it could be Al himself calling to tell me where'd he been all night and telling me to relax, he was home safe and sound.

Or, it could be the kidnappers.

I held my breath and pulled my phone from my pocket.

Francesca looked up at me. "Who is it?"

My heart dropped. Restricted. "It's Dexter."

"Well, answer it!"

My heart throbbed wildly in my chest as I did. "Drunk here."

"You tired of playing games with me yet?"

I crumpled into my squeaky office chair. "Completely tired." And this time, it was the truth. I wasn't sure how much more of this I could take. "Is Pam okay?"

"Oh I've got no need for her anymore," said Dexter, followed by a throaty little maniacal laugh. "I've got someone better."

My heart immediately froze as panic filled my blood with a rush of adrenaline. "What?" I breathed into the phone.

"Not *what*, Daniel. *Who*?" Dexter laughed. "I've left you a little present back at your place. You might want to get back there and check it out. Then we'll talk."

The phone clicked.

I stared at Francesca.

This was bad.

Really, really bad.

"What?" she squealed. "What happened?"

"I don't know," I said, feeling like I'd been punched in the gut.

"Well? Does he have Al?"

"I didn't ask and he didn't say."

"Okay, so then why do you look like that?"

"He said he doesn't have a need for Pam anymore. He said he's got someone better."

Francesca's face went pale. "Oh my God."

"He said he left a present for me back at my place. We gotta get back there, now!"

Francesca's eyes widened. "Oh no. Hugo!"

WE COULD HEAR Hugo barking even before Francesca turned off the ignition. He was barking as though the devil himself was in there with him.

She looked over at me. "Something's not right. Hugo doesn't generally bark like that." She pulled her gun from her center console. "They might still be in there."

I pushed the barrel of the gun down. "This is my mess, Frankie. I'm going in first."

She shook her head. "You're unarmed, and that's my dog in there. I'm going in first. If anyone messed with him, they'll have to answer to me."

Meeting her eyes, I looked at her sincerely. "Frankie, I've already gotten Pam into this, and Mack, and now possibly Al. I can't have you in the middle of this too. Please. Just this once, I'm asking you to let me go in first. You'll be right behind me, so you can set your FOMO dial to simmer. All right?"

She closed her eyes and sighed. "Fine. But I'll be right behind you."

"Thank you." We both climbed out of the vehicle, neither of us closing the doors, and we approached the porch carefully. My eyes scanned the area for any signs of a disturbance. Seeing nothing, I motioned for Francesca to take the other side of the stairs. She nodded, and we flanked the doorway. I reached down and slowly turned the handle, then pushed it open with my foot.

Hugo came rushing out to the porch, barking like crazy.

"What is it?" asked Francesca, lowering the weapon.

"Woof woof woof!" the dog insisted, bouncing around in the doorway.

I stuck my head inside, careful not to get it blown off, and when I didn't see anything, I cautiously moved my whole body inside. "Looks clear to me."

Francesca followed Hugo as he bounded towards my bedroom. "What are you barking at?"

I held her arm. "They could be in there," I whispered.

She nodded, and together we approached the open doorway in the same manner we'd approached the front door. Hugo bounded in ahead of us and began barking wildly again.

I went in first to find Earnestine dancing in my windowsill. *"Rawck! No morning kisses! No morning kisses! Rawck!"*

Hugo ran right up to the window and barked wildly at the dancing parrot.

I slumped forward. "Fuck! Earnestine! You scared the hell out of us!"

"Yeah, she did!" said Francesca. "That's what had Hugo so worked up!"

I threw my hands up to shoo the bird out of my window. "Shit! My heart's racing now."

"Mine too." She looked down at Hugo. "I thought something happened to you, you big dummy. What's the matter? You can't handle a little bird?"

I held a hand to my chest. "Yeah, Hugo. Geez!" I glanced over at Francesca. "But Dexter said he left me a present. I wonder what it is?"

Francesca and I walked back into the living room, her keeping a hand on Hugo's collar. I scanned the open floor plan. My kitchen and living room were really just one big room. My eyes crawled across every square inch, looking for anything that didn't belong. My eyes finally settled on a small white box on my kitchen counter. It sat amongst the cluttered mess of candy wrappers and tequila bottles, and I just about missed it.

I strode over to it and lifted it off the counter. "This isn't mine." A closer inspection told me it was a watch box from a fancy jewelers, and it was tied shut with a ribbon.

"Be careful, maybe it's a bomb…"

I shook my head. "Nah, I don't think it's a bomb. It's too light." I gave it a little shake. Something was in there. Curious, I pulled the ribbon off and let it fall to the floor. I pulled back the hinged lid.

My eyes widened when I saw the contents. "Holy shit," I said before snapping the box shut and dropping it onto the counter. I pushed myself back and spun around, giving Francesca my back.

36

"Oh my God, Danny, what is it?"

Standing with my back to the counter, my knees threatened to buckle and I felt light-headed. Anger, fear, and sadness all bubbled up inside my chest. I couldn't speak.

I heard her walk over to the box.

I held a hand backwards towards her. "You don't wanna look at it," I whispered, over the lump in my throat.

She stared down at the box weakly. "What is it?"

"It's the engagement ring I gave Pam."

Francesca was silent for a moment. "They gave you back the engagement ring? What's so wrong with th…"

I turned in time to see her opening the box. Her eyes were huge as her hand moved to cover her mouth. She snapped it shut almost immediately. "That's not…?"

"It is." I went to the sink and opened up the faucet to let cold water pour over my hands. I leaned in and splashed my face with the water. I had to wash away the image of Al's pinky finger wearing Pam's ring from my brain.

"B-but how do you know it was…"

"I know, all right. I know what Al's gnarled old hands look like. I know. It was his."

Francesca swallowed hard. "I know they told you not to get the island police involved, but maybe it's time we get Sergeant Gibson in on this. We're in over our heads, Danny. We can't do this alone."

"They'll kill them both if we do," I whispered. "If Pam's not already dead. I almost feel like she's dead now. There's no way they pried that engagement ring off her finger if she's still alive. She loved that ring."

"You'll do a lot of things if a gun's pointed at your head," said Francesca.

My head began to spin. This seriously wasn't happening. Pam was dead and Al was next. How would I ever tell Evie that I'd gotten Al killed? How could I ever forgive myself if Al died due to my recklessness? What would I do without my best friend in Paradise?

I had to sit down before my knees buckled beneath my weight. I stumbled over to the sofa and fell down onto it. Hugo plodded over to me and put his head on my lap like he understood the utter sense of defeat I felt to my core. "I don't understand, Frankie. How did they know?"

Still in shock, she looked down at me. "Know what?"

"About Al? And about Pam? And about Mack? And about the money? Who the hell *is* this Dexter guy? How did I ever get on his radar?"

She shook her head. "I don't know. It's what we're going to have to figure out if we want to find him."

"No." I waved a hand in the air. "We won't need to find Dexter. Dexter's going to find us. He's desperate now. He wants that money. And I'm going to give it to him. Every last red cent of it. It's blood money now. I have to do whatever it takes to get Al and Pam back. I only pray they'll still be alive."

Francesca lowered her head, and Hugo trekked over to be by her side. She patted him softly.

When the room had gone still, my eyes suddenly began darting around. "It's like he's got a fucking bug in here. Is that it?" I jumped up and spun around. "Does he have a fucking bug in here? Is that how he knew about Al? And Mack? And Pam?"

Francesca looked around too. Like my idea had merit. "Maybe. Obviously we were talking with Al in here last night. I assume Mack's spent a little time here."

I couldn't even look her in the eye as I nodded.

"What about Pam? Has she been in here?"

"No, never!"

"Had you ever spoken about her in here?"

I couldn't think of a single time before Pam had been taken that I'd spoken her name aloud. Not in my room. Not outside of my room. Not since she'd shown up on the island. "I don't think so…" And then a memory hit me. "Oh, wait! I did have a conversation with Mack about her."

"When?"

"The night Pam showed up at the resort. Mack saw us together in the lobby that morning, so that evening we had to have this whole long conversation about the status of our relationship."

"You and Mack's relationship?"

"No, me and Pam's relationship. It was like Mack was kind of jealous or something. I think she was concerned that Pam and I might be getting back together."

"And Pam was taken that next morning?"

"Yeah."

"Did you ever talk about the money in here?"

I didn't even need to think about that. My hands cut the air. "No, absolutely not. I've never spoken to anyone about the money. And I haven't been flashy with it either. I've barely spent any of it."

Francesca strode into the living room and sat down on one of the cushioned bamboo chairs. She drew her knee to her chest so she could rest her chin on it. Hugo moved across the room to the blanket he'd claimed on the floor and plopped down onto it. "This all had to start with someone finding out about the money. Think about it, Danny. Who else knew about that?"

I sat back down on the sofa and tried to think. Who else knew about the money? Al knew. And Artie, of course. The geriatric squad who had helped me get the money in the first place knew. Manny knew, but I doubted he'd tell anyone else after I'd asked him not to. "I don't know. I don't think Al would've told anyone, and those old guys he hangs around with, they're not gonna tell either. The swim-up bartender, Manny, knows, but he's a friend of mine. I don't think he'd tell anyone."

"You're sure that's all the people that knew?"

And then a memory hit me. I slammed a hand into my knee. "Shit. I just remembered. Mariposa mentioned something to me the other day about me being richer than God. It completely caught me off guard when she said it. Apparently she knows, but I have no idea who told her."

"Who is Mariposa?"

"She's in charge of the front office staff and the cleaning staff."

"Do you get along with her?"

I pulled my lips back and widened my eyes. "I mean, I *try* to get along with her."

"What does that mean? You *try* to get along with her."

"It means I've been trying to win her over since I got to the resort. She just doesn't seem to like me."

Francesca tipped her head sideways. "Does Mariposa know about your relationships with Pam, Mack, and Al?"

I nodded. "Definitely. Everyone here knows about Al and me. She hated the fact that Mack and I were hooking up. And Pam made a scene the day she showed up here. Mari saw it for sure. But, to be fair, the whole resort heard about it."

"So, Mari knew about the money, and about your relationships with the three people taken. It's not that big of a stretch to think that perhaps she's the one that's been talking to Dexter," said Francesca.

I shook my head. "I just can't picture Mari selling me out like that. She seems like a nice person besides the fact that she's not my biggest fan."

"Danny, some people will sell their own mother out for money. Dexter could be giving her a big slice of the pie. Is she struggling for cash?"

"I don't know. She's a single mom. What single mom doesn't struggle for cash?"

Francesca shook her head. "I hate to say it, but this woman is looking guiltier and guiltier." She began to tick things off her fingers. "She knew about the money. She knew about your personal relationships. She's not your biggest fan. She's a struggling single mother who could use some quick cash. And she knows where you live. It's all adding up."

"I would be shocked if it were her."

"We don't have a lot of leads, Danny. We've gotta start somewhere. Maybe we need to find out exactly how she discovered the fact that you'd gotten that money."

I nodded. "Yeah, I'm definitely curious about that too."

Francesca nodded and strode towards the door. "All right, then. What are we waiting for? I think it's time we pay your friend Mariposa a little visit."

I stood up.

Francesca held a hand out as a thought hit her. "Wait. What are we going to tell Al's wife? We can't just leave her hanging. Al lost a finger. Dexter's got him, Danny. We have to tell her something!"

I swallowed hard. The thought of telling Evie about the finger and Al's abduction made my stomach churn. "I'll call her while we're on the way and tell her we're working on finding him."

"But are you gonna tell her about Al's finger?"

I winced and carried the box with the finger in it to the

sink. "Hell no. In fact, I'm gonna wrap it in wet paper towels." I pointed at one of my cupboards. "Hand me a Ziplock."

She opened up my cupboard and pulled out a little baggie.

When I'd wrapped the finger, I slid it inside. "There, now we'll keep this on ice and maybe if we get Al back in time, they can sew it back on. I'll meet you out front in a minute."

37

A Seacoast Majestic shuttle bus sat empty beneath the porte cochere as a whole new crop of men in shorts and flip-flops and women in summer dresses and sandals filled the air-conditioned lobby. Francesca and I stood off to the side, watching Mariposa Marrero work diligently to accommodate the influx of new arrivals. Usually she only oversaw her staff, but since Mack wasn't there, Mari had taken over her computer and was currently helping an elderly couple get checked into their room.

Francesca and I stood with our arms crossed, watching the vertically challenged woman work and waiting for her to finish. Our unwavering stares followed her every movement, and yet, she refused to make eye contact with us.

Francesca leaned sideways towards me. "Looks like she might be a while. Can we interrupt her?"

I shook my head. "As much as I wanna find Al, I don't think interrupting Mari while she's checking in new arrivals is gonna make her want to talk to us. Let's go talk to Artie first. I need to update him on the Al situation anyway. Maybe when we're done there, Mari'll be free."

I led Francesca through a door marked Employees Only

and through a series of hallways to Artie's office. I took a deep breath and knocked on his door.

"Come in."

I opened the door and stuck my head inside. "Artie. May I have a word?"

"Of course. What's going on? I assume you found Al?"

I opened the door wider to let Francesca inside. "Artie, you remember Officer Cruz?"

Artie blotted at his forehead with the white towel on his desk and then stood up to extend one of his meaty hands in her direction. "Of course I do. Officer Cruz, it's a pleasure. Artie Balladares. Have a seat." He gestured to the chairs in front of his desk and then sat back down and looked at me, annoyance covering his face. He cleared his throat. "I thought we agreed to handle this situation *internally*, Drunk."

Francesca held up a hand before I could say anything else. "I can assure you, Mr. Balladares, I'm on my own with this case. I've taken a few personal days' leave from the PIRPF so I could help Danny out with this. No one at the station even knows I'm working on it."

Artie let out a heavy sigh. "Good. The bad publicity would eat my business alive."

I cleared my throat. "Artie, I've got some bad news. I really don't even know how to tell you this." I looked down at my hands and then back up at Artie. "Things have taken a more serious turn."

Artie's brows knitted together. "Turn? What do you mean?"

"It's Al," I said, rubbing the palms of my hands against my shorts to dispel the stickiness.

"Al?" Artie looked confused.

I glanced over at Francesca. I wasn't sure that I could actually say the words.

Francesca nodded at me and then turned to look at Artie. "Mr. Balladares, Al's been taken."

"Taken!" gasped Artie.

"Abducted," she added.

I sighed. I really didn't want to tell him the rest. "And listen, Artie. It's not just that they abducted him. They fucking cut his finger off!"

Artie's usually squinty eyes practically bugged out of his head. "They did *what*?"

"We have the finger," I added, as if that made anything better. "I've got it on ice back at my place."

"On ice? You're serious? Someone *actually* cut off Al's finger?"

"I'm serious as a heart attack, Artie. Things are all kinds of messed up right now."

"Oh my God, Al…" Artie leaned forward over his desk. His sausage fingers covered his face as he sucked in a deep, asthmatic breath. Finally, after an extended silence, he leaned back in his chair again. It made a groaning sound beneath the pressure of his weight. "Drunk, tell me what I can do to help. You wanna call the cops? Let's call the cops. Resort be damned." He reached forward and put a hand on the phone on his desk.

My hand lurched forward to settle over his. "It's only gonna make it worse for Al, Artie. We can't."

"But, Drunk! Al Becker is one of my oldest, dearest friends. I can't just sit around and not try and help him."

"I know exactly how you feel, Artie. Al's been my best friend since I got to the island. We're going to do everything we can to find him, but if we get the island police involved, the kidnappers are just gonna kill him and Pam. We can't let that happen," I said firmly.

"But they already took his finger. What's to stop them from killing him?"

"They want the money. I don't think they're gonna kill him until they get the money. Otherwise they lose their bargaining chip."

Artie shook his head. His eyes darted between us. "Then what can I do? I have to help."

I leaned back in my chair, pulled one of my ankles up to rest on my knee, and ran my hands through my hair. My hair felt greasy, like I hadn't showered in months. I hadn't even bothered to look at myself in the mirror before leaving. I probably looked like hell warmed over. "Well, for starters, Artie, you can keep this to yourself. Whatever you do, for crying out loud, don't tell Evie. She's gonna lose it when she finds out. We're hoping we can find Al before something else bad happens to him."

"Of course, of course," said Artie. The color had drained from his usually white face, making him appear pastier than usual.

"Besides that? You can get an orthopedic specialist geared up and ready to reattach the finger. It's in my cottage if you want to send someone over there to grab it and have it prepped for when I get Al back."

Artie's head bobbed. "I'm on it. I'll get the best surgeon money can buy!"

I sighed. "Otherwise, there's not much else you can do. We're waiting to speak to Mariposa. But she's busy right now, so we thought we'd update you on the situation while we were waiting."

Artie looked confused. "Mariposa? Why do you need to speak with her?"

Francesca leaned in, resting her elbows on her knees. "We think she might be involved. It seems that a lot of the signs are pointing towards her as possibly being the kidnapper's informant."

Artie's head jerked back. "You're kidding me? You think Mari's involved in Al's abduction?"

I nodded. "And in Pam's and in Mack's."

"Mack's? You never told me Mack was abducted!"

I sighed. "Oh, yeah. Shit. Sorry. But don't worry, we got her back. Last night. We were supposed to trade the money for Pam, but when we got there, it wasn't Pam, it was Mack. But she had a bag on her head, so we didn't find out who it was until after we'd already made the exchange. That's why Mack was a no call, no show at work yesterday. So hopefully, you'll be willing to give her her job back. If she even wants it back after everything that's happened."

Artie looked at me with a tilted head and narrowed eyes. "Now explain to me why you think *Mari* is involved in all of this?"

Francesca took the reins on that one. "Well, for starters, she knew all about Danny's relationships with Pam, Mack, and Al. And according to Danny, Mariposa never liked him much. She's also got access to his house. And most importantly, she knew about the money."

I nodded. "Yeah, there aren't that many people that knew about the money. You, Al, Manny, and the guys down at the clubhouse, but none of those guys are telling anyone. Although I haven't figured out exactly *how* she knew about the money. But I'm sure she did. She made a comment to me about it the other day."

Artie's face froze. Only his eyes darted from me to Francesca and back to me again. "Ooooh," he groaned. Then slowly he raised one of his hands. "That would be me. I accidentally let it slip one day."

My eyes widened. "Artie! You told Mari about the money? Why would you do that? I asked you to keep that on the DL."

His head bobbed. "Yes, yes. I know you did. It was a mistake. It slipped out. She was in here one day complaining about you. She was upset because you were sleeping with her girls, and she didn't think you were doing a very good job as resort security. On and on she went. She wanted me to fire you."

Francesca quirked a brow and gave me a sideways glance,

as if that somehow proved that Mari was indeed Dexter's snitch.

"She actually *said* she wanted you to fire me?" So much for trying to win the woman over with chocolates.

Artie nodded. "Yes, sadly. I convinced her that you were just going through a tough time and you would do better with time. We just needed to let you have a little time and room to breathe."

I smiled at him. "Thanks, Artie. I appreciate you having my back."

"Well, I tried," he said, dipping his head, his hat covering his eyes for a split second. Then he straightened. "She said she didn't like all of her girls fighting over one of the employees. She said it disrupted their work. And that was when your secret accidentally came out. I told her that I hated to break it to her, but even if I fired you, it was more than likely that you'd just stay living on resort property because you had the money to do it," he admitted. "Then it was too late. It was like I'd opened a can of worms. She asked me a million questions about what that meant, and I was forced to admit that you'd come into a windfall after that whole Jimmie fiasco."

I palmed my forehead as I breathed, "Oh my God, Artie!"

His head bobbed. "I know, I know. I kicked myself after that. I know I shouldn't have told her, and I didn't mean to. I'm so sorry, Drunk."

"It's Pam, Mack, and Al that you should feel sorry for. They're the ones that have had to live through this horrible ordeal!"

"So now what?" asked Artie. "You just think it's Mari because she knew about the money and about the relationships between you and those three?"

Francesca pointed a finger. "And because Danny mentioned that she's a struggling single mother. She probably needed the money."

Artie lifted his brows and his head slowly bobbed like for

the first time he might be buying the theory that Mari was involved. "She *is* trying to save up enough money to send Giselle, her oldest girl, off to college next year."

"It's gotta be her," said Francesca, shaking her head. "It's just gotta be."

Artie sighed. "But Mariposa is my best employee. I just can't imagine she'd risk her job to do something like that. It would be very out of character for her."

"That's what I said," I said to Artie, "but Frankie's convinced."

Artie lifted the handle of his phone. "Well, we're going to get to the bottom of this once and for all. If she had something to do with Al's disappearance, we're about to find out."

"What are you doing?" I asked.

"Calling her in here. I think it's time we had a word with Ms. Marrero."

38

"HAVE A SEAT, MARI," SAID ARTIE, GESTURING TOWARDS THE empty seat next to Francesca.

I stood with my back pressed against the wall, watching the woman enter.

Mari's brows knitted together as she looked around the room curiously. "What's this about?"

"Just have a seat. We're getting to that," said Artie.

Mari took the seat and looked at Francesca. "Who's she?"

"Just a friend of mine," I cut in. I didn't want Artie accidentally telling Mari that Francesca was a police officer. If she really *was* Dexter's informant, that could prove to be fatal for Al and Pam.

"Well, what's she doing here?"

"I'm helping Mr. Drunk and Mr. Balladares with a resort issue," explained Francesca.

Mari turned to look back at me and then at Artie. "I don't understand. What resort issue?"

I stalked around Artie's desk so I now stood directly behind him. I leaned against the wall and crossed my arms over my chest. "We think you know exactly what resort issue."

Mari shook her head, seemingly confused. "No, I have

absolutely no idea what you're talking about. What's going on?"

"Mari, they know it was you," said Artie weakly.

Mari frowned. "Well, I'm certainly glad someone knows something around here, because I sure as heck don't have any idea what's going on. Maybe one of you can enlighten me, because I'm confused."

"You remember me accidentally telling you how Drunk is worth seven million dollars?" asked Artie, glancing back at me nervously over his shoulder.

Recognition finally registered on Mari's face. "Oh. That? Is that what all of this is about?" She put a hand on her chest. "For heaven's sake, I thought that someone had *died* by the looks on all of your faces."

Francesca and I exchanged a look.

"Mari, what did you mean when you said 'oh, that' just now?" I asked.

Mari lifted a shoulder along with one thick black eyebrow. "Well, obviously you're sore because I mentioned it to you the other day. I don't know what you want me to say. You walk around here acting like you own the place. I'd just kind of had enough. Some of us actually have to work for our paychecks."

"Mari, I asked you to keep that information to yourself," snapped Artie. "I wasn't supposed to have mentioned it to you. You know that."

She waved it off. "It really wasn't that big of a deal. It just kind of slipped out. I was in a mood, and he had me fired up."

I frowned at her. "You told someone else about the money, didn't you, Mari?"

Mari's mouth went to open and then snapped shut immediately. She glanced from me to Artie and then over Francesca. Then she looked back up at me again angrily. "So what if I did?"

I took two steps forward and leaned my palms on Artie's desk. "So you *did* tell someone. I knew it!"

"Mari!" breathed Artie, his eyes widening. "So it *was* you!"

"Was me what?!"

"That told about Drunk's money!"

"Yeah, I mean, I'm not denying it. What's the big deal? It takes three people to chew me out over spilling a secret?"

"What's the big deal?" I barked, my face now hot. "Mari, you have no idea what you've done!"

"What I've done?" She looked at me like I was crazy. "I said it wasn't a big deal! Okay? You've been nothing but a big pain in my ass since you got to the island. You deserve whatever repercussions that money has gotten you."

"Mari!" bellowed Artie. With his palms flattened on his desk, he pushed himself up so he was standing now. "How could you?"

For the first time since she'd gotten into the room, Mari visibly shrank. She looked around at all our faces. "Why are you all getting so upset? You act like I killed someone!"

"Maybe they aren't dead yet, but they could be close," I whispered.

A deep V formed between her brows then, as if something had finally clicked and she had a reason to be concerned now. "What are you talking about? Who's almost dead?"

Francesca, who had been taking everything in quietly, finally turned to face Mariposa. "Ms. Marrero. We're going to need the names of the person or people whom you're working with?"

"Working with?"

"Who did you tell Mr. Drunk's secret to?"

"Just the girls. I only told the girls."

"The girls?" said Francesca, unsure of who she was referring to. "Can we have names, please? For the record?" She took a pen and a notepad off Artie's desk.

"Names?" Mari's face paled.

"The names of the people that you told," said Francesca, her pen poised to write them down.

"Oh, well, I mean, I only told Alicia, but I think she told Anita. Okay, I *know* she told Anita." She held up her two flattened palms up by her shoulders. "But technically, I *personally* only told Alicia."

"You didn't tell anyone else? Someone off resort property, perhaps?"

"Off resort property?" Mari's face crinkled again. "Oh no. Absolutely not. Resort business is resort business. I abide by our strict confidentiality policy. I don't bring work home with me at all."

"But you didn't abide by the strict confidentiality policy when it came to telling Alicia about Mr. Drunk's money," said Francesca. "How are we to believe that you abided by the policy at home?"

Mari frowned. "That's different. Drunk's money had nothing to do with *work*. I considered it personal in nature and just office gossip. Nothing more. But I don't even bring office gossip home. It's just me and my kids anyway. They don't care about who's messing around with who. Why would they care if some man their mother works with suddenly came into seven million dollars?"

I'd just about had enough of the back and forth. I couldn't tell if I should believe her or not, but something in my gut told me she was telling the truth. But I had to be sure. "Mari, you and Al get along well, don't you?"

Mari's brows furrowed. "Yes, of course. Mr. Becker is my favorite long-term guest. He and his wife have even had me and my children over for dinner."

That was something even *I* was unaware of. I rubbed a hand across my forehead and swallowed hard to keep my emotions in check. Al was such a good man. I found it difficult to continue.

"You wouldn't want anything bad to happen to Mr. Becker, is that correct, Ms. Marrero?" asked Francesca, filling in for me when she saw I couldn't continue.

Mari's eyes widened. "Of course not! He's a wonderful man. I'd be devastated if something happened to him." She grasped her hands tightly in her lap, like she was worried now. "Why? Has something happened to him?"

I swallowed hard. It wasn't Mari. I could hear it in her voice. She loved Al like I did. There's no way she would have given Dexter his name. "No, Mari. Nothing bad has happened. I was just upset that you told Alicia about my money. You know, rumors have gotten around and all and it's frustrating. I'm really sorry I bothered you with this." I walked around the desk and held the door open.

Francesca looked up at me curiously.

Mari looked up at me curiously too, turning her gaze from Artie to Francesca before finally standing up and striding towards the door. "Y-you'd tell me if something bad had happened to Mr. Becker, wouldn't you?"

I nodded. "Yes, yes, of course we would. I'm sorry to make you uneasy. But he'll be fine."

"Mari, I'm going to ask that you please keep this conversation completely confidential. No discussing it with the girls?"

Mari nodded. "Of course, Mr. Balladares." She looked up at me sheepishly then. "I'm sorry I told Alicia about your money. It was none of my business and very out of character for me to break Mr. Balladares's confidence like that. And if it's caused you problems, I am very sorry."

I squeezed her arm. "I'm sorry I caused you problems that you had to go to Artie to complain about me, Mari. I promise. Very soon you'll see a new, improved Danny Drunk. And you can take that to the bank."

39

Sitting atop one of the barstools in my cottage, Francesca shook her head. "I can't believe you just took that woman at her word, Danny!"

I threw my arms out wide. "She had nothing to do with it. I could tell."

"How could you tell?"

"Something in my gut. I don't know what to tell you. Mari isn't the one."

"So if she's not the one, then who is? Because *someone* is feeding information to Dexter, and it made a heck of a lot of sense that it was her."

I shrugged. I couldn't answer that question right now. Nothing was making sense to me. "I don't know," I finally said, giving Hugo a distracted pat on the head.

We were silent for a little while, each of us lost in our own thoughts, when finally, Francesca piped up again. "Well, now that we know Mari knew about the money, she admitted that she told Alicia and Alicia told Anita, we have to consider them suspects. Do you know those women?"

"Of course I do. They both work the front desk."

"Could it be either of them?"

I let my head roll backwards on my shoulders. "I mean, I don't know Anita very well, so I couldn't tell you. I do know Alicia." I swallowed hard and cast a shifty glance in Francesca's direction. "She's not real fond of me either."

"Yeah? Why not?"

My lips puckered as I stared at Francesca. "Mmnnmm?" I murmured, shrugging. "Some girls just don't, I guess."

Francesca stared at me hard before putting a hand on each hip. "Danny! You slept with her too?"

My brows knitted together. "What? I was trying to get over Pam. Whaddaya want me to say?"

"I don't know. But it sounds like we need to burn sage in your house when this is all said and done."

I couldn't help but laugh. "You wanna smudge my house? Seriously? It was just sex, Frankie. It wasn't an exorcism."

Francesca's eyes scanned the walls. "I don't know, Danny. This place suddenly feels pretty gross."

I rolled my eyes. "Listen, if we get Al and Pam back, I will *personally* smudge the shit out of every corner of this house. All right?"

Francesca smiled. "Okay. Now, back to what we were talking about. Alicia doesn't like you. Could it be her?"

I shrugged. "I mean, it's possible."

"Do you think those two girls would've told anyone else?"

"It definitely would not shock me," I said, nodding my head. "Rumors and gossip travel at the speed of light around here."

"Did either of them know about your relationship with Pam?"

"Well, everyone knew about it the day that she arrived. She made a huge scene in the lobby. Word spread around the resort like wildfire."

"Okay, so let's think about this logically. Mariposa knew about the money. She told several of the front office girls, and what was to stop them from telling the maids, you know?"

I bobbed my head. "Exactly."

"And all of those people she told also knew about Pam coming to see you."

"Yup."

"Did any of them know about your friendship with Al?"

I nodded. "Oh, sure. Everyone here knows about my relationship with Al. We're like this," I said, holding up two intertwined fingers. "We go everywhere together."

"Okay, so then it's not such a stretch to imagine that Dexter knew about that relationship. Whoever told him about the money likely told him about Pam and your relationship with Al. What about Mack? Did any of the front office girls or the maids know about your relationship with Mack?"

I sighed. "Yeah, that was common knowledge too." I groaned and let my head fall forward. "In fact, a few of the girls were burned over the fact that I'd hooked up with the new girl. Alicia being one of them."

As if he'd just been spooked, Hugo jumped to his feet and trotted back to my bedroom.

Francesca climbed off her barstool. "All right, I think we're getting closer! One of those girls *has* to be working with the kidnapper. Maybe you pissed one of them off enough to come after you. We're just going to have to interview all of them until we figure out which—"

From the bedroom, Hugo started barking wildly again. I sighed. "Shit. Earnestine's back."

"Hugo! Come here!" shouted Francesca.

His barking continued.

I grabbed a handful of hair on either side of my scalp and groaned. We had so many people to interview. Now was not the time to hear that bird's incessant squawking. Why hadn't I killed the fucking bird when I'd had the chance? I jumped to my feet and went to my bedroom.

Sure enough, Earnestine was on my headboard again. She was dancing about, her little feet clicking against the wood.

Her head bobbed as she moved, as if she were laughingly teasing Hugo.

"Earnestine!" I barked. I flapped my arms at her to chase her back out the window. "Go! Go!"

But instead of flying out the window, she flew over my head and out my bedroom door towards the living room. Hugo practically knocked me over trying to chase her out the door. "Woof! Woof!"

I closed my eyes. *Fuck.* I didn't have the energy to deal with a fucking bird and a dog! I was trying to concentrate and figure out who could've possibly been Dexter's informant.

In the living room, I found that Earnestine had landed on Francesca's shoulder. *"Pretty bird, pretty bird, pretty bird,"* she squawked.

Francesca smiled at her. "She remembers me!"

"She's a smart bird," I admitted. I waved my hand at Earnestine. "Come on, birdy, time to go bye-bye."

Earnestine swayed from side to side. *"No morning kisses, no morning kisses, rawck!"*

"This bird really doesn't like morning kisses, huh?" said Francesca.

I rolled my eyes. "Every fucking morning."

"You taught her that?"

"She overheard a conversation between me and Mack," I explained. "The morning that Pam showed up."

Something about that thought made me take pause. I tipped my head to the side for a moment and furrowed my brow.

"What?"

"Well, we sorta just came to the realization that maybe it's one of the front office girls that's Dexter's informant."

Francesca nodded. "Yeah?"

"Mack's new to the Seacoast Majestic. She's only been working here a few weeks. And she was actually the one that sought *me* out down at the pool bar that night. I didn't even realize that Mari had hired a new girl."

"Okay? Where're you going with this?"

"Think about it. Mack's new. She probably heard from the girls about me having that money. She sought out a relationship with me. Then Pam shows up, Mack grills me on my relationship with her, and the next thing I know, Pam's kidnapped."

Francesca furrowed her brow. "But didn't you tell me that Mack sought reassurance from you that you and Pam were over? If that's the case, then why in the world would she suggest that Dexter kidnap Pam? I mean, who in their right mind would kidnap an ex that someone detested? It doesn't make any sense."

I shook my head. The pieces were falling into place now. "Well, that's kind of the thing. I *didn't* tell her I detested Pam. I told her we'd always love each other. I didn't want to sound like a dick, you know?"

I sat back down and Earnestine flew from Francesca's shoulder to mine, but I hardly even noticed as my brain began to put the pieces of the puzzle together. "I don't know why we didn't think about her before, but Mack was the last one to see Al before he disappeared. And we watched all that security footage and we never saw another vehicle leave that we could tell had Al or any of Dexter's other known goons in it."

"Right?"

"Well, what if Al was in the car with Mack?"

"We watched the security footage, Danny. There wasn't anyone else in the car."

I shrugged. "He could've been in the trunk." I took a deep breath and smiled. "Oh my God, Frankie. What if Mack was Dexter's informant?"

Francesca swished her lips to the side as she thought about it. "But what about last night? Mack was abducted too. She had that big bump on her face. Remember? That girl was a mess when we found her. You really think they'd knock her around if it was all fake?"

"They would've wanted to make it look real. Right? If they returned her to us without a single scratch, that might've been suspicious."

Francesca thought about it for a long moment. "You seriously think she could be the informant?"

I shrugged. "I mean, I don't know. How wild would that be? Mack's new to the resort. I don't know a heck of a lot about her, to be honest. All I know is that her aunt and uncle are wealthy and have a nice place they're letting her stay until she gets on her feet."

Francesca nodded like she was getting it now. "You know, if she did nab Al, maybe she's in this more than just being Dexter's informant. Maybe she's a part of this whole thing."

My eyes widened. I'd been played! I slammed a hand down on my leg. "I can't believe it. I was sleeping with the fucking enemy! What an idiot I've been!"

Francesca held out a hand to steady me. "You just take a deep breath. We don't know it was Mack. We need to find out more about her before we go making any accusations."

"Maybe we should pay her a little visit."

Francesca's eyes brightened. "You know where she lives?"

"I do. She's staying at her aunt and uncle's vacation villa. It's not far away. I'll get the exact address from Human Resources."

"Well, then, what are we waiting for? I think we have a serious lead to investigate!" Francesca opened the front door and lowered the bird to the porch railing. She patted her leg. "Come on, Hugo. It's time to tell your new friend goodbye. We're outta here."

40

AFTER DROPPING HUGO OFF AT COURTNEY'S DOGGIE DAYCARE center just down the street from Francesca's apartment, we stopped by her apartment so she could change her clothes, brush her teeth, and grab the Ruger LC9 she kept in her nightstand, along with some extra ammunition.

"You know, the smart move would've been to buy your own weapon with a little of that found money," she said, sticking her head out of the bathroom while brushing her teeth. "It seems like trouble follows you wherever you go."

"Weapons are for amateurs." I smiled at her and lifted both arms to curl my biceps in front of her. "Who needs a 9mm when they've got guns like these?"

Francesca couldn't help herself. Toothpaste sprayed out of her mouth as she laughed. "Oh my gosh, Danny! You're hilarious."

When she disappeared back inside the bathroom, I twisted my wrists and looked down at my biceps. While my arms weren't as big as they'd been when I was working out every day back in the States, they still showed a *little* definition. Okay, maybe I'd put on a few pounds and lost a little muscle over the last several weeks of resort living. I shook my head and decided then and there that when this was all over, I was going to start visiting the resort's on-site gym daily.

After we left her apartment, the next stop was Bubba's Supa Valu Station around the corner from her place for a quick gas up and breakfast. Then we headed towards the Avalonian Peninsula, where one of Paradise Isle's most exclusive residential communities was located. Mack's family owned a vacation villa along the southern edge of the peninsula on the idyllic turquoise waters of Herman's Bay.

As we wound our way down the tree-lined tropical street where mansions and vacation villas dotted the beachfront and lush, intricately manicured lawns were second to none, I peeled back the wrapper of my second Snickers bar and bit off a third of the candy bar in one bite.

"That's what you eat for breakfast?" asked Francesca, one brow lifted.

With my window open, I leaned back into her seat. The warmth of the island air blew through my hair and made me miss having my own vehicle to drive whenever the urge struck. "Breakfast of champions," I said through a mouthful of chocolate and caramel-covered nougat.

She took a sip of her iced vanilla latte and shook her head. "That's not very healthy."

"Like that crap's healthy?" I asked, gesturing towards her coffee.

"Hey, I had a yogurt and some granola," she said, chuckling at me.

I shook my head and took two big swigs from my extra-large fountain Dr. Pepper. "Listen. Life's too short to eat *yogurt* and *granola*. I'd rather die young drinking Dr. Pepper and tequila than to live forever because I choked down yogurt and salad, or whatever else you skinny chicks eat."

She looked out her window. "The way you're going, that might just be your undoing."

"Drinking Dr. Pepper?"

"Drinking tequila!" she said. "Maybe you're blind to it, but you had seven empty tequila bottles at your place. *Seven!* And that's not even including the whiskey bottles! Danny, you've been on the island less than two months. I don't think I've downed seven tequila bottles in my *life*."

"Seven bottles?" I shrugged. "That's like a bottle a week. That's not that much."

"Whatever. I'm all for living your best life, but all I'm saying is, that can't be good for your liver."

"My liver's impenetrable." I shot her a cocky grin.

"No one's liver is impenetrable. Maybe you should take it down a notch."

"We've only been hanging out a few days, and already you're telling me to quit drinking so much?" I lifted my left hand to stare at it, flicking my wrist back and forth. "Fuck! I don't even get a ring before the nagging starts."

She swatted at me playfully. "Shut it. I'm just giving you some friendly advice."

I reached over and squeezed the hand that had landed on the gear shifter between us. "I know you are. And I appreciate your friendly advice. I appreciate everything you've done to help me. You're a really great person, Francesca Cruz."

She shot me one of her killer smiles. "Thanks, Danny. I appreciate that."

The car fell silent for a moment.

Feeling uncomfortable, I had to break the silence. "So, we going in guns blazing or what?"

"You really think that's wise?"

I shrugged. "I don't know. I haven't done many stakeouts in my career. In fact, this might be a first."

"Yeah, well, unfortunately, I haven't had a lot of experience with this either. Sergeant Gibson doesn't have a lot of faith in me. He keeps me on a pretty tight leash."

"What an asshole."

She shrugged and turned the vehicle down a long driveway. "I'm used to it. My brothers don't have a lot of faith in me either."

"Yeah, I noticed. What's up with that?"

She let out a heavy sigh. "I'm the baby, obviously."

"So? What does birth order have to do with it? I'm the oldest. I hear that's supposed to mean I'm responsible or something. I think it's pretty obvious that the rules of birth order don't apply to everyone."

"I don't know about that. You're also the only. That's different."

"Regardless, it shouldn't matter that you're the baby. You're an adult, and you're a kick-ass chick. I have faith in you. Your brothers should too."

"Thanks," she said, staring ahead at the road. "But when it comes to my family, they don't see me as a kick-ass chick. They just see me as a girl, and I think brothers by nature want to protect their kid sisters."

"Seems like they just don't even want you in this line of work."

"It's kind of a long story. I'll tell you about it sometime." Francesca pulled the car to a stop a few yards in front of a set of black wrought-iron gates.

And I was suddenly curious to learn more about the woman sitting beside me. "Promise you'll tell me?"

Her head bobbed. "Promise."

I nodded and turned my attention to the property in front of us. On either side of the gates, a row of neatly trimmed ficuses lined the property. Hot-pink bougainvillea flowed like hot lava over one side. I vaguely wished it grew over the other side too to suit my innate need for symmetry. There was no guard shack, simply a pair of black swinging gates likely activated by a remote control in Mack's vehicle or inside the house somewhere.

She looked over at me. "Here we are. Got a key?"

I climbed out of the car. "It's not Fort Knox. I'm sure we'll find a way in."

She sucked in her breath. "Danny! I'm a cop. I can't break into someone's house."

"Frankie!" I mocked in a high-pitched voice matching hers. "How did you think we were getting in?"

Wilting slightly, she shrugged. "I thought Mack would be home, and we'd just ask to speak to her."

I groaned. "Look, Al's life is in jeopardy. I'm not gonna wait around for the maid to invite us in so we can calmly ask Mack a few questions. We need answers now! We need to find him before these lunatics decide a finger isn't the only thing he should lose."

"I get that, but I could lose my job if I'm caught breaking into the place."

I sighed. "Wait here, then. I'll be right back."

41

Several minutes later, the gates swung open and I strolled through them grinning like a Cheshire cat. I gave Francesca a low bow. "Madame. I'd like to formally invite you inside. No breaking in required."

"Well, that was quick."

"What did I tell you? I'm fast," I said, grinning ear to ear.

Sauntering up to me, she slowed beside me and winked. "You do everything that fast?"

My heart stopped for a split second as a coy smile formed across my face. "Ha-ha, no. Definitely not *everything*. There are certainly a few things I prefer to take my time on."

Her chin jutted out slightly as she looked up at me. "Yeah?"

"Yeah."

Laughter trailed behind Francesca as she walked away. Even that tiny bit of flirting had my testosterone pumping wildly through my veins. Wiping tiny dots of perspiration off my brow with the back of my hand, I shoved the feeling down and followed her up the flower-lined driveway. I led her to the mansion's side garage entrance, which I'd discovered to be unlocked.

"The garage is empty. I'm pretty sure no one is here," I

whispered as we made our way into the house through a long marble-tiled corridor that ended at the kitchen. The kitchen, which was fully equipped with every modern stainless-steel appliance, long granite counters, and antique white cabinets, looked completely spic and span, like no one had cooked anything in it in days. We went from there to the living room. The ocean-facing wall had been fitted with floor-to-ceiling windows and French doors that led out to an oversized deck overlooking the bay. Sleek furnishings made the meager rattan settee in my cottage look like the furnishings of a homeless man.

"Wooow," said Francesca, her eyes wide.

"Yeah," I whispered. "So this is what millions buys a person." I tried not to think about the fact that I could've lived like this if it weren't for the fact that I would soon be giving away my millions to rescue Al and my ex. The fact pained me to no end, but the thought of me and Evelyn having to live life without Al pained me even more.

"Should we split up?" asked Francesca, looking around.

I shook my head. "Oh, hell no. We're sticking together." Not only did I not want something happening to her, but I also didn't want something happening to me, and I figured we were better as a team. "Let's go this way. We'll check all the bedrooms." I pointed towards a long hallway.

It took us a solid fifteen minutes to explore the entire house, bouncing from room to room, each one more impressive than the last. The master suite had been my favorite, as it boasted a full-size hot tub, his-and-hers jetted showers, and walk-in closets the size of my apartment back in Kansas City. When we were done searching the main house, we ended the tour back in the kitchen.

"Now what?" asked Francesca. The disappointment on her face mirrored the disappointment I felt in my heart. I think we'd both been hoping to find Mack, or at least some clue that told us whether or not she'd been Dexter's informant.

"I don't know." Shaking my head, I sighed as I stared out the window at the beautifully serene water in the bay. I pointed at a little cottage-style boathouse just off the pier. "We could check down at the boathouse."

Francesca looked out the window and followed my finger. She brightened. "Oh, for sure. That's where I'd hang out if I had a place like this. Let's go."

We went outside to the deck and took the stairs down to the backyard. Just off the patio at the bottom of the stairs was a carpet of lush green grass. A pool sat between the patio and a small putting green, and a stone path woven with moss led down to the beach. Partway there, the path forked. The left trail led down to the beach while the right trail led to the pier and the boathouse. We took the right fork and soon found ourselves standing in front of the boathouse.

It was a small cottage, about the size of the one I lived in at the Seacoast Majestic, but this cottage was newer, with crisp grey lap siding and white window trim and shutters. Surrounded by green island vegetation and colorful flora with the dock and the turquoise waters behind it, the cottage looked like it should grace the cover of a vacation magazine.

"It's crazy. Their boathouse is nicer than my apartment," said Francesca.

"It's nicer than my resort cottage," I agreed in awe. "Hell, it's nicer than my folks' place back in the States."

We found the door locked, but a quick search under the rocks around the stone path revealed the hide-a-key had not been so cleverly hidden. "Amateurs," I said with a grin, holding up the key.

Inside, the boat house was simply decorated. It was obvious it was used as a beach destination. Sand covered the tile floor, beach blankets were strung out over the furniture, and a big inflatable yellow duck sat staring out the window in the living room. This was the first real sign we'd seen in the entire house that the villa was actually being lived in.

A wall of photographs in the living room caught my eye. "Frankie, check this out."

Framed photographs of family members enjoying various parts of the villa covered the wall. Pictures of what I had to assume were aunts and uncles, cousins and friends sitting in padded Adirondack chairs down at the beach were numerous.

Francesca tapped me on the shoulder. "Danny, check it out."

I looked over her shoulder. A man and a woman holding a champagne bottle stood on the deck of a yacht. She pointed at the photo. "It's a yacht christening."

My eyes were mesmerized by the picture. The yacht looked very familiar. "Do all yachts look alike?" I asked, having never been around them much in my life.

"Some do," she said. "Is that the one you were on?"

"I can't be completely sure, but it really looks like it," I admitted. I pointed to the name printed along the front hull. "*Better Late Than Never.*" My eyes widened as my jaw dropped.

"You recognize that name?"

"Mack mentioned that once. She said it was her aunt's motto."

"You're kidding."

I shook my head as another picture on the wall caught my eye. I zoomed in on it. "Look at this."

"You recognize those girls?"

The photo was of two teenage girls wearing swimsuits. Their hair was wet and their arms were slung casually around each other's shoulders, and they both were cheesing out for the camera. But it wasn't the girls that caught my eye. It was the thing on the wall between them. Between the two faces, a brass rhinoceros bust hanging on the wall photobombed the picture. "I don't know the girls, but something about that rhinoceros bust has set a bell off in my head, and I'm trying to understand why."

And then it hit me.

I sucked in my breath.

"What!"

"When I woke up on the yacht, I was in a stateroom. It was dark, so I had to crawl around to find my way to the door, and at one point, I hit my head on this—this *thing*. I wasn't exactly sure what it was. It had this horn and ears and I..." I wagged my finger at the picture. "It was a rhinoceros."

"This rhinoceros?"

"Wow. Yeah, I think it was *that* rhinoceros. I think that picture was taken on the yacht that I was on, and I think *this* is a picture of that yacht!"

Francesca beamed. "Oh my gosh, Danny. We've got 'em!"

I threw my arms around her excitedly. "We've got 'em!"

When we parted, Francesca took a step back and pulled her cell phone out of her pocket.

"Who are you calling?"

"I'm calling my brothers. They have to have seen this yacht. Now that we have a name and a picture? There's no way they can hide from us. If they're in the waters around the area, someone's bound to have seen them. We're going to find them, Danny! And we're going to bring them home!"

42

SEATED IN FRANCESCA'S SUV IN MACK'S DRIVEWAY, I STARED AT
Francesca expectantly as she hung up her phone. "Well?
What'd they say?" I was hoping that one of her brothers had
seen a yacht called the *Better Late Than Never* riding around the
island and they'd be able to point us to it.

"Solo said he'd do some digging. He knows a lot of people
with boats. If it's out there, he'll find it."

"But he hadn't heard of it?" I felt my body crumple back
against the seat with disappointment.

"No, according to his records, that yacht's never been in his
marina. But there are a lot of other marinas on the island, and
he knows all of those people. He's going to put out some calls.
Don't worry, Danny, he'll find it."

"But what if they don't find it fast enough?" I was beginning to feel like we were never going to catch a break. "What if
they kill Al and Pam?"

"We can't think about that now. We just have to focus on
finding the yacht. It's out there somewhere."

"So what do we do in the meantime?"

Francesca backed out of Mack's driveway and headed back

up the peninsula towards the main part of the island. "I don't know, I—"

My phone rang, making my adrenaline surge. I pulled it out of my pocket and stared down at it. "It's them."

"Answer it, answer it. Set something up. Let's get it going."

I nodded and took a deep, calming breath before answering it. "Drunk here."

"Did you find the little gift I left for you this morning?" asked Dexter's annoyingly evil voice.

"I did, and I wanna speak to Al and Pam!"

"Oh, you think you're in a place to make demands now?" He chuckled. "Daniel, what are you thinking? I hold all the cards now. I have who you're *really* concerned about now."

"Are they alive?"

"Wouldn't you like to know," said Dexter. "But you know what? There's only one way to find out. You need to bring me the rest of that money."

I glanced over at Francesca.

She nodded encouragingly.

"Fine. Where do you want to meet?"

"Meet? Oh, no. Meeting time is long gone. You'll drop off the money. After I've had a chance to inspect it and prove that it's all accounted for, then I might consider returning any spare parts I might have laying around to you."

My anger, which had been set to a low boil, flared. "Spare parts? You motherfuck—"

"Tsk tsk tsk. You better watch your language, Daniel. You wouldn't want to blow your last chance, would you?"

"Listen, there's no way I'm giving you the rest of the seven million dollars without even knowing if Pam or Al are still alive. If I'm only going to get back a bag of body parts, what's the point?"

"It's just a chance you're going to have to take."

I gritted my teeth. If he'd killed Al, I was going to find him and make him pay. "And exactly how in the hell am I supposed to trust you after what you did to Al?"

"*You should have thought about that before double-crossing me, Daniel!*" he hollered. He took a deep breath and seemed to be trying to calm himself. "If you'd done as you were told, none of this would be happening right now."

"But you double-crossed me too!" I argued. "That wasn't Pam in the boat, that was Mack."

"I was going to drop Pam off when it was all said and done and I was sure you'd given me the money, but now…"

"Now *what*? Is Pam alive? Is Al alive?"

"Harbor Street Park in one hour. Be there."

The phone went dead.

I looked over at Francesca. "Harbor Street Park in one hour. Go!"

MACK'S AUNT and uncle's villa was only fifteen minutes from the Seacoast Majestic, so we made a quick pit stop back there to get the money from where I'd hidden it.

"It's around here somewhere," I promised Francesca as we wandered the jungle behind my cottage, carrying a pair of his-and-hers shovels.

"I can't believe you buried it. Who buries seven million dollars, Danny? Someone could've found it!"

"Seriously? *We* can't even find it, and I'm the one that buried it! No one else even knew it was out here. This place doesn't exactly get a lot of traffic, you know."

She sighed and kept her eyes glued to the ground, looking for a mound of recently upended sand and dirt. "You said it's under a big tree, right?"

"Yeah. A big palm tree. There was this lizard there." I poked my shovel into the ground as I continued walking again.

Francesca stopped walking and stared back at me. "Danny! You can't be serious. The lizard was your landmark?"

I straightened and held my arms out wide. "You shoulda seen the size of the thing! I've never seen a lizard so big."

"But, Danny, lizards move. Why would you pick a lizard as a landmark?"

I shrugged. "I don't know. Gut instinct?"

"And who hides seven million dollars in the ground and doesn't draw a map? Even pirates know to draw maps when they bury their treasure."

I grinned at her. "Are you comparing me to a pirate?"

"Aye, Captain!" she said with a laugh.

"Oh my God," I groaned, palming my forehead. "No worries, lassie. I know exactly whar I hid me gold."

"Then get to finding it, Captain Drunk, because we're running out of time." She looked at her watch. "We've only got thirty minutes left to get to the Harbor Street Park."

I sighed and looked out across the jungle. I was sure I'd counted twenty paces from my bedroom window to the tree and then twenty paces to the right. I must have swerved somewhere along the way. It had been dark when I'd buried it, after all.

I backed up and recounted my paces from the tree at more of an angle this time. When I did, I landed next to another tree where an enormous lizard stood, seemingly asleep. Next to him was a pile of fallen palm fronds. I cracked myself over the head with the butt of my hand. "Oh!" I called out to Francesca across the jungle. "I forgot! I covered up the dirt with palm fronds. I found it!"

She jogged over to me and came to a screeching halt when she saw the lizard. "Oh, wow. That *is* a big lizard. I can't believe he's still here."

"I told ya," I said as I used my shovel to move all the debris off the mound. "I had a gut feeling that this was the place to put the money." I began to work at unburying the treasure.

She tipped her head sideways. "This lizard doesn't look so good."

I stopped shoveling for a moment to look at the lizard. "Mmm. Pretty sure that's how lizards look."

"Maybe he's dead?"

I started shoveling again. "You're asking the wrong guy. I have absolutely zero skills in lizard care."

Francesca squatted down and poked a finger into the lizard's side. His whole body tipped over stiffly. "Yeah. He's dead."

An exposed handle in the sand made me smile. "Found it."

"You didn't bury it very deep."

"It was dark when I buried it, and I was in a hurry." I grabbed hold of the handle and gave a tug. Sand fell away as I slung it over my shoulder. "Okay. We got the money. Let's go."

She looked up at me sharply. "But what about the lizard?"

"What about him?"

"He's dead!"

I stared at her like a cow stares at a new gate. "And?"

"Danny! We can't just leave him out here."

I furrowed my brows. "Of course we can. He was dead before we got here and he'll be dead for years to come."

"But he deserves a proper burial. Look at him! He's gotta be at least twenty years old! Something that's been around that long deserves to be properly honored."

"Are you kidding me right now, Frankie? We gotta be at the Harbor Street Park in less than thirty minutes and you wanna give this lizard, whom we've never met before, a proper burial?"

She tipped her head sideways and gave me one of those pleading looks that women do so well. "Please, Danny?"

I was pretty sure no man on earth could resist that look. My shoulders slumped forward. "Okay, how about this? When all of this is over and we're *not* trying to save Al and Pam's life,

I'll come back here with you and we'll give the lizard a proper burial. Deal?"

She looked down at him and sighed. Then she stood up and dusted off her knees. "Deal."

43

THE HARBOR STREET PARK WAS LOCATED IN THE BUSY DOWNTOWN area just across the street from Paradise Elementary School. A fountain sat in the center of the park with six cobblestone sidewalks radiating out from it like rays from the sun. The wedges of grass between the sidewalks housed palm trees, park benches, and picnic tables, and on one end of the park was a swath of children's playground equipment.

Chickens pecked at the ground, roaming the area freely, and a few dog walkers were out, enjoying the morning sun. Around the park, several vagrants claimed benches as their own. Some fed the chickens, others napped. A food truck was parked along the curb. Captain Vinnie's Surf & Turf was painted in scrawling reds, yellows, and blues along the side. The scent of fried fish overpowered the scent of the yellow-and-white frangipanis skirting the park's northern perimeter.

I wandered the sidewalks, the duffle bag of real money now hanging heavily from my shoulder. It was much heavier than the fake bag of money I'd given to ponytail man. At this point in the game, I was fully prepared to do whatever it would take to get Al and Pam back, and that meant finally turning over the money. I gave a skittish glance across the park at the parking lot across the street, where Francesca was seated inside her vehicle. Even though I had pulled my eyes away, I could still feel hers following me as I paced the sidewalks, waiting for the call.

I glanced down at my watch. "Any minute," I whispered under my breath. My stomach was a mess, and my heart beat wildly in my chest. All I could think about was how to get Al back. What would my options be?

The phone finally rang. I sent a furtive glance around the park before answering it, my eyes finally rested on the food truck across the street.

"Drunk here."

"Daniel. Good of you to come."

"I wanna speak to Al."

"Al's unavailable at the moment."

I took four long strides towards the parking lot. "Then I'm afraid I'm not going to be able to play this game with you. I need to know he's all right first." I kept walking.

Dexter was silent for a few beats. When my feet finally hit the outer sidewalk surrounding the park, he sighed. "You are such a pain in my ass, Daniel!"

"It's what I do best," I promised. "Put Al on, or I leave right now and you never see your money."

"Al's not feeling so well right now," said Dexter. "But here, I'll let you talk to someone else."

There was some background static and the next thing I knew, Pam was on the phone. "Danny? Is that you?"

My heart soared. Pam was still alive! "Pam? You're okay?"

"No, I'm freaking out, Danny! They said this is your last chance to give them the money. If they don't get it, they're killing me. They have a friend of yours. Al?"

My knees buckled. I had to fall to a park bench nearby. "Oh my God. Is Al all right? Have you seen him?"

"They cut his finger off, Danny!" she sobbed. "There was so much blood!"

"But is he okay now? Is he alive?"

Pam's voice was shaky. "Y-yeah, he's still alive. He's right here with me. He's knocked out. T-they gave him something."

"I'm gonna do whatever it takes to get the two of you back, Pam."

"Well, that's good to hear, Daniel."

"Let them go!" I hollered. My raised voice garnering a look from a nearby homeless man.

"In time, Daniel. In time. First things first. Turn around."

I stood up and turned around. My heart throbbed against the inside of my chest.

"Follow the sidewalk to the other side of the park. I want you to keep walking until you get to the Harbor Street Pier. Understand?"

"I'm not familiar with this area. How far is it?"

"It's only about a five-minute walk," he said. "When you get there, I'll call you."

The line went dead.

Fuck.

The adrenaline in my veins raced wildly out of control as my anger seethed in the pit of my stomach. I wanted to lay a fist into Dexter's face so badly that my hand ached.

I threw as casual of a glance as I could muster over my shoulder towards Francesca. She was still seated in her car. My hands shook as I looked down at my phone and turned on the eavesdropping app once again, then slid my phone into the front pocket of my shirt.

"I'm headed to the Harbor Street Pier. He said it's only about a five-minute walk," I said aloud as if I were talking to myself.

I took off towards the pier.

My long legs made the walk take less than three minutes. There was a parking lot that faced the water with a dock for putting in small fishing boats. I stood at the end of the pier and looked around. There were a handful of vehicles in the parking lot. Each had an attached empty boat trailer. The water looked calm, but there wasn't a single boat in sight.

My phone rang again.

"Yeah?"

"Finally, you're following directions."

My eyes scanned the area as I turned in circles. Wherever he was watching me from, I couldn't see.

"What now?"

"In a hurry?" Dexter chuckled.

"I want Pam and Al back. Al's missing a finger. He needs to be taken to a hospital."

"Mmm," purred Dexter. "All right. Do you see that brick building to your right?"

I glanced in the direction Dexter was talking about. "The bathroom?"

"Yes. Leave the money under the sink in the men's room. Then head back to the Harbor Street Park. I'll call you with further directions."

The phone went dead again.

I crumpled. I hated the idea of leaving seven million dollars in a stall in a park men's room. But I felt like I had no other choice. I followed his directions and opened the door. "Hello?" my voice echoed off the walls.

There was no answer.

I put the money under the dingy porcelain sink's corroded plumbing and then sprinted out of there and towards the park. "I'm headed back to the Harbor Street Park, Frankie. He's going to give me directions to get Pam and Al when I get there. Be ready to pick me up."

My legs carried me as fast as they could back to the park. When I got there, I almost couldn't breathe I was so winded. Doubled over, I sucked in air while waiting for my phone to ring. Finally, it rang. "Okay. I'm going to need some time to go through the money to make sure you haven't fucked with it again. You have exactly thirty minutes from now to get to the courtesy phone in the lobby of the Seacoast Majestic. I will call you there with the exact whereabouts of your friends."

When the phone went dead, I raced towards the parking lot across the street. I could see Francesca behind the wheel. I waved at her wildly.

She pulled the car into the street and I jumped inside, barely having time to slam my door before she took off again.

"We have thirty minutes to get to the courtesy phone in the Seacoast Majestic lobby. He's going to give us the location of Pam and Al from there. Let's go!"

44

WHILE WORKING THE FRONT COUNTER, MARIPOSA AND ALICIA didn't even pretend to try and hide the fact that they had their eyes glued to Francesca and me as we leaned against the wall, flanking either side of the courtesy phone in the lobby. It was funny; I'd worked for the Seacoast Majestic for almost two full months and this was the first time I'd even realized there was a phone in the lobby. And now here I was, waiting for one of the most important phone calls of my life in front of it.

I glanced down at my watch. "He should've called by now." We'd already been standing there for twenty minutes, but it had been a full fifty minutes since I'd last spoken to Dexter and he'd only given us thirty minutes to get there. It wasn't like him to be this late with a phone call. My stomach twisted nervously.

Francesca rolled from her shoulder to her back against the wall. "He said he was checking the money out first. Maybe it's just taking longer than he thought."

"Like it really takes that long to flip through some stacks of bills?" I shook my head. I took a couple steps forward, rolled my head around on my neck, bent at the waist and bounced slightly, touching my toes. I wanted to make the gnawing in the pit of my stomach go away. "No. Something's not right. I can feel it in my gut."

"That's just nerves," she said. "I feel it too."

"It's not nerves. He should've called by now. I think he's double-crossing me again." Adrenaline pulsed through my veins. I wanted to come unglued on Dexter. I wanted to put my fist into his face so badly that I could almost feel the bristle of his beard against my knuckles. "Can you call Solo and see if he's heard anything about the yacht? They have the money now. We can't let them get out of local waters."

I didn't have to ask her twice. Francesca pulled her phone from the back pocket of her shorts and dialed. "Hey, Solo, it's me. I'm just checking to see if you've heard anything about that yacht?" She spent the next thirty seconds uh-huhing, ohhing, and okaying him.

When she finally hung up I stared at her. "Well?"

"He said he was just about to call me. The yacht's been spotted. You were right. They're headed out to sea."

"Oh my God," I breathed, my head rolling back on my shoulders. "This is really, really bad. What if they're taking Al and Pam with them? That is, if they aren't already dead. What are we gonna do?"

"Solo's got us covered. He's already spoken to Miguel and the rest of the guys. They're bringing the boat back in. He said they'll have it fueled up and ready to go by the time we get there."

"Get there?"

She nodded. "They're giving us a ride out to the yacht. We're going to follow them. They said they want to help save Al."

Relief flooded my body. I threw my arms around Francesca's shoulders and buried my face against the top of her head. "Oh, Frankie. Thank you!"

"It's Solo and the boys you need to thank. You still owe them a boat, you know."

I nodded. "I know, I know. I haven't forgotten. We'll figure something out." Then I looked at the phone. "But what about the phone? We can't leave. What if they really do call?"

"Danny, we don't have time to stay. They'll be too far away for us to catch up with if we stay."

My eyes glanced over at Mari and Alicia. I had no other choice. Without another word to Francesca, I strode over to the counter. Both of the women pretended to suddenly be busy when they saw me coming.

"Mari, may I have a word with you, please?"

She gave me a courtesy smile. "Sure."

I strode over to the end of the counter, leaving Francesca to watch from afar. Mari followed me to the end of the counter. "Mari, I know we haven't always seen eye to eye about everything. But I have an emergency situation happening right now, and I could *really* use your help."

Mari's head bobbed. "I knew there was something going on. Does it have to do with Mr. Becker?"

Pursing my lips, I inhaled deeply. As I let it out, I nodded. "It does. But I need you not to say anything to his wife yet. I'm trying to help him, and telling *anyone* could make things worse. Do you understand?"

She nodded.

"You won't tell anyone?"

"I swear, Drunk. You have my word."

I had no choice but to trust her. "Thank you. I'm waiting for a very important phone call on that phone. I don't know if it will come through or not, but I have to leave right now. If that phone rings, will you answer it?"

Her brows furrowed. "Of course."

"If the person on the other end says anything, you have to call me immediately with the information. Okay?"

"Yeah."

I reached across the counter and squeezed Mariposa's hand. "Thank you, Mari."

"You're welcome, Drunk."

I gave her a tight smile and started to walk away before she stopped me.

"Hey, Drunk."

"Yeah?"

"I'm really sorry I opened my mouth about your money."

"I know, Mari. For what it's worth, I probably deserved it. And I accept your apology." I turned around and strode towards Francesca, hooking my arm through her elbow. "Come on. We gotta go save Al and Pam!"

FRANCESCA and I were met at the marina by a line of five angry-looking Cruz brothers. Each of their faces were set rigidly, only softening to give their sister a nod hello.

"We're not doing this for you," said Solo stiffly as we joined the party.

Glancing across the angry faces, I nodded humbly. "I figured as much."

"We're doing it for our sister, and for the old man that you were with the other day."

"Al," I said, reminding them that the old man had a name.

Solo seethed in my direction, one brow lifted ever so slightly. His jaw clenched when he spoke again. "Yes, Al."

"Right. Well, thank you. I appreciate it, and obviously, Al will appreciate knowing that you were involved in his rescue."

All the Brothers Cruz stared at me.

I shifted in my boat shoes. Clearing my throat, I looked behind me at Francesca. "Well, I suppose we should get going, huh? We don't wanna let them get too big of a lead on us." I took a step towards the idling boat.

Solo put a hand on my chest to stop me.

I glanced sideways at him.

"Are you sleeping with my sister?"

"Solo!" breathed Francesca. "That's none of your business!"

Solo closed his eyes. He could have been meditating, but I was pretty sure he was just trying to keep from ripping my head off. "Panchita!" he countered. "It is very much my business. I don't want this joke of a man in your life."

Joke of a man? I winced. I had to admit, that one stung a little bit. I mean, I knew I didn't have my shit together, but joke of a man? I shook my head. I wasn't *that* bad, was I? "Don't worry, Solo. Your sister's too good for me. I'm completely aware of that fact."

His head bobbed seriously. "Yes, she is."

"I have too much respect for her as a woman to subject her to someone like myself. I swear."

"Good." His frame relaxed slightly.

"For right now, anyway."

Solo's eyes narrowed as he looked at me. "Excuse me?"

I shrugged. "I can't say that if I ever got around to cleaning up my act, I might not ask your sister out on a date."

Solo peeled his squinty eyes off me and focused them on his sister. When she didn't say anything to counter that, he looked at me again.

"Of course, at that point, if she wanted to accept my request, she wouldn't have to ask your permission. You know that, right?"

Through gritted teeth, he growled at me. "I know Francesca. Her family's approval means everything to her."

"I believe that," I said in agreement. "And if Francesca and I ever decided we wanted to date, I know that I'd be a good enough man at that point that I'd get her family's approval. But her deciding whether or not she wants to date me will be her decision to make. And her decision alone."

Solo's jaw clenched tighter.

Despite my rapidly pounding heart, I patted him on the shoulder. "But don't worry. I know I have a lot of work to do on myself before I get to that point. There's plenty of time for me to convince you to like me."

I strode past Solo and the rest of the Cruz brothers. Aside from Solo, the rest of the men wore expressions of surprise and almost shock on their faces. As I boarded the boat, I heard Francesca's feet on the dock behind me. Then, slowly, the sound of her brothers' casual chatter filled in the silence. I'd managed to stand up to Solo. And if I hadn't known any better, I might've thought they all respected me just a little bit more because of it.

IT WASN'T until five o'clock that afternoon that Rico, standing at the bow on the foredeck, finally pointed out at the horizon. "There she is!"

Sure enough, a yacht dotted the distant horizon.

"You're sure it's them?"

"It's them all right," said Solo, sitting next to Miguel at the helm. "We've had multiple sightings reporting back to us."

Eager anticipation bubbled up inside of me. I couldn't wait to get my hands on Dexter and make him pay for what he'd done to Al and Pam, and to find out what role Mack had played in the whole duplicitous scheme.

Francesca turned to me then. "We need a plan."

"The plan is to save Al and Pam!" I said, my hands flaring out in front of me. "What more of a plan do we need?"

She shook her head. "Danny, it's not just about grabbing those two and throwing them onto our boat. They could have a small army up there. We need to be prepared."

"We won't let you go up there alone," said Diego. Reaching down to a bag lying on the deck behind him, he pulled out a rifle. "We're going with you."

"Oh, you don't have to—" I began, my head shaking determinedly. This was my fight, not his. I couldn't have any more people getting hurt because of me.

Francesca held a hand up to my mouth to silence me. "Thank you, D., We'll gratefully accept your help."

I stared at her in surprise.

"Any idea how many guys we gotta worry about on that boat?" asked Solo.

"Five men for sure. One woman," I said. "Smitty's a big guy. Fists the size of cantaloupes. He's the one that laid into my face. There's another guy with a ponytail. I'm pretty sure he's the one that laid into Pam."

Beto's jaw tightened. "Any man that lays hands on a woman needs to have his ass whooped."

"You're certainly welcome to whoop any of their asses," I said with a smirk. "Although I'd like to be the one to wipe the smug smile off their boss's face."

"You can have the boss," promised Beto. "I'll be watching for anyone with a ponytail."

"Deal."

Miguel pointed at the yacht. "It's going to be hard to get close without being spotted. And I don't think we're going to be able to get anyone on board while they're moving."

"You can't just cruise up behind them and throw a grappling hook over the swim platform and walk on or something?" I asked.

Miguel chuckled. "Maybe in a James Bond movie they do some crazy shit like that, but no, man. They're going pretty fast, and the prop wash on a yacht of that size could swamp us."

"So what do we do?" I asked, feeling the excitement I'd just felt slowly draining from my body.

Rico pointed up ahead at the sky. "I think we're about to get some weather tonight."

"Even more reason to catch up to the yacht and board it now before a storm hits!"

Miguel glanced ahead at Rico. "Hey, Rico. What would you do if you were the captain of that yacht and a big storm is about to hit and it's nightfall?"

Rico shrugged. "Well, in their case, they're trying to sneak out of the area. So if I was sure I wasn't being followed, I might find a nice little isolated island cove and hunker down until morning. How 'bout you?"

Miguel nodded. "Same."

I stared at Miguel, wide-eyed. "You want us to hang back until dark?"

"Would make it a heck of a lot safer climbing aboard if the ship's sitting still," said Solo. "It'd be what I'd do."

"I get that," I said, nodding in agreement, "but Al and Pam could be dead by then!"

"Listen, Drunk, if your friends are still alive right now, they'll still be alive by nighttime. If they're dead, they'll still be dead by nighttime. I don't think waiting them out is going to make a difference."

"*If* they're dead?" My mouth gagged on the words. I let out a sputter. "They can't be dead."

Solo shrugged. "There's no way of knowing. But the one thing I do know is, if we catch up to that yacht while the sun's out, there's a very high probability that they're gonna see us following them. That doesn't make for a very good surprise entrance."

I couldn't disagree with him there. "But what about a storm? Then we're dealing with the storm too."

"We'll be fine," said Miguel.

"Yeah, my brothers and I have been through all sorts of storms. We're pros," said Diego proudly.

I glanced over at Francesca. "Well. According to you, you're running this operation. What do you think?"

"I think it's best to trust the experts," she said, looking up at me. Her big brown eyes sparkled in the sun.

The big breath I'd been holding exploded out of my mouth in a loud puh sound. "All right. Fine. I'll trust the experts. Just tell me you know what you're talking about."

Miguel chuckled. "No worries there. We know what we're talking about."

45

TRUE TO THEIR PREDICTION, A STORM HIT THE CARIBBEAN SEA JUST after dark that evening. Lightning flared brightly in the distance, and the air around us erupted with a rolling baritone of thunder. The dark clouds drowned out the moonlight. And as the wind whipped up, the waters became choppier and choppier.

Rico pointed up ahead at the yacht we'd been tailing from afar. "I was right!" he hollered over the wind and the ocean spray. "They're mooring up in that little cove off Starfish Island."

Miguel smiled. "What'd we tell you?"

I threw my hands out. "What can I say? You were right."

"Damn straight I was right. I'm always right where the water's concerned."

"So, what do we do? Motor over there and climb aboard?"

"No way," shouted Diego. "If they're keeping an eye on their radar, they'll see us coming in this boat. No, we'll moor up far enough away that we won't be detected. We've got a little inflatable dinghy I can take us over there in."

"I'll stay here," said Miguel from the helm, "and man the

boat while you all go looking for Al and Pam. Then if you get into any trouble, I can race up there and get you back into the boat quicker."

A streak of lightning cracked open the dark sky, and a kaboom followed it. Then the rain started.

"We better hurry!" shouted Solo. "This storm could get really bad."

"Diego and I will go get the dinghy ready. Gather whatever supplies we're bringing along," shouted Rico.

"Supplies?" I asked.

Solo strode over to the bag that his brother had extracted a rifle from earlier and took out a second one. "We came prepared." He looked at me and then his sister. "You two just worry about finding your friends. Rico, Beto, Diego, and I will handle whoever gets in your way."

Francesca reached out and squeezed her brother's arm. "Thanks, Solo."

Twenty minutes later, the group of us sat in the small inflatable dinghy in the water. Trees shrouded our view of the *Better Late Than Never*, but we could see the lights shining from the vessel from between the branches. The rain pelted us all, soaking us down to our underwear. My hair was matted to my face as we motored away towards the yacht using only the dinghy's small outboard motor against the rocky waves.

Each of the men sat stoically in the little skiff, their rifles in hand. Rico was the only one who carried a speargun instead of a rifle. Francesca quietly pulled her Glock 19 from her appendix holster and checked the magazine before reholstering it. I fingered the Ruger LC9 she'd let me borrow. I had no holster, and I refused to blow off one or both of my testicles by shoving it down my pants, so I just had to keep ahold of it.

Proper gun handling was one of the few things I'd actually paid attention to in the academy, as my instructor had been a well-regarded "gun guy" and had been able to recount many instances where a lack of proper training had resulted in one of two things. A, the owners forever walked with a limp; or B, they were unable to procreate. And that was just not something that I wanted to see happen.

The waves made the journey more difficult, but we were close enough that it didn't take long to get to the back end of the yacht. The sheer size of the larger vessel provided a bit of cover from the raging storm. Rico and Beto worked quickly to lash the two boats together and to make sure that they were secured enough that they weren't going anywhere.

Solo's feet touched down on the yacht's swim platform first. He leaned forward and reached a hand out for Francesca to take. Rico and Beto didn't even give me time to help her onto the ship, as they both pushed and Solo pulled. When she was securely on the back end of the yacht, the rest of us followed, stepping from the dinghy to the swim platform. Solo opened the cockpit's knee-high transom door, and the group of us rushed to take cover against the cockpit's fiberglass hull.

The whole process of getting on board happened in complete silence. Only the sound of the storm booming around us could be heard. At the bottom of the stairs up to the aft deck, with his back to the wall, Solo held his rifle at the ready and motioned his brothers to hold steady. He wanted to take the lead.

I grimaced. This wasn't the way it was supposed to happen. This was *my* battle. I needed to take the lead. I slid from the back of the line to the front. Solo put a hand on my shoulder to stop me from going up the stairs. I gave him a look of appreciation but climbed the handful of steps to the aft deck anyway. I had to find Pam and Al.

Stealthily, I slid across the fiberglass sole, to the stainless-steel-framed sliding glass doors facing out over the stern of the ship. Solo followed behind me, both of our backs now pressed against the cabin's shell. Inside, it was brightly lit, and the heavy beat of music trickled out through the doors. I held the Ruger in my leading hand and slid forward so my back was now against the glass. In time with the thunder booming around me, I slid the door open. When I heard no objections, I began to move.

Swallowing hard and leading with my gun, I stepped around the corner so that I was now in full view of the saloon. A large U-shaped sofa took up much of the space on the port side and a shorter three-person sofa on the starboard side. There were built-in counters and a wooden entertainment center with a flat-screen TV. On it, a news reporter in a navy suit relayed stock prices.

Forward of the saloon was a round glass dining table with a buffet and a china cabinet. Bottles of liquor, glass tumblers, and plates of partially eaten food were scattered around the table. Across from the table on the starboard side was a set of stairs that led down to the staterooms below. I remembered being led up those same stairs with a gun to my back only a few days prior. I'd seen enough of the dining room and saloon to know that there was a galley straight ahead of us, and there we'd find stairs that led up to the top deck. The same top deck where, days earlier, Dexter had had his goons toss me overboard and then leave me to sink or swim.

Though the lights and television were on and music played from somewhere, the long room was empty. But when a break in the storm silenced the thunder, we heard the sound of feet pounding on the sole above us. I had a strong feeling the party was up there.

I turned to look at Solo and Francesca, who were right behind me. I jerked my head towards the ceiling. They both nodded. They'd heard it too. Though I knew Dexter and his goons were likely celebrating their victory on the top deck, the people I really wanted to see were more likely being held in the lower deck's staterooms. With my gun at the ready, I padded across the polished teak flooring, leaving water dripping in my wake, being careful not to make any noise to alert anyone of our presence.

I peered over the staircase railing and down into the lower compartment. I couldn't see anyone, but that didn't mean someone wasn't sitting in the little landing area below. I held my breath and slowly descended the stairs. Solo was right behind me. When my head sank low enough, I was relieved to find the landing area empty.

Wasting no time, I rushed towards the room that I'd seen Pam in days earlier and flung open the door. A lump of a blonde woman lay unmoving on the bed. My heart stopped beating for a moment. Was she dead? I rushed to her side while the rest of the crew all slid into the stateroom. Diego, bringing up the rear, shut the door behind us.

"Oh my God," I breathed. "Pam?" I rolled her limp, lifeless body over. Her face was even more swollen and bruised than it had been before. Guilt flooded my body. Had they finally killed her. What the hell had I done?

Francesca and her brothers' eyes widened when they saw her battered and bloodied face.

Beto stared at the door. "These guys aren't getting away with this," he said, his jaw clenched tightly and the hand that didn't carry his rifle squeezed into a fist. "If someone did this to my wife or my sister or one of my daughters, they wouldn't live to see the light of day."

"Is she alive?" asked Solo.

Cupping her jaw, I shook her lightly. "Pam?"

And then I heard a tiny sigh, like a gasp for air. It was barely audible, but I'd heard it.

"Pam!"

"Danny…" she whispered through pale, chapped lips.

"Yeah, Pam. It's Danny. I'm here. We're gonna get you outta here!" Rage at what they'd done to her boiled my blood.

"Oh, Danny!" Slowly she began to awaken.

I tried to pull her from the bed, but she was chained.

Without a word, Francesca's brothers all knelt to the floor and began to work on her bindings.

"Pam, where's Al? Do you know?" I asked.

She shook her head listlessly. "I don't know. I-I… I think they gave me something. I think they gave him something too. My head hurts."

Francesca shook her head. "We've got to get her to a hospital, Danny."

From the floor, Rico looked up at me. "They've got her chained to the bed, and the bed is attached to the floor. We can't budge it, and we don't have any tools. We're gonna have to shoot it off."

"But they'll hear us!" I countered. "They can't know we're here. We still have to find Al and get him off the boat."

"We don't have a choice," said Solo. "She needs medical assistance. We don't have time to go looking for the key to her cuffs. We have to get her off this boat now!"

"Al needs medical assistance too," I countered. "They cut off his fucking finger!"

"We'll wait for another bolt of lightning and time the thunder," said Solo. "It's our only chance to get her out of here."

I stared down at Pam and then looked up at Francesca and her brothers. If this went wrong, we could very well be sentencing the whole group to disastrous consequences.

Francesca put a hand on my arm. "It's our only choice, Danny. We don't have any other way to get the chains off her."

I sighed. "All right. We need to be ready to run." I kneeled down to scoop her up.

Rico shook his head. He shoved me out of the way and handed me his speargun. "I'll take her back to the dinghy. You've gotta find Al."

Pam's face broke out into a panic, and she practically climbed me, grabbing me around the neck and squeezing as tightly as her weak arms would allow. "Danny, don't leave me!" she begged.

Gently, I unleashed my head from her terrified grip. "Pam,

this is my friend Rico, all right? He's gonna take good care of you, I promise. He won't let anything happen."

She panted wildly. "Danny, you have to come with me. I'm so scared they're going to kill me!"

When Rico had her scooped up in his arms, I pressed the Ruger into his hands and squeezed his shoulder.

"I know you're scared, Pam, but you're in good hands," I promised.

"He's right," Rico agreed. "I'm not going to let anything happen to you. Okay?"

Though she began to sob, she nodded through her tears. "O-kay," she cried.

Before anyone had time to discuss the getaway plan, a flash of light lit up the sky outside of the porthole in Pam's stateroom.

Solo sighted in his rifle, aiming at the foot of the built-in bed where the chain was wrapped around the leg. "Everyone get back."

When the boom fired in the sky, Solo fired. The bullet glanced off the side of the chain and dug a hole into the sole of the ship.

"Shit!" he cursed.

But almost immediately after, another strike of lightning flashed past the porthole, followed by another boom of thunder. This time, he nailed the target, and the chain link exploded open.

"Hurry!" said Rico, wanting to bolt to the door. "Someone could've heard the shots. We gotta get outta here."

Solo and I worked together to unwrap the chain from the bed, but it was still attached to the iron cuffs around her wrists. I piled the chain onto her stomach. "You've gotta hang on to these, Pam. Don't let them fall while he's running, all right?"

Her head bobbed wildly as tears coursed down her cheeks.

"Let's go," said Francesca, rushing towards the door. She opened it to find a surly Smitty standing in the doorway.

"So I did hear something!" he snarled, pointing his gun at her. He reached forward and, grabbing a fistful of Francesca's hair, jerked her around into a headlock. He pressed the muzzle of his gun against her temples. "Looks like I got me a room full of dead guys."

46

WE ALL TURNED OUR WEAPONS ON SMITTY.

"Let her go, Smitty," I growled, aiming the speargun Rico had given me in his direction.

With his arm still wrapped around Francesca's neck, Smitty released his hold on her hair. With his free hand, he racked his gun, then pressed it harder into her temple.

Francesca's head dipped sideways. A tiny grunting sound escaped the back of her throat as her eyes closed.

"Weapons on the bed," he growled.

My pulse surged. If anything happened to Francesca, I didn't know what I'd do.

Solo's jaw tightened. Rifle drawn, he took a cautious step towards Smitty as the rest of us threw our guns to the bed as instructed. "You shoot my sister, and I shoot you."

Smitty grinned and pulled the gun off of Francesca's head and aimed it at Solo. "Well, then, I guess you'll just have to be the first one that I shoot."

Solo cocked his rifle and tipped his head sideways slightly, staring at Smitty down the barrel of his gun. "Take your best shot, *cabrón*."

Francesca's hands shot forward, palms facing us. "Solo,

no." But before anyone could shoot, she smacked both of her hands against Smitty's, knocking the gun loose. It went clattering to the floor and slid beneath the bed. In one smooth step, Francesca pivoted around and hammer-fisted him in the throat.

Shocked, Smitty's eyes bulged as he grabbed his throat, gasping for air.

But she didn't stop there. Francesca grabbed hold of his arm and hip-tossed the barrel of a man to the floor. His back hit the floor with a thud. Then, still holding his arm, she dropped into an arm bar and heel-kicked him in the chin, momentarily dazing him.

"Holy shit," I murmured.

Her brothers and I all stared at her in stunned amazement as she climbed to her feet again. She'd no sooner recovered from her defensive move than Smitty tried to raise himself to his elbows.

"Panchita! Watch out!" hollered Solo, pointing at the man behind her.

Francesca spun around. Bouncing on one foot, she stomped her heel into his jaw, knocking him completely unconscious this time.

With Smitty now down for the count, we stared at Francesca. All our mouths gaped open like we were members of the asthmatic mouth-breathers' club.

A slow grin poured across my face. I suddenly felt like raising her arm up and declaring her the winner by first-round knockout. I'd never seen a woman do anything so unbelievably cool. In another time and place, that might've been the match that lit my candle and then went on to burn the whole fucking house down.

"Panchita! Where did you learn to do that?" asked Solo, his face full of shock.

"Yeah, sis. We had no idea you had that in you," breathed Diego.

"There's a lot of things you don't know about me." She grinned while readjusting her ponytail. "I told you I could handle myself."

"Yeah, but we had no reason to believe you," he said, still stunned.

Wide-eyed, I stepped over Smitty's limp body towards the door. I chuckled. "Looks like you got a reason now."

"Yeah, it does," said Beto, giving his sister a smile. "Impressive."

"Thanks, but we really need to get upstairs and find Al before someone else realizes we're on this boat."

"But what about him?" asked Rico. Still carrying Pam in his arms, he gave Smitty a tap with his boot.

Solo nodded. "Yes, we should probably secure him." He patted his shirt and pants. "I don't have any rope on me, though."

Francesca stepped forward and pulled a bag of zip ties from her back pocket. She handed them to her brother. "What is it that my big brother always says? By failing to prepare, you're preparing to fail?" With a hand on her hip, she shot him a wink.

A slow smile crept across Solo's face. "Maybe I've underestimated you, Panchita."

"I could have told you that." She pretended to think about it for a second, tapping a finger against her chin. "Oh, wait. Seems like I already did."

Solo sighed. "So you did."

Francesca pointed at her brother. "I saved your life, Solo. I think you owe me one."

He nodded, resigned to the truth. His sister had indeed saved *his* life. "So I do."

Diego stepped forward then and took the zip ties from Solo. "Listen, I'll take care of this guy. You guys go get Al. I'll be up when I've got him secured."

I patted Diego on the back. "Thanks, man. All right, guys,

let's move out." I led the group out the door, though the corridor, and back up the stairs to the saloon. When I was sure that the coast was clear, I motioned to Rico, and he followed me up, carrying Pam in his arms.

"Go, go, go," I said quietly as he dashed past towards the aft deck. Then I turned and gestured towards Francesca, Solo, and Beto to follow me to the galley and the stairs that would lead up to the top deck.

As soon as I turned the corner into the galley, I ran into the tall ponytailed man that had abducted Pam from the resort. Behind him, seated around the L-shaped table beneath the large forward-facing windows, were the two monstrous guards I'd seen the last time I'd been on board.

"What the fuck?" said the ponytailed man, clearly shocked to see us. "Where the hell did you come from?"

I pointed to the air behind him. "He invited us."

When ponytail man turned to look, I gave him my best right cross, sending him stumbling backwards further into the kitchen.

The two big guards immediately jumped to their feet, but my backups behind me had their guns drawn.

"Don't move," said Solo.

The two guards' hands instinctively went up.

Ponytail man stood back up, holding his jaw. "Ahh, is that all ya got?"

Beto took a step towards him. "Is this the tough guy that likes to beat on women?"

"That's the guy," I said.

Beto nodded at me without peeling his eyes off of the ponytailed man. "We'll take it from here. You guys go find Al."

"He's all yours." I reached back and pulled Francesca towards the stairs. Seconds later, the distinct smack of flesh on flesh echoed in the galley, followed by the thud of a body hitting the floor.

47

NO SOONER HAD MY HEAD CROSSED THE THRESHOLD TO THE TOP deck than I heard Dexter's crackly voice calling out across the room. "Well, hello, Daniel. So good of you to join us. I must say, I'm more than a little surprised to see you here. You're more tenacious than Mack gave you credit for." He tipped his head towards the sofa across the room, where Mack and Al were seated.

Al's eyes were closed, and his head bobbed forward slightly. His right hand lay across his lap, bandaged in a blood-soaked white cotton wrap, and his shirt was drenched in blood. His other arm was slung across the back of the sofa. He looked like he'd been through hell. I could've crawled out of my skin, I was so furious. I wanted to leap across the room and scoop Al up and get him to an emergency room, but Mack sat to the right of him, aiming a gun at his head.

"You motherfucker! What did you do to Al?" I bellowed at Dexter.

"It's not what *I* did to Al. It's what *you* did to Al. You weren't following directions, Daniel. I had to send you a warning that you'd heed."

My eyes zeroed in on Mack then. "You bitch, I knew it was you."

"Oh, Drunk. It's nothing personal," said Mack, a smile curling the sides of her mouth into a smarmy grin.

"Nothing personal? You let your goons take Al's fucking finger!"

"That wasn't personal either," she said with a shrug. "I told you you should've handed over the money to my brother."

"Your brother!" I bellowed. "This asshat Harry Potter wannabe is *your brother*?"

Mack's smile vanished as she turned the gun on Francesca then. "Make fun of my brother one more time, and I bury a bullet in your new girlfriend's head."

I held my hands out in front of myself. "Whoa! Whoa! Mack! She's not my new girlfriend!"

"As if I believe you. You've got a real problem bouncing from woman to woman. You know that, Drunk?"

I nodded. "Yeah, I know that. I'm working on it. Put the fucking gun down, Mack."

She turned the gun back to Al's temple. "You know, I do kind of feel bad about getting him involved. Mr. Becker's always been nice to me."

"Then what the fuck were you thinking?"

She furrowed her brows. "I was thinking seven million dollars in my bank account would provide a much better lifestyle than being a stripper in Vegas for the rest of my life."

"But you've got a fucking gorgeous mansion and a yacht, for crying out loud. Why the hell do you need seven measly million dollars?"

"Duh, haven't you figured it out yet? That's not our aunt and uncle's villa. Our aunt and uncle live in a trailer in West Virginia. The villa and the yacht belong to some shmuck who thinks he's my sugar daddy. He said I could crash at his villa while he takes his wife on a European vacation. Who knew his offer included the use of his yacht?" She giggled. "He sure didn't."

"But now my sister and I want our *own* villa and yacht. And that's where you came in, Daniel. When my sister mentioned that one of her new coworkers, this idiotic manwhore, was worth seven million dollars, we knew we had to figure out a way to get our hands on that money."

I shook my head. "But I don't understand. How'd you even know about Pam? You couldn't have possibly known that she was gonna show up at the resort. *I* didn't even know she was gonna show up at the resort."

Mack laughed. "I didn't know about Pam. My plan was just to sleep with you, get you to marry me and then take your money. But then, lo and behold, Pam showed up. I thought kidnapping her and demanding ransom sounded a hell of a lot easier than trying to convince you to marry me."

"You were going to convince me to marry you?" I said, astounded.

"I know. You would've been a lucky man. It would've been a win-win, honestly. I would've gotten your money, and you would've gotten to be married to me."

I rolled my eyes. "Oh, please! I wouldn't have married you if my life depended on it! You were a distraction. A flavor of the week. Sorry to break it to you, little girl, but men don't marry flavors of the week."

Mack pursed her lips and pushed her hair back over one shoulder.

Nothing made me happier than to see that I'd wounded her pride after everything she'd put all of us through.

"Well, I admit, it might have taken me a while, but I would've gotten there eventually. Which is why, when Pam showed up, it sounded like a much faster plan just to kidnap your old fiancée and hold her for ransom. But you *fucking lied to me* and told me you still loved her."

"Oh, let's talk about who fucking lied to who, shall we?" I bellowed.

Mack waved a hand in the air dismissively. "Oh, Drunk. Can't we let bygones be bygones?" She patted the green duffle bag on the sofa next to her. "After all, I've gotten what I came for. I think I can finally forgive you."

I grimaced. "Oh, gee, thanks."

She smiled. "My pleasure."

Dexter stood up and looked at Mack. "I don't know about you two, but I've had enough of this chitchat."

Mack rolled her eyes. "Whatever."

He turned his gaze on me and Francesca. "Daniel, you and your new girlfriend have hitched a ride on my boat long enough. I think it's time for a repeat of the other day. Don't you?" He smiled, his eyes widening with glee. "I actually never thought I'd get to say it again. Of course, this time there's not going to be any boat waiting for you." He pouted out his bottom lip. "Only sharks."

Francesca looked at me, worry in her eyes.

Dexter put one hand on his chest, and with the other pointed towards the ocean, like he was fucking Lewis and Clark, he said, "Now I think it's time for you to walk the pl—"

I pulled the speargun out, and before he could finish his sentence, I fired. The spear soared through the air, piercing through his hand and sending blood splattering against the back wall.

Mack whipped her gun around at me as her brother screamed in agony.

"Ahhhhhhhh! My finger! You fucker!" Dexter screamed.

That was when the lights went out. The room went dark. Thunder growled around us as lightning flashed out on the horizon. Through the thunder and Dexter's wild screams, I could hear the sound of a scuffle breaking out on the sofa across the room. And then a shot rang out. I heard the bullet whistle through the air and shatter the window behind me. I tackled Francesca to the floor.

Dexter continued to holler. "You fucker! You shot my fucking finger off!"

"You took my brother's finger, you asshole!" shouted Mack. I could hear her moving across the room towards Dexter.

"A finger for a finger, you piece of shit!" I yelled back, unsure of what was happening.

"It's an eye for an eye, Drunk," shouted Al from somewhere near the sofa.

My eyes still hadn't readjusted to the lack of light. I couldn't see anything and was shocked to hear Al's voice. "Al?" I breathed. "You want me to take his *eye* too?"

"Drunk, I'm gonna kill you, you motherfucker," shouted Mack.

"It's gonna be pretty hard to kill him when I've got your gun," said Al.

"Al? You have her gun?"

"Yeah, Drunk. Here, catch!"

"Al, no!" I heard Al's grunt as he tossed the gun across the room in my general direction. I ducked. The gun smacked against something hard behind me and bounced off things on its way to the floor. A shot rang out, causing to me to duck again. "Shit! Frankie, are you all right?"

I felt Frankie move next to me. "Yeah, I'm fine, Danny. Hurry, get the gun."

I crawled forward, feeling around on the floor, searching blindly. "For crying out loud, Al, who throws a fucking loaded gun?"

I could hear Mack on the other side of the room, rifling through Dexter's desk now.

I patted around to the right of me, still unable to find the weapon Al had tossed.

"It's on your other side, Drunk. Don't you see it?"

"No, I don't fucking see it. I can't see shit."

"I can see it. It's right there. Move your hand."

My hand moved. Still nothing.

"No, move your other hand. Your left hand."

I followed Al's directions, patting the floor. Suddenly the lights turned on.

I spun around to see Mack standing behind Dexter's desk, holding a revolver on me. Dexter lay on the floor behind the desk, seemingly unconscious.

"You always were one step behind, Drunk. When are you gonna get your shit together?" Mack shot me a smarmy grin, then hoisted the bag of money up onto her shoulder and cocked her gun. "Now you're gonna walk the plank, and I'm gonna sail out of here with all of your money because this should've ended days ago. But like my aunt always says, better late than never."

Two back-to-back shots fired out, hitting Mack squarely in each shoulder. I looked back and saw Francesca kneeling on the floor with her gun drawn.

Stunned, Mack looked down at herself as her gun clattered to the floor. Blood gushed from both bullet wounds. "Fuck!" screamed Mack. "You bitch! You shot me!"

The duffle bag of money slid off her shoulder and dropped to the floor with a heavy thud. Mack slid to the ground.

"Frankie!" I said, my smile widening. "You got her!"

Frankie grinned. "What can I say? I'm a crack shot."

"Yeah, you are!" With the lights on, I finally saw the gun that Al had thrown me in the darkness. I reached down and picked it up. "Thanks for the gun, Al." I glanced over at him to see him now lying facedown on the ground. "Oh my God, Al!"

Francesca and I rushed to help him.

"He's alive," she said.

Relief washed over me just as a noise behind me caught my attention. I spun around to see Dexter grabbing the bag of money and rushing towards the outer deck.

"I'll take care of Al. Go after him, Danny!"

I fired the gun in my hand at Dexter. Three shots sank into the bag of money he carried over his shoulder. Dexter kept running. I followed him out onto the outer deck.

The rain had finally stopped, but the wind blew fiercely. I chased Dexter, cornering him near the bow of the ship. Weaponless, he swung the bag of money at me. I ducked and he missed, but the bag hit the railing. He swung wildly at me again and again hit the railing. This time I heard the sound of material tearing apart. He swung at me a third time, and this time the bag tore open. Money began to pour from the bottom of the bag. Apparently when they'd checked the money for authenticity, they'd unwrapped all the bundles. Now crisp green hundred-dollar bills flew up into the air, the storm sucking them from the open bag. They swirled around in the sky like a cyclone of cold, hard cash.

"My money!" screamed Dexter, reaching wildly for the money as it whirled around his face.

I reached out, grabbed ahold of his shirt and pulled him into me. Finally, I had a chance to do what I'd been wanting to do. I kept a hold of his collar and punched him repeatedly in the face until blood spurted from his nose and his eyes went blank. I gave him one more punch, sending him over the railing of the yacht to the water below. "No, Dexter," I sighed. "It was *my* money." I looked down at the nearly empty bag. "At least, it *was* my money."

Then I heard the sound of a scream from the cabin. I went racing back inside to find Mack holding a gun on Francesca. "What the…"

Mack stood with her back pressed up against the bulkhead. Blood oozed down both sides of her body, and she was barely able to hold the gun up. "This bitch ruined everything!" said Mack weakly. "She's gotta go."

"Drop the gun, Mack," I said evenly, holding my gun on her.

"No, you drop the gun, Drunk," she spat back. "Or else your girlfriend eats a fucking bullet."

I slowly lowered my gun to the ground.

Francesca had her hands out defensively. "Just relax, Mack. Let's get you some medical attention."

"Shut up! This is all your fault!"

"*My* fault?"

Mack nodded weakly. "Drunk couldn't have figured out how to find us if you hadn't gotten involved. He's fucking clueless."

"You underestimate him, Mack. He's a smart guy. *He's* the one that figured out it was you all along. Not me."

"Took him long enough," she spat. Her words were now slurred as she slowly backed out of the open hatch towards the outer deck.

When she got outside, her back hit against the railing. She gave a half-smile. "Bye-bye, Francesca."

A shot rang out. My heart lurched as my head swiveled to look at Francesca. I rushed to her side. "Frankie!" I yelled, holding her, my eyes searching for her bullet wound. "Where're you hit?"

"I wasn't hit, Danny. Look!" She pointed in Mack's direction.

I turned to follow Francesca's finger. Mack had a bullet hole between her eyes. She sank to the deck.

I couldn't believe what I saw, I looked behind me to see Solo holding his rifle on Mack. He put the gun down and smiled at his sister. "Now we're even, Panchita."

Francesca rushed to her brother's side and threw her arms around his shoulders. "Totally even."

"A little help over here?" called Al. Francesca had gotten him as far as the sofa before Mack had pulled the gun on her.

"Al!" I said, rushing to his side.

"Holy moly," said Al, shaking his head, as Solo and I each got an arm under his armpit and helped him to his feet.

"Al, are you all right?" asked Francesca.

Al looked down at his bandaged hand. "I dunno," he slurred. "But I think when whatever they gave me wears off, this might hurt a little."

"Yeah, I think so too. Come on. We gotta get you out of here."

We helped Al back down the stairs, where we discovered Beto and Diego finishing up tying up the three men.

"Al!" said Diego. "You're alive!"

"I'm alive," parroted Al with a weak nod. "Thanks for helping Drunk rescue me."

"We were glad to be able to help," said Diego.

"And we're glad you're all right," said Solo. "Now, we really should get moving. I think we'll drive the yacht back to Paradise Isle. The police are going to want to have it for evidence. We'll tow Miguel's boat back."

"I'll go tell Rico to have Miguel pull the boat up here," said Diego, starting towards the stern of the ship.

Seconds later, he was back. "They're gone!"

Solo's brows lowered. "What?"

"Rico and Pam. They're not back there. The dinghy's gone."

Francesca and I helped Al to the sofa in the saloon and then met up with her brothers at the stern. The dinghy was indeed nowhere to be seen.

"What the hell?" cursed Solo, looking around. "Where'd they go?"

"Rico must've taken Pam back to the boat," said Francesca.

Solo shook his head. "Even if he did, they should be back and waiting for us by now. Something must've happened."

He climbed the steps back to the aft deck and scanned the horizon looking for his lights. Finally, he heard the sound of shouts on the starboard side of the ship.

"Someone wanna give us a hand?" called out Miguel. We all rushed to the port side of the boat and looked down to see

Miguel and Rico idling in their charter boat next to the ship. A water-logged Dexter was lying on the floor of the boat, and Miguel and Rico were busy seining hundred-dollar bills off the top of the water.

My eyes brightened. "My money!"

48

THE SUN WAS JUST STARTING TO COME UP WHEN WE FINALLY MADE it back to the King's Bay Marina. Francesca had called ahead, and a team of officers and paramedics were waiting for us at the dock. Dexter, real name Sam Decatur, from Hinton, West Virginia, was handcuffed now and chained up in the stateroom that Pam had been kept in. I'd checked on the man several times to ensure that he hadn't figured out a way to escape and found that he'd finally cried himself to sleep after discovering that his sister, whose real name was Alison Decatur, was dead.

Pam and Al both spent the ride back dozing on the U-shaped sofa in the saloon. Despite the fact that they'd woken during the action, the drugs in their systems still fought against their consciousness, and they'd had difficulty staying awake during the return sail back to the island. I still hadn't called Evie to tell her what had happened. But I had shot her a text saying that I'd found Al and he was alive, but that we weren't able to talk. I figured I'd ask her to meet us at the hospital once we finally set foot on Paradise Isle sand.

Francesca and I had taken up residence on the smaller three-person sofa across from Pam and Al. We'd spent much of the ride talking about everything that had happened and keeping a close watch on the battered duo. Eventually Francesca's head had gotten heavy on my shoulder and I'd leaned my head against hers, and the next thing I knew, we were being awoken by the sounds of her brothers preparing to dock.

At that point, Solo strode over to me and handed me the bag of money he and his brothers had managed to recover from the ocean. Both the bag and the money were soaking wet, and it was only a small portion of the original seven million dollars, but it was still a hefty chunk of change. "Well, I guess this rightfully belongs to you, Drunk."

I took it from him and nodded. "Thanks, Solo. I sure appreciate everything you've done for Pam, for Al, and for myself."

Francesca stood up then and looked at her brother. "Hold up, Solo." She turned to look down at me and then promptly retracted the bag from my lap and handed it back to her brother. "Miguel and Rico collected the majority of this money, Solo."

I gawked at her, unable to speak.

She scratched her chin. "What was it that you said to me, Drunk? Finders keepers, losers weepers?"

"No, I couldn't," Solo began, handing me the bag back.

Before I could get a word out, she continued.

"I mean, unless you want to explain to the cops up there at the marina where this money came from originally and see if they agree that the cardinal rule is indeed finders keepers, losers weepers." Francesca grinned.

I stared at her, my eyes wide. Then I looked at the bag, and then I glanced over at Al and Pam, who quietly dozed. We'd gotten them back. That was all that mattered. I nodded. I was pretty sure I'd have gotten to that conclusion on my own at some point. Even without her help. I pushed the bag back towards Solo. "I owed your brother a boat, Solo. There should be enough in there with interest." Even though I didn't know how much was in the bag, I was sure it was a hell of a lot more than the price of a new charter boat. But without the Cruz brothers, I wouldn't have Al back. And instead of calling Evie and telling her to meet me at the hospital, I'd be telling her to meet me at the morgue.

Solo tried to hand the bag back to me. "You really don't have to give it all away."

I shook my head and shoved the bag towards him again. "I do have to. I appreciate all of your help. You guys deserve that money. And besides, I've got a great job, some great friends, and the interest that had accrued on seven million dollars over the last two months. I'm gonna be just fine."

Francesca smiled and sat back down next to me. I put my arm over her shoulder, and she took hold of my hand. "You're well on your way to being a good guy, Danny. I have faith in you."

I snuggled in close to her and kissed her forehead. "Thanks, Frankie. Thanks to you, I have faith in me too."

49

I pulled the resort car to a stop in front of the Paradise Isle International Airport, popped the trunk, and glanced over at the woman sitting next to me. Sunglasses covered the lingering bruises on her face. Her tanned skin, borderlining on pink, glowed, and her long blonde hair was tied up on top of her head in a simple bun.

"Thanks for everything, Danny," she whispered, turning to look at me.

Two weeks had passed since her ordeal had ended. Pam had spent the first week at the hospital and the police station, both getting over her injuries and answering questions about the Decatur siblings. And she'd spent the second week on the beach, trying to regain some semblance of normalcy. The PTSD she faced after the ordeal made her scared to stay in a room alone, so I'd let her stay at my cottage with me. Of course, I'd slept in the living room on a blowup mattress and she'd taken my bed, but we'd made it work.

"I'm sorry you got mixed up in all of that."

"I know you are," she said, tears springing into her eyes for the millionth time that week. "I'm sorry for what I put you through too. I know now that I shouldn't have come after you."

I sighed and leaned my head back against the headrest. While it was true that things would've been a lot better for me if Pam had never come in the first place, mainly because I'd still have my seven million dollars and Al's finger would still be able to bend at the knuckle, it would've only been temporary. Ultimately, Mack would've probably found another way to swindle the money out of me. But truth be told, she'd probably done me some good. "We were able to talk things out," I said. "I probably needed that for closure."

She nodded and dabbed her tissue against the corners of her eyes. "Yeah. I needed the closure too. But it was silly of me to have held out hope that you'd be able to forgive me."

Forgive.

Manny's words that I'd heard when all this had first begun replayed in my head. *"Hate's a double-edged sword, man. You can't cut her without cutting yourself."* I hadn't taken him seriously then, but the week's events had proven firsthand that he'd been right.

I shook my head at Pam.

"No, it's not silly of you, Pam. I forgive you." I knew the last thing she needed was my anger and my hatred riding on her shoulders while she tried to deal with the abuse she'd suffered during her abduction. I knew she needed my forgiveness in order to put all of the ugliness behind her. And I knew I needed to let the hate go in order to move on with my life. I couldn't let that double-edged sword cut either of us anymore. I wanted us both to be able to heal.

She looked at me with surprise. "You do?"

I nodded. "I mean, don't get me wrong. I wish things hadn't gone down the way they did, but I'm not gonna hold on to that anger anymore. It's not healthy for me, and after everything you've been through, it's not going to help you recover." I smiled at her. "And I want you to recover, Pam."

She smiled and then leaned across the center console and threw her arms around my shoulders. "Oh, Danny, thank you!"

Even though I'd forgiven her, I wasn't exactly excited about the hugging. I patted her back stiffly and let her have her closure.

She sat back up in her seat, sniffling. "You have no idea what that means to me to hear that you forgive me."

"I think I get it," I promised her. "It needed to be done. And I hope that you'll be able to forgive me for being so cavalier with the kidnappers."

Pam blotted her eyes. "How about we just call it even?" she said, giggling through her tears.

I smiled. "Sure."

We sat in silence for a long moment. She looked out the window at the airplane on the tarmac. "Well, I suppose this is it, then."

I nodded. "Yeah."

"How long are you gonna stay in Paradise, Danny?"

I shrugged and looked back towards the main part of the island. "I don't know. As long as I feel wanted here, I guess."

"I really like Al."

"Yeah," I said with a smile. "He's a great guy."

"And Evie."

I nodded.

"I'm glad they'll be here to take care of you, Danny."

"I can take care of myself, Pam. I'll be okay."

She reached out and squeezed my hand. "I know you will be. I'll miss you."

My mouth opened. I knew the right thing in that moment was to repeat the sentiment. But I wasn't quite there yet.

She patted me. "It's okay. I know you won't miss me. But I really will miss you. You were good to me, Danny. And I know I was the one that messed everything up." She leaned across

317

the center console one more time and kissed me on the cheek. "Goodbye, Danny."

She climbed out of the vehicle then and grabbed her bags from the trunk. When the lid slammed and I saw her walking towards the terminal, rolling her bags behind her, she gave me one last wave.

I waved back.

"Goodbye, Pam."

50

THE HEAT OF THE DAY WAS SHIELDED BY THE PALM TREES SWAYING overhead. I wore my Sunday best. My boat shoes, the pair of navy Bermuda shorts I'd purchased in the hotel gift shop and a simple white polo shirt. I also wore the brand-new black fedora I'd purchased in the airport gift shop after dropping Pam off the day before.

With my hands folded in front of me and my head bowed reverently, I cleared my throat. "We are gathered here today to celebrate the life of Diablo de Reptilian."

Francesca stood beside me, her shoulder pressed up against mine. Her head was also bowed and her hands folded. Around us stood Solomon Junior, his wife, Marina, and their children. Beto and his wife, Selita, and their children stood next to Solo's family. Miguel and his new wife, Kayliana, were there, as were the single Cruz brothers, Rico and Diego.

Directly across from me, Al and Evelyn Becker stood arm in arm. Al's hand was still wrapped. He'd already undergone surgery to have his finger reattached, though we were still unsure how useful it would prove to be, and I was half-afraid to lift my head lest I catch another of Evie's angry stares. She still hadn't quite forgiven me for getting Al mixed up in the kidnapping. Even Artie Balladares and Manny Velázquez had turned out for the event. Everyone held a flower in their hands.

Squeezing my eyes shut, I continued. "Diablo was a good lizard. Judging by his size, we believe he lived a very long and happy life. Even though we did not know him personally, I'm quite sure that he ate many bugs in his lifetime. He was a good-looking lizard, as far as lizards go, so it's very likely he enjoyed the company of many female lizard friends. Perhaps he even has children walking around to this day. If so, we offer up extra blessings to those he leaves behind."

I pinched one eye open and lifted my head enough to peer around me. Everyone's heads were still lowered. "And at this time, I'd like to open it up. If anyone has anything they'd like to say about Diablo, they're welcome to." I took Francesca's hand and gave it a squeeze.

She nodded. "Like Danny said, we didn't know Diablo, but he has been on this earth for a very long time. It's hard to believe that he didn't affect someone's life in some way. So we pray for Diablo's safe journey to the other side of the Rainbow Bridge and hope that he finds lots of bugs to eat and lots of new friends."

I nodded and lifted my head, looking around. When no one else seemed to want to speak, I stepped forward and shoveled dirt back into the hole we'd placed Diablo in.

"Go in peace, Diablo," I said, throwing my flower onto the unmarked grave.

"Go in peace, Diablo," said the rest of the crowd, tossing their flowers onto the pile.

Then I looked up at everyone. "I'd like to thank everyone for attending this memorial service today. It was important to Francesca that we honor Diablo in this way. And because of that, it was important to me too. I owe her a lot for helping me find my friend Al and for helping me bring him home to Evie." I smiled at Evie and was thankful to see her smile back at me.

"I also want to thank my new friends, Solo, Miguel, Beto, Diego, and Rico, for everything they did. They made it possible too."

"Hey, man, we're glad we could help," said Rico.

Solo nodded. "We are very thankful that Al and Pam made it out of that situation all right."

"So I'm glad that we could all gather today to say our goodbyes to Diablo and to celebrate Al being alive and back with us again."

Al gave everyone a little wave with his good hand. "Thank you, Drunk. I know what you all went through to find me was difficult as well, and I'm thankful that I got another chance at life. I got to come back to my dear sweet Evie." He squeezed her arm. "And I'm thankful that the villain of this story will get what's rightfully coming to him."

"Hear, hear!" I shouted.

The crowd chuckled.

"And even though this might have all gone differently if Drunk had just given the kidnapper the money to start with," said Al, lifting his arm.

I grimaced.

"The important thing is that I believe Drunk learned a very valuable lesson."

I bobbed my head. "Indeed I did. I'm very sorry about what happened to your finger. I'll forever be in your debt, Al."

Al lifted a shoulder. "I know you will," said Al, pointing at me with his good hand. "And it can't be all bad. At least I've got a story to tell now."

I smiled and rolled my eyes. "Oh, now it begins."

"But I'm thankful to everyone that brought me back, and I'm glad we could all get together and celebrate."

Evie nodded. "I'm also thankful to all of you for bringing my sweet husband back. Without him, I don't know where I'd be. So thank you, Cruz Brothers. Thank you, Francesca. And thank you, Terrence." She strode over to me and gave me a hug while the crowd cheered. When she'd let me go, she looked around. "Now, with all of that being said, everyone make your way back to Terrence's cottage. There's a feast fit for a king waiting up there. Everyone help yourself!"

Several people clapped and began to head back to my place for the picnic we'd invited them to join us for. Before he could get away, I stopped in front of Al. "Hey, buddy. Once again, I'm really sorry. I hope you know that."

"You're like a broken record, kid. I know you're sorry. I already accepted your apology and told you none of this was your fault."

"I know. It's just… you had your finger cut off! I mean, I know you got it back and all, but that's a big fucking deal."

"Yeah, it's a big deal, but kid, here's the good part of the story. I'm still alive. And even if this finger proves to never be functional again, at least I had a good eighty-seven years with it."

I smiled at him. "All right. I'm just glad to have you back, Al."

He nodded. "I'm glad to be back." He shook his head. "I got bad news, though."

I curled my lip. "Yeah? Worse than finding your best friend's finger in a box in your kitchen?"

He nodded. "Yeah. Worse than that."

"What's that?"

"Evie says I don't get to do missions with you anymore."

"Yeah?" It didn't shock me in the least.

His head bobbed. "Yeah."

"You gonna listen to her?"

"Of course not."

I smiled. "All right, then. We're good."

Al patted me on the back. "Yeah, we're good."

He lumbered back towards the cottage, leaving me with the last two partygoers at Diablo's grave site, Francesca and Solo. I walked over to them.

"Hey, thanks for coming, Solo," I said, shaking his hand.

He actually smiled at me as he shook it. "I gotta hand it to you, Drunk."

"Hand it to me?"

"Yeah. There's not a lot of men out there that would hold a funeral for a lizard that wasn't even someone's pet."

I grinned. I wondered if I'd catch some flack for that. I shrugged. "It was important to Frankie, and I made her that promise."

Francesca smiled up at me.

"And that's why I gotta hand it to you. My sister used to make us hold funerals for every pet we ever had. From the dogs all the way down to the goldfish. It used to drive all of us boys *nuts*, but we did it because we loved our sister, and it was important to her."

"Yeah?"

Solo nodded. "So for some other man in her life to do that for her?" He threw an arm over his sister's shoulder. "Well, I guess it just means that you appreciate her as much as we do."

"Of course I appreciate her. I told you, Solo. Francesca's a kick-ass chick. She's sweet and smart, and I'mma be honest, she ain't too hard on the eyes. Plus, you saw her skills on that yacht for yourself. She can take care of business."

Solo's brow raised and his lips tightened as he nodded his head. He almost couldn't speak. Tears welled up in his eyes. "I know she did," he whispered. "Our dad would've been so proud of her."

"Solo!" said Francesca, her own eyes now filled with tears. "Quit, you're making *me* cry."

He shook his head. "No, Panchita, I won't stop. You handled yourself like a pro on that ship. I'm so proud of you, and I just want to say that the rest of the guys and I are going to give you the respect that you deserve when it comes to your job from here on out."

She smiled from ear to ear. "For real?"

He nodded. "For real. We love you. And we just want you to be safe."

She hugged him then. "Thanks, Solo. I love you."

"I love you too."

When he let go of her, he dried his eyes with his shirt. Then, clearing his throat, he shook my hand again. "So if the time ever comes that you want to date my sister, I'm going to trust her judgment."

I smiled. "Thanks, Solo."

"But just because you held a funeral for a lizard doesn't mean you're ready yet," he cautioned, squeezing my hand and pulling me closer to him.

I laughed. "Yeah, Solo. I know. I still have work to do on myself before I'm going to be worthy of Frankie. But I'm sure as hell gonna try."

HEY THERE, IT'S ZANE...

I'm the author of this book. I've got a huge favor to ask of you. If you even remotely enjoyed Drunk, Al, and their predicament, I'd be honored if you left a review on Amazon. I'd love to see this book reach more readers, and one way to do that is to have a whole bunch of feedback from readers like you that liked it.

Leaving reviews also tells me that you want more books in the series or want to read more about certain characters. Or, I guess, conversely, if you didn't like it, it tells me to either try harder or not to give up my day job.

So, thanks in advance. I appreciate the time you took to read my book, and I wish you nothing but the best!

Zane

MANNY'S BLUE HAWAIIAN RECIPE

1 oz light rum
1 oz vodka
3/4 oz blue curacao
3 oz pineapple juice
1 oz sweet & sour mix

Combine rum, vodka, blue curacao, pineapple juice, and sweet
& sour mix in a hurricane glass filled with ice. Mix well.
Garnish with pineapple slice and maraschino cherry. Enjoy!

SNEAK PEEK - DRUNK DRIVING

THE MISADVENTURES OF A DRUNK IN
PARADISE BOOK 3

1

Valentina Carrizo approached *me* first.

Now, I won't lie and say that I didn't find her attractive. The woman could set a wet sponge on fire, she was that hot. And truth be told, she *did* catch my eye. But let's not get it twisted.

She.

Approached.

Me.

But despite the fact that Valentina Carrizo was hot, she was by no means the type of woman I would've ever hit on in a bar. And *not* because I thought I couldn't score with someone that hot. So let's just drop that notion right now, shall we? There were numerous reasons *why* I wouldn't have approached her, *none* of which being that I thought I'd be unable to score.

No. I knew from the moment I laid eyes on her that sex was kind of a given. Her clothes kinda told the story. Red skimpy dress, clinging to every nook and cranny of her body. The slit in the front of the dress riding clear up to her lady bits. Big bulging breasts on display and as inviting as the last two peanuts in a bowl on top of a bar. They dared every man around to grab 'em for a taste, but in the back of that man's mind, he had a nagging curiosity as to how many hands had been there before him and just where, exactly, *those* hands had been.

No. Scoring was most definitely *not* the reason I wouldn't have approached Valentina Carrizo. The real reason, I actually attributed to my mother. And she wasn't even in the bar that night. She was twenty-two hundred miles and an ocean away.

Go figure.

But it was her words that rang truth and wisdom into my head that evening. "Only hookers wear that much makeup."

Thanks, Mom.

I was pretty sure her advice saved me several hundred dollars that evening and quite possibly an antibiotics prescription.

So when Valentina Carrizo approached me at the bar—and in lieu of a handshake as a greeting, her hand immediately grabbed my junk—my head tilted approximately fifteen degrees to the right. I squinted and frowned at the same time, having the instant urge to cough. I imagined the conversation she'd just been having with her girlfriend on the other side of the bar. I figured it had to go a little something like this.

"Hey, Valentina, you see that hot guy over there?"

"You mean the one with the big nose?"

"Yeah. You know what they say, 'big nose, big hose.'"

"You know, I've always wondered if that was true."

"I guess we'll find out…"

Challenge accepted.

"Well, hello to you too," I said.

She let out a giggle and then a sultry, thickly Spanish accented, "Just checking." She ran a hand through her long, wavy black hair, pulling a lock over her bronzed shoulders.

I leaned both elbows back against the bar and chuckled. "Checking to make sure I am what the beard says I am?"

She held out her hand then, her long red fingernails looking like daggers covered in blood. "I am Valentina."

Taking her hand, I gave it a small pump and then leaned into her slightly. "I'm Drunk."

She put her ear against my mouth then. "What do you say?"

"I'm Drunk," I repeated over the pounding bass.

She giggled. "Yeah, me too."

"Can I buy you a drink?"

"Sure. Rum and Coke."

I turned and flagged down the bartender whom I'd been chatting with before Valentina had arrived. "Rum and Coke." I held up my tumbler and gave it a little shake, making the ice that was left clink against the sides. "And I'll have another."

The bartender grinned at me. I was sure he thought I was some poor shmuck that didn't know a hooker from a ho when I saw one. He probably assumed I thought I was getting lucky tonight by buying the woman a drink. But that's not what I was doing. I was actually buying the woman a drink so she wouldn't be offended when it was time to excuse myself.

Is that wrong?

Well, then, let's just put it to a vote, shall we?

Ladies, would you be offended if a man bought you a drink just so you wouldn't be offended that he *didn't* buy you a drink?

I didn't think so. A free drink's a free drink.

I was playing it safe, folks. I'm not stupid. The bar scene used to be my jam. And I knew how to work a room.

Rule #1. Keep the women happy.

Rule #2. Don't take home hookers. Just don't. I don't care how hot they are. Just don't do it.

Rule #3. Tip your bartenders well.

And rule #4. Never eat the peanuts.

I slid the bartender some cash and handed Valentina her drink.

She took a sip, then smiled up at me, batting her long dark eyelashes. "Thanks. So what do you do, handsome?"

"I'm in security."

She cuddled up to my side. "I feel safer already."

I smiled at her. She was cute. That much was for sure. "I like your accent. Where's it from?"

"Colombia," she said, sounding a little like a cross between Sofia Vergara and Charo.

"You're sure a long ways from home."

She took another sip of her drink and shrugged. "You're American?"

"Yeah. Why?"

"You're a long way from home too. Maybe we were destined to meet."

I could play along. "Were we?"

She nodded. "We could go back to your place and get to know each other a *leetle* better."

"Mmm, I don't think my better half would like that very much," I said, giving her a tight grin.

"Aww, you're married?" Though her bottom lip plumped out when she said it, her body language said the opposite. She cuddled up closer to me as if the idea of me being married had made her *more* interested.

"Something like that."

She stood on her tiptoes, nuzzled my ear, and whispered, "I don't care." Her hand cupped my junk again.

I glanced over at the bartender. He was smiling. This was his silent *I told you so* moment, even though he hadn't said a word. Only his shit-eating grin had spoken for him. Without moving, I looked down at Valentina. "Do I get a discount for all these free feels?"

She giggled. "Oh, honey, if that's not a rolled-up sock in there I'll do it for halfsies."

"Halfsies, huh?" I sighed and glanced around, wondering

just where exactly my other half was when I needed him. That was when I spotted him.

Eighty-seven-year-old Al Becker was a small man with hunched-over shoulders that made him *barely* five feet tall. Aside from the two small patches of white hair behind his ears, he was bald. He wore his usual uniform. Khaki shorts. A white ribbed tank top under a Hawaiian button-down. White New Balance sneakers and long white socks pulled up to his knobby knees. He hobbled over to me at the bar.

"Al. What took you so long?"

When he looked up at me, his whole torso moved, like he had a stiff neck or something. "We gotta go, kid." He said it low, like he'd been chased to the bar by a mafioso.

"Go? Why?"

"The line for the john's too long."

"You been in line this whole time?"

"I mean it, Drunk. Let's go."

"Why we gotta go?"

"Which one of us has the bad ears here? You or me? I told you. The line to the john's taking too long."

"Your point?"

"Do I really gotta spell it out?"

"Fuck, Al. I can't take you anywhere. We just got here."

"Don't 'fuck, Al' me, kid. We've been here for over an hour."

I glanced backwards at the bevy of beautiful women on the dance floor. I hadn't even gotten started yet. I was still waiting for my first three drinks to kick in and give me rhythm. "An hour? That's nothing."

"An hour in a bar is like dog years to a hooker. Trust me, it's plenty."

My eyes widened and I glanced down at Valentina. "Did you seriously just say that, Al?"

"I did. Now can we go?"

I cleared my throat. "Hey, Al. I'd like you to meet my friend, Valentina."

Valentina's right brow rose, but she extended her hand to Al.

Oblivious to the fact that her hand had just been cradling my boys, he took it and gave it a polite shake. "It's nice to meet you, Valentina."

"Valentina's a hooker, Al."

He cupped his ear. "A what?"

I leaned closer and hollered, "A hooker."

Al's brows lifted up towards his bald head, lifting the bags beneath his eyes and making his watery blue-green eyes more pronounced as he looked her up and down. "I'll be honest. That doesn't surprise me."

Valentina didn't even pretend to look offended. She leaned in a little closer to me. "I'm sorry. Who is this man?"

I tipped my head towards Al. "My better half."

She quirked a smile. "You are kidding."

I grinned cheekily.

Al's head gestured towards the door. "Come on, Drunk. We're leaving. I need to make. Those taquitos you forced me to eat aren't sitting right with me."

Al started towards the exit, but my hand shot out to grab his arm. "You're not even gonna say goodbye to our new friend?"

He nodded amicably to the bombshell clinging to my side. "It's been a remarkable pleasure, Valentina." Then he turned his narrowed eyes on me. "Now let's go, kid. I gotta take the kids to the pool."

When he'd disappeared into the crowd, Valentina looked up at me curiously. "He is your grandfather or something?"

"Nah. My wingman."

"He's fun," she said dryly.

I tried to pry myself out of her viselike grip. "He's a cool cat. He's just not used to leaving the resort. Especially after the sun goes down."

"Resort?"

"The Seacoast Majestic. That's where I do security."

"Oh, so you *live* on the island?"

"I do now." I didn't think she needed to hear the whole story of how I'd come to move here from the States. I was over all of that. I was an official Paradise Isle resident now. For better or worse.

She curled into me again and purred, "Niiiice."

I chuckled while trying to escape again, but shaking Valentina was like trying to flick a booger off your finger. "Sorry, Valentina. I gotta go before Al deuces in the resort rental and we get our driving privileges revoked."

"How about a raincheck?"

I glanced back at the bartender again. He'd moved on to a group of college-aged girls down the bar and wasn't watching me and Valentina anymore. I shrugged. Just like I'd bought Valentina a drink so as not to offend her, I decided to agree on a raincheck for the same reason. Hell, she didn't need to know I had no intention on cashing it. "Sure, a raincheck would be great."

Magically, she plucked a business card out of her cleavage and handed it to me.

"Valentina Carrizo, Professional Escort." I looked up at her in surprise. Though I knew prostitution was legal on the island, this was my first experience with it being so blatant. I smiled at her. "You have *fucking* business cards?"

"In case you ever need a date to the ball, but the fucking part is extra," she said, giggling.

"Next ball I go to, I'll look you up."

"Promise?"

I grinned. "You have my word." Valentina grabbed my face and kissed me on the lips then. It was pretty PG and not anything I would've been embarrassed for my mother to have seen, but somehow it made me uncomfortable. I pulled my head back and cleared my throat. "It was nice to meet you Valentina."

As I started to walk away, she called out to me. "Hey. What's your real name?"

"Drunk."

"It's really Drunk?"

"Sure is."

She smiled at me. "Well, it was nice to meet you, Drunk."

Outside, Al waited for me in the resort car that Artie Balladares, the owner of the Seacoast Majestic, had let us borrow. It wasn't the first time we'd been loaned the car, and it always came with the stipulation that Al had to be present when it was used, and I had to be the one driving. I wasn't sure if that was Artie's way of making sure Al was always entertained or if it was his way of making sure I always had a chaperone.

I crawled into the driver's seat. "Jeez, Al. I barely got a chance to look around."

But Al wasn't one to be sidetracked. "What took you so long? Those taquitos bought my stomach a one-way ticket to Shitsville."

"Hey, man, I'm sorry. You didn't have to eat 'em. I mean, you know what they say. 'Greasy in, easy out.'"

"You said you ordered them for the table, Drunk. I was being polite."

"In that case, you get two gold stars. You were extra polite."

"Let's just go. I gotta find the nearest john."

I pointed to the nudie bar next to the Blue Iguana, where we'd just been. "I bet Club Cobalt next door has a bathroom you could use."

Al's eyes widened. "Are you nuts? You don't sit on a toilet seat in a place like that unless you wanna get pregnant, and I'm too weak to squat."

"You're also too old to get pregnant."

Al pursed his lips. "Are you gonna start this car, or do I have to get out and push?"

"In your current condition, I advise against pushing. You'll shit your shorts."

Al shook his head. "I think it's time you bought your own vehicle, kid. I can't keep hauling you around like this."

I tried to restrain my smile as I started the engine. "You can't keep—" Steering the vehicle out of the parking lot and onto the main road, I shook my head. "Who's hauling who around here?"

"Look, you've got the cash. How about I take you shopping for a new ride one day this week?"

I shrugged. The thought had crossed my mind a time or fifty. Only every time I wanted to run into town for something and had to ask Artie's permission to use a resort car and then persuade Al to ride along. I'd tried to convince Artie to give me my own private business car, but he said he'd seen the bullet holes we'd gotten put into Gary Wheelan's ride my first week on the island and he didn't trust me to keep his small fleet of cars safe. They were for guests to be shuttled around in, not for my personal escapades.

"I'm not sure I wanna part with that kind of cash, Al."

"You're not exactly a pauper, kid. You can afford to spend a little of that money."

"But it's my nest egg." Al was referring to the money I'd made solving a big theft my first week on the island. Even though I'd made off with nearly seven million bucks, I'd lost the majority of it in the fucking Atlantic—a ransom drop gone bad. And the small amount that we'd been able to fish out of the ocean had gone to pay for the damages to the Cruz brothers' fleet of boats. In the end, I'd wound up with only the interest I'd earned on the money for the couple months that I'd had it. It wasn't enough to live the rest of my life on, but with

Al's help, I'd invested it properly and it was already growing steadily. I really didn't feel like touching it.

"You need your own car, kid." Al held up his hand and pointed at his little finger. "Besides. You owe me."

"Oh, come on. You're gonna bring *that* up?"

"The fact that you got my finger cut off? Yeah, I think I earned the right to bring that up a time or two a week for the rest of my life."

"It's not like I was the one that cut it off, Al."

"Really? That's how you're gonna spin it?"

"Spin it? I'm not—look. I put it on ice for you, didn't I? They sewed it back on. It hardly looks used. Well, except for all those wrinkles on it. But those are your fault, not mine."

"Hardly looks used? I can't bend it anymore, kid!"

I fought back a laugh. Watching Al drink a cup of coffee now was like having a tea party with the queen. I had to look away to convince my lips to cover my teeth again. When I had myself under control, I turned to Al.

"Fine. I'll look at cars."

Al's head bobbed as if it was settled. "We'll go see Steve Dillon this week. I think Artie knows the guy. He'll give us a good deal."

I glanced over at Al as I hit the main road that would take us back to the resort. "You're kinda bossy, you know that?"

"Yeah, well, you're pain in my ass." He was quiet for a minute. "And you drive like an old woman."

I pulled the car over at the first convenience store I could find. "Yeah, well, I took lessons from you."

ALSO BY ZANE MITCHELL

Drunk Driving is now available!

Want to be the first notified when the book is released?

Then consider joining my newsletter.

I swear I won't spam you, I'm really not that ambitious.

I'll only send out an email when I write a new book or have something to give away that I think you might like.

So what is that?

A couple emails a year?

You can handle that, can't you?

Sign up at www.zanemitchell.com

ABOUT ZANE

I grew up on a sheep farm in the Midwest. I was an only child, raised on Indiana Jones, Star Wars, and the Dukes of Hazzard. My dad was a fresh-water fish biologist and worked on the Missouri River. My mom was a teacher when I was young, and then became the principal of my school around the time I started taking an interest in beer. My grandpa, much like Al in my Drunk in Paradise series, actually owned a Case IH dealership, and I thought the world of him and my grandma.

I've been married twice. I'd say the first was a mistake, but that marriage gave me my four kids. Marriage numero dos came with two pre-made kids. So yeah, we're paying for Christmas presents for six and college for three. So buy my next book, *please*. I'd say that was a joke, but jeez. College is expensive.

In a former life, I was a newspaper columnist, and I actually went to journalism school but eventually dropped out. I did go back to school and eventually got a teaching degree, but let's face facts. I sucked at being a teacher. I was just as much of a kid as the kids were.

The love of my life and I live in the Midwest. We go about our boring lives just like you do. We parent lots of teenagers and twenty-something-year-olds. We watch superhero movies and Dateline on TV. We're a little obsessive in our love for the Kansas City Chiefs. We take yearly visits to the Caribbean because hey, tax deductible. And now, I write books - sort of a life long dream, to be honest.

So thanks for reading. You have no idea how cool I think it

is, that you picked *my* book out of all of the choices you had to read and you made it to the end. You rock. Don't ever let anyone tell you otherwise.

Zane

Oh. P.S. I don't do Tweets. Or Insta. I do have Facebook and a website. www.zanemitchell.com. You're welcome to come over and hangout. BYOB.

Made in the USA
Middletown, DE
04 February 2020